The Lion Sleeps

A novel by

Peggy Poe Stern

Moody Valley
Boone, North Carolina

Published by
Moody Valley
475 Church Hollow Road
Boone, N C 28607
moodyvalley@skybest.com

Cover painting by Peggy Poe Stern
Cover design by David K. Stern

First Published 12/11/2023
Edited 01/02/24

ISBN: 978-1-59513-075-4

Dedicated to Our
Beloved Family
Past, Present, and Future

Chapter 1

~~– Bennie Jack ~~
In the jungle, the mighty jungle

"**D**o you want to live or die?" Brigham asked as though there was a chance that I would answer the latter.

"Need you ask? I returned with my usual degree of sarcasm.

"Then you have one chance and one chance only."

"I refuse to run and hide like I'm the criminal," I told him stubbornly. I have worked undercover for the past five years. "I've survived this long, and I can continue to survive."

Brigham shook his head as though I was being totally ridiculous. "You're supposed to have some intelligence, but I'm beginning to wonder if that's true. Walk out this door with nothing other than your arrogant defiance and you will be dead before morning comes."

I knew he had a point, and he could be right if he was referring to anyone other than me. I'd been through many dangerous situations and escaped. I'd been trained by the best in how to take care of myself, how to survive against the odds. I wasn't the kind to turn tail and hide just because my life was in danger. Being in danger was nothing new.

His eyebrows lifted. His lips puckered for a moment as he looked me in the eyes. "You have done a great service for your country by gathering information of great importance. Unfortunately, your cover was blown, and we were only able to prosecute one man from the information you provided, and he was only their scapegoat. As you know, there are many more out there who will be seeking revenge by making an

1

example of your death. They have a thousand ways to Sunday at getting revenge. I dare say you will wish for death many times over before they finish you off."

One small-time, unimportant person had been sacrificed for their cause? If it wasn't so sad, I'd have laughed at that.

Brigham put several pictures on his desk in front of me. I looked at them and cringed even when I tried not to. There were dismembered human parts along with the remains of women and men's dead bodies. Those pictures would turn the most seasoned stomach. What had been done to humans was unthinkable. It said a lot about who we were dealing with.

"This is what you will look like – or worse," he told me in a voice that held no room for questions. "You can't fight them regardless of how well you've been trained or how hard you want to fight. Your only choice is to disappear off the face of the earth."

"How many people have successfully disappeared?" I asked as I tried not to let my real fear show. Those pictures of torture and dismemberment were enough to shake up those who were braver than I would ever become.

"Far more people than you know about or could imagine. We're good at assisting people in disappearing. You won't be put in one of our so-called safe houses. It isn't safe enough for someone such as you. Unfortunately, your picture was caught on a hidden camera and your identity was discovered. Your service will be terminated immediately, and our agency will deny ever having known you. You will not be given a false social security number or a false identity. Such as that can be traced. You will not step into the shoes of another person in hopes of living a somewhat normal life. Only a dead person will be forever safe. Your death needs to be believably faked. The only drawback will be that your friends and family will never know one single thing about your faked death, but fortunately you've led a rather exclusive life. You do understand the necessity of faking your death, don't you?"

I understood, but I didn't like it. Not that I had friends and relatives that would miss me. I was an only child – a late in life baby. My mother was forty-nine years old when she unexpectedly got pregnant with me. My father was fifty-six. I'd lost them both when I was in my early twenties. I likely had a few distant cousins scattered about, but none that I was close to. There were no bosom buddies, only a few acquaintances. That was one of the reasons I had been good at my job. It had been years since anyone cared about my existence. To put it concisely, I was as close to being alone as a person could get.

"I need to get a few things in order before I disappear," I finally said in my most agreeable tone of voice to let him think I was in agreement with what he was offering, which I was not.

"No time for such as that. You will be taken to a safe space while your faked death is being arranged. You'll be leaving in the next five minutes. There is a helicopter on the roof warming up to take off. We can't delay if you want to stay alive."

"But . . ."

"There are no buts."

"I'll need my things," I objected. There were clothes along with special items I was fond of. If I were to agree to such, I didn't want to leave everything behind. I would also need my equipment along with my bank account.

"Taking things with you is a dead giveaway that you've gone into hiding. If every single thing is left behind, including your bank account and clothes, it will appear someone knocked you off and disposed of your body. At least that's what we're hoping for. If worse should come to worse, we can always change plans."

Sure, they could. Were the pictures still lying in front of me faked? I didn't think so.

"Wait a minute. I don't intend to leave a lifetime of income behind. Regardless of where or how I disappear, I'll need money to live on."

"You will leave it all behind if you're dead."

"I don't plan on being dead – one way or the other."

"No one plans on being dead. Let me be crystal clear. No one is trying to rip off your hard-earned finances. We're trying to keep you alive. Period."

Sure, I believed the government had arrived to help me. Like president Ronald Regan once said, "I'm from the government and I'm here to help you," were the scariest words ever spoken.

"We will devise a way to get your cash back to you. Until then, everything you'll need will be taken care of."

Like I also believed that. "Wait a minute . . ." I started to object.

He stood up, pulled out what looked like a book from the bookcase behind his desk that caused a section of the bookcase to swing open. He then clutched both my arms and dragged me through the concealed door. There were stairs going up and stairs going down. I considered giving him a shove downward. Nope. A bad idea. I needed to find out what his plans were before I took action.

"I have no concern about you divulging the location of my secret escape hatch as you will be living far away never to return to my office again. Understand," he added without it being a question.

His words caused a chill to creep up and down my spine. What he said about my disappearance hadn't sunk in thoroughly until this moment. It was hard for me to believe such a thing would happen. I had chosen to send Brigham a copy of the documents I had discovered because he was one of the head men in the FBI. He was the one with the power to take action against those who were committing treason. When he requested my presence at his office, I thought it was to find out more about what I had discovered.

The stairs led to the roof where a stocky built man met us. He took a firm hold on my arm and rushed me toward the helicopter, which I hesitantly allowed, as we dunked to avoid the blades. I was not sure what was up and not exactly willing to find out, but I was held firmly in his clutch. He all but shoved me in the seat and then got in himself.

I had no doubt my life was about to change drastically – and not for the better.

"Go," he ordered the pilot. The blades increased speed as the roar of the engine filled my ears. I felt as though my very breath was being sucked out of my body, not that I hadn't ridden in a helicopter before, but because I'd allowed myself to be put in this position.

I didn't even have my weapons on me, which should have been a warning in itself. I had to go through a check point before I entered a government building. I had stashed my weapons behind some shrubby next to the door where I planned on retrieving them when I left. I should have bolted out of that office, used my own training in how to disappear. I had been trained in how to take care of myself, but I hadn't expected my bosses to turn against me.

"Where are you taking me?" I asked in hopes one of the men would answer.

"Dropping you off in about an hour." The huge man who had rushed me into the helicopter said with a smirk. The pilot acted as though he hadn't heard me, which might have been the case since he was wearing earphones.

"Where?"

"Top secret," the man answered with infuriating arrogance that instantly raised my hackles. Never trust an arrogant man.

It took control not to knock his front teeth out of his mouth with a hammer-fist, or at least strike him in the nose with a ridge-hand. Might have if he wasn't big, muscled, and appeared to be tougher than I was, not to mention the Glock that was almost concealed at his waist. I got the impression he wouldn't hesitate to coldcock his own sweet, little, old grandma, much less me. I wasn't in the mood to be coldcocked. I knew better than to become defensive. Acting helpless, if not scared, was my best bet. Let him think I wasn't capable of fighting my way out of a wet paper bag. Surprise was a great aid in defense.

I had the unpleasant realization I'd allowed myself to be blindsided when I should have known better. It wasn't like I could leap out of the helicopter or overpower two burley men. My training included how to fly an aircraft, along with helicopters, but I had only a very limited amount of training. I'd never flown anything without a trainer assisting me. If I wanted to escape, It would be best to wait until the opportunity presented itself instead of trying to force a confrontation where I might not have the advantage.

"Are you sure you can give me protection?" I asked as though I was scared and trying not to show it. Truth was, I really was scared, but not of what they thought I feared. I had found out too much information about what was going on behind the scenes. I turned in my report along with the necessary evidence to back up what I had discovered. Only one small-time criminal had been zeroed in on and then convicted, which had surprised me to no end. FBI, CIA, ATF, and others in command of justice were acting like his conviction was a big deal. It wasn't. He was nothing more than the sacrificial lamb set up to take the fall away from the elite power players I had delivered concrete proof of their corruption.

I had and still did consider myself to be an excellent collector of secret information. I was known as an invisible shadow with a camera who took real pictures of secret documents and managed to listen in and tape secret meetings. I had obtained and tweaked my very own snoop devices along with the best way to use them. In other words, I had devoted my entire life since I turned eighteen to finding out information I sought, regardless of what I had to endure.

What I had verified so far was unbelievable. Not only did I find information on common everyday criminals, but I also had information that went all the way to the top – the most powerful people in the world.

I sat there in the seat being extremely still, looking out the window as the helicopter climbed to its maximum height. Without oxygen masks we couldn't go higher than 14,000 feet. It was easy to tell we were leaving the city far behind and heading out over the ocean. After flying over water, the helicopter made a sharp turn and came back over land. I did my best to keep track of where we were going, but after about an hour flying over what appeared to be government forest land, I was becoming confused as to our exact location as well as to why we were flying in that direction.

I hadn't been dropped off yet.

Suddenly, the hair on the back of my neck lifted, my skin prickled, my hearing intensified, my breathing slowed down.

During training I'd been told over and over gut instinct was your guardian angel talking to you. I was listening and taking everything into consideration that my guardian angel was trying to tell me.

Things weren't adding up – or maybe they were.

I glanced at the pilot while pretending to be looking out the windows at the ground we were flying over. His teeth were clenched. His jaw muscles twitched every so often. A thin show of sweat glistened in the beard stubble on his upper lip. It was chilly in the helicopter.

He was young, at least younger than I was. Probably in his early twenties. His hands were soft looking and not exactly shaking, but not steady either. His body appeared tense instead of relaxed. I got the feeling he was paying no attention to me but was focused on the man behind us with every fiber of his being.

He's afraid of the big man, I decided, which made me more cautious than I already was.

"Stay on course," the big man told him.

"I am on course," the pilot said.

"No, you're not. You're over land. You're supposed to have turned back over the water by now."

"I was ordered to take a short cut over the mountains."

"By whom?"

The pilot took a card from his shirt pocket and handed it back to the big guy. I got a glimpse of a map along with numbers I took to be coordinates for him to fly by. The big man took the card and looked it over. Much to the pilot's surprise, and mine, the big man ripped it to pieces.

"Not the directions I received," the big man said as he took his own card from his jacket pocket and handed it to the pilot. "This is the direction you're going to fly in. Got it?"

The expression on the pilot's face remained blank – almost.

"I've got my orders. I won't change them," the pilot told him through clenched teeth.

"Yes, you will," the big man said with a sneer that chilled me.

I saw the muscles in the pilot' jaw twitch a moment before the big man stuck his hand in his pocket, pulled out a knife and clicked the release on the switchblade.

"Change course, now," he demanded as he pressed the tip of the knife into the side of the pilot's neck near the jugular. "It's time for our guest to take a permanent dip in the ocean." A tiny drop of red showed. The pilot lunged sideways in an effort to escape the knife and the helicopter shot upward.

I reacted without realizing what I had intended to do as my survival instinct kicked in big time. My left hand struck fast and furious with a heel-hand to the big man's nose resulting in a pop that shattered the bone and sent fragments upward resulted in profuse bleeding from ruptured blood vessels. I followed up with a crushing right-handed ridge-hand to his Adam's apple with all the power and precision I'd been trained to deliver. He uttered a grunt and a gurgle as his eyes bulged. I followed up with strikes to his solar plexus and groin. Recoil did the most damage to body tissue, much like the snap of a whip.

I had lightning recoil along with precision as both my fingers gouged at his eyes. When my life was in danger, I had to make sure I disabled the danger while I had the chance. The big man fell backward, his weight causing his body to wedge face up tightly between the narrow seats. His huge bulk had him wedged solid without being able to free himself.

When the pilot had lunged sideways, the knife had flown upward from the pilot's lower neck to the top of his head before the movement caused it to be flung from the big man's hand. In what appeared to be slow motion, I watched the gash open up from the base of his neck to the top of his head. There was the white bone of his skull followed by a red prickle of blood an instant before a flood of dark red came. Both men were down, and the helicopter was going crazy.

"Oh, shit," I mumbled. Now, I was in a fix. The pilot was bleeding out, and I had disabled the big man the way I had been trained to do.

"When you have one chance of survival, make it count," my trainer, A. J., had drilled into me.

The big man was lying near my feet bleeding from his busted nose almost as badly as the pilot was bleeding from his neck wound. Not only that, but both were also making similar gurgling sounds as they struggled to draw a breath. I grabbed the gun from the big man and the knife from the floor, jerked the pilot from where he was slumped in the seat and took his place. I wasn't the best of pilots, but I was now the only pilot.

What happened next was entirely up to me.

I hadn't slit the big man's throat as my trainers would have told me to do, but I held the knife in my hand just in case he unstuck himself. He didn't.

I leveled the helicopter back out, relieved that what little training I had in flying a helicopter was still somewhat viable.

That gave me only a small amount of momentary relief. I had to decide what I was going to do next.

"Survive," I could hear A.J. whisper.

That went without saying. I had always managed to survive – up until now.

I looked at the bloody pilot. It was obvious he was in his last throes of life. His jugular had been severed. I had heard that a severed head remained conscious for twenty seconds. Did the pilot know he was dying?

Had my attack on the big man caused the pilot's death, or had the big man's movement been intentional? If so, would the big man have flown the helicopter while I was still alive?

As for the big man. I had no trust in him from the get-go. He had a mean streak I recognized from experience. I looked back at him. He was on his back with his arms and legs jerking. Not a good sign – for him.

"Oh, shit," I mumbled. My ridge-hand to his Adam's apple has stopped his breathing, while the heel-hand to his nose was causing the blood flow to strangle him further. He might survive if I roll him onto his side. He was extra big, extra heavy and lodged firmly between the seats. If I made such an attempt, I would have to stop flying the helicopter.

Had I inadvertently been the cause of the pilot's death? I was definitely caused the big man's death.

But I was alive.

Now, I realized why I hadn't been allowed to take anything with me other than the clothes I was wearing.

I was expendable.

Permanent dip in the ocean, he'd said.

I continued flying the helicopter.

I flew the helicopter back over the ocean. I had grown more comfortable with flying as my training kicked in. I made sure to fly over the water until I saw no houses or boats. I searched the pilot's pocket taking his billfold of money along with his identification. I was flying low enough to make radar tracking difficult if not impossible. I managed to push the pilot out the open door without crashing. The big man would prove too difficult for me to continue flying while pulling him from between the seats.

Why would I need to push him out of the helicopter? He didn't have an obviously slit throat. If the helicopter crashed, it could explain his busted nose and crushed Adam's apple – maybe. With luck, it would take a while for his body to be discovered. Salt water and flesh-eating aquatic life might take care of his soft tissue.

The question was how would I get back on land if I dumped him and the helicopter in the ocean? Would it be better if I crashed the helicopter on dry land? There were problems with that idea. A helicopter crash on dry land would be easier to spot. There was a small chance radar was already tracking the helicopter even with me flying low. Someone somewhere might hear or see a crash, especially if there was a fire. Even more important, how could I crash and remain alive? There was no parachute for me to jump out.

My dilemma was resolved after I had the forethought to look at the fuel gauge. Why hadn't I noticed before that the fuel tank was empty?

"Okay, fly as low as possible back toward land," my trainer words ran through my brain. At the last minute, I planned to ease the helicopter down a few feet above the water until it sputtered out of fuel. It would be safer than letting the helicopter crash into the water. I'd had a very limited amount of HUET training. Mostly reading the survival instructions on how to survive a crash into water. I knew this type of helicopter was top heavy and would roll almost instantly once it hit the water.

I tried to guess the water temperature. I figured the water was warm enough not to cause hypothermia, which was a plus, but cold enough to make my body temperature drop. I needed to get as close to land as possible while trying to remain undetected when I ditched the plane. I had not had

Navy Seal training as such, but I was a good swimmer even with my clothes and shoes on.

The trick was to get as close to shore unseen and yet stay far enough out not to be detected. Oil, hydraulic fluid, remainder of fuel, if any, and other liquids from the helicopter would likely rise in the water, which could cause skin burns and eye damage. Anything loose would also float in the water leaving evidence of a crash behind, but I had no choice in what was about to happen.

I heard, felt, and saw the warning signs that the fuel was running out and the engine was cutting off. I quickly reached back and got the big man's billfold. I would need all the money I could get if I was going to survive. Fortunately, I had also been taught to have secret compartments sewn into my clothes and under the insoles of my shoes where I could hide cash. I wasn't in the least surprised that both billfolds had a considerable amount of cash, but not nearly enough for me to survive for an extended period of time.

I took out the money from both billfolds and secured it in the secret inner pocket sewn into my pants and tossed the billfolds in the water. It was a no-brainer that I was to have been disposed of by taking a permanent dip in the ocean. Therefore, my survival depended on remaining as dead as the two men who would be checking out the ocean's depth.

Chapter 2

I made sure my feet were away from the seat as the helicopter touched the water. I knew through HUET that most helicopters seats would collapse, and I certainly didn't want to be trapped or have broken legs. I dived out of the door moments before water ran into the helicopter and it started flipping over. I stroked hard with determination to make sure I got out of the way and didn't get trapped by the helicopter and taken under by the sinking debris. I had to swim away with my eyes closed to make sure I wasn't blinded by the helicopter fluids that were already rising to the surface. Hopefully, being covered in fluids would be a deterrent to sharks.

The shock of the unexpected cold water hit me. I was immediately coming face to face with hypothermia, panic, and disorientation. I swam away with all my strength before I dared open my eyes. I had no way of knowing which way land was or which way would take me further into the ocean. Don't panic, I told myself as I felt panic trying to take over common sense.

What would a Navy Seal do in this situation?

What would my trainers tell me?

Their answer was also a no-brainer. They would tell me not to struggle or panic. Struggling was more likely to attract pretors than remaining still.

Swim or float gently and let yourself feel the flow of the water.

What time was it? Morning or evening? Was the tide going out or coming in? I determined it was evening and the tide was coming in. I should swim in the direction the tide pulled and hope it would take me to land. I had no doubt I would eventually wash up on land. I just hoped I would still be alive when it happened.

I hadn't swum far when the helicopter disappeared, and paraphernalia started floating around me. Something was coming toward me. It appeared to be some kind of seat cushion. I grabbed onto it and was relieved to discovered it would continue floating while holding up a portion of my weight. The cushion allowed my head and shoulders to stay out of the water while my legs dangled.

I thought of shark infested water. I knew those body snatchers were out there somewhere looking for a fresh, hot meal of flesh and blood. Hopefully, they were not close to me. Maybe oil and hydraulic fluid would repel them instead of attracting them. I had some on my wet clothes. I hadn't been able to completely out distance the flow. I calmed myself the best I could and allowed myself to drift with the tide.

I wasn't sure how much of a chance I had of not getting that permanent dip in the ocean as had been planned for me. I closed my eyes and hung on, and hung on, and hung on. The temperature was getting colder and the tide stronger.

My arms had gone numb, but I still managed to cling to the cushion. I could feel the pull of the tide continuously getting stronger. I was growing weaker even though I was fit, well-muscled, and did physical endurance training daily. Stress was having an effect on me, making exhaustion worse. Stay calm. Think of something pleasant.

I thought of the one person I could trust. My trainer, A, J. He had spent years making me the person I now was. He made sure I had a chance of survival in a world where people who did what I did were often eliminated – permanently.

"What you're wanting to accomplish won't be fast or easy," A.J. had warned me. "You must have a raging fire in your gut, heart, and brain," he said. "If it's not there, if you can't keep it there until you're old and permanently disabled, give up now and go live an easy life."

I had the fire then.

Still had it.

But the cold ocean water was cooling that fire off. How could the water be this cold when the burning sun was shining down from a cloudless sky?

"Think of revenge," my trainer, seemed to advise me, although he wasn't struggling in the cold water up to his armpits hanging onto a floating cushion waiting and hoping I would hit land as darkness set in. "Plan out how to get even with them while you are resting."

Resting! Oh, could I tell him a few things for that advice if he was within hearing range.

The sun finally sunk into the ocean. A blue haze came over the water. At first the sinking sun brought relief from its burning reflection. I still wore long sleeves on my arms, but my head, face and hands were exposed to the merciless sun for hours on end even when the water kept getting colder. Even though I was in water, I could feel my body drying out. I was so thirsty my lips were cracking. All I had to do was lower my face into the water and drink. I would die faster if I allowed myself to do that.

Many times, I had thought about turning loose of the cushion, sinking down into the depth. If I was going to die anyway, I would rather do it sooner than later. I had never enjoyed pain of any kind, and I was now undergoing slow, painful torture.

I took a deep, shaky breath of the salt air. What had gotten into me to think in such a way?

I wasn't injured.

I still had arms and legs.

I had all my body parts intact.

I had no intentions of dying even if I had to hang onto this cushion until my upper body fried and stuck to the cushion while my lower body shriveled up in the salt water and rotted off. My trainer was right. I wanted revenge. I wanted it badly enough to stay alive days or weeks in this salt water if necessary.

I grew illusional and considered letting go of the cushion and swimming for the shore several times before common-sense hit.

If I turned loose of the cushion, it would drift away from me. My body would freeze up and not be able to swim or float. It was better to be patient than dead. My ghost might not be able deliver adequate revenge.

The night had become pitch black. I couldn't see a thing even if I had been able to hold my eyes open. The wind picked up. I grew more chilled and started to shiver. Again, I thought of taking a permanent dip in the ocean. It might become a reality regardless of how determined I was not to let it happen. I had no doubt the only thing keeping me alive was that my arms had become so paralyzed they had locked themselves onto the cushion similar to rigor mortis setting in. If they relaxed, I would sink. I closed my eyes and took in deep, slow breaths of the salty night air.

What would befall me was surely to come soon.

~~~~

I opened my eyes to feel rain pattering down on my head. It had taken great effort for me to open my eyes. When I finally got them open, I was shocked at what I discovered. I was lying on top of a rock. An actual rock at the bottom of what appeared to be a rock cliff. How I got here was beyond me.

My body could still feel the movement of the ocean, but the cushion was gone from my arms. Yet, it seemed I was clutching at something hard. Somehow, the rising tide must have lifted me up until I was washed on top of the rocks that protruded out of the ocean. Fortunately, I had been deposited into a crevasse between the cliff and the protruding rocks. My arms were clutching at a small rock protrusion for dear life.

Am I alive? I tried to make my lips say the words, but the movement made them crack in pain. Feeling the pain told me I was alive faster than my words would have. Still, I felt more words come into my mind.

Thirsty.

Dehydrated.

Desperate.

I had no idea how long I had gone without water. At least a day and a night. Maybe longer depending on how long I had lain unconscious in the crevice. However long it was, it was now imperative I gather what was left of my strength and find a source of fresh water if I wanted to survive.

I was desperate to survive.

The fact that I had killed one man, and most likely caused the death of a second man did not diminish my need for revenge. I wanted to bring justice to those I had gathered information on. I would have laughed if I could have.

Cracked lips didn't stretch willingly.

Those who deserved justice were the ones who seldom if ever received it.

It was laughable to think I could accomplish what many others had failed to do. Especially while I was lying on a rock with only a flicker of lifeforce left inside of me.

Get up, I told myself. Get up now or give up now.

The choice was mine to make.

I moved my toes and then my fingers. My hands and my feet. My arms and my legs. They worked. Slow and painful, but they worked. My hand moved to determine if the ocean had ripped my pants and shoes off. If it had, survival would be more difficult. My exhausted, slow moving fingers touch material. I was wearing my pants and amazingly enough my shoes. I felt the small bulge of money where I had put it in the inner pocket of my pants. Oddly enough, it gave me hope.

I have no idea how long it took for me to crawl out of the crevice. Everything about me ached and barely moved, but it did move. I climbed the rock cliff like a slug struggling to find safety away from the burning sunshine, while the sun grew higher in the sky. I grew even weaker. Twice I came to some kind of bushes growing from crevices. I lay in what little shade they offered and made an attempt to regain some strength along with determination.

You've not survived this long to give up, I told myself. You've lived through pure hell before, you can surely survive nature's elements. Nature had no wish to kill me, but it would if I allowed it.

I wouldn't allow it.

Crawl, rest, crawl became the words my mind repeated over and over until I felt actual dirt beneath my body. I would have cried with pure joy if I'd had enough fluid inside of me to do so. Instead, I rolled onto my side and looked about as best I could.

There was one big white house perched atop of the rise. Its owner obviously wanted a view of the ocean. It certainly had that.

That house would have water.

Probably food too, but I wasn't interested in food. Neither was I interested in being seen by anyone. My brain was still working enough to realize my survival not only depended on finding water, but that my dead body would be thought to be somewhere in the ocean's depth.

I didn't move a single muscle as I heard the engine of a car start up along with the sound of a garage door opening. I watched as a white car drove away from the house. I wished I knew if the driver was alone or if there were people still inside the house. I didn't know, so I had to assume there were still people inside.

It was my luck that the place had been professionally landscaped. Which meant there was an overabundance of trees, shrubs and flowering plants surrounding the house. The more plants there were the better camouflage for me. I crawled my way to a cluster of green shrubby. The eye was slower to detect a slow-moving object than a fast-moving one. To my credit, I always wore dark clothing, nothing bright and noticeable that would reflect the light.

I had barely reached the shelter of the shrubby when I heard a noise only a few feet from where I was hunkered. Much to my regret, I no longer had the strength to fight a mouse much less a person. I best be coming up with a good story. One that was believable.

My heart slowed its panic when I realized the sound came from the sprinklers being activated. Precious, life-saving water started spraying over the lawn and shrubbery. I cupped my scraped and dirty hands and lapped at the drizzle of water I collected in them. It was only a few drops at a time, which was exactly what I needed. If I guzzled water, I would surely die. I wasn't sure I would have had the resistance not to guzzle if more water had been available.

Thankfully, the nearby sprinkler not only gave me water, it soothed my sunburnt skin as it washed some of the salt brine off my body and clothes. I hadn't drunk nearly as much water as I dared when I closed my eyes to ease their burning from hours of salt and sun exposure.

It was getting dark when I opened them again. I wasn't sure if I had been asleep or passed out. Whichever it was, I wouldn't mind going back to that state again. Everything about me was in pain from the top of my head to the bottom of my feet. Pain is a reminder that you're still alive, my trainer had once told me.

Boy, was I ever alive.

I looked about in hopes the sprinklers were still on. They weren't. The leaves of the shrubby were dry, but the grass beneath them held drops of water, which I took to be fallen dew. I licked off every drop I could find. It wasn't enough water, but it was a comfort to my swollen tongue.

No one realized how much they needed water until they didn't have any.

I lifted my head out of the shrubby to look about. There were lights on inside the house. Fortunately, they were shining in a different direction than I was hiding in. It was dark enough for me to crawl closer to the house if I could make my body do so. I was counting on there being a water spigot near the house. If I was to gain strength, I needed to hydrate myself. What little water I had consumed helped, but it wasn't enough.

I longed to jump up and run, but I knew better even if I had been able to do so, which I wasn't. I would need time to regain strength. Considering how vigorously I had trained to build up my endurance and muscle mass, I should be able to recover faster than the average person.

Still yet, I was a lightweight. A hundred and fifteen pounds of solid muscle with the reflects as fast as those of a striking snake according to my trainer. My trainer also commented that I didn't have an ounce of fat on my entire body. If I had a little fat, it would sustain me until I found food. Fact was, a person could survive for weeks without food, but only three or four days without water. I'd had a taste of water. Now I needed more.

I must have gotten to the house unseen for I heard no commotion or angry voices. It was my luck that the house was built high up to give a better view of the ocean. It was light enough outside for it not to take long for me to spot the water spicket against the rock foundation of the house. I turned the spigot on dribble and drank as much water as I dared. I saw a door not far from the spicket and made my way to it and slowly opened the door. Underneath the house was a large crawl space that was used as storage considering the objects that were barely visible from the small amount of light that still shown through the crack in the door.

I tried to determine a safe spot where I could lie down and spend the night in a protective shelter. In the far back under tarp covered equipment would be best, but I didn't have the strength or the light to get far. I closed the door and stumbled to the first tarp covered equipment I came to. I laid down on the concrete floor beneath it. Hopefully, I would be covered if someone opened the door.

"Help me put the garbage out. It's trash pick-up day," the sound of a woman's voice woke me up. "It's time to go to work and I don't want to be late."

I lay still in case the garbage had been stored in the crawlspace. It had. The door creaked open and both a man and a woman grabbed a bag each sitting against the wall near the door. Thankfully, they closed the door back without so much as hesitating or looking about.

"What time will you be home this evening?" the woman asked.

"Usual time. Don't have to work late today."

"Good. We can have a good meal together."

"Right on. I'm sick and tired of eating pizza," the man said.

The thought of pizza made my mouth water. I was both thirsty and hungry.

"Then I'll get the left-over pizza out of the frig and put it with the trash," said the man.

Happy words to my ears. With luck, I could eat pizza soon. I stayed put and listened as the trash can lid dinged open and closed. The sound of two car engines sounded moments before the garage door opened. First one vehicle and then the other drove out. The sounds of cars driving away disappeared in the distance. All was silent.

I eased out from under the tarp, made my way to the door as silently as my stiff, aching body would allow, felt for the door handle and eased the door open. Thankfully, the hinges were well oiled and didn't make a squeak, which I hadn't even taken into consideration last night.

The brightness of the morning sunlight hurt my eyes. Too much salt water and reflected sun rays had surely done a job on my eyes as well as my body. It was going to take more than one night of rest for me to recuperate. Was I willing to spend the time here in the crawl space, or should I be moving on the best I could? Once I had more water and some food in my belly, I could think more logically about what would be best.

I tried to be invisible as I slunk along the side of the house to the water spigot. I turned on a trinkle and drank again. Again, it wasn't enough, but I feared to drink my fill until later. If there was pizza, I didn't want to vomit it or the water up. I knew all too well what trauma and stress did to my body. Food and water would help, but time was the miracle worker.

I listened to sounds as I looked about. I could see the roofs of two houses in the distance and determined the trees and shrubbery would conceal me as I carefully made my way to the garbage cans at the end of the driveway. Whoever lived here had enough money to do things right. They hadn't skimped on building the house or the landscaping. I slunk from grouping of shrubby to grouping of shrubby like a hungry raccoon until I was within reach of the trash cans. I lifted the lid, still on my knees, looked in, and lifted the pizza box lid.

Did I ever hit the jackpot. There was a good half pizza left in the box, along with an empty liter drink bottle. I took both out, closed the box, put the garbage can lid back in place as silently as possible, and slunk back into a clump of shrubbery. I gobbled down a slice like I hadn't had food in days. It was hard to stop myself from eating it all, but I knew better. Not enough was better than too much. I closed the pizza lid and slunk back to the water spigot, filled the bottle, and slunk back to the crawl space with my prize possessions. I went inside and closed myself in the semi-darkness.

Odd how precious food and water became when you didn't have any. Money meant nothing when you couldn't buy what you needed with it. So, exactly what did I need right now? What actions was I to take next? Those were the same two questions I'd asked myself many times over when I found myself in a desperate situation.

Exhaustion was my enemy. Now that I had eaten and gotten fresh water in me, I needed to rest in order to have a clear mind. I found a darkened corner and curled up like a rat hiding itself from danger.

Being in danger was not unusual for me. My chosen profession always put my life at risk. This was the first time the people I worked for had turned on me. The first time I had real evidence they wanted me dead. Had my death order come down from the top or was it from a rogue branch of the Freedom Group I'd learned too much about?

There was no such thing as the good guys and the bad guys. There was a mixture of both in every organization.

Chapter 3

~~Bennie Jack~~

I drew in a deep breath and let it out slowly. I had expected primitive, but this went beyond expectations. A good description of the road I was driving on was on the prehistoric side. I could only assume the road had been traveled once upon a time, but not recently, which was alright with me. That was exactly what I wanted for now. And perhaps for an unknown amount of time to come. If a person needed to disappear, it was best to do a permanent job of it.

Oh well, I never had a guarantee that life would be easy. I still didn't expect easy even at my most optimistic moments. Actually, I'd always chosen the opposite for myself. I lived for the challenge of the impossible as well as the dangerous. My trainer claimed I had a death wish, but that wasn't true. My wish was to live life to its fullest and die at an exceedingly old age.

I continued driving the ancient Ford truck up the overgrown, rutted, washed-out, muddy, excuse of a road. My head hit the cab of the truck so many times I'd lost count. From now on I would have to get a hat with padding in the top, or perhaps a football helmet. I'd finally geared down the truck to groundhog to avoid a concussion.

The truck and I had traveled over five miles of the delipidated road before the road took an upward turn that kept getting steeper and narrower. The old four-wheel drive truck had been chosen for a reason. Now, I found out why it was a good idea to have undercarriages jacked higher than normal. Unfortunately, I hadn't yet learned where the big rocks and deep holes lay hidden, or which mud holes had no solid bottom.

This was an unknown place to which I was moving to. A place where no modern conveniences existed. A place with no computers, electricity, or WIFI. All of which I thought I wanted and needed if I were to remain dead at the bottom of an ocean.

I had purchased the place sight unseen with seeing only a deed of the land and a few outdated pictures of the house and outbuildings. I was not trying to purchase a lifetime investment knowing the property would increase in value. Actually, I was hoping to obtain the opposite. My main purpose was to purchase a place that no one other than God was willing to venture into much less want to live. A place as far away from other human inhabitants as possible.

The farther I drove, the more I realized I might have succeeded.

As for disappearing, a dead person was harder to trace than a live one. When a person did their job and then needed to disappear, it was helpful when the right decisions were made. And that was exactly what I was doing. I had made the decision to disappear for the rest of my life – in order to save my life.

But I knew better than to be too optimistic.

I learned long ago no one did favors unless they expected a lot more favors in return. That's why I was determined to do everything on my own and in my own way. There was no other person in the entire world I trusted other than myself, and that included my trainer. That cautionary fact had been proven many times over. That's why I chose this secluded place. I wanted to go back to nature and live my life in peace and solitude without anyone knowing I still existed.

It didn't bother me that the house I bought was built over a hundred years ago. Actually, its age attracted me. I liked the idea of owning a home with a lot of long-ago history. The house appeared to be in habitable condition according to the pictures the owners' real estate agent had shown me. The house and large acreage belonged to six grandchildren who hadn't visited the place – ever. All they had were pictures of the property that had been handed down from their great grandparents, grandparents, and parents. The real estate agent made a point of stating the land was what was being sold. The old house and outbuildings were not calculated into the price. Therefore, there was no fiduciary guarantee of their condition.

The one heir who had been paying the taxes for many years had taken the other five to court in an attempt to get them to pay for their fair share of the taxes, which had added up to be more than the value of the property. The five had gotten together and decided to sell the property. And, for spite, not to the one who had been paying the taxes.

There had been others who showed interest in purchasing the land at a lowball price because it was so remote, almost non-navigable, mostly uninhabited mountains. I had been the only one who had shown interest in the property at anywhere close to fair market value. And the only one who did not require a bank loan. There were many factors that stopped banks and loan companies from being willing to finance the place at any price. One of the factors was the lack of ingress, egress, and regress. The only possible entrance to the tract of land was a logging trail that was a few feet of width winding up the side of a rocky mountain. It was mainly a wagon road where the Whiting Lumber company timbered a portion of the mountain many years before.

I had cash money. A lot of it. Got some of it illegally, although a good portion of it was a replacement for my own money. My supposed death had defiantly been to my advantage. It was only my basic instincts, along with my training, that saved my life.

After barely managing to survive, I went after those who planned my death and took back what rightfully belonged to me. My anger had me wanting retaliation for those who tried to kill me. Therefore, I took all the cash-money Brigham was holding for those higher up crooks, which wasn't a small amount. I considered a portion of it as being interest on the time spent during my suffering and recuperating. Not to mention that loss of the money would bring Brigham worse punishment than I could ever dish out.

It was difficult to prove a person, who had been killed before the theft occurred, had been the one to take all the money out of a hidden, supposedly secure safe.

I felt a touch of glee at that.

The further I drove, the more thankful I became that I had stopped at a small town fifteen miles before reaching this logging road to stock up on food stuff and other necessities. I dared not over fill my cart at any one store. It took three stops in different areas to get enough food to tide me over for a month, including a lot of dried beans, rice, and canned goods. I knew fresh foods would not last long. I had no idea when I would make another trip out of the mountain. Considering the condition I found the road in, I wouldn't be in any hurry to make the trip a second time.

This long, so-called lack of a road was only one of the factors that put buyers and loan companies off. The isolation and lack of inhabitants were only two of the many more reasons. Reasons that led to me buying it.

To make matters worse, it started to rain. It was an early spring cloudburst. One minute the sun was shining, and the next minute dark clouds boiled up over the tree covered mountain like black smoke from the burning of old tires. Daylight turned as dark as night once rain spatters started hitting the windshield of the old truck. Hail was pounding down with the intended to shatter glass. I reached forward and turned on the truck's headlights, which helped only a marginal amount. All I could see ahead of me were the lights reflecting off weeds, underbrush, and tree trunks.

My first instinct was to stop right where I was and wait out the storm, but I had driven for so long that I was exhausted and impatient to get to the old house. My rearend ached from sitting on the worn-out padding of the truck seat. Not to mention how my legs and feet hurt from driving a straight stick. To added to everything, I was struggling to guide a vehicle without power steering. But, to the truck's credit, it was well built and dependable. It was traveling over ground I didn't think a tractor could go.

I thought the road couldn't get any worse, but I was wrong. The road got steeper as it climbed and twisted its way upward. The headlights reflected on wet, drooping branches that touched each other over the cab of the truck. There were terrible ruts and mudholes that I unsuccessfully tried to steer the truck around.

The road got even narrower with steep banks on the upper side along with what I could determine in the dim light to be dangerous drop-offs into a ravine on the lower side. There was barely enough room for the truck tires to travel on. Vegetation scraped the bottom and both sides of the truck making me cringe with every knock and bump.

The longer I drove the more the rain increased. The cloud cover was making it get dark earlier than it should be. The wind began to shriek strong enough to blow half-grown leaves and snap branches out of the trees. The windshield and truck hood were covered in debris. Overhead the sky sizzled with forks of lightning. Claps of thunder rumbled with enough vibration to shake the ground beneath the truck.

The rain gushed down harder than I thought possible. I could no longer see the hood of the truck much less the road. I decided it was best to stop driving and wait out the storm. I lifted my foot off the gas just as the truck hit something hard and came to stop so powerful that it jarred my teeth and threw me against the steering wheel. The cab of the truck was tipped down lower than the bed.

I cranked down the window slightly and tried to get a good enough look to determine the situation. The sound of rushing water increased. From what little I could see; it appeared I had come to a spot where I had to ford a creek bed that was overflowing with a sudden flashflood.

The force of the water moved the truck until I feared the truck and I would be washed downstream to an unwelcome ending. I didn't dare try to escape the confine of the truck, and I didn't dare stay in it. I closed my eyes, gritted my teeth, and started praying even harder than I was accustomed to doing on a minute-by-minute basis. My survival had a way of ending up with prayer and luck regardless of intelligence and planning. Sometimes I wondered to what purpose God kept me alive. Considering my profession, He surely had a powerful reason.

The truck had only moved a few feet when it came to a jarring halt as the engine stopped running and the headlights went out. A tree had uprooted and blocked the truck from being washed down the embankment into a black chasm. I rolled the window up and said a heartfelt prayer of thanks to the Almighty.

The storm continued to rage as the water increased until it was washing in one side of the truck and out the other side. I considered opening the lower door to see if it might stop the water from rising in the cab, but reason hit me. I didn't want the force of the water to jerk the door from its hinges. It was best to leave things as they were. I feared for the supplies I had stored in back of the truck along with what I had stored in the cab. Hopefully, the things I had on the seat and behind it would stay dry. The few things I had in the floor of the cab were already wet, but they would dry okay.

I lifted my feet onto the seat to keep them out of the water. I feared I would be right where I was sitting for a long time to come.

After some time passed, my situation altered my thinking until I started laughing right out loud. It seemed ironic that after all the hair-raising, death-defying circumstances I had participated in, Mother Nature just might be the one to end my existence. It seemed rather fitting when I thought my life would finally become somewhat normal, perhaps even happy, I would end up in a watery grave after all.

Chapter 4

~~- Aunt Polly~~

Shivers crawled up my arms and down my back. It brought that chill I'd experienced ever since I was little. Didn't have any idea what it meant this time. It could be good, or it could be bad. Whatever it was, I feared it would affect my life. The feeling could be a warning that my beloved daughter was going to show up again. It was not in her nature to leave me alone to live in peace. It could also be a warning that the sin eater would show up to pray over my dead body before eating my sins. I hoped neither of those things was the cause of what I was feeling. Whatever it was, I'd best get myself prepared for it.

The smell of rain was in the air as I gathered enough deadfall to warm me up some supper in the old cook stove for several days. There was one thing for certain, these old virgin woods provided all the wood for my fire that I would ever need.

I was thankful for it.

Little things made a big difference in my life.

I can't begin to thank God enough for what came easy, what God allowed Mother Nature to provide in abundance. The wind and snow were better than any ax to take down deadfall. And the wind and rain, oh my, the rain could be the mightiest force of all. It could give gentle life to all that lived, or it could be a flooding torrent that took life away, including the thin mountain soil.

If my nose and eyes were holding true, there was a humdinger of a storm in the making somewhere near at hand,

31

but I didn't think that was what caused my body to go on cold alert.

Earlier in the day, the sun had come out too hot for the spring day, and my old milk cow had laid down in the shade of a hickory tree with her tail end to the east. A bad sign where the weather was concerned. The spring robins had gathered early in the day to fill their craws with worms that were sheltering under the cow patties. It wasn't long until they stopped their search for food to seek early shelter as soon as the sunlight crept behind clouds. Even the insects had become silent as though they were waiting for Mother Nature to let loose of whatever she had in mind.

I had soup beans warming on the stove from where I had soaked and then cooked a pot full yesterday, along with cornbread mixed up to fry as soon as the stove was hot enough to sizzle the hog lard in the frying pan.

Living in the backwoods of these old mountains wasn't the easiest kind of life, but it was the kind of life I'd always known. The kind of life I still wanted to live even at my age. Not that I was dead old, but I sure enough was staring eye to eye with my maker. I no longer could do what I once did as far as just about everything went, but God had granted me enough strength to get by on. I could ask for no more than that. Didn't want God to think I had done gone and got greedy by asking for what he had no intention of giving. He'd already given me more than I deserved, all things considered.

Most folks wouldn't understand how I could love this place where I'd lived in hardship all my life. It didn't matter that winter's freezing winds blew through the cracks of my parents' old log cabin, or how the winds whistled down my rock chimney when a storm was whaling its fury. It didn't matter that I was always chilled to the bone during the coldest part of winter while I barely managed to keep myself from freezing to death. I was convinced spring and summer were worth the cold of winter, but I wasn't so certain I was right about that during winter's deep freeze.

Fall of the year was right good. It did bring on lonesome feelings that rumbled inside my guts and kept me from sleeping good at night. Fall of the year didn't used to feel that way – not when my George was still alive. I knew I could depend on George to keep the lonesomeness away – or at least keep it at bay. George was a lot older than me. His oldest boy, he called little Gee, was almost my age. If little Gee had been a girl, George would not have been willing to marry me. An old enough daughter could have done all the things a man needed a wife for, almost. There was that one thing women didn't talk about. The thing a man would never do with his daughter – at least a decent kind of man wouldn't. The good Lord knew there were plenty that weren't decent.

George was a decent man.

A man willing to take on a child-bride if she was willing to work her fingers to the bone for the rest of her life. I was willing back then. Still was.

George hadn't been the man I thought I would marry, the one I dreamed about marrying, but he was the one I had married – and that was enough. I was hardly more than a little ole thing when he agreed to take me on. His wife had died and left him with a house full of hungry boys to raise. He needed a wife, and I needed a place to live as far away as I could get from my folks. A place where I could hide without bringing shame down on my family as well as myself.

I still cringe when my mind brings all that up – usually late at night when sleep won't come. The worst thing that could happen to a girl happened to me. I was attacked on my way back from the toilet one dark night by one of them not so good men. I had barely come out of the toilet door when he stepped from the shadows and hit me on the side of my head with something hard. That's all I remembered until I came to my senses a good while later. I was cold and shaking all over. Pain was so great it took all my determination to get to my knees. I vomited twice before I was able to stand up. My shaking legs managed to get back to the house. I opened the door, stepped inside, and tripped over a chair, making enough noise to wake up my momma.

There was no question as to what had happened to me. The blood staining my night gown and running down my legs was evidence enough without me going into detail, as was the knot in my hairline just above my temple.

"I'll kill him," my daddy said. "Who was he?" he asked as he went for his squirrel gun that always remained loaded.

"I don't know," I sobbed out. "He knocked me out as I came out of the toilet. I never saw his face or heard his voice." I did get the idea he was there about a grown man instead of a youngish boy.

Momma helped me wash my body in lukewarm water and clean my privates out with vinegar water several times. Momma knew as bad as the attack was, it would be much worse if I had to give birth to the baby of an evil rapist. But, just in case, the vinegar wash wasn't enough, it would be best for me to find a husband right away. That way I could claim it was his, while saving my family and myself from being disgraced forever. Folks on this mountain weren't the forgiving kind. Being an unwed mother was the worst thing that could happen to a girl, her parents, and all her relatives. It was a sin that would never be forgiven or forgotten. She would be better off dead than unwed.

Momma gave me barely enough time for my bruises to fade before she had my daddy contacted the widower, George, and offered me up in marriage. Daddy knew of George and his plight and his need for a wife. He was a poor man who had nothing to offer a wife other than poverty, hard work, and a house full of young'uns to care for that wasn't hers. No girl or young woman in her right mind wanted to fall into something such as that. I was desperate and so was George. He accepted my daddy's offer of me without question.

The night before the wedding, my momma gave me some advice that I heeded all my life. "Don't you ever tell a soul what happened to you – and that includes your husband. It makes a difference to a man, even if he claims it doesn't. He'll think about it. Dream about it. And end up blaming you," Momma warned. "A girl always gets the blame for what happens to her, regardless."

I never did know for certain if my Meadow Lark belonged to George or the attacker. She was born two weeks less than nine months after I married George. She was a mighty big baby. Weighed more than any baby I ever heard about. I do know she was far prettier than any child George fathered before. I had such a difficult time giving birth that I was never able to give birth again. Though my baby and I would die before I managed to push her out. George wasn't disappointed in her being a girl and neither was I. Although I would have liked to had a son of my own, my sweet, little Meadow Lark was enough.

She grew up as pretty as the little bird I named her after. Her voice was as sweet and welcoming as the songs of the springtime. I wasn't sure who my little bird took after. Not only did she grow into a beauty, but she also grew hardheaded, stubborn, and willful. There was nothing on God's green earth that would settle her down or control her. Which, in a way, wasn't a bad thing.

I guess she could be called a free spirit who was determined to do exactly what she wanted to do since she drew her first breath of air. In a way, she kind of reminded me of my mother. Both thought they knew what was best for them and everyone they came into contact with. Especially where I was concerned.

When George died, I only got a little of what he left behind. Once everything was divided among his children, I didn't hardly have a pot left to piss in. By that time my Meadow Lark had left the mountain and gotten married. Between her and me we owned two slivers of the house and land. George's other children insisted we sell the property and divide up the money. Meadow Lark and I had no choice other than do exactly that since we didn't have the money to buy them out.

Meadow Lark insisted I could come live with her, since she used both her small amount of money along with mine to put a down payment on a house, but I declined. I'd about mommyed myself to death getting all George's children grown. I didn't want to move in with Meadow Lark to be a servant again to her and her children. So, I moved back in with my parents. Didn't occur to me at the time that taking care of two elderly people was much more difficult than taking care of children.

After years of their sickness and then their departure into heaven, I got their run-down cabin for my very own along with a large hunk of rocky, steep, side of a mountain. There wasn't one soul who would take what little I now owned away from me. I would see to that.

Much to my regret, Meadow Lark didn't take back after me in her love for her mountain upbringing. I'd always believed if I could make home a happy enough place for the children, they would be willing to return to their happy place, but I was wrong. My Meadow Lark hated the mountains and so did George's boys. My Meadow Lark was ambitious and as restless as a cat in season. I realized early on that she had dreams bigger than this mountain could possibly give her. She had always wanted bigger and better. That's why she ran off to up and marry who she did at a young age. He was a rich boy from off whose parents had bought a whole big acreage adjoining George's land that I was forced to sell. His folks planned on building a fancy summer cabin on the land, but never got around to it. Don't know if they still owned that piece of land or not. It was a far piece away from where my parents lived on their high mountain land most folks claimed was less than worthless.

I'll have to admit the land Meadow Lark's in-laws bought was a mighty fine piece of bottom ground. Ever since I was little, I would watch my daddy look at that piece of ground as we passed by when we went to buy supplies. He longed to make it his. He knew, as did I, that it would never happen. Poor folks had poor ways. Ways that would never bring in enough money to buy what was needed, much less what was wanted.

I often wondered how rich folks got rich. I figured they had to squeeze dollars out of about everybody they came across. I remember Momma saying a rich man could no more go to heaven than an elephant could squeeze through the eye of a needle. If it was poor people who went to heaven, I suspected both Momma and Daddy both entered heaven's door with ease.

Don't know why my Meadow Lark had a different mindset than I did. It was her nature to question everything people told her regardless if it was me or the preacher man.

All the preachers I ever listened to claimed that God was a vengeful God ready and able to punish those who didn't go exactly by his word. Meadow Lark disagreed with that kind of thinking from the very beginning. In her sweet little voice, she'd say: "God ain't vengeful. He's a loving God. He makes beauty and happiness out of everything he shines his light on."

I did my level best to teach her it wasn't right to contradict what the preachers claimed, especially to their faces, but it did no good. She always spoke the truth as she saw it.

My Meadow Lark had set her mind on marrying that boy from off the mountain and nothing would do her until she did. The bad thing was he and his family were off. And that's what he did with my beautiful Meadow Lark. He took her off. Far away from the mother who loved her.

I'd get to see her only when she came with him to the mountains on a very short visit. Her man's daddy owned a car dealership way down in hot country. Her man worked for his daddy. They made money hand over fist, but I knew deep down in my heart that my Meadow Lark wasn't happy. Although she never said a word, I still knew.

I didn't rightly know what it would take to make my sweet girl happy. If I had, I'd have done my best to make sure she got it, although I was as poor as Job's turkey. I loved her enough to do whatever it took unless it was selling my land and moving off my mountain.

Much to my regret, I suspected my sweet girl had taken back after her daddy, or the one I suspected was her daddy. The one I never knew for certain who he was. Still didn't want to know, although I always suspected his identity. Him and his folks lived down off the mountain, but him and his buddies came on the mountain to hunt and kill whatever animals they came across.

For years, when our paths happened to cross, I'd see the longing in his eyes when he looked at me. I reckon he knew from the very beginning that his folks would never allow him to marry such as me, so he took what he wanted knowing he would ruin me for somebody else.

My family and kin were rough mountain folks brought up on hard work and determination. His momma and his daddy were both schoolteachers. High up in society people who made a whole lot of money from being paid by the government itself. He had a mighty good future in front of him when I didn't. His folks would undoubtedly send him off to college to become a teacher like them.

I suspect it didn't stop him from wanting me even after I was married. Guess he was afraid to bother a full-grown woman instead of a helpless young girl. Not to mention me having a husband like George.

Mess with a man's wife and you just might find yourself dead.

Sometimes I thought about attacking him in the dark, knocking him out cold, and then cut him like cutting a boar pig. I never did but just thinking about it gave me a sense of revenge. Sometimes, to this day I thought about doing it.

After George died and Meadow moved away, I just might have traveled off this mountain and given it a try if I ever got the right chance.

I know it went against God's commandments, but I never forgot a wrong done to me. Neither did I forget a kind soul who when out of their way to help me. A good turn was worth a good turn in return.

Chapter 5

~~Bennie Jack~~

Sometime during the long night, my mind must have gotten exhausted to the point that my body took over and allowed me to fall into a deep, black sleep. It was nearly morning when I opened my eyes, slightly confused for a moment before memory came back to me, which was something I never wanted myself to do. Confusion was not a beneficial state of mind. I needed my mind to stay sharp at all times, even when I thought I was in a perfectly safe situation, which I wasn't at all during the night. One never knew what Mother Nature would do. Fortunately, she had gentled during the night.

I was left alive.

The cloud burst had wrung itself dry.

The black of night was slowly turning to morning gray. I could detect the pale outline of the moon in a clear sky. There were even a few stars to be seen through the leaves of the trees. It was an entirely different world from last night. I got out of the down sleeping bag, rolled down the window and looked out. I no longer heard the sound made by rushing water, but the truck was still lodged against the uprooted tree. A morning drop in temperature had arrived, and I was chilled all the way to the bone, so I turned the key in the ignition with hopes the engine might miraculously start. It didn't turn over. There wasn't even a click from the battery.

A trash bag of clothes was behind the truck seat where I had put it. I fished it out, opened it up and put on a coat to warm up before it was light enough to see what circumstance

I was in along with exactly what damage the storm had caused during the night.

I sat on the seat bundled in my coat as the light slowly continued to creep in until I could see the outline of trees against the morning sky. And then, like a miracle, the gray sky turned to the palest of pink. The sun was finally rising over the eastern mountain. I opened the passenger door and stood on the running board as I looked down into the washed-out trench the truck was sitting in.

It was obvious a flash flood had hit the mountains last night as darkness set in. A river of water washed out a deep gully down the mountainside taking soil, rocks, and debris with it. Unfortunately, it had also taken a section of the so-called road while the truck was still on it. The truck was sitting in a ditch two feet lower than both sides of the road. If that wasn't bad enough, the truck wasn't starting.

Okay, I told myself, refresh your mechanical training and get out to take a look under the hood. I did and discovered the bottom of the washed-out gully was more solid than I had expected. Somewhere down below this area, the flat land had gotten some good mountain soil. With flash floods like last night there was no wonder mountains consisted mostly of rock.

I opened the hood and climbed up on the bumper. It didn't take a nuclear physicist to see the hard knock the truck took when it landed against a tree trunk had merely jarred the battery cable loose on one of the posts. I reconnected it, got back in, and turned the key. It started. I got back out and turned the hubs into lock. I hoped having four-wheel drive would be enough to get the truck out of the gully. It wasn't. The truck couldn't pull itself up the steep bank of the washout. Looked to me like I had two choices. I either shoveled down the banks until the truck could pull itself out, or I could carry enough rocks to fill in the gully enough to make the tires ride higher. Most likely it would take both to get the truck out.

I would start with the shovel.

But first, I needed to find out how close to my property I was. I took out walking in the direction I should have been driving. I walked about half a mile before I realized the only change was that the so-called road got rougher and steeper the farther I walked. I gave up, turned around and went back to the truck. I started shoveling to discover rocks and roots were keeping me from digging the sides down. I would need to bring in rocks in an effort to build the road up. I spent hours searching the woods for rocks small enough and flat enough for me to carry and place in the washed-out road. It took me hours to get one layer of rocks. I got in the truck, started it up and rocked it back and forth enough to pack the rocks down. I did the same over and over again until the sun was high in the sky and sweat was sliding off my face and body.

I took a break, got peanut butter and crackers out of my food supply inside the truck, knifed the peanut butter on the crackers and ate a few.

"All that water," I mumbled, and I didn't have any to drink. I had assumed there would be a spring at the house I was traveling to. I found the remains of the soft drink I had been sipping on yesterday and drank it down. I began my rock hauling again.

Hours passed until the sun was sliding down behind the mountains, and I still didn't have enough rocks piled up to get the truck out. So, I kept at it until it was too dark for me to find rocks in the woods.

"Tomorrow is another day," I told myself as I climbed into the cab of the truck and ate a few more crackers spread with peanut butter. I opened the half-gallon of orange juice I had bought and drank half of it down. I would save the rest until morning.

I laid down in the truck seat and tried to rest, but my body was aching similar to pain from a rotten tooth. After all my training, why was I not in better physical condition? The time I spent in the ocean, plus going without food, must have weakened me more than I anticipated. Nothing I did eased the aches I was feeling. So much for my arrogance in thinking myself being in topnotch physical shape. I had lifted weights, run miles on end with weight strapped to my back, endured military tactical courses, gone through several types of self-defense training, not to mention the other physical devastations that had befallen me during my career, and my muscles were still aching from doing something as simple as lifting and carrying rock all day long.

I tossed and turned on the old truck seat until I finally fell into an exhausted sleep. I opened my eyes to broad daylight. I sat up and let out a scream of surprise – along with fright. There was a face pressed against the passenger window, with hands cupped around the face, looking in at me.

It was the leathery wrinkled and grooved face of a very old person. I couldn't tell for sure if it was a man or woman. Sprigs of white hair stuck out from under a dilapidated, grayish, sweat stained, felt hat. Two dark lines of what looked like snuff-spittle stained the wrinkles going down beside the mouth and chin. I had to grin at my sudden fright. I had woken up to see the faces of a lot worse.

I rolled the window down.

"Not meant to of scared you?" the apparition said. "'Pears you're in a fix."

"Yes," I admitted. "It does appear the flood put me in a fix."

"Water warshed the road out," the apparition needlessly said. "Does it at times. Clouds split wide open and floods this ole mountain something awful."

"I was trying to build the road up enough to get my truck out." I decided this had to be an old woman although her voice had grown deep with age.

"Why for?" she asked.

"So, I can continue driving?" I told her what I thought should be obvious.

"Why are you here in the first place?" she made her question clearer.

"I bought the old Slaughter place," I told her, although I didn't think I needed to explain myself to anyone. I wasn't entirely sure if she was real or if I was still asleep and having a nightmare. I pinched my arm just to make sure I was awake.

"Do tell? Well, I'll be. Never thought I'd see the day any fool would do a thing such as buy that old place. Not in my lifetime anyhow."

"How far is it from here?" I asked.

The wrinkles on her face grew closer together as she considered what I'd asked. Finally, she answered. "I calculate another three or four miles going by the road. Not so much as the crow flies."

Unfortunately, neither my truck nor I was a crow.

"What road?" I mumbled.

"The onliest one here abouts," she told me. "Reckon it'll take you a spell to tote enough rocks," she said, turned, and disappeared into the undergrowth of the woods. I pinched myself again to make sure I really wasn't in the middle of a nightmare.

I opened the door and got out. I was awake, but I could still be in the middle of a different kind of nightmare. The old woman's appearance had been unsettling to say the least. I might as well start carrying rocks. I couldn't leave my truck and all the supplies I bought sitting in this washed-out ditch.

I had cleared a half-mile circle of rocks when I finally had enough rock, moss, and dirt piled high enough to drive the truck out. My hands were raw with blisters while every fingernail had been pinched black. Every inch of my body now ached with equal pain as to having every tooth in my mouth abscessed and ready to rupture. I couldn't begin to describe how badly my back hurt. But then I had hurt equally as much many times before while gathering information for the Freedom Group. Thing was, I had thought my life would be easier on me from now on. It appeared I was wrong.

Three or four miles. I assured myself wasn't far – not compared to how far I'd already driven on the goat path of a road. I reminded myself I had chosen this place for its isolation. I didn't want visitors of any kind and this road would assure me of that. Or was I wrong about that also? I hadn't even reached my new home when another human being had shown up. At least, I assumed she had been human. The good thing was – well, I wasn't sure there was a good thing unless it was how scary she had looked standing on the running board and peering in the window at me.

She wasn't the type to draw a lot of visitors. She certainly didn't go out weekly to sip tea with the ladies. But then, I had no right to be sarcastic. I wasn't the tea sipping kind myself. I was more – well, the kind you didn't want to know existed.

~~~~

I continued traveling on a road that got worse the farther I drove. The rain had settled the mud somewhat but left what appeared to be near bottomless mud holes. I had to give credit to the old truck. It kept on going regardless of bouncing and sinking in washed-out ruts. Its undercarriage stayed solid. Its tires held together. The road topped a steep slope, and I came out of the woods to see what might have once been a meadow that hadn't been mowed in many years. Grass and weeds appeared to be waist high in the April sunshine. The soil must be fertile. It hadn't been eroded away the way the road had.

I drove a little farther in the high grass until a house came into view on top of another rise. The morning sun shone its light on the front of the house. My breath caught. What a house. The pictures I had been shown did not do it justice. Even with all its once-upon-time grandeur it was now a falling down reminder of what it had once been. I quickly concluded I had paid too much for the place in its present condition. The roof was of orange rusted tin with several sections blown loose but at least the tin roofing was still hanging on. The boards that remained were weathered gray without any paint evident. As for overpaying for the many acres of land I'd bought with the house would remain to be seen.

As I looked at the old house, my imagination began seeing it as a once regal lady. One that had become aged, lost her beauty and her teeth, along with a bent back and nearly blinded eyes. Some of the windows were broken. The roof over the upper and lower porches were sagging. Siding boards were missing. Some of the porch posts were hanging on at an angle. To the builder's credit, four rock chimneys were still intact.

The old woman who peered through the truck window came to my mind. She and this house had surely aged similar during the years they remained on this mountain. I couldn't get the old woman and where she came from out of my mind. It was like she appeared out of nowhere, like an apparition. I'd seen no sign of a house, or even smelled a hint of smoke coming from a chimney. One thing was for certain, there was and never had been electricity on this mountain. I hoped there never would be. Modern conveniences came with population.

As for this old house, repairs on it would keep me busy for years to come. I did plan on restoring the old place as best I could. Be it what it was, it was now my home. Fortunately, I had thought to bring hammers and a lot of nails.

I drove the truck through the field, hoping I wouldn't run into dangers hidden by the tall grass. I jumped, hitting my head on the roof again as I was startled by a doe deer leaped up in front of the truck and bounded out of sight. I hit my brakes to allow two small fawns to disappear after their mother. I smiled. I really had gone from city life back to nature.

I started the truck up again and drove as close to the front porch of the house as possible. I stopped the truck and got out. I had the strangest feeling that I was being watched. It was most likely by the deer that I had scared away. Still, I felt the warning prickles on my skin. Trust your intuition, my trainer's words came to me. Most likely watching eyes belonged to the old woman. No doubt she could walk faster through the woods than I had driven on what could barely pass as a road.

There were five wide steps leading up to the porch. Some sort of creeping vines climbed up all four of the chimneys. Spindly weeds had sprouted up and grown through the cracks of the porch. Along with the signs of decay, there were also signs of nature's beauty. Lilac bushes, way taller than my head, were in full bloom at each end of the porch. Forsythia grew in wild yellow profusion along the sides of the house and all the way to the barn and outbuildings, which were many. It was obvious that outbuildings were just as important for survival as the house was. Needless to say, I was pleased with the outbuildings even though they were also in need of repair. There was a barn with a corn crib, and other sheds I wasn't sure of their purpose. Somehow, they were not visible in the picture of the house I had been shown.

I carefully placed my feet on the steps and was surprised to find they felt solid enough. I climbed onto the porch, steeping on a few weeds, and went to the door. I don't know why I was surprised that it wasn't locked, being it would be easy to climb through a broken windowpane if someone wanted to enter. I always thought it interesting how doors were locked when windows were breakable.

I entered a large room with a huge rock fireplace against one end of the room. A window was on one side of the fireplace looking out onto the meadow. Two windows faced the porch. The room had two closed doors, not including the entry door. I assumed the doors led into other rooms. Not so much as one stick of furniture was in the room. I wasn't surprised, but I was disappointed. I had hoped the house would come furnished. I had to grin at my hopefulness. A house abandoned for as long as this one would have been raided of everything of value years ago.

I opened one of the inside doors. It led to a long narrow kitchen. At least there was a heavy looking wood cookstove against the wall. Its stovepipe still attached to one of the chimneys. No doubt it remained because it was too large and heavy to be moved without several strong men straining their backs. I was thankful for it as there was obviously no electricity or any other amenities in the house. I had expected such deprivation and had the bed of the truck filled with things I would need. I had covered everything up with a canvas tarp, but I hadn't counted on such a sudden storm. I hoped the cloudburst hadn't ruined anything.

I had brought a large box of different sized candles along with several boxes of kitchen matches and a few dozen cigarette lighters. Being without the ability to start a fire was a real danger. I had also added two old style oil lamps with two five-gallon jugs of lamp oil. I had no idea what I would need that I hadn't thought of, but I assumed I would be able to leave the mountain to purchase it before I settled in for good. I had done my best to change my appearance. I had lost at least twenty pounds of weight, cut my tangle of hair so short my head was all but shaved, and dyed the stubble a pale shade of red. I could pass for a young boy if one didn't look too closely. One thing was for sure. I wouldn't be leaving the mountain often. Actually, I hoped I wouldn't need to leave it at all once I got settled in with everything producing the way it should.

What was the use of leaving the grid and going back to nature if I had to keep seeking stores in order to survive? I had undergone a degree of training in order to live off the land for a short period of time, but I didn't want the permeance of it to be too difficult. Living off roots, worms and insects wasn't what I had in mind when I chose to become a recluse for my own survival. What I wanted was a life of self-sufficiency in an area where I would never be found. I'd had enough of serving my country the day my government decided I knew too much about what was going on.

I went out an inside kitchen door to find a small, attached dark room with a concrete trough running along one side. It also had a door to the outside that I opened to bring in more light. There was a pipe leading into the trough and one leading out of it. I'd seen such in pictures of old houses. It was a built-in spring house. Such as that was evidence of a well-to-do family during a time long past. I felt fortunate I wouldn't have to carry water from a spring once I found the headwater and got it running back into the trough.

I went back into the front room and opened the other door. It was a hallway between two rooms that I assumed had been bedrooms. The rooms were empty except for peeling wallpaper hanging from the walls in long strips. One of the rooms had a narrow staircase against the far wall leading to the second floor. I went to the staircase and very carefully placed my feet on the steps to check their strength. The stairs were solid. I went up them and looked around. The stairs ended in a narrow hall with four small rooms. Two bedrooms on each side of the hall. Each room had a window and a chimney with a hole in the wall for a stovepipe. All the floors in the house were made from wide planks of what appeared to be oak or maple wood. There were also signs that the roof leaked, which wasn't a surprise since the tin had obviously blown loose.

Okay. What was I to tackle first? Water. I need to find where the spring was headed up and get water into the concrete trough. The trough had to be gravity fed, which meant the spring was located higher up than the house.

Chapter 6

~~Aunt Polly~~

I didn't know what to think when I heard the sound of a vehicle climbing up the mountain. My first thought was that my Meadow Lark was coming for me. As much as I wanted to see my Meadow Lark, I didn't want her to come back if she thought she could take me away from my beloved home. She claimed I was too old to live by myself in a desolate place like this mountain. Surely, she had to realize I didn't want to leave my home. Although it was true that much had changed with my ability, nothing had changed where my willpower was concerned. Age and hard survival had taken its toll on me as it had with my folks' cabin, but I still wanted to die in the same place I had been born and lived in. I didn't think it too much to ask my only child to grant me my wish.

The last time my Meadow Lark was here was when the timber had changed color four years ago. Since then, I'd managed to mail her a letter several times a year telling her I was happy and healthy. I'd get letters from her right often when the only other person who lived on the backside of the mountain happened to go into town and then stick the letters under my front door late at night. He'd always stop at my cabin to see if I needed anything and mail my letters. He was an odd sort of fellow who stayed to himself and bothered nothing and nobody. I thought of him as a hermit. His hair, mustache and beard were so dark and thick all I could see of him were his eyes. When he first allowed me to see him, his appearance just about scared the breath outta my body.

The last time my Meadow Lark showed up, I'd had a summer of good conditions, and things were looking good. I'd gathered a large stack of deadfall for the coming winter. Plus, I'd grown a mighty good garden and filled every canning jar I could find. Not only that, I'd dried apples, leather britches beans, and corn along with a few other things. I'd even spruced up the old cabin a little.

My Meadow Lark had decided I was doing okay but lacking a few necessities. She made the trip off the mountain to buy a hundred pounds of flour and fifty pounds of sugar. Which, she thought would be a treat for me. I ground my own corn meal and robbed honeybees of their honey. I also grew a small patch of molasses cane to press and boil them down. I kept two nanny goats for milk, along with an aggravating billy-goat that was no use other than to eat briars and breed the nannies. My Meadow Lark didn't realize I had everything I needed right here.

I certainly didn't want my Meadow Lark to show up before I had a chance to recover from the long, hard winter. That's one of the reasons I checked out the vehicle once the rainstorm had passed. I was both relieved it wasn't my Meadow Lark and upset to find it was a stranger. Never in my life had I thought it would be some outsider who bought the old Slaughter place. Lawsy me, that place had been some kind of fancy many years in the past. It had been built and passed down by a long line of moonshiners back when moonshining was profitable.

Old lady Slaughter was a prolific woman with the strength and endurance of a team of oxen. She gave birth to a pile of children, all of them boys, before her juices dried up. There were so many Slaughter kin who shared ownership of the place that none of them could get together on a single thought much less on selling the place. Talk about a bunch of jealous, greedy folks, the Slaughters took the whole cake and then some. All any of them ever cared about was themself. They'd skin a neighbor for his hide if it benefited them.

That's another reason they had such a fancy house and a whole bunch of acreage.

I was so shook-up I didn't even ask questions or find out who the stranger was. I wanted to get away from her as fast as I could. Strangers of any kind on this mountain could mean a world of trouble. Didn't matter if it was a woman or a man.

Used to be a lot of men came to the mountain on drunken hunting trips even though the top and most of the back part of the mountain was privately owned. Hunting wasn't allowed on privately owned land either, but hunters didn't care. They came hunting and drinking anyway.

I wasn't the only person who lived on this old mountain. There was one other person who valued his privacy far more than I did. I wasn't exactly sure when he'd arrived or even who he was. He'd slunk in as silent and unobtrusive as the oncoming night. Thankfully, his place was on the back side of the mountain over the rugged top. He stayed to himself, and the dark haired, dark bearded man only showed up on occasions when I was in great need of something.

I figured it was the folks down off the mountain who told my Meadow Lark there was a rogue sin eater who hid out on the mountain. I had to laugh at that. Still, the mention of a sin eater put fear in some people, which I didn't mind in the least. The only other human living on this mountain was just like me. He wanted to be left alone to live in peace. I figured he was the one who put a stop to those hunters. Their belongings kept disappearing. Even the ones who weren't passed-out drunk lost their guns and ammunition. All of them lost whatever supplies they brought to the mountain, including their liquor. Those who talked about it, claimed their belongings disappeared like mist in the wind. They said they never saw a thing or heard a thing, but there had always been a spooky feeling surrounding them.

Some of them even accused me of taking their things until they had a look at me. They figured there was no way an old woman such as I could climb the rocky mountain, much less be stealthily enough to take their things without them seeing me. I could have done it even at my age, but I hadn't.

I knew who had taken their things. Sometimes a portion of their belongings ended up at my place when the cold weather set in. That's how I got a down-filled sleeping bag along with a rifle, bullets along with a shotgun and shells. There were even times when firewood showed up during the night along with a box of matches. I was thankful.

I had to chuckle every time I thought of a sin eater. Even I didn't believe in such a thing as taking on someone else's sins. It wasn't possible. Nobody could take on another's sins. But then, there was a whole bunch of folks who thought paying a priest to listen as they confessed about their sinning ways would be enough to get rid of their sins. It was called confession. Reckon they didn't know much about repenting and redemption. As for me, I believed the only confession of one's sins ought to be directly to God. I had a direct pathway to God the same as every anybody else did.

I didn't believe there was, or ever had been, such a thing as a sin eater. A man such as that had come about only to make the kin of an unsaved dead person feel better. If it worked for them, so be it. I wasn't going to waste a minute of my life trying to straighten out anybody's thinking, unless it was my Meadow Lark's.

I wondered if this stranger would be somebody crazy or somebody trying to hide from something or someone. No sane person would be willing to live on this mountain without a good reason.

I had only seen the one woman sleeping in the truck, but I feared there would be more than her coming to this mountain. She was still young enough to have a man and houseful of young'uns. If she didn't already have one, she most likely would before long. A woman her age always had a longing streak running in them to reproduce. No matter how independent they thought they were, a need to be held and loved snuck in before a woman knew what was happening to them. I know. I was young once upon a time. Kind of missed it even at my age.

Chapter 7

~~ Bennie Jack~~

I left the house to check out the old barn and the other outbuildings, going to the smallest outbuilding first. It was leaning slightly and looking none too stable. Just as expected, it had a wooden box built against the back wall with two holes cut in the top plank for people to sit over. I had to grin at the two holes. I suppose those who peed together stayed together. At least the old-fashioned toilet hadn't been built over a creek as I'd read many had been. I'd expected to dig a deep hole in the woods, but this would suffice much better. There was a supply of bathroom paper in my stash of necessities. Using leaves wasn't what I had in mind. I got a lesson on wiping with poisonous plants that my trainers hadn't warned me about. It was an unforgettable lesson.

The next outbuilding was a woodshed. There weren't any big sticks of firewood, but there were lots of wood chips that could be used to build a fire in the cookstove. Much to my delight there was a double bitted ax sunk into a wooden stump used to split wood on. How did this tool not get taken if all the furniture in the house was gone? I certainly was glad it was there as I had brought a hatchet instead of an ax. My reasoning was that I could get other necessary things after I checked the place out.

I left the woodshed and walked through the tall weeds to the barn. The door was hanging by one hinge. The other hinge was still attached to the side of the barn with the nails missing on the door side hinge. I entered to the smell of dust and molded hay. I walked down the narrow hall inspecting four stalls, two on each side. There was also an enclosed room with a button holding the door closed. I turned the button and opened the door. Much to my surprise and delight there was a whole grouping of tools hanging on the wall. Shovels, rakes, hoes, pick and mattock and more. There were also stairs leading into the loft. I carefully walked up the stairs in case one of them wouldn't hold my weight. Like the stairs in the house, they were still solid. An eerie feeling came over me as I investigated the almost empty loft, and I couldn't figure out a reason for it.

Trust your instincts, came to mind. I walked farther into the loft, but there was nothing there other than a scattering of hay as old as time. So, why was I getting chills running up my backbone? There couldn't possibly be one of my enemies here. I went to a small door in the loft and opened it up to air out the moldy smell of hay and propped the door open.

The chill I was feeling now was similar to what I felt after I escaped the ocean. I'd made triple sure I had been declared dead along with the two men in the helicopter. The discovery of the helicopter crash made front page news in the local newspaper two weeks after it had happened. The names of the two men along with the name on my birth certificate were in the article. The article stated the helicopter had gone down too far out in the ocean for anyone to survive, although search planes had combed the area. So far, no bodies had washed ashore and were not expected to do so. It was a well-known shark infested area. However, if anyone spotted anything unusual, including articles of clothing etc., let the law official know. I grinned at that and wondered if this was the outcome expected. I knew no one expected me to show up – ever, but I wasn't sure about the two men. I was well aware how events could be manipulated to any specific outcome.

The day after I left the basement, I had hidden in the loft of a barn. As I buried myself in the hay, I found a hen's nest and consumed three raw eggs. I didn't get the chills then like I was getting now. I turned and walked down the stairs. Once my feet touched the bottom stair, the eerie feeling left me. I didn't know what my instinct was telling me, but I would keep my eyes wide open when I was near the barn and every place else.

I walked from the barn to what must have once been a garden spot. There were the remains of a barbwire fence sagging from leaning locust posts. Berry briars were tangled on one side of the fence with their pale leaves starting to bud out. On the other side of the fence were asparagus shoots about six inches high. The soil appeared fertile with an abundance of weeds growing. I recognized lamb's quarters and chick weed. I was well familiar with what greenery and berries were eatable and which ones were poisonous. I had survived on weeds and roots before. They would keep a person alive, barely.

I had brought a large variety of seeds with me, including two fifty-pound sacks of potatoes and twenty-five pounds of both onions and garlic sets. Living off the land meant growing my own food, which I was prepared to do the best I knew how. I had never grown my own food before, but I was both willing and able. I had even been leery enough not to buy a large amount of anything in any one store. I shopped at several stores and garden centers purchasing a few things here and a few things there. I knew how an excess of anything triggered scrutiny. I always paid in cash. I knew having a bank account or any other form of identification provided a way for the government to trace people.

I spent my young life as a city girl. After my parent's death, I started working as a congressional staffer in Washington D.C. while also attending college to get a law degree. I was told as soon as I got a college degree, I could become a congressional aid. I never completed my law degree, but I got one heck of a job offer, which I took because it sounded both exciting and challenging. I hadn't realized at the time that it would also become a form of mission impossible as well as life threatening.

At first what the Freedom Group wanted from me was easy. It required little effort on my part. Plus, the pay was great. It was later on as the jobs became more difficult, that I realized there was never-ending danger that came with what they asked me to do. If I didn't agree to do what they wanted, my past degressions would be made public and I would face prosecution. As on tv production of Mission Impossible, if I was caught, those who employed me would claim no knowledge of my crimes. Never again could I hope for a normal life. Especially now – after I had been declared dead.

I should stop thinking about your past and focus on the future. I'd been put out to pasture, and the real pasture I was walking through was where I planned on remaining for the rest of my life.

I almost made a sound when a pheasant rousted from under my feet and flew into the air and disappeared into the woods. I'd automatically reached for my Glock only to realize I didn't have it with me. How could I have been this foolish this soon? Had my trainer not warned me over and over that there was never a safe place to hide, or a single person to trust?

"Fool," I whispered. What was I thinking when I left my Glock inside? I knew to keep my weapons on me at all times - even when I slept. I had gone against that advice when I left my weapons under the shrubbery. I knew better than to retrieve them as the government knew they belonged to me. It would be best if they were found on a homeless person. I did have the dead man's Glock and knife. I had an idea neither could be traced. I headed back to the house to get the gun, knife, and pepper spray. The pheasant had made me realize again that I was never safe – but I wanted to be.

I had been reckless in pretending I was.

When I took on the name of Bennie Jack, I tried to become who I imagined her to be. I was determined never to utter the name of Fizz or any of my aliases ever again. That person had become fish food at the bottom of the Pacific Ocean.

Me, as Bennie Jack, had arisen from a dead girl's bones. Bennie Jack had disappeared right off the face of the earth leaving her parents to grieve the loss of the youngest of their many children. Where she had disappeared to, no one knew.

"Poor little thing," Momma said. "She was born into a no-good family, plus she was too pretty for her own good. Being a pretty little thing just don't pay when she had their kind of siblings and kin."

Momma had told me back then a missing girl was of little importance and never reported to authorities. Momma had also warned me to listen to my instincts and trust no one, especially when they were being overly friendly. "You're not as pretty as Bennie Jack was when she was little, but you've not turned out ugly either," Momma had warned. "It doesn't pay to be too pretty."

She was right. I wasn't ugly in face or body. When I was still a teenager one schoolteacher told me I had bedroom eyes. I didn't know what he meant by that at the time, but I never forgot what he said. When I was in high school another man looked me over and said, "Everything in portion, nothing in excess." A dangerous combination for a girl with no caution.

I later learned that a pretty face and body were of value to organizations with a purpose in mind. Especially when the naive girl had no relatives to watch over her.

The women's rights movement started in the nineteen sixties. Up until that time women were little more than unpaid slaves to men. My mother had explained all of that to me while I was growing up. I never intended to become a slave to a man or anyone else. And yet, I had become one to the government and then the Freedom Group. But no longer. I had finally found a way to free myself, and I took it. Being in the government's clutches was like being in the mafia. The only way to get out was after you were dead.

It was even worse for a government spy. Young girls were trained how to worm their way into the whitey-tidies of old men as well as the younger men. The younger, prettier, and more innocent a girl looked the better. Get the men hooked on sex, drugs or both and a spy had it made. I didn't become a government spy. I was spying on the government.

I never wanted to be the kind of girl involved in such activity. I played the sweet and innocent type and figured out a way to steal secrets when no one was expecting anything from a dumb naive kid who barely looked sixteen and gave the impression of being a step above dumb, which worked well for me most of the time.

I knew I would be tortured and killed if my true purpose was ever found out. I had to perform a disappearing act more times than I ever dreamed possible. I had come within a hair of my life so many times fear became a habit, but I never thought those who hired me would be the ones who wanted to kill me. How had they found out I had discovered more than they wanted me to know?

"Paranoid," I said to myself as I strapped my Glock under my baggy shirt and secured my knife in a sheath and attached it to my thigh under sweatpants. Pepper spray was put in the left pocket of my sweatpants.

Old habits die hard.

After I armored myself, I headed out with a purpose. I needed to find the spring and get water running in the trough if possible. There was blue-eyed grass and white clover growing in perfusion along the overgrown path I followed up the hill in the direction I though the spring was located. Honeybees gathered on the clover blossoms and flew up as my feet disturbed them. I wondered if there could possibly still be beehives somewhere, or had the bees gone wild and moved into hollow trees. Wild honey would sure come in handy if I was able to harvest it without getting stung to death.

Just as I expected, I found a rocky spring branch running down the hill and disappearing behind the barn. A rock and concrete reservoir had been laid up under a large rock in the edge of the woods. A metal pipe had once been fastened to a spout coming out of the reservoir. I cupped my hands, held them under the spout, and caught water in them to drink my fill of the icy cold water. I picked up the pipe that had come loose and fallen on the ground. I reconnected it the best I could without tools. At least some water was running into the pipe for the time being, and hopefully filling the concrete trough at the house.

It was getting late by the time I got back to the house and checked to see if the water was running into the trough. It was, but the water was washing mud out of the pipe into trough. I assured myself once all the muddy water ran out the overflow there would be clear, clean water in the house.

I got a five-gallon bucket out of the back of the truck and went to the woodshed for wood chips to build a fire in the cook stove. The chill of a spring evening was coming on fast. After that, I would unload the truck before dark set in.

Everything in the back of the truck that could get wet was wet. Thank goodness I had been studious enough to fill the cab of the truck with whatever the elements might destroy. I sat things on the porch to dry out and put other things in the kitchen near the cookstove where the heat would dry them faster.

I had thought to bring a broom, mop, detergent, and bleach. I had an idea the old house would need a good going over. Such cleaning would have to wait until tomorrow. There wasn't enough light at this time in the old house to see how to clean properly. I swept the kitchen floor as best I could, placed a plastic tarp on the floor and put my goose-down sleeping bag on it. Morning would bring another day.

Chapter 8

~~Bennie Jack~~
Revenge

Sleep brought dreams if not actual nightmares. As soon as I fell asleep, I was back in the barn loft after I left the basement. I had to get as far away from the ocean as fast as I could. At the same time, I couldn't take a chance on being spotted during the light of day. My appearance, after spending time in the ocean, would be a dead give-a-way that something was off. My hair had to be a tangled mess. My skin was sun, and wind burned, while my entire body was stiff and salt covered. I could feel that my ears, face, nose, and lips had cracked and peeled. My clothes were ragged, baggy, and caked with salt brine and dirt from where I had crawled and hidden in the basement.

I considered finding clothes to steal but what I was wearing had secret pockets where my money was hidden along with the Glock and knife I'd taken off the dead man. Plus, there was a chance clothes could be missed. I wouldn't dispose of what I was wearing until I had a better alternative. My best plan of action was to rest in the hay until night came. I alternated between sleeping and making plans. My priority was to stay alive and undetected. Once I was safe and had my strength back, I would commence my revenge. I couldn't rely on anger and luck alone. I needed to be prepared and know exactly what I was to do every step of the way.

I heard the sound of animals moving about not far from the barn and a man's voice talking to someone.

"Back 'er in the barn hall, while I let the mare in."

I heard the sound of the barn door opening on rusty hinges, and the starting up of a diesel engine. I had glimpsed a truck with a fancy fifth wheel horse trailer attached to the truck when I had crept to the barn.

I heard the sound of sliding metal and assumed the door to the trailer was being opened. A few minutes later a barn door opened, and a horse snorted and whinnied.

"Atta' a girl," the man said. "Get in there like a lady. Good girl."

"Must know where I'm takin' her," a younger man's voice said with a touch of humor as metal sliding sounded again.

"Maybe," said the man. "Make sure the stallion breeds her first thing when you get there and then again right before you head back home. Twice ought to do the trick. Don't want you and the mare staying overnight.

"Will do," the young man said. "I've put a couple bales of hay and a sack of grain in the storage area."

"I filled the storage tank with water. It'll warm up by the time you get there. Don't want her drinking different cold water than what she's used to. And don't feed her grain. Excitement and grain can colic her the same as cold water. You can give her hay a little at a time."

"Okay," the young man said.

"Come on in the house and I'll get you a check for the stud fee. I'd say your momma has packed you enough food for an army by now."

I grew brave enough to leave the hay and look through a crack to see the two men walking toward the house. I climbed down the ladder, opened the horse trailer door, and looked in the storage area where the hay and grain were stored. I was surprised to see a narrow bed covered with quilts. Two horse blankets and a saddle were lying on the floor against the bed. I heard the men talking as they left the house. I had to make a decision fast.

I closed the storage area door, moved one of the horse blankets, and squeezed myself under the few inches between the floor and the bed as silently as possible. I pulled the horse blanket back in place. I was taking a tremendous chance of getting caught, but I also needed to get as far away as possible as fast as possible.

"Drive careful, son," the man said as one of them opened the storage area door and sat something inside. "Go slow and stop about halfway there to fill up and make sure the mare is riding okay."

"Will do," the young man said.

"Wish I could go with you, but I best go with your mom."

"Wise decision," the boy said with a touch of humor.

I might have made a mistake by not staying in the hay loft. I might have a better chance of escape if everyone was leaving home and I could pilfer a few much-needed supplies, but regret was useless now.

I never realized how uncomfortable lying on the bottom of a horse trailer could be. I felt ever dip and bump in the highway. After several miles, I eased out from under the narrow bed and peeked out. We were traveling on the interstate. I saw the cooler resting at my feet. I opened it to find food. Three ham sandwiches, two apples, two bananas, and a large slice of cake were in the cooler along with a thermos. I couldn't resist eating one of the sandwiches and one of the bananas. I opened the thermos expecting coffee. It was milk. I drank as much as I dared. I wanted the energy the sugary cake would provide but feared the young man would miss the cake.

Now what? I needed to leave the storage area sometime, but I'd have to wait until it came to a stop. I sat down on one of the horse blankets and waited. One good thing was if the young man looked into the mirrors, he wouldn't be able to see me.

After about an hour, temptation got the best of me. I opened the cooler, took out the apple, and stuck it in my pocket to save it for later. After another hour, the truck slowed down and took an exit. I eased back under the bed and pulled the horse blanket in place before the truck came to a stop. I heard what I thought was the young man filling up the tank. The strong smell of diesel told me I was right.

I thought about making an escape, but it was broad daylight at a gas station. I couldn't take a chance, but would I be taking a greater chance if I stayed put? I heard people talking and knew I couldn't leave the trailer yet. I felt the movement of the trailer as the young man climbed up on it. The horse nickered.

"Good girl," he said in a soothing voice. "You're doing great. We'll be there shortly, so stay calm."

The young man didn't open the door to the storage area to get the food. Instead, I got a whiff of fast food as he passed the storage area.

Once I felt the truck traveling on the interstate again, I got back out and waited. What I estimated to be another hour, the truck left the interstate again. I got back under the bed and waited again. The truck slowed and it felt like it was on a regular highway. He slowed down again and made a turn. A few miles later he came to a stop and got out of the cab.

"See you made it right on time," said another man. "Get 'er out and we'll see if she's standing."

I stayed under the bed as I listened to them unload the mare. The two men talked as they moved away from the trailer. Once I could no longer hear them, I eased from under the bed and looked through a crack. The trailer was parked in front of a fancy barn. I could no longer hear the men talking, but I could hear the horses snorting and whinnying from what I took to be inside the barn. I observed the area the best I could. There were several buildings, all a long distance from a fancy house. A larger, more expensive horse trailer was parked next to the one I was in. There were several different fenced in paddocks with horses grazing in them. Unfortunately for me, there were no trees or places where I could hide nearby. If I stayed in the trailer, I would surely get a ride back where I came from. I didn't want that.

My only other option was to hide in the other horse trailer. The other horse trailer appeared to have a larger and fancier enclosed storage area. I heard the horses making a louder noise, and hoped they had the men's attention. I eased the door open and looked about. I saw no one and made a run for the other horse trailer. Just as I expected, the storage area was larger and nicer although containing similar items. I wasted no time hiding under the bed and settling in for a long duration.

Again, I had no idea where I was, but at least I was several hours away from the ocean where I had washed up on the rocks. I wondered if there was anything else that had washed up, or if the helicopter wreck had been discovered. All I knew was that I couldn't trust anyone at all. I was on my own from here on out.

~~~~

Morning came and I awoke with a start. I thought I had heard a noise. I eased my hand under my pillow and gripped the Glock as I looked about the kitchen. At first, I wasn't sure where I was until reality hit. I heard the noise again and eased the barrel of the gun in the direction of the noise. A mouse was trying to get into my jar of peanut butter. I had no doubt this place was infested with pests. Too bad I didn't think to bring a cat along. Even better, some type of terrier dog who hated varmints and intruders.

Relief washed over me. I detected no other sound. I wasn't in danger. I got up to start my day. There were so many things that needed doing, I didn't know where I should start first. Breakfast was a good idea, but the fire had gone out during the night. I would have to build it if I wanted to cook something. Like a few of the two dozen eggs I had brought with me, or even boil some of the grits. I decided on crackers and a glob of the peanut butter the mouse was trying to get at.

After my meager breakfast, I decided to check the upstairs. I had been foolish not to do it yesterday when I arrived. I had assumed there was nothing threatening up there. I was right. It was as empty as the downstairs, unless more spider webs, dead insects and dried out bodies of vermin counted. I even discovered two snake skins that had been shed. The snakes weren't doing their job if there were still mice.

I opened a door in one room thinking it was a long, enclosed closet. It was the stairs leading to the attic. I took the stairs only to find another door at the top. I forced its rusty hinges to open, but it was too dark to see anything. I went back to the kitchen and got the flashlight. If I was investigating the place, I might as well get a look in the attic.

Much to my surprise, it wasn't empty. There was dust covered furniture along with boxes stacked up against the back wall. From what I could tell, the furniture was crude and handmade, but I was glad to get it. Something was better than nothing.

Seeing the furniture gave me enough encouragement to clean the downstairs. To do a good job I needed hot water, which meant I had to build a fire in the wood cookstove. No sinks with running water. No hot water heater. No electricity for lights or electric stove. How did people survive without such conveniences? Guess I was going to find out.

At least the concrete trough next to the kitchen was full of water. It took me a while to get the fire going with the wood chips. Then came the problem of having wood large enough to get and keep the stove hot enough to heat a bucket of water. I found deadfall and cut the limbs to size on using the ax. By the time I had the right size wood in the house, the woodchips had burned out. I had to rekindle the fire. I would need to learn more about being self-sufficient than I anticipated.

I had to laugh at my frustration. Hopefully, I would get my survival skills together sooner or later, but it was going to take a while for a city girl to get used to going off the grid even with all the survival training I had undergone. But I was determined, not to mention I had little choice. I had to remind myself of the horrible conditions I had lived through. Surely, I could conquer something as simple as existing with nature.

Chapter 9

~~Aunt Polly~~

I couldn't get that young woman off my mind. I spent hours thinking about her and wondering what her purpose for being here was. I had lived on this mountain by myself for so long I had become more like the animals that inhabited the mountain than the people who lived down in the valleys below. This kind of life suited me partly because it was all I had ever known and partly because it had always been the way I wanted to live.

This girl was different than me. I could tell by her innocent looks. She was delicate. Even her hands were delicate looking. I wondered if they had blisters and blackened fingernails after she hauled all those rocks through the woods. I had to give her credit for getting that truck out. She said she'd bought the old Slaughter place, and I reckon she probably had. What puzzled me was why. It wasn't the kind of place most people would want to live at, especially a woman who was as young and pretty as this one, although I suspected her life had taken a turn for the worse considering how she had tried to make herself look like a young boy. When a pretty girl whacked off her hair and hid her attributes under baggy men's clothing, she had a reason for doing it.

I wasn't altogether sure, but I thought the so-called sin eater stayed at that Slaughter place on occasion. I reckoned he had some kind of place somewhere over the mountain, but I had never crossed the mountain to know where or what kind of place was over there. I had only seen him a few times in passing, but never long enough to get a right good look at his face being he was so hairy. He appeared to be a normal sized man with a wild head of hair and full-face of ragged beard and mustache. He hadn't been and still wasn't of my concern. The young woman was.

I couldn't resist letting my curiosity get the best of good sense and headed through the woods to get a better look at the situation. It was a right smart walk up the mountain to get from my place to the old Slaughter place, but I made it in short time. Back when I was a young thing, I could make it at a fast run. My legs were right nigh as nimble as a cricket's way back yonder. Now I was kind of crippled up and slow moving as a garden slug, but I was determined to find out what was going on with this young woman.

I didn't think she had anything to do with me or my Meadow Lark. By the way she reacted when she saw me, she didn't know I existed. She sure got an unexpected welcome to her new home. It was a welcome she would never forget. It was only by luck of an uprooted tree that she hadn't been washed down into the steep ravine. Don't know if she would have survived that. I had to give her credit for the way she worked to get the truck out of the wash. Hauling all those rocks along with shoveling what little dirt she could gouge from the roots of trees wasn't an easy thing. I figured her truck would stay right where it was for a long time to come, but I was wrong. She kept at it until she got that truck out. I had to give the wimpy looking woman two thumps up for that.

I ran her appearance through my mind again. The way a person looked told a lot about them and how they lived. When I first looked through the truck window, I thought she was a young boy. Her hair was no more than two inches long all over her head. Her face and arms had a kind of roughed up look to them like they had been badly blistered by the sun and were at the end of skin peeling off. Her eyes were big and round with a childish innocent look about them. Her body was just a little ole thing without an ounce of fat anywhere. I wasn't sure if she'd been half starved or a natural puny thing. If she had been mine, I'd have given her a dose of wormwood and a lot of fried apple pies swimming in goats milk.

I wasn't too badly winded once I reached the old Slaughter place. Springtime had perked me up a bit. The warmer weather had helped ease my aching bones. Time summer finally reached these mountains, I'd be going right good, at least that was what I hoped. I sat down on a nice big rock that had been warmed by rays of the sun peeking through the trees. The rock was high up on a rise, but still was in the shelter of the woods where I could watch the house while remaining unseen. I wasn't ready to confront her right up front until I'd judged her for a while.

I was getting right comfortable with my legs hanging down the side of the rock. I had learned as a girl not to move about if you didn't want to be seen, and I didn't. I was so quiet that little ole ground squirrels were checking me to see if I was food. They had gotten so bold that I had used my hand to brushed one off my leg.

It was then I heard it – the sound I had grown to fear all my life. I looked down and my guts turned to ice. Near my feet was a quilled-up timber rattlesnake, Its tail was sticking straight up and quivering to beat the band. I saw its mouth open and in preparation for a coming strike a millisecond before a loud blast sounded right near my head. The snake flew backward and rolled over and over in a death twist. I whirled around to see the young woman standing behind me with a pistol in her hand.

"That was close," she said.

"That's a pistol," I said. "You hit it with a pistol."

"Luck," she said. "Snakes are known to strike at heat. It met the bullet."

But I knew the luck part wasn't true. She handled that pistol like it was a part of her hand. It didn't appear she even took aim. Didn't know what to think about her knowing how to shoot a pistol the way she did. She surely had a lot of training in the use of it. Made an old woman right leery.

"Lucky for you," she added. "But not for the snake. Did it bite you?"

"No, thank goodness," I told her. At my age, I wasn't sure I could fight off the poison. "Thank you wholeheartedly," I told her.

"I hate snakes," she said, still standing on the ground slightly behind me.

"As a woman ought," I said as I thought of Eve in the Garden of Eden. "I give you my thanks," I told her again.

"Glad I was gathering wood for the cookstove," she told me. "Do you live close here?"

"Down in the swag a little ways," I told her. "Not far. I was coming to check on you," I reckon that was the truth. "Just sat myself down to warm my old bones for a while," which was also the truth. "See you got out of the warsh."

"Warsh?" I questioned.

"The warshed out hole your truck was in."

"I did," she told me. "How long has it been since the road was traveled?"

I wondered why she'd ask me such a question, but I answered her just the same. "Some time back when my Meadow Lark paid me a visit. Nobody since then." I saw the puzzled look that came to her face.

"Meadow Lark?" she questioned. "A bird?"

"My girl. I named her Meadow Lark. She don't like it none. She insists on being called Larkin by some. You got young'uns?" I asked.

"No," she told me firmly.

"You got yourself a man?"

Again, she was quick to answer no.

"What you doing in a place like this all alone? It hain't fittin' for civilized folks," I wanted to know and didn't mind asking.

"Going off the grid," she told me. "Is Meadow Lark the only child you have living on the mountain?"

"Only 'un I birthed. She don't live here," I dared to tell her. Might be foolish, but I had an idea I could put some trust in her. I eased down off the rock and picked up the dead rattler. "I'll skin and gut it for you to cook," I told her. "It's rightfully yourn since you're the one who killed it."

Her eyes widened, and she looked at me a bit strange.

"Cook it?" she questioned.

"You hain't never eat snake? Lawsy child, you don't know what you've missed. They're good food. Their skin tans good, and their poison can be used to make powerful medicine if you milk 'um."

"I'll pass on all three," she told me. "It's all yours."

"Got bit by a copper head snake once about twenty years past. Not usually on this high mountain, but they'll climb up if the weather down below gets too hot and dry for 'um. Timber rattlers are a differed matter altogether. They like the high places. I poured the bite full as I could of turpentine and sliced me a hunk off the fattiest part of a chicken and tied the raw fat on it to draw out the pizen. Got over it in hardly no time."

"Timber rattlesnake carried more poison," she said as though I didn't know such as that.

"Did you know if you lay a snake belly up, it'll rain?"

"Then by all means, keep its belly down."

"Reckon you've got a point. You might ought to get used to those kinds of rains up here on this mountain. A right plentiful down-pour happens right often," I told her, although I reckon she'd got a right good belly full of rain before she got a chance to expect it. "We get plenty of rain here. Mountains tend to poke a hole in those rain clouds a-fore they can move out. Meadow Lark claims weather off this mountain can be right pleasant. Where you from?"

"A long way from here," she said.

It was obvious she didn't want to tell me anything about herself. It was a dead giveaway she was running from something or someone and thought this place was a good place to hide out. I decided not to push her on it. Things usually came to light when left out in the open long enough. Besides, a body was entitled to their own privacy.

"I'll help you tote some wood in return for killin' the snake."

"No need for you to do that," she assured me quickly. "The more snakes I kill the less chance I'll have of getting bit," she told me with a right powerful intent.

"There's need a-plenty. I always repay my debt. No question I'd be in a mighty bad way if it hadn't been for you. Ought to of knowed, springtime, rocks, sunshine, ground squirrels and snakes go together. Might ought to get away from this here rock. Where there's one snake, there's usually two. Did you know that timber rattlers mate in the fall of the year and then hold the juices inside of themselves until June of the next year before they allow the juices to fertilize them? Young are usually born in the fall."

"I didn't know that," she said. I saw a mixture of disbelief and interest come to her face.

"Poison snakes most likely give live birth, while non-poison snakes lay eggs."

"Really," she said as a dismissal. Reckon she wasn't in a snake learning mood.

"Well, now. I'll help you tote wood and then be moseying on my way. Want to gather me enough herbs for a spring tonic. Blood's been running a little slow during winter months. Cold winter weather thickens the blood up a right smart, you know." I reached down and started filling my arms with deadfall – making sure I was on the lookout for more snakes.

She started to object again but changed her mind. I could see a whole pile of questions gathering in her mind. I figured she'd start asking them a-fore long. I was right.

"How long have you lived on this mountain?"

"Born here," I told her.

"How old are you?"

"How old do I look? Don't sugar coat it none."

"Eighties," she told me.

According to her, the years had worn on me more than I thought. "Sixty-one this past winter." I told her and saw the surprise on her face.

"These mountains are hard on a body, especially when you're a woman living alone." Skin becomes like tree bark and has a way of roughing up before its time. I got a good closeup of her face. Appeared to me she'd sunburned it all the way to the bone not so long ago. It still looked kind of tender.

"You live alone?" she asked.

"I do. Done it ever since my George died a whole lot of years ago." He died a short time after my Meadow Lark left out to find her a man. At least she got a good 'un ad far as I know. The few times she's showed up here, she never complained about him beatin' her or drinkin' himself stupid the way some men do. My Meadow Lark and George's boys came back for his funeral.

"His boys had up and left out as soon as they growed into long britches. Those boys of his ain't never come back to visit me, but my girl comes every so often. Meadow Lark claims she wants me to go back home with her, but I refused. I told her I wanted to die on and be buried in the same ground I'd been birthed on. She didn't see the reasoning behind such as that, but it made no never-mind to me." I always figured my girl must have taken back after that daddy of hers, but I couldn't hold to it as being a fact being I wasn't entirely sure who he was.

"Must have been the very next day that George's boys made up with each other to sell what George owned, which wasn't much, but plenty enough. Didn't know for certain who bought the place as they've never showed up to this day that I knowed of. Reckon it was ownership of the land they wanted, nobody ever moved into the old place. Never showed up to claim the house and land either. Old house sat right there and ruined. Fields and pastureland turned itself back to briars and brambles in no time a-tall."

I had my suspicions those Slaughters pilfered everything of value that his boys didn't take with them when they left, but I couldn't prove it. All I knew was that the place had been picked clean.

"His boys?" she questioned.

I knew what she was questioning. "I was his second wife. His first wife died. Most women don't last long where there's hard times, especially if they have to give birth every year or less. Don't know if it was luck or not, but my juices dried up after my first 'un was born. Had a rough time of birthing her, I did. I was no more than a bean pole of a girl when I had to push her out. Damaged something inside me, I reckon. What's your story?" I made a direct point of asking. I watched her as she considered what and how much to tell me.

"Like your Meadow Lark, I was an only child. After my parents died, I survived the best I could going from one job and one place to another. I found myself being nothing more than a small mouse in a big rat race world. Finally, I got tired of going around in circles and getting nowhere. When this place came up for sale, I scraped together enough money to buy it. And here I am. End of story."

We both carried our armload of wood down the hill to the old woodshed. I saw that she'd already chopped some up. I was surprised when I looked at the double-bitted ax. Both blades had been sharpened to a shiny cutting edge. She might not be as helpless as I thought.

"Thanks for helping me with the wood," she said. "I'll not keep you from your spring tonic any longer. Enjoy the rattlesnake and be careful."

I had to chuckle at how nicely she had dismissed me. She hadn't invited me back with a *come again*. I hadn't invited her either. I went back to where I'd left the snake, gathered it up, and left for home. I'd learned a right smart more about the young woman, but it wasn't nearly enough to satisfy me.

Chapter 10

~~Bennie Jack~~

I didn't know what to think about the old woman showing up the way she had. I did know that she was lucky to be alive. If I hadn't been there at that very moment with my Glock, she would most likely have died from the bite – and in a slow and very painful way. From now on, I would have to watch when I gathered firewood. I hadn't brought anything for snake bites, but I had brought a pair of thick, heavy boots for winter. I should have asked the old woman if there was some kind of native cure for snakebites. If a woman lived on this mountain for as long as the old woman had, she would have knowledge that would be beneficial to me.

Not only that, I hadn't even asked her name. She hadn't asked mine either. In an odd sort of way, knowing I wasn't the only one living on this mountain was comforting. The fact that it was an old woman who couldn't have a thing to do with what I had run away from was even more comforting. As was the fact she had lived here alone and was still alive was even better.

I filled the stove full of wood, poured what water was hot in a plastic bucket, filled the metal bucket with water and put it back on the stove to heat. I swept and then scrubbed the front room, two back rooms and kitchen floors.[1] I was surprised at how much better the wood floors looked. Whenever I left the mountain to get supplies, I planned on buying some polyurethane to put on the floors. It would help preserve the old wood along with making it easier to keep the floors cleaner.

After I had the floors scrubbed, I decided to check out what was stored in the attic. I found the flashlight and took it into the attic with me. I had never realized how handy electricity was until I was in a house that had none at all. There were some streaks of light coming from cracks in the walls and under the eaves. Little birds had built nests or were building nests in the rafters. Insulation would be needed before winter set in. The scuttling of tiny feet let me know other varmints were living in the attic.

I came across a metal bedstead leaning against the wall. It was dirty and dusty with loops of rope hanging on it. I had always heard of a rope bed, but this was the first one I'd ever seen. A feed sack tied with twine lay on the floor beside it. I opened the sack to find a feather tick. It smelled musty but looked to be in fairly good condition. Thankfully, rats hadn't made their nests in it. I would take it to the spring branch with a bar of soap and wash it the best I could before I dared sleep on it. Until then, I would be a lot more comfortable to put my sleeping bag on the old rope bed than sleeping on the hard, drafty floor. There were also some old quilts in a cardboard box. A handmade table and several chairs were pushed in a corner and covered with dust and cobwebs.

I held the flashlight until it cast a glow on the wall. Several pots and pans were hanging on nails. I was sure I could use each and every one of them for one thing or another. I managed to drag the bedstead down the attic stairs, which wasn't easy. I pulled it and the feather tick outside in the yard where I could scrub all the buildup crud off. I had no idea how many years of dirt and animal droppings were caked on everything, but it had to be several. There were other boxes and sacks stored in the attic that I would go through later. For now, I'd had enough of dust and animal droppings. Just cleaning this place would take all summer long. Not to mention any repairs to the house I wanted to make.

I took what was left of the lukewarm water to scrub my body and hair. I missed being able to turn on hot water in a shower. I gained a whole new respect for people who tried to keep clean with a washcloth and pan of water.

Once I washed, I put on clean clothes and found myself something to drink and eat. I was used to roughing it on occasion. My trainer made sure of that, but I hadn't expected so much needed doing to assure my future survival. I was lucky it was springtime, and I had time to work all summer long. One of the things I needed to do right away was plant a garden. Maybe I should have asked the old woman about that. Further contact with her would probably be alright. I was rather confident she knew nothing about the kind of life I had lived up until now.

I sat down in the sun to let my stubble of hair dry as I thought about my escape out of the ocean.

~~~~

I listened to the men talk as the boy put his mare back in his horse trailer. I was hoping one of them would say something that let me know the location I was in. There were things I needed to do in a hurry. Not one word was said that would help me figure out where I had landed.

"You're welcome to leave her here over night," the man said. "You're even welcome to spend the night in the spare room. My wife isn't the best of cooks, but she'll feed you a-plenty. Just make sure you don't let on that I said such about her cooking. She got that red-headed temper."

"Thank you, but I best get on back home. Dad said breeding her twice today would be enough."

"Maybe," the man said. "I like to breed 'um again on the second and fourth day, but it's up to you."

There was little more said as the boy loaded his horse and left.

I settled under the bed in hopes I could rest if not actually sleep until I could safely leave the horse trailer without being seen. I still didn't know where I was, but I did know I was going to need food, water, clothes and a way to disguise myself. It shouldn't be too difficult since I had done similar dozen times before when I was in as bad, if not worse, situation than I was now in.

I stayed hidden until night came on enough to give me cover, and then crawled from under the bed and slowly opened the door a crack. There were lights on in the house along with dimmer lights on in the barn where the stallion was kept. Riding a horse would be faster than escaping on foot. I grinned at the thought of me getting on a horse. That had been part of my training A. J. hadn't put me through. I think I might have enjoyed it more if I'd had time to get used to horses. I eased out of the trailer without hearing a dog bark. Thank goodness for answers to small and large prayers. I rushed from shadow to shadow until I reached a wooded area.

I sank down in the underbrush where I could take time to inspect the area. I hadn't taken time when I arrived to observe anything about where I was at. From what I could tell it was definitely a horse farm, but not a large one. It had a few paddocks and a barn with smaller out buildings. The light from the house showed it to be a nice, well maintained farmhouse with smoke rising from a chimney.

The smell of woodsmoke filled my soul with longing. I imagined a sweet little momma cooking an evening meal for her family. I could also imagine how happy they would be while gathered around a table eating their evening meal. A family. A real, happy, ordinary family. How I longed for such as that. It made me even sadder than I already was to realize I would never have such a thing as a family again.

I was well aware of that fact when I signed up for the job. I had been warned that my life would no longer be my own. I would be owned forever by the Freedom Group - at least as long as I was young and useful as a spy. A.J., the trainer who had been assigned to me, told me there would never be anything normal and orderly in my life, which I thought was somewhat amusing. I had learned to be orderly, but I wasn't sure what normal was. Orderly was definitely needed when someone was being trained how to become a silent and original killer who was required to cover their tracks.

I didn't like being referred to as a killer, but that was exactly what I was trained to become when necessary. "It's best to kill than be killed," my trainer told me repeatedly. Of course, he was right about that, as he was about many other things. He told me that an effective spy needed to fear neither danger nor dagger. Neither capture nor torture. What I was trained to fear was failure. What I feared was pain. No training or wishful thinking could take that fear away from me. I came to the conclusion such fear was a good thing. It made me extremely cautious. I agreed to live for my country, but I didn't want to die for my country.

Chapter 11

~~A. J.~~

I was to find the most capable young woman to do the much-needed job of becoming a successful spy. I knew looks mattered, but not to choose the best-looking woman or the ugliest. She had to be average looking and yet pretty enough that men would find her tempting. Too pretty could be a giveaway as could a homely woman. I also wanted one who had high morals, or appeared to have them until the time came not to. I looked at the pictures before me. Six young women were staring straight into a camera as their pictures were being taken. It was my job to pick the one I would spend my time and ability training. I couldn't afford to pick the wrong woman. My time and expertise were too valuable to waste.

I remembered what my grandfather told me when he was a boy. "Become an honorable man by doing your duty unto the country in which you live." It was similar to what President John F. Kennedy had said. "Don't ask what your country can do for you, but what you can do for your country." Things had certainly changed from that long ago time. Now everyone, especially politicians, was only after what could be done for them. Even to the degree of being a traitor for a foreign nation in return for money.

Honor, I had, but duty was another question altogether. How could I possibly serve my country from a rogue, deep swamp that was being highly paid to destroy this beloved country? That was why I joined the Freedom Group who were determined to put their country before their wealth by exposing the traitors of this the greatest country on earth.

The answer was confusing while at the same time, simple enough. I needed to do everything in my power to eliminate anything and anyone who would do harm to my country. Much like a priest who gave himself to God. My country became my wife, my children, my heart, and my soul. I would protect her with my life – but was that enough? Would one determined man be enough to protect this country? The answer was no, never. But I could learn enough to help train those who could pick up where my ability left off.

There was something about this girl's picture that appealed to me. It was her eyes. They were big and innocent in appearance, much like a puppy dog who only wanted to give and receive attention. And yet there was more. There was naivety along with a deep-down intelligence. I wasn't at all surprised to find she was working as a government staffer, which was also a plus. Unless I was mistaken, she was the kind who was looking for a higher purpose in life. I had to grin at that. No question, a higher purpose was a good idea, but not a feasible one. It was little more than idealistic, wishful thinking of a person who wanted to do something that matters in the scheme of their lives.

Her appearance was the kind that got jobs as aids to men in power who had a roving eye. Men who were past their prime got stimulation from having pretty, young girls around. The more innocent they were, the better. Innocence stimulated their memory as well as their failing libido.

She would be the perfect type to gather the information his group needed. That was if she was willing and proved to be trainable. Another good factor, was that she was an only child with no close relatives to keep track of her. According to my research on her, there was no one who would miss her, not even a boyfriend.

If I chose her over the other young women and arranged a meeting, would she proved to be everything I wanted her to be? Plus, there was one thing more which surprised me. Even I felt an attraction to her picture. Something that had never happened to me before. I marked it up as another advantage for using the girl. If she appealed to me, a hardnose where women were concerned, she was sure to appeal to other men.

I arranged a face-to-face meeting with her. All the information I had gathered on her was useless if this girl proved to be a featherbrain or have a mouth that couldn't stop talking. Rachet-jawed was the term I called those types.

I was even more impressed with her as she sat in front of me. She watched my every move, listening to my words, questioning everything I was saying as well as asking questions of her own.

"Who wouldn't want to work for the betterment of their country?" she questioned me.

"More people than you would believe," I answered.

"Like who?"

"Those who are being bribed in one way or another," I told her.

"Bribed? For money?" she questioned.

"Wealth is a universal enhancer. It usually starts as a slight infraction that blooms rapidly. Once a person has gotten the taste of easy money, it becomes more powerful than any drug in existence."

She thought a minute, and then nodded as though she understood how it could happen. "My parents were poor, but they never once gave in to immoral temptations."

"How do you know?" I asked.

"I listened. I watched. They had their own way of dealing with what they considered wrongdoing. For example, Dad once came upon a stranger picking apples from Dad's favorite apple tree. 'Let me help you with that," Dad said as he started picking apples and putting them in the man's sack. 'Who owns these apples trees?' the man finally asked Dad. 'Reckon God does, but it just so happens I'm the one who

gets to pay taxes on this place since my own Dad passed.'
The man turned red in the face, jumped in his car and drove
away without taking his sack of apples. Doubt the thief ever
forgot the man who allowed him to be a thief without
condemnation."

I had to grin at her story and the way her dad handled it.
I wondered if her dad's kind of wisdom had rubbed off on
the girl. If so, she might be too much of a do-gooder for what
needed to be done in a life and death situation.

"Did either of your parents ever kill anyone."

Her eyes narrowed as she looked me over carefully. I felt
like squirming under her scrutiny.

"Dad fought in the Vietnam war. He was a sniper. He did
what his country asked of him. Although, he knew it would
haunt him for the rest of his life."

"What did you think about what he did?"

"Sacrificing one person's values, or their life, means little
when it comes to saving thousands of innocent people."

"You actually believe that?" I was quick to ask her.

"Yes," she gave her simple, yet strong answer.

"You believe your dad killing other human beings was
justified?"

She hesitated only a moment. "I wouldn't say it was
justified or even necessary in a broad picture, but it was what
was required in order for the betterment of his country as well
as the safety of his unit. Our country sends our people out to
fight and kill others and call it war. I have no doubt all those
who survive are haunted for the rest of their lives. I know my
dad was."

"May I ask if you would kill for your country?"

"Like my father, I believe I would kill to save my own
life or the life of someone I love. I definitely love my country
and my freedom."

Again, she gave me a scrutinizing look. "Suppose you
come to the point and tell me why this meeting and all these
questions?"

"Would you consider working for the betterment of your government?"

"Is that not what I'm already doing?"

"May I ask why you are only a staffer?"

"What better way to learn the ins and outs of our politicians and policy makers."

"And what have you learned?"

"I've learned to be disappointed in both."

"And why is that?"

"In their dirty dealing ways," she said without hesitation. "It's more like I'll do this if you'll do that instead of doing what best for everyone."

"Are you willing to do something about their dirty dealing ways?"

"Yes," was her answer.

"Does anyone know you're meeting with me?"

"No."

"Why not?"

"Because I know you're meeting with me for a specific reason. So, stop fishing and get directly to the point."

I had to grin. "You may not be worthy or capable of the job I'm considering you for."

"Only one way to find out," she said with a slight grin.

"Okay," I said. "Let's find out what you're made of as well as capable of."

She nodded in agreement.

~~~~

She was taught to shoot a pistol from a one-handed crouch instead of a traditional upright position while holding the gun with both hands. There will never be time for a fancy stance when killing speed was need. Another thing she wouldn't have time to do was use the sights. You shoot where your finger points. A gun fight can be a matter of a split second. Make sure you hit your target first shot. You may not get a second shot.

She was a natural with a handgun. She fired instinctively at both moving and bobbing targets. I made sure she trained outside and inside buildings with poor lighting and bright lights as well as total darkness. She was also taught how to use shotguns, rifles, submachine guns, and machine guns. I didn't want the girl to lack anything, including how to put a detonator into a primer, and then the primer into the explosives. I also taught her about fuses and their timing so she would have time to escape before the explosion happened.

After passing those training skills, next came knife fighting. Knife fighting could be called a close-up sport. A bloody and dangerous one. It required speed in deflective movements as well as slice and jab movements. The girl was fast as a striking snake. She was quick to learn to get in and get out with blinding speed. Move your body, dodge, block, and slash. Run away.

Her training also included how to poach, steal chickens, wring their neck, trap rabbits, and cook over an open fire long enough to kill parasites and bacteria. She could also drive boats, canoes, and planes, along with navigate by the stars.

Her biggest asset was her intelligence along with her little-girl innocent looks. She had a naive appearance that left people thinking she was of little consequence, which was a big mistake. Her mind could sum up a situation in an instant. Her instincts were usually spot-on. She never took anything for granted and always prepared for the worst. A trait a lot more people should strive for.

Yet, she wasn't perfect. She was temperamental, arrogant, impulsive, hasty, opinionated, and hardheaded. She had a tendency to act rather than take time to let things work themselves out slowly. She always believed she was right until proven over and over that she was wrong. Plus, she wanted to do things her own way. She had such a distrust of others, that she hesitated to work with anyone. She had deep set trust issues. She trusted herself and only herself. He could tell she didn't entirely trust him, her trainer and trainer. The man who had to teach her all the ways that would keep her alive or get her killed.

"What name do you want use?" I asked her after she passed my expectations. She wasn't perfect, but she was the best I had found.

"My own."

"No can do."

"You pick one, then."

"Fizz," I said. Short for Fizzle. Something you're never allowed to do. "One mistake and you're out. Once you accept this job, you're virtually on your own as far as your own safety is concerned. If you get caught, I, nor anyone else, ever knew you. Understand?"

"Perfectly."

She was hired, and she did far better than expected. She became a shadow moving in the night with an inborn instinct where secret documents were kept hidden and how to ferret them out. The one area she failed in was the one thing no one could convince her to do. That was sleep with the men she was spying on.

"Why not?" I had once asked her.

"I detest being slobbered on," she told him.

If she could do her job without being slobbered on, so be it.

It would appear that men's want-to was far more powerful than the having. The challenge of seducing her was a powerful drug she knew how to use. After all, such men could buy sex every hour of every day and night. The challenge of subdue and conquer was definitely an ego booster.

No one expected how good she would become at her job. Not only that, but she also decided on her own to delve deeper than her job permitted. When I received copies of the documents she had discovered, the very hair on my head rose. If she turned those documents in, she was done for. She must have known that when she provided me with a copy of the flash drive. I hoped beyond hope that no one knew she had given me a copy. I also suspected there were more copies than the one she gave me.

She provided her own death sentence if she gave the information to anyone else. A woman who knew too much wasn't tolerated. After reading what she had given me, I rushed to find where she had gone. I had to make her realize what danger she had put herself in by obtaining such information.

Chapter 12

~~Bennie Jack~~

I clung to the concealment of wooded areas near main highways as I made my way north on foot. The process was too slow. I was ready and willing to get revenge before I pulled a forever disappearance. I was drawn to the aroma of a truck stop dinner. There was always a lot of extra food tossed in truck stop dinner dumpsters late at night, and I needed food. There was also simi truck parking for overnighters which weren't in use at this time.

I was hiding in the shadows waiting for the place to close down before I raided the trash bins when I saw a semi pull into the almost deserted parking area. I got a good look at the truck's license plate and knew I'd hit a home run. There was a good chance the semi was heading north to or near the exact place I wanted to go.

A very tired looking, pop bellied man got out of the cab without even locking his door. I guessed him to be in his sixties and close to retirement age. I got the impression he had been a driver for all his adult life by the way he stretched his body after he got out of the cab, yawned long and deep, along with a bow-legged walk. He was dressed comfortably in overly wrinkled clothes, which told me he was returning from a long drive instead of starting out on one.

Once he had entered the building, I left my hiding place and kept to the dark shadows as I went to the semi, opened the door facing away from the truck stop and quickly got inside. The light came on, but no one seemed to notice.

The cab of the semi smelled of sweat, old food wrappers, along with other body odors. I got into the sleeper and covered up with the many piled up, musty blankets that had been used for some time without washing. I found the man's smell repulsive but not enough for me to get back out. Once I had myself concealed, I eased the Glock from my pocket to hold in my hand in case I was discovered and the man needing a little encouragement. My appearance alone was enough to convince the man I was desperate and not in the mood for bluffing. I was placing my bet on not being discovered. A plus was that I found a pack of cheese crackers lost under the blanket and gobbled them down while I waited for his return.

I put my exhausted body into rest mode while waiting approximately thirty minutes before he returned. He climbed into the seat, belched, farted, and grunted before he started the engine. A cell phone rang. He answered.

"Hello," he said in a tired voice. "I just stopped to eat a bite. I'll be home in about two hours. Bye."

He pulled out of the parking lot, and relief settled over me.

I had spent a lot of time hiding and thinking during the daylight hours. I was still hiding under the cover thinking. The information I had turned over to Brigham, the big boss, was not what he wanted or expected. It was obvious that was why he called me into his office with the intent of having me killed, while I had expected praise for a job well done.

My initial mission this time had been to find out names of members in a criminal organization who was laundering money. I managed to do exactly that with only one minor player being sacrificed. The biggie was the other information my investigation led to that I hadn't been told or expected to investigate.

I had discovered a list of people in the upper echelon of government who were on the take along with undisputable proof of individuals, as well as countries, who had given them money in exchange for secret, classified information. Not only was it the illegal enrichment of politicians, but it was also iron clad proof of treason at the highest levels. I was both naïve and foolish to think this was breakthrough information that would be both needed and welcomed by Brigham. I had been questioned repeatedly in the pretense of validating the information I found. On hindsight, I realized it was little more than trying to find out if I had made copies or given copies to anyone else. I was a good enough liar for him to believe I hadn't. The lie didn't save me from my supposed death, but it most likely saved others. It certainly hadn't saved the lives of the two men in the helicopter.

Time eased on and so did the semi-truck.

I found myself beginning to relax at not being discovered when the big semi-truck finally came to a stop. The man let out a long sigh, cut the engine and lights and got out of the truck. I didn't make a move for at least another ten minutes. As I eased myself out from under the cover, my foot hit a satchel in the far corner. I unzipped it to find clothes the man had taken with him on his run. They even had a clean smell to them. Not that the smell would have mattered considering how much I wanted clothes. I took out pants and a shirt and left the rest and put the satchel exactly where I had found it.

When I got out, I was relieved to discover I was in an area that wasn't overly populated although I could see lights from several other houses. I hid behind an unattached garage to put the clothes on over the top of my own clothes. I wouldn't dispose of my own clothes for several reasons. One reason was the hidden pockets containing money. Another reason was I didn't want even a scrap of my own clothing to be found. It would be too easy to detect salt from the ocean not to mention containing my DNA. I had learned never, ever underestimate what the government was capable and willing to do. They have the ends and the means to everything, and I do mean everything.

I've always heard that money talks. I also learned money is the one thing that has total control. Money is more powerful than fear. Put money and fear together and you've got the ability to control the outcome of just about everyone and everything. More and more the rogue government officials remind me of the mighty ruler with citizens as peasants. Once the peasants are powerless, hungry, and afraid they are controllable. Go against the rulers and they have a million ways to torture or eliminate you. I'm not surprised they decided to eliminate me – a peasant who would never be missed. That's why I created and set up a secret plan and a way to escape. But I craved revenge first and I intended to get it even if revenge cost me my life. After all, I wouldn't be missed by anyone.

Chapter 13

~~ Bennie Jack~~

Once I figured out my location, it didn't take too much effort to walk or manage to hide in transport vehicles until I reached my destination. There were so many homeless people on the streets dressed in baggy, filthy clothes with tangled wild hair that I fit right in. I went over my plan many times while seeing in my mind every move I was to make. What I really wanted to do was come up with a feasible plan to assure Brigham met the same demise he had planned for me, but without risking anyone finding out I wasn't dead. Therefore, I needed to set things up so someone else would be the one to eliminate Brigham.

My first feat was slipping into Brigham's office building unseen, which required me to disable all the security cameras and codes to the alarms. I already knew how to accomplish that without much effort thanks to the fact that I had scoped the place out when Brigham summoned me to his office. Always put an escape exit foremost, A.J. had drilled into my head. It always paid to research all the details in a building when you wanted to be able to get out of it alive if something went wrong. My mistake was going up those stairs to the roof. It never pays to be too sure of your own abilities.

Finding construction blueprints of the building was a no-brainer as was the wiring system along with the locations of the cameras and security systems. There were also blueprints of the ductwork in the building. A.J. had spent considerable time teaching me skills a good cat burglar knew. He taught me how to enter and disappear from a building so many times

I wanted to refuse to do it again, but I always did as he directed me over and over. A.J. said I wasn't perfect but acceptable. So far, I had proven to be perfect enough to stay alive.

I stopped at a dumpster and emptied the two least dirty black garbage bags. Not only was black difficult to see on a dark, moonless night, wearing garbage bags could provide good cover. Hunker down, don't move and few people would take a second look at a bag of garbage.

I put both garbage bags on my body to provide more thickness, and carefully knotted the top together, poked small eye and nose holes in the plastic and ripped open a small space in the bottom of the bags for my feet to be able to move fast. Once I stopped and squatted down, my feet didn't show. That was how I got to the basement of the building and into the area where the garbage was stored for pickup.

Thanks to the training I'd received from A.J. along with my own knowledge and determination, I'd managed to turn off the power to the building I was in for a total of three minutes. That was enough time to get in the building undetected, go directly to Brigham's hidden storage room make a slit in the bag large enough for my hands, crack his safe and take out the money he was holding for criminal organizations as well as other antifreedom groups, and stashed it inside my pants pockets.

All went as planned except it took me a few minutes longer than the three minutes I had estimated to get back into the garbage area. Alarms started going off in the building seconds before I made my exit. I didn't dare chance leaving the building. I wasted no time climbing in the middle of the huge garbage receptacle full of both black and white trash bags and waited, fearful that I had made a terrible mistake in timing. "Don't panic," I could hear A.J. tell me. A mouse hides best when it blends in with its surroundings without moving.

I didn't move for what felt like hours as security searched the building. I could hear men's feet stomping on floors and opening doors as they called out "All clear." Two men came into the garbage area in order to secure it. One came to the receptacle where I was hiding and looked in. He used something to poke holes in a few trash bags I was hiding under. I smelled the stink of rotten food and other unknown stinks. It turned my stomach even though I was near starvation.

"Crap," the man who poked the holes said. "This place stinks. Let's get outta here. There's nobody here. Must have set off the alarms when the electricity malfunctioned. Happens sometime."

I was able to breathe again once I heard their footsteps leaving the area. I was ready to get the heck out of the stinking garbage bin. I waited another twenty minutes before I eased out the same garbage chute I had used to crawled in. I squatted down against the building as I peeked out the holes in the garbage bags. Once I thought all was clear, I moved an inch at a time making sure I stayed out of range of outside cameras that could be in operation. Once I felt I was in the clear, I ripped a larger hole for me to see though and took off running. I left the garbage bags on just in case an unexpected camera was in operation. I didn't stop running until I came to a river. I jumped in the cold water, ripped the bags open, got out and weighted the bags down on the bottom of the river with rocks. I used sand to scrub the stink off me, clothes, and all. The early spring weather was chilling me to the bone, but I would survive, and my clothes would dry eventually.

~~~~

I woke up in a cold sweat not knowing where I was for a moment. It was barely light enough for me to see the dim outline of the room. Relief flooded me when I realized I was still sleeping on the hard floor of the old house in my sleeping bag. The bed and feather ticks had not gotten dry enough for me to bring them in the house last night. I had been dreaming about the cold river water where I scrubbed myself clean and what I had gone through to escape undetected. I wondered if bad dreams would ever come to an end. I feared not.

I relunctly crawled out of my sleeping bag to find that the house was almost as cold as the river water had been. Nighttime on this mountain was colder than I expected. I slept in a clean pair of pants, t-shirt, and socks. I hurriedly put on a jacket and shoes as I tried not to think about how cold it would feel in the wintertime. I wasn't a carpenter by any means, but I was determined to work every minute I could to make my life here comfortable, which would include insulating the place.

I found it irritating to know I had to build a fire in the cookstove before I could perk myself a cup of coffee to warm my insides up. A.J. had trained me well to survive in hostile environments, but it didn't make discomfort any more pleasant.

"Might as well get at it," I mumbled to myself. "You've always liked a challenge." I didn't want to admit this would be the kind of challenge I had never encountered before. I had an idea A.J. never thought I would be doing something like this or he would have trained me better. I wondered what he thought about my supposed death. Most likely he would say the risk of an early death was part of the job I'd signed up for. Spies were always at risk for short lives. I let out a derisive sound wondering if all the information I had uncovered had been of any use in the betterment of our country.

I had been gung-ho to change the workings of the government for the better. What I got was a stinging slap of reality. It didn't matter how much I exposed treason along with other crimes, the deep state had set up an impenetrable defense. They had many ways to get rid of those who tried to expose them. A permanent dip in the ocean was only one of the many ways. Threats of harm to those someone loved was a real clencher in getting hesitant people to do what they wanted. I had no one. Control over me wasn't as easy as those with families. I had given my all for my country and what good had it done? I didn't even know if my taking all of Brigham's hidden money supply had worked as I hoped it would. Regardless, he was nothing more than another fly on the rotting flesh of treason.

One thing was for sure, our country had enemies who wanted to destroy our country from greed, jealousy and a wide range of other reasons including the triumph of knowing they were powerful enough to do it. I could not understand how some of our own citizens would assist the enemy in doing such a thing. I had risked my life to ferret out traditors and it appeared no one seemed to do anything about what I had discovered.

And then it hit me. I was now doing exactly what millions of other people were doing. I was trying to take care of myself instead of taking care of my country. I felt guilty for not doing more. Surely there had been a way for me to have done a better job. I had already killed a man, maybe two. What was there to stop me from doing similar to others? As the old saying goes, might as well hang from stealing ten horses as for stealing one.

I consoled myself a little by the assurance I had been doing a good job and that was why my death had been ordered. But it hadn't been enough. I wanted to accomplish more.

"I did my best. Others will have to do the rest," I mumbled as a bit of comfort for my failure to do more.

I stuck the lifter tool into the slot on the stove eye so I could fill the fire box with small kindling. I struck a match and held it to a handful of dry leaves and carefully fed woodchips into the fire. It blazed up as I continued feeding it more chips and twigs. One thing was for sure, I would have to purchase a wood heating stove, or maybe two to go with the chimneys, when I left the mountain to buy building supplies.

It would be a while before I left the mountain. I needed to figure out what I would need to purchase as I didn't want to make another trip. Plus, I just might need to fill a lot of chugholes with rocks if there were more washed-out places, which could take years considering the miles of road it took to get up the mountain. I looked at my blackened fingernails and cringed at the thought of carrying more rocks. Oh well, I might as well get used to black nails, blood blisters, splinters, callused hands, and aching muscles if I did all the work I planned on doing before winter set in.

I finally got enough chopped-up deadfall in the firebox to get the coffee perking and the frying pan hot. I put in two eggs along with a slice of bread. I needed all the energy I could get for the day ahead. I had stacked flour, meal, sugar, shortening, coffee, soap, detergent, and dozens of canned foods along the wall in the kitchen. I needed some kind of shelves or cabinets to put everything in. At least I had thought to buy metal containers with tight fitting lids to keep vermin out.

There were many things I was going to need. Like chickens to lay eggs and a cow to give milk if I lived off the grid like the old folks did a hundred or so years ago. Self-sufficiency was what I wanted to accomplish, but I was willing to admit I had a lot to learn before I reached that place. I wished I had a back-to-nature trainer similar to what A.J. had been able to teach me about being a spy.

It was then I thought of the old woman. If she had lived on this mountain all her life, she surely knew the way of survival. Perhaps she would be willing to teach me things I needed to know. I missed a good opportunity to ask her about things when I had killed the snake. As soon as I got this place cleaned up a little more, I would go looking for her.

As soon as I had finished eating, I put a bucket of water on the stove to heat up to wash dishes along with cleaning more of the house. I thought cleaning the house should be my first priority. Once that was accomplished, I would go in search of the old woman to ask about planting a garden.

I longed to have books telling what all was needed to live successfully off the grid, but I was too afraid to be seen in bookstores, or any other stores for that matter. I had made sure I had stopped to buy things approximately seventy-five to a hundred miles from the mountain. I'd have to shop at many different stores to buy supplies. When I left the mountain again, I would make sure I never shopped at the same place twice. Repeat customers were remembered. I would prefer to find small stores that were unlikely to have cameras. The more I left the mountain, the more likely I would be recognized. I wished I could find a way to disguise myself even more, but I would worry about all that later. Right now, I had enough supplies along with enough work to keep me busy for a long time.

At one small hardware store I bought a machete and a scythe.

"Plan on doin' a little hand work, young fellow?" the old man at the checkout counter asked me. Young fellow, I liked him saying that. My almost shaved head under a John Deer cap along with my now skinny body was coming in handier than I thought. I had gone several weeks without eating much food, not that I had any extra weight to begin with.

I'd did my best to make my voice sound gruff as I nodded my head. "Kinda," I said as I picked up a tin circle of chewing tobacco sitting in a shelf on the counter. I was hoping it would make me seem more like a boy who was pretending to be a man.

"Reckon you might not be old enough for me to sell you that, but I won't say a thing if you won't."

I'd grinned and nodded my head. I paid the man in cash and left. Somehow, I would make myself look even more like a young boy when it came time to leave the mountain again to buy more supplies. I'd hurried to the truck where I hoped to have parked out of sight and drove away at a slow enough pace not to draw attention.

I took the scythe from where I had put tools in an empty bedroom to make sure they were safe and took it out to the front yard to cut the tall grass while water heated. Tall grass and snakes went together. I made sure to wear my winter boots in case I came across more snakes.

How in blue blazes people used this thing was beyond me, and yet I knew they did. There were two knobs on the curved handle to hold onto. I held onto them, swung the curved blade and stuck the tip end in the ground, but I didn't give up. I would learn to use this thing if it took me all spring and into the summer. I assured myself I wasn't a quitter, and I never gave up on something I was determined to do. I finally managed to whack off a ragged section of grass in front of the porch, but not enough to brag about.

I used the excuse of carrying in more firewood to keep the water hot to stop whacking at the tall grass for a while. I didn't want to blister my hands right off even when I was wearing latex gloves that I always kept a good supply of.

I scoured the downstairs floors again with detergent and a broom, then rinsed them with hot water and a mop. I then started on the stairs and upstairs floors. Once I finished with the floor cleaning, I carried the bedstead into the bedroom and figured out how to set it up.

Now came the part that made me feel dumb and incompetent. I needed to thread the ropes through the holes in the bedstead tight enough to hold up my weight. At least the rope had not deteriorated enough to lose its strength. Once I decided to leave good enough alone, I brought the feather tick in and placed it on the ropes. Then came my down sleeping bag. I grinned at the thought of being buried in feathers like a baby chicken. I would be a lot more comfortable than sleeping on the hard floor.

This time I tied a cloth over my nose and mouth to go into the attic in search of useful things. I found an old handmade dresser covered up with a ragged quilt. I could certainly use the dresser and the quilt if it didn't come further apart when I washed it. I had been thoughtful enough to bring several packs of different size needles and a lot of different colored spools of thread. One thing was for sure, I didn't plan on raising sheep to spin their wool on a spinning wheel. Some things were beyond even my attempt. After all, I was raised as a city girl who was trained to be a capable spy instead of a back-to-nature survivor.

"That's something to be proud of," I assured myself out loud. But I wasn't proud of myself yet.

~~~~

Again, I couldn't set aside the fact that more hadn't been accomplished with all the documentation I had discovered. I felt as though I had failed big time. To think I had spent years of risking my life to gather secret information about high-ranking officials – and for what? Handing the information over to those who were supposed to be the proper channels had only been enough to get me to be the one who was killed, but what could have I done differently? That haunted my mind continuously and will probably continue to do so for a long time to come.

I assured myself that my supposed death had allowed me to start out on a different journey. One that was for me alone – forever. That forever bothered me. Did I really want to be a hermit for the rest of my life? Deep down inside I knew the answer, What I wanted more than anything was a happy family life with a husband and children who loved each other, but that could never happen. The life of any person I loved would be in danger. I couldn't allow that to happen to innocent people. My own mother used to tell me I was old enough until my wants would hurt me, but that wasn't true. My wants had always hurt me and would continue to do so most likely for the rest of my life. From my disappointment in myself, I tried to work hard enough to find some consolation.

I had dragged the entire continents of the attic into the yard, washed everything the best I could and placed each item into the house. I now had a bed to sleep on, chairs to sit on and a table to eat at. It was enough for now.

I had also whacked at grass and weeds in the yard and around the barn and outbuilding until I had a somewhat cleared space. I found a place that was surely once a garden spot. There was a fallen down locust rail fence surrounding the section of ground. Asparagus and raspberries were growing on two sides of the sagging fence. I knew it was time to get the garden going if I was to grow enough food for me to last until next year. To do that I needed to find the old woman and get advice from her if I planned on doing things right the first time. I didn't think I had time to learn as I went. The fact that I couldn't take doing any more work in the house or outside was a good incentive for me to go in search of her.

I headed out to find her on what was a perfect, warm morning in late April. This highest section of the Blue Ridge mountain had to be as close to heaven as a person could get without leaving the earth. The wildflowers were blooming everywhere and filling the air with a delicate aroma. The birds were calling to each other from the treetops, while honeybees and bumble bees were busy collecting pollen from every bloom available. Squirrels were chattering at each other and perhaps at me for disturbing them.

A sudden kind of peace came over me. I was happy and thankful to still be alive instead of being fish food. I had no idea where the old woman lived other than the direction she had walked off in. I entered the woods at the same place she had. I had gone a good way down a slope when I heard the sound of water flowing. I followed the sound until I came to a spot where water was tumbling down rocks, not large enough to be called a waterfall, but maybe a miniature one.

The floor around the waterfall was a garden of ferns and delicate looking flowers. Trees and other vegetation had put out small green leaves that whispered gently when the wind blew. This spot reminded me of a magical make-believe place I'd seen in picture books when I was growing up. It wouldn't have surprised me to see tiny fairies flying about. I never imagined such a place existed in real life. I wondered if this place was part of the land I had purchased. I hoped it was.

I sat down on a rock and absorbed the peacefulness of the place until the moist chill got to me. I drew in a deep breath, stood up and continued on. I had gone for a long distance or so when I wondered if I had made a mistake going through the woods instead of taking the road. A.J. had trained me to survive in a wooded area, but there was still a chance I could get turned around in a place as thickly wooded with as many hollows and rises as this mountain had. If that happened, I would learn a lot more about maneuvering in these rocks and ridges than I planned for today.

I climbed on top of a rock cliff above a gully. I got a slight whiff of wood smoke lifting into the air. I climbed back down and followed my nose until I came to a clearing with a small, rough looking log cabin hunched in the center. I spotted the old woman coming out of a leaning shed that appeared to be struggling to stay upright. The old woman was carrying what looked like a quart lard bucket in her hand. It had a wire handle fastened to it so she could hold it in her hand with ease.

"Lordy be," she said as she saw me. "You skert the breath right outta my chest. I hain't seen a-body on my place in a coon's age."

"Sorry to frighten you," I told her. "It was such a pretty morning I decided to take a walk." I didn't tell her I was trying to find her. She gave me a long look as if she knew I wasn't telling the truth.

"Come on inside then, while I strain this goat's milk. It's about all that eases the ache in my belly these days," She finally said. "Living long is a might hard on a body. I've spent eighty-one years on this earth."

I followed her inside the dark little cabin. The place wasn't as large as the kitchen in the old Slaughter place, but it seemed to have everything the old woman needed including a table, two chairs, and a bed against the wall near a heating stove with an iron teakettle sitting on top along with a cook pot with something that smelled good simmering in it.

"Pull yourself up a chair and set a spell," she said as she took a cloth from a nail in the wall and put it over a quart jar. She poked part of the cloth into the can with two fingers and poured the goat's milk in it. She took the cloth off the jar and dropped it in a pot of water and then screwed a lid on the jar and sat it in a pan of cold water she had sitting on the table.

"Let's have us a cup of tea?" she offered as she took two tin mugs off a shelf and dipped out a tablespoon of good smelling crushed herbs into each cup and lifted the kettle from the stove top and poured hot water in both cups. I considered refusing but decided against it since I didn't want to seem rude. She then took a pint jar of honey from the shelf and added a teaspoonful to each cup.

"Want a drap of milk in it?" she asked.

"No thank you," I told her as I took the tin cup. It was almost too hot to hold.

"I have to put a drap in mine. Can't stand to drink hot stuff. Burns my mouth, it does. Always has. Reckon it always will. Take my George afore he died. He could just about drink his coffee scalding hot. I don't have no coffee no more unless the sin eater brings me some when he happens to show up."

"Sin eater?" I questioned just as she knew I would.

"You never heard of a sin eater?"

"No, I haven't."

"Ah, well. They're a legend that goes back to olden times. They're usually men who take other people's sins on themselves. Reckon women could be sin eaters too, but I've never heard tell of one being such as that."

"Exactly what does a sin eater do?"

She poured a little more goat's milk into her tea and took a sip. "I don't hardly believe in 'em myself, but they have a purpose, I reckon. Why you're not drinking your tea?"

I put the tin cup to my lips and took a tiny sip. It was too hot but delicious. "It's good, but too hot. I'll have to let it cool a little."

"Milk?" she questioned again.

I shook my head. I'll let it cool a little longer. "Tell me more about your sin eater."

"I've got an idea their purpose was to make folks feel better about their kin who died before getting right with God. Folks would take a portion of the dead person's worldly possessions, be it clothes, money, or what not and put it out in the woods with a bit of food on top. The sin eater would come along during the night and eat the food and take the dead person's possessions. After he done that, the dead person's sins would be laid on the soul of the sin eater. The sin eater always kept himself covered up and wore a mask. He made sure nobody ever looked at him, especially his face. He was both hated and feared, but folks thought he was needed."

I felt like laughing at such a story but didn't. The old woman seemed to be sincere.

"There is a sin eater living on this mountain?" I asked.

"Not exactly on this side of the mountain. I suspect he has him a place on the far side."

"And he brings you coffee?"

"On rare occasions he'll show up to see if there's anything I need. It hain't often, but I like it when he does show up. I believe he's a God-fearing man."

"Does he wear a mask?" I couldn't resist asking.

"Not exactly, but I've never seen what he looks like. His face has more hair growth than a werewolf's does. He wears a hat pulled way down on his head that makes his face hard to see. I've got to say he has kind eyes and a nice voice. He's always been mighty good to me."

"You're not afraid of him?"

"Never did hear of a sin eater who harmed anybody."

"Then why were they hated?" I wanted to know.

"Folks were afraid to have anything to do with one in case some of other people's sins enter them instead of him."

"Interesting," I said. "Who else lives on this mountain?"

"Just me and now you as far as I know."

"What about the Slaughters?"

"All the children moved away from all the hard work their daddy made 'em do. Never come back for longer than it took them to pilfer things. Old folks died off and that was it. None of 'em wanted the place. Surprised you do."

"I've always wanted to go back to nature and live off the grid."

"How's it suiting you so far?" she asked with a twinkle in her beady little eyes.

"I'm liking it, but I'm finding it more difficult than I thought it would be. I hate to admit it, but I don't know nearly as much as I thought I knew."

The old woman nodded as though she understood. "I feel that way myself at times."

"I want to grow a garden. I'm hoping you might give me some pointers on how to do it."

"Well now, I reckon we just might be able to work things out. I'll be mighty willing to help you out if you're willing to help me out in return.

"That sounds fair," I told her.

"I spread goat manure and chicken manure on my garden spot, but I hain't turned it over yet. If you'll help turn mine over, I'll help you with yourn."

"Okay," I told her. "Sounds fair," I repeated.

"We could start right now, but I've only got one shovel. You got one?"

"I've got one."

"Good. Want to start in the morning?"

"Yes, that will work for me."

"Then drink your tea and show up around seven o'clock in the morning with your shovel. We'd start sooner, but I've got to do up the work. Not to mention that it takes a few hours for my bones to warm up right good. I tend to stiffen up if I stay still."

"This tea is delicious," I told her. "What is it?"

"I put several different herbs in it, but it's mainly Sassafras. God provides right good for a body if they'll pay attention to what He grows. Say, how did you come here? Through the woods I reckon."

"Right. I passed a tiny waterfall."

"I call it the narrows. Little rocks pinch the branch water up before it falls over the big rock. That's the long way through the woods. Here, give me that," she said as she took my cup and rinsed both cups in a pan of water and set them on the counter. "I'll warsh 'em later. Come on, I'll show you a short cut from my place to yourn. No need to dally about when we could spend walking time working."

"What is your name?" I asked as we left her cabin.

"Polly. Folks call me Aunt Polly. What's yourn?"

"Bennie Jack," I told her.

"Penny Jack," she repeated.

"No, not Penny. It's Bennie with a B."

"Oh," she said. "Never heard of a woman named that. Where did you come from?"

I hadn't expected her to ask me that. It made me realize I needed to invent a background for myself. It also made me think I had made a mistake by seeking out the curious old woman. I surely had a momentary lack of intelligence.

"Have you ever heard of Killdeer, North Dakota?"

"I know of North Dakota. They say it's mighty cold out there."

"Right," I told her. "I never did like to be cold."

"And you picked this mountain? It gets cold here too."

"Not nearly as cold as it does in North Dakota."

"Your folks still live there?"

"No, they died when I was eighteen. I was a change-of-life baby."

"You're not much older than that now," she said.

"Not much," I fibbed. "I sold their little house for enough to buy the Slaughter place. I longed to live my own life. You might call it trying to find myself." Which had a small amount of truth to it.

"My Meadow Lark was always wanting to *find herself*, to quote her. That's one of the reasons she left here. Now you've come here trying to *find yourself*," she said with a chuckle. "Seems like I'm the only person alive who is satisfied with who they are and where they're at."

I wanted to tell her I could find the rest of my way home, but I didn't. For some reason she tagged right along. I wondered how long it had been since she had someone to talk to. "You get much company on this mountain?"

"Nary a one hardly. Just the sin eater and my Meadow Lark once in a long while. Used to have hunters now and again. Hain't heard one of 'em on this mountain in about ten years or so. Reckon it'll be just me and you living here."

That was what I wanted to hear.

"Let me tell you, life hain't easy, but it's a good life if you're willing to work hard and expect little."

I was certainly willing to work hard. I wasn't entirely sure what I expected or what kind of life I would end up with.

"If you don't mind me stating the truth, considering your age, I don't expect you to hold out here for long," she told me.

"Why shouldn't I? You've held out here all your life," I pointed out.

"I was born here and never knowed much of anything different."

"But your daughter left," I pointed out.

"Her and George's boys walked off this mountain to attend school some. They brought books home about different places and other ways of living. That's how I learned to read and write at the same time my Meadow Lark did. I tried my best to absorb every word in those books. I didn't want my Meadow Lark to think I was plum ignorant."

"Good for you," I told her.

"Yeah, it was good for me," she agreed. "Hope you don't mind me tagging along with you. I want to see how much work you've got done with the repairs on the old Slaughter place," she said as though she didn't expect me to have accomplished much, which I hadn't.

I had worked from daylight to dark and planned on continuing to do so. Yet, I couldn't see that I had improved things much. I felt as though I was trying to dip the ocean dry with a teaspoon.

Chapter 14

~~A.J.~~

All the bad words I uttered were definitely not acceptable language for human ears when I received the information that Fizz had given the documents to Brigham. She didn't have the intelligence of a bed bug if she thought she could get away with gathering such confidential and explosive information and then giving it to Brigham. I already knew about his treason, as did others, but we also knew it would take a lot more than exposure to stop him and the other perpetrators. It involved more than what was easily comprehended. Our select team has been gathering information for years without a sure-fire conclusion on exactly how to eliminate those who were so powerful. Once they were put into office, they were extremely difficult to get rid of. Once a politician, always a politician.

The information our team had been gathering for several years was getting us closer to having enough proof of treasonous conduct to expose the traitors. What Fizz had discovered was a big step in that direction. What she didn't realize was now the traitors would be able to set up contradictions to what she had discovered. Not only that, but chances were also that a tortured woman would squeal her guts before allowed to die. In other words, Fizz could blow our own secret operation.

I couldn't believe the helicopter had gone down in the ocean a short time after takeoff. Hopefully, they hadn't had enough time to torture her. Could it be possible that she told Brigham what she knew before he put her on the helicopter?

According to the tracking devices I had plated in her shoes, she hadn't been in his office very long. I regretted not also having her wired so I could hear her conversations, but I didn't want her to know I had her bugged or her whereabouts traced.

I regretted her loss, although her fast death might be the best thing that could have happened for our organization. Personally, I missed her and regretted her loss even though this hardheaded, stubborn, arrogant Fizz had jeopardized our own secret operation by putting every one of us, along with all we had learned, in jeopardy.

I admired her determination, but that didn't stop me from being angry at her. Surely, she realized her own life was in danger from many different angles. How she had managed to get her hands on such highly classified documents was beyond me. I didn't think a fly on the wall could get the information she'd already gotten.

It was necessary for me to go over what had happened in an effort to eliminate mistakes. Knowing what I should have done better was an important learning lesson. While I was making arrangements to see that she would safely disappear, she headed straight to the wrong person – the crooked FBI agent who was having his future well provided for in a foreign bank account. I knew about him, but Fizz didn't. Her knowledge was limited for a reason. My team also knew about his treason and double dealing, but the crazy little Frizz thought she was accomplishing what no one else ever had. She'd played with fire one time too many and it was going to cost her life unless I found a way to stop her immediately.

Not only would she be in trouble, but I would also be in trouble as well if she told she had given me a copy of what she had discovered.

I had failed her and the Freedom Group. I was the one who trained her and recommended her for the job. I was at fault for not getting it through her head that she was only a small speck in a very large operation where total secrecy was necessary, although I thought I had done so many times over. The little idiot obviously thought she was an indestructible spy with everything under control. She didn't realize it was going to take more than one person, or even a small army, to accomplish our mission. It wouldn't be as easy as finding a needle in a haystack, it would be like finding a needle in the middle of the ocean to stop this treasonous group. But we were determined to accomplish our mission.

Now, it was too late. I had failed in my job, failed Fizz and my country. I needed to review everything that had gone wrong until I came up with a better solution in how I would train future recruits.

~~~~

I had headed straight for Fizz once I discovered that she was meeting with Brigham. I had to stop her before she got to him. Double agents were everywhere. I thought I had made it clear that she was only to report her findings to me and no one else.

But she hadn't listened.

I condemned myself for picking her in the first place. I saw the intelligence in her as well as her determination to never give up. That wasn't all I saw in her. I had a tendency to be drawn to her in a physical way. She had the kind of innocents along with sex appeal that I knew older men would find hard to resist. I found it hard to resist.

Men in power became controlled by power. They came to believe they deserved everything they wanted, including young women to fulfil their sexual desires. In a way I felt guilty by putting Fizz in their clutches. I figured such men would be able to eat her up alive, but I was wrong. It seemed she realized she had greater control by their wanting her than by them having her. I got a lot of pleasure watching how she was able to use that fact to her benefit. Just when the men were ready to pounce on her, she moved slightly out of their reach. She was a challenge, and they tried again and again without blaming her.

What she had managed to discover on both men and women was astounding. Even I would have deemed her as heroic if she had given only me the information instead of going straight to Brigham. At least she had been wise enough to send me a copy. I had no idea who else got a copy, which concerned me to no end.

Anger, frustration, along with a devastating feeling of loss filled me as I saw the helicopter lifting off from top of the building.

I had been minutes too late to save her.

She hadn't been smart enough not to get in the helicopter. She would be no match for what was about to happen no matter how well I had trained her.

So be it. I tried to soothe my feeling of loss with those three words. I could do nothing to save her now. I had to concentrate on how to counter whatever damage she had done to our intelligence operation. I had no idea if she would be thought to be an independent agent or if she would be traced back to our organization. My fear was the latter.

I tried my best to get a fix on where they were taking her. Another of my fears was that she would be sequestered and tortured until she told them everything she knew, which included me as her trainer. No one, especially a young woman, would be able to remain silent for long. She would spill her guts before they put her out of her misery.

She had no idea I had planted tracking devices in her shoes, as I did all the recruits I trained. It was my way of finding out if t I was able to get enough faint signals of her going over the mountains and then cutting back over the ocean. I was able to continue getting faint signals until the helicopter went down into the water where the salt water shorted out the devices.

My consolation at the loss of someone I had spent a considerable time training, and that I was genuinely fond of, was two-fold. She would not spill delicate information and she would not endure their torture.

~~~~

I did my best to put Fizz out of my mind. She wasn't the first person our organization had lost, and she wouldn't be the last. Each and every one of us realized our life was at risk, but we were willing to take that risk. I wasn't the only trainer, but I had arrogantly thought I was the best. I thought I had trained Fizz to near perfection. I wasn't sure I'd be given the chance to train another person. I might as well face it. I failed with Fizz.

I was thinking about her when I received information that Brigham's office building had gone black. It was something that never happened. Something our organization never wanted to happen. There had to be a reason for it, and we needed to know what that reason was. I wasn't sure Brigham was capable of blacking out his own office building, but he was the most likely one to do it.

My question was why?

"What the hell is going on?" was his question sent to us.

"Not of our doing," was the reply sent to him. "Suggest you explain."

"I've been targeted," was the last we heard from him.

I didn't know what had happened to him, and I didn't care. My concern was who was to take his place. I had an idea the person would be a lot worse than Brigham if that was possible.

Chapter 15

I wasn't the least bit surprised when the girl showed up at my place. I had gone back to get a look at her twice to determine what she was about. She was a worker alright, but she had a way of doing things backward to the way she ought to do them.

I wanted to know more about her, but I wasn't about to butt in on her business. She and I both had a right to live our lives the way we wanted. Still yet, I found it mighty odd for a young girl to buy such a backwoods place on a remote mountain like this one. That was if she wasn't squatting on it. I would like to see her deed, but I wasn't about to ask for such as that. Maybe I could take a look at it in the courthouse when I walked all the way off the mountain to pay the confounded taxes the government had started robbing people with. I had to gather enough ginseng, plus sell a baby goat to pay them. Way back my folks didn't have to pay a red copper for taxes. Things sure had changed for the worse since then.

On the good side, maybe I could hitch a ride with that gal when she went to pay her taxes. It sure would save me from having sore feet along with having to spend the night in the woods. It took me a sight longer to walk back up the mountain than it did going down it. There were bobcats all over the place along with a few mountain lions and bears that came through every once in a while.

Can't say as I liked or didn't like that girl being here. If she proved to be a good neighbor without any unlawfulness about her then I welcomed having another woman on the mountain. If she proved to be nothing but aggravation, well then, I'd have to think on her a while. If it had been my Meadow Lark who bought the place, I would be the happiest old woman living.

"I want to buy a milk cow and some chickens," she told me as we walked through the woods.

"You don't need a cow," I told her. "You'd have to have a bull to breed her if you wanted to keep her giving milk. What you need is a nanny goat or two like I've got. You could use my billy for breeding or get your own. They don't take much feed to keep them going like it does a cow. As for chickens, I reckon I can set a hen for you. I wouldn't charge you for 'em if I didn't need cash money for the confounded, no-account government who's laid taxes on the backs of us poor folks.

"I wouldn't expect them for free," she assured me. "I've never had goat's milk before."

"It's the best milk a body can drink. Folks used to feed babies on it all the time. It's a lot richer and easier on the belly than cow's milk," I told the girl, but I wasn't sure she believed me, her being a city gal and all.

"You don't have to take me all the way home," she told me. "I know my way from here."

"I reckoned you do at that, but if you don't mind me being nosy, I'd like also to take a look inside that Slaughter place. I've always wanted to know what that fancy place looked like on the inside."

She looked surprised. "You've never been inside the house?"

"I hain't," I told her. "I've made a point of never going where I'm not invited. It hain't respectful."

"But it's been empty for years," she said as though I didn't already know that.

"A body ought to respect what hain't theirs regardless if it's occupied or not. I know I do."

"Then I will certainly invite you to come inside any time you want to."

"That's mighty nice of you, but I only want to take a look to ease all the years of my curiosity."

I had looked on the outside of that place for years and wondered what it would be like to live inside that place. I had never known living in a place that wasn't a log cabin, and I didn't want to. I was happy to have my own parent's place. It was good enough for me. I know I could go live with my Meadow Lark in her fancy place. She told me she had hot and cold water running in the house along with a tub where a body could wash all over at one time. She also said there was a toilet in the house where a body could relieve themselves in warmth and privacy. She said folks pushed a latch and water would wash the human refuge down into a hole in the ground. I could only imagine how that would smell after a spell. That wasn't all. Her place had electricity that could keep the place hot in winter and cold in the summer.

I had read about all that in one of the magazines my Meadow Lark brought me, but I wasn't much interested. I had no inclination to live in such a way. A body would grow fat and lazy living like that. Not to mention being bored all the way to your grave.

I looked about her raggedy mown yard. I'd seen her trying to use the scythe and had to grin right big. She was beating the grass and weeds to death instead of cutting them.

"I'll show you how to use the scythe. Appears you've not got the hang of it yet. You'll need to put up hay if you buy one of my goats," I told her.

"I'm willing to learn," she told me. "Nothing is as easy as I expected."

"Never is. This place needs a lot of work. Too bad you don't have a man to help you," I said just to see what she would say in return.

"Did you have a man to help you?" she came back with.

"Not after my George died. His boys left out about the time they wore long britches. Didn't blame 'em none."

"You managed and so will I," she said with confidence.

"It's the only way I knowed to live. You're different. You're a city girl. You're used to all that easy living my Meadow Lark is always bragging about."

She looked like what I said aggravated her some. "I'm a fast learner," she was quick to tell me. "Come on inside the house. I'll show you around."

I did want to take a look at the inside of that place. Lord knows I'd thought about that place and the folks who once lived there a plenty.

Chapter 16

~~Bennie Jack~~

I found it difficult to believe the old woman had never been inside the old Slaughter house considering how long it had been empty, but I did find her rather odd in her own way. I suppose living on this mountain alone all these years would make a person odd. I almost let out a groan at what I had to look forward to.

"Lawsy me," she said as she went from the living room to the kitchen. "A spring house right there inside the kitchen like that. Now, if that hain't fancy living. I have to trudge through the snow and brake ice with my ax to get water in the wintertime. You've got it made."

When I took her into the bedroom, a big grin came to her face. "Was them ropes rotten?" she asked.

"No," I told her. "They weren't. I had trouble getting them not to sag."

"I'll help you with that, if you want. Sleeps a lot better if they don't sag in the middle."

"I really would be grateful if you show me how it's done."

She didn't hesitate to flip my sleeping bag along with the feather tick and quilt off the bed and went to work on the ropes. I was amazed at how strong her hands were even when they were drawn and knotted with what I took to be arthritis. Her small hawk-claw hands moved with speed and capability. She certainly knew what she was doing with the ropes and did it well.

"I hope you biled that feather tick and quilt right good," she said. "Birds and vermin carry mites and fleas. I had an infestation of 'em once. Had to bile everything and then scald furniture, floors and walls. Took me several days to get it all done. Don't reckon they left a scalding pot behind. I'd say them Slaughters carried off everything that was worth two coppers. Surprised they left this much behind. But then those boys never did put much value in women things."

"Sounds like you didn't have a high opinion of the Slaughters," I couldn't resist saying.

"Reckon the old woman was alright, poor ole soul. Felt right sorry for all she had to put up with. Never did have a girl young'un to help her out none. Kept spitting out boy babies like a cat having kittens. Had to do all the work to keep that bunch going. May the good Lord forgive me for say so, but it was the old man and them boys I didn't care for. Couldn't trust a one of 'em. They'd skin a flea for its hide especially if the flea belonged to somebody else."

That wasn't a good recommendation for a place to live. I was hoping the place had good vibes about it instead of giving off an unhappy past.

"I can tell you those Slaughters made the best white liquor of anybody here abouts. It'd take the hair off a hog's back. Never used old car batteries or nothing that would kill a person. I can say that for 'em. I drunk a drap once when I had a bad sore throat. It tasted like water till it hit the back of my throat, and then it set me on fire. Liquor has a lot of good uses. Too bad men took advantage of it and drink enough of it to make them crazy."

"The Slaughters made illegal liquor?"

"Lawsy honey, it wasn't illegal way back then. It was about the only way folks high up on this mountain had a way to make cash money. Couldn't grow enough stuff to haul down the mountain to sell. Folks were willing to travel up the mountain to get good corn liquor. Some brought cash money, while others brought things to barter. I have to say those

Slaughter never allowed themselves to be cheated. Folks off the mountain learned it was best not to try. Folks call the old man and them six boys the seven devils. Earned the name most every day of their lives if you asked me."

"What happened to the six boys?" I asked.

"They done like George's boys. Got tired of how hard their daddy worked 'em and took off. Got married and had young'uns of their own, I reckon. Once the old folks died, some of 'em come back to tote things off, but that was all. Hard life living on this mountain, I can tell you."

"And yet you refuse to leave the mountain and go live with your daughter," I couldn't resist saying.

"Never did want to live the kind of life they have off this mountain. Most of the folks might be God fearing folks, but the times I do go off this mountain to pay my taxes makes me think different. That reminds me, if you drive off this mountain, reckon I can hitch a ride? I've got a goat to sell to pay my taxes with. Hain't due till the end of the year but I like to pay 'em before bad weather sets in."

"I plan on going in before summer is over," I told her, but I didn't want to take her with me. I didn't want her to know I planned on driving a long way to different stores to get supplies. "When do you want to pay your taxes?"

"I usually go when the timber starts to change color. Hain't too hot and hain't too cold to walk. Don't like to pay 'em afore then. Ask me, that confounded government robs a poor person. Government don't care if they leave a body starved and ragged so long as they get your money."

I agreed with her on that. I just as soon she hadn't mentioned the government. I moved here to put all that behind me, but their long arm reached even here on this remote mountain.

"Don't hardly want to climb them stairsteps," she said, as she looked at the steep stairs. "My joints hain't what they used to be. Let's go take a look at the garden spot. Reckon it'll be right troublesome to dig up dirt that's been fallow for all this time. It'll be a job to keep down all the weeds that's reseeded themselves. You'll have calluses on your hands as big as banty eggs from all the hoeing you'll have to do. This mountain will find out what you're made of by the time bad weather sets in."

"How much do you get for a baby goat?" I asked.

"Don't let 'em go cheap. Most folks don't know what a prize a goat is. Like I done said, don't take much to feed 'em, plus they keep down briars and the like," she said before she quoted me a price. It was dirt cheap.

"I'll give you twice that amount if you'll teach me how to take care of it."

She cocked her head and looked at me. "I'll take you up on that, but you'll be the one getting cheated at that price."

"I'm not paying that much for the goat. I'm paying for your years of experience and knowledge."

She chuckled. "Come to think on it, you'll be the one getting a deal."

~~~~

I decided to make a trip off the mountain as soon as Aunt Polly and I had shoveled our gardens over, as she called it. She was also right about my garden being like new ground. Talk about a job! My hands had blisters on them for two weeks straight, not to mention how every part of my body ached. How the little old woman held up was beyond me. I decided right off that I would buy a garden tiller along with a lawn mower and ten more gallons of gas. I wanted to go back to nature without having to work myself to death.

"Wimp," I accused myself. I was proud of being an excellent spy. I knew how to ferret out secrets others tried to keep hidden, but I wasn't much when it came to farm work. "You'll learn," the old woman kept telling me. I was more than willing to learn, but I didn't like feeling 1 was inadequate.

The one good thing for me and Aunt Polly was we were keeping each other company. I decided she had been in need of someone to talk to for a lot of years. She was now showering me with all the words she hadn't said. "Lawsy me," she would end up saying. "Just listen to me running my mouth. Never expected to ever talk this much. You're a good listener."

"I'm going off the mountain to buy more vegetable seeds and get supplies to repair the house. Is there anything you want?" I'd made a trip to her house to ask. I knew she would *take it hard*, as she had a way of saying, if I left without telling her. Working together had brought us close.

"Don't know of a thing I need that I hain't got," she told me. "When you aim to take off?"

"Early in the morning," I told her.

"When will you be back?"

"Tomorrow evening."

"Drive careful," she said. "I've got kinda used to having you around. Already spoke more words to you than come outta my mouth for the past twenty years, but I've got a sight more to say."

That was one of the best compliments I'd gotten in a long time, maybe ever. Even A.J. never seemed to appreciate me or my abilities. He was always trying to make me be better than I was.

That night I prepared myself for the trip by cutting my hair down to half an inch of my scalp. I'd been out in the sun enough to darken my face and hands a lot. Still, I looked more like a woman than I did a boy. I found a ragged sheet and tore a strip to bind my chest with. Too big of a man's shirt would hide my breasts a little, but it might not hide them enough. As for my lack of beard, there wasn't much to do about that. I couldn't even fake peach fuzz. I had gained a little of my weight back, but I was still too skinny. Thinking of peach fuzz made me think of Fizz. I really would like to know what was going on in the world I'd left behind. Was I still considered dead? Had the documents I'd risk my life to copy done any good? Did A.J. morn my death, or did he have another young woman in training?

I headed out the next morning as soon as it got daylight enough to see how to drive safe on the sorry road. I left with an almost shaved head, dirty cap, bound chest, and too big men's clothes on that I deliberately made sure smelled like sweat and old barn yard dirt. I had the tin of tobacco in my shirt pocket in hopes it would add conviction to my disguise.

The road hadn't gotten one bit better than what I remembered it being, but I drove a lot slower trying to dodge as many potholes as possible. Telling myself the rough goat path of a road kept people off the mountain did little to make me appreciate being bounced about. Again, I was thankful for the toughness of the old four-wheel drive truck.

I came to the washout where I had gotten stuck. The rocks and dirt had settled somewhat. I held my breath and eased the truck over it. It held, thankfully. I got a queasy feeling as I looked down into the ravine where the truck could have gone if it hadn't been for the tree that kept it from going over the bank. The rocky drop-off was breath taking to say the least.

This was without doubt one of the most remote mountains I could have found. I could understand why young people wanted to leave as soon as possible. I feared that I might want to leave after a while. Right now, I loved everything about the mountain that I had encountered, especially Aunt Polly. She had been a blessing I hadn't expected. Without her I would have felt completely isolated if not deserted on a mountain I knew nothing at all about.

By the time I'd made my way off the mountain, I smelled more like sweat than I wanted. Even my too big shirt had sweat stains under the arms. Sweat ran down my back and front as it dampened the rag I had wrapped my chest with. I was nothing like the city woman who was neat as pin, always well-groomed and sweet smelling with expensive perfume. The storm had made the road a lot worse than when I arrived.

I expected to get stuck or pop a tire before I got off the mountain. I wiped sweat from my face and said a prayer of thanks to the power above when the truck and I arrived on a smoother gravel road with me and the truck still in one piece.

I drove miles away from the mountain until I came to a town large enough to have a Home Depot. I knew they would have cameras, but I didn't think I looked anything like myself. I kept my head down when I went to the lumber desk and ordered what I wanted. The checkout girl hardly looked at me as I paid her in cash. I noticed how her noise wrinkled slightly at my sweaty smell. I took my receipt and drove around back to the lumber yard where I handed a man my receipt. He and another man loaded my purchases, and I drove away.

Next stop was at a feed and seed store closer to the mountain. I bought bags of fertilizer and lime, along with more seeds than I knew what to do with, including two fifty pounds sacks of potatoes. I also purchased goat feed along with three fifty-pound sacks of corn. I planned on planting as much of the corn as I could turn over ground for. As I was going out the door, I heard the peep of baby chicks. I turned around and went back. I bought a dozen females and two baby roosters, along with two fifty pounds of chick starter. The clerk put the chicks in a cardboard box with several newspapers in the bottom.

"You going far?" he asked.

"Not far," I fibbed.

"Then they ought to ride fine in the cab of your truck."

I then drove a few miles to a hardware store and bought the garden tiller and lawn mower along with two five-gallon gas cans and had the dealer load them on top of the lumber I had bought. I moved the sacks of feet and fertilizer against the tiller and lawn mower to keep it from bouncing about. From there, I drove to a gas station and filled up the tank of the truck along with the two gas cans and bought a whole case of oil. Last on my list was to stop at a grocery store and buy enough supplies to last until my garden started producing.

As I left the store, I saw several newspaper dispensers against the grocery store wall. I bought a newspaper from each one of them. I hope they had at least a few of the answers about the world I'd left behind. I would read them once I got back home. The sun would be going down by the time I got back up the mountain.

Across the highway from the grocery store, I saw a goodwill store. I decided I might as well stock up on clothes and whatever household items I might need in the future. I also wanted to get warm clothes for winter for Aunt Polly as well as myself. I bought shoes, boots, shocks caps and all the blankets they had. I also bought every knife and hammer in the store and made room for my purchases in the cab of the truck.

Just as I had dreaded, it was much slower going up the mountain than driving down it. The load I had in the truck was heavy enough to worry me, but the old truck kept plugging ahead in groundhog gear. I would like to have thanked the factory that built the sturdy old truck, along with the old man who sold it to me. At the time I thought I had paid too much for it. Now I realized it had been one of the best deals I'd ever gotten.

The sun was getting ready to set by the time I finally reached home. Again, I was wet with sweat perhaps even more so than when I had driven off the mountain. I kept thinking about what I would do if the old truck didn't make it.

Aunt Polly was sitting in a chair on the porch when I arrived.

"Lawsy mercy, child," she said as soon as I got out of the truck. What on earth hain't you brought back? Good thing you tied all that pile of stuff down real good or it would have bounced off and landed down in the ravine. We best get to unloading it afore your tires go flat."

There was a smile on her face and a twinkle in her eyes. She seemed as excited as a young child on Christmas morning at seeing the load I had. I knew she could hardly wait to see what I had bought home.

"I tried to get all the things I thought we would need for a long while," I told her.

"It's a load alright. Heard that truck straining all the way up the mountain. I hurried here to make sure you and that truck made it back in one piece."

Again, I was surprised at how strong the little woman was. Even A.J. would be impressed with her. We had unloaded every single thing by the time the sun was sinking behind the mountain.

I had made two piles on the porch of clothes, boots, shoes, caps. blankets and kitchen utensils.

"That pile is yours," I told her. "And this pile is mine."

"Lawsy me. I can't take all that stuff. I've never seen the like."

"I bought those things for you. Besides, it's not nearly enough to pay you for helping me unload the truck."

Tears dampened her eyes before she could blink them back. "My Meadow Lark never did bring me things like this. Only the sin eater ever brought me what I was in need of." `

"I tried to get some of the things I thought we would need come winter," I told her. Mention of the sin eater put an odd feeling inside me. I didn't know what to make of the feeling. I wasn't exactly afraid of him, but I did hope I never came into contact with him.

"How you gonna keep all of them little biddies warm?" she suddenly asked. You know they'll die if they get cold."

"I didn't know that," I told her.

"Looks to me like I'll have to bring you my old broody hen to put in with 'em. Good thing they've put some of your stuff in that big cardboard box. You'll need to keep them biddies and hen in that big box next to the cook stove until she takes 'em and you build a chicken coop to keep 'em in."

"I can't just turn them loose outside?"

"Lawsy child, they wouldn't last no time. Looks like I'll have to show you how to take care of 'em," she chuckled a little. "You brought back enough feed and corn to last a mighty good while. Not to mention all them seeds and things. I've never seen the like."

"I hope I got everything we'd need," I told her. "Don't plan on traveling that road again until we go to pay taxes."

"I reckon not," she said. "Looks to me like we've already got all we'll ever need right here."

I had a good feeling inside about Aunt Polly. I had come to think of her as a gift from God. I had expected to be all alone on this mountain. Finding Aunt Polly was an unexpected blessing– for both of us.

"Be right back," Aunt Polly said as she took off through the woods. Her little legs and stooped body going almost at a run carrying the things I had bought her in her arms. I was busy trying to find a place to put all the things I'd brought home. Most everything would be stored in the spare bedroom, except for the lumber that we put on the porch to stay dry in case it rained. The tiller and lawn mower would go into the barn hall.

It wasn't long until Aunt Polly returned carrying a black hen under her arm and a shotgun resting under her other arm. She was holding onto the gun with one hand and the hen's feet with the other hand. She laid her shotgun on the top step to the porch and came inside.

"I see you done put those little biddies in the big box," she said before I could ask about the shotgun. "Go ahead and poke some air holes in the box. I'll put this hen in with 'em and cover up the top with one of those blankets. The hen will most likely take 'em if it's dark inside the box, but we don't want to smother 'em."

As soon as she had the hen and chicks covered up, she took the knife from my hand and poked a dozen or so more air holes.

"Don't have time to help you no more right now," she said. "I best get back to the house afore darkness sets in. I saw some big cat tracks near my goat barn. Glad I had my goats closed in. I'm thinking that old mountain lion is passing through again. Gotta keep a sharp eye out for it. Don't want it making a meal of my livestock."

"Mountain lion?" I questioned.

"All kinds of vermin on this mountain. Bobcats, mink, and weasels are always after my chickens. Mountain lions and bears show up every once in a while to go after my goats. My animals don't have much of a way to protect themselves. It's my job to do it for 'em. Mountain lions and bears usually pass by on their way to somewhere else without doing any harm, but I keep my shotgun handy just the same. They can kill more than I'd ever be able to replace."

"I'll walk you back home," I told her.

She chuckled, amused. "Lawsy child, there's no need for that. I've taken care of me and mine all these years. I killed a mean bear once with this here double-barreled shotgun. Let him have both barrels right in the face when I was ten feet from it. Then had to jump behind the trunk of a big old tree to keep it from mauling me to death. Killed my baby goat it did. Had to shoot it two more times near its heart. Didn't die until I slit its throat with my knife. I'm telling you a mad bear is a hard thing to kill good and dead."

I was stunned at what she said.

"My daddy used to tell me I couldn't sell the hide until after I killed the bear. I killed that bear and tanned its hide and then canned the meat, although it weren't much good considering how mad it was, but it helped get me through a long winter. Still got that hide up in the shed loft. Never did find nobody to sell that bear hide to."

With those words she was back out on the porch, grabbed up her shotgun and was trotting off through the woods.

~~~~

It was after midnight when I was woken up by the sound of a woman screaming. I jumped straight out of bed and grabbed my rifle and pistol. I knew that mountain lion was killing Aunt Polly by the way she was screaming.

I ran out into the yard yelling her name. The moon was bright enough for me to see the outlines of things, but there was total silence. I didn't know which way to go to find her. I called out her name again as fear tightened my chest. Silence was not a good thing. I turned in a circle hoping to hear some kind of sound. It was then I heard a slight noise coming from the barn. A shadow leaped out of the barn loft door I'd left open to air the loft out and disappeared into the woods. I knew it was the big cat I heard screaming. I lifted the rifle I had purchased the same time I bought the truck and shot into the woods where it had disappeared. I knew I wouldn't hit the mountain lion, but the noise might scare it enough until it wouldn't come back.

Once I was back inside the house, I got the shakes. It was similar to the feeling I got after I'd managed to barely escape being caught when I was spying. I'd never expected to get that kind of feeling here. As the old saying goes, wherever I go, I take me with me.

"Did you kill it," were the words that brought me out of a deep sleep to see Aunt Polly glaring down on me with a double barrel shotgun in her hand. It had taken me a long time to fall asleep after I'd shot at the mountain lion. I was so startled I came in a hair of pulling my pistol on Aunt Polly before I realized it was her. Looking up at her was even more foreboding than standing face to face with her.

"What tha . . .?" I said.

"Didn't mean to intrude on you," she said. "When you didn't answer from my calling out your name, I feared it had got you. So, I trespassed and went inside to make sure you were still alive. Did you kill it?" she repeated.

"No," I told her. "I was hoping to scare it off."

"Heard it squalling and then heard you shoot the gun. Hoped you might have got it being the crack shot that you are."

"It leaped out of the barn loft and was in the woods before I knew what was happening."

"They're like that. Can't judge what they'll do next. Seen you left the barn loft door open. Might ought to keep it closed. All cats like laying up in high places. We both best be keeping our guns handy for a while."

"Good advice," I said as I got out of bed. "Have you eaten breakfast?"

"Nope. Come to check on you as soon as it was light enough."

"Good. You build a fire in that hateful cookstove, and I'll fix us both breakfast."

"You got a deal," she said. "I get tired of my own cooking ever year or two."

Aunt Polly ate twice as much as I did. I wondered if she ate that way all the time. If so, she surely must work it off because there wasn't an ounce of fat on her bones.

"That was plain good," she told me. "I done checked on the hen and biddies. She's hovering them like they were her own hatchlings. They've still got plenty of water and feed. Since I'm already here, we can get right to work. Want us to finish planting your garden, work on the roof, or build you a diddle house?"

I could just imagine frail little Aunt Polly on the roof trying to help me. "What about your animals? Don't you need to be home taking care of them?

"Done fed them while it was pitch dark. I hain't letting any of 'em out until I'm certain that mountain lion has left out for good. Usually stays around for several days when it comes through.

"Okay," I agreed, although I had rather rest for a few hours and read the papers I bought, but that could come later. "We'll plant the garden, and then we'll go to your place."

"Done finished up my garden. "Besides, if I stay still for long, all my parts get stove up."

"What needs doing at your place?" I asked.

"Nary a thing. I already done up what needed doing. Momma always said if you didn't have half your work done by ten o'clock of a morning, you most likely wouldn't get the other half done."

"It's only six o'clock," I told her.

"Won't get half of your work done by ten o'clock if we don't get at it," she told me.

I had an idea I'd never gain my weight back with Aunt Polly around. She was driving me almost as hard as A.J. did.

I was amazed at how effortlessly Aunt Polly built the chicken coup. I cringed at the amount of plywood she used. She even found a used roll of chicken wire in one of the sheds.

"Hawks," she said. "Have to keep the whole thing enclosed so the hawks won't get at 'em. Snakes, rats, snapping turtles, mink, weasels and only the good Lord knows what all else eats biddies along with grown chickens. Got to keep your eyes on 'um all the time. Same way with goats and cows. You've got to take care of things if you have anything."

I agreed with her, but there was more to take care of on this place than I could ever imagine. Yet, I looked forward to it. I wanted to make this place my own, and the best way to do that was by doing all the work myself. That was with help from Aunt Polly. She was determined I didn't make too many mistakes.

She stopped working on the chicken coup, tied a knot in her apron, and started picking weeds and cramming them in the pocket she'd made by tying the knot.

"This is broad leaf plantain. This here is lamb's quarters just coming up good. And lookie yonder at the garden fence. There's a bunch of poke just the right size to eat. Have to be careful on poke so it won't pizen you. Have to boil it just right and then fry it in grease. You got any vinegar, grease, and a dap of sweetening?" she asked.

"I brought a supply of all three." I had brought two gallons of apple cider vinegar and another of white vinegar to pickle things like cucumbers. I had even brought three cans of Crisco shortening and four ten-pound sacks of sugar. I had tried my best to bring all the major supplies I thought I'd need, but there seemed to be no end to the supplies I had forgotten to bring until I learned enough to be self-sufficient. "Do you keep a supply of such things?" I asked her.

"I make my own vinegar, grow molasses cane, rob bees, and make goat milk butter."

"Amazing," I said. "You're self-sufficient. I want to learn how to do everything myself."

She kind of grinned. "Time," she said. "It'll take a lot of time even with me helping you."

I didn't doubt that. I was already learning how much I didn't know. Sometimes I felt so lost I wanted to burst into tears. It was one thing to use what A. J. had taught me to survive in the elements, and quite another thing to do it on a day-to-day basis for the rest of my life, but I would have to learn if I wanted to stay alive.

Chapter 17

~~A.J.~~

I hadn't been told to train another spy recruit and that concerned me. Something was up and I needed to know what it was. What Fizz had uncovered was far more than I had ever expected her to be capable of. It was proof positive of what was going on with the highest bureaucrats of our government. The money they had been paid under the table for handing over our highly sought after classified documents was mind blowing. It was treason without any question about it. How many people she had sent copies of the documents, I still had no idea. I did know treason and the setup for it had been going on for some time. It was a carefully laid out plan that had been put into action years before until it escalated to what it now was. Such plans had worked to destroy other countries, and it was now working to destroy my country.

A type of chemical warfare was a surefire way to win without spilling any of your own blood from retaliation. Get rid of old people who were wise of evil ways by giving them a disease their bodies couldn't recover from. Get rid of the young by getting them hooked on drugs, or preferably killed by them. To add to that, put in teachers that would convince their students the propaganda they were being fed was the truth they should accept without question. Such as that wasn't difficult when the brain was fogged up on drugs and surging hormones.

And last but not least, get rid of all the old law enforcers who believed in doing what was right, and replace them with officers who would stand up for the criminals instead of the victims. All it took to accomplish this destruction was money. Lots and lots of bribe money along with people who could be easily bought.

"Fools," I wanted to shout. "Don't you know you will be the first to get eliminated once the enemy has what they want from you?" How anyone could be stupid enough not to realize such as that was beyond me.

I did find out that Fizz wasn't one of the stupid, unless believing Brigham was on the side of those who could be trusted was stupid. I took full responsibility for her believing Brigham was one of our trusted men. I hadn't warned her of Brigham's double dealing – hadn't though she needed to know. My silence had cost Fizz her life. It was up to me to avenge her death. To do that I would need to put a failproof plan into action – like there was such a thing as failproof.

I had a copy of what Fizz had discovered as did Brigham. The question rattling my brain was what could my group do about it? I knew my group didn't have the power, time or the backup to take the perpetrators to court for treason, but if something didn't happen soon our country was at risk.

Anyone willing to take a good look around them should see what was going on, but maybe they didn't. It always amazed me how blind people could be to what was an obvious threat to their freedom. It reminded me how thousands of people were loaded onto trucks and trains to be shipped off to gas chambers without putting up a fight. Hitler was an evil man, and yet people refused to admit it and fight back. Just like they were doing now.

A similar takeover as Hitler did was going on today, while thousands of people were taking a blind eye and refusing to see it. They wanted to believe the propaganda that was being fed them. They wanted to continue their easy life without realizing their freedom was at stake. I longed to grab everyone I saw and give them a good shaking. Don't trust all that soft spoken, sweet talk that's being spoon fed to you, I wanted to yell in their ears until they would listen. It seemed people chose to believe lies when they suited them better than truth they didn't want to hear. They were like sheep following a leader who was a greedy wolf disguised in sheepskin.

The first step in taking over was to convince people to trust you. The next step was to have them dependent on you. Taking away their means of self-defense would be a major win. Taking away their means of earning a living was another. Fear was a major tool in controlling people. Division was another undisputed weapon. Turning one race against another race was a major tool. Having people fighting with each other instead of fighting the enemy was a sure means of winning a battle the enemy didn't have to fight.

It was obvious that well-fed animals made no attempt to feed themselves. It wouldn't take long until they became fat and lazy enough until they were dependent on handouts. I saw that happening every day with government handouts, and I knew it would get worse until something drastic took place.

I had even wondered about assassinating the higher ups that were now in power, but they were only puppets on a string. They were not the ones who were making the decisions. They were only mouth pieces for those who did. And at the same time, it was possible the ones who took their place might not be as easily controlled, which could be a good or a bad thing.

The major weapon our country had was its people. There was still power in our country if our people banded together to see clearly what was taking place and then did something about it. Unfortunately, our enemies were controlling not only the news media but the social media as well. Plus, people were too occupied with trying to take care of their own family and pay the ever-increasing bills to take time to analyze what was happening. Americans wanted to trust the government and the people they elected to represent them.

If only they knew the truth and believed it.

Our enemies were allowed to do whatever they wanted while our leaders rolled over and bellied up. Were there no longer men with big enough gonads to stop what was going on? Was I not man enough to give up my own life by trying to take them out by any means necessary?

Chapter 18

~~Aunt Polly~~

I just didn't know what to think about that girl, but in a way, I was glad she had bought the Slaughter place. I had worried about that place for years. I feared some outsider would move into it before I died. The kind of people nobody wanted as a neighbor. At least this girl wasn't the sort I feared, but I had a need to check her out more closely. No better way to find out about a person than to offer them free help.

She changed the way my days went, plus, she was right entertaining. She was also gritty and determined for a city girl who didn't know a thing about living on this mountain. She had an expectation of how life ought to be without the reality of how it was.

Judging from all the things she had bought when she went off the mountain into town, she must be one of those cradle rich who had inherited a lot of money. It was obvious she had money to throw away. She brought stuff the likes I'd never seen before. Wasteful, that's what she was. At the same time, I could sure use what she'd given me. Not that I was going to take it for free. I would help and guide her enough to pay her back in full plus some. I never did like to owe a body anything, and I wasn't going to start at my age. Not only that, but this girl was as dumb as a rock about how to survive on this mountain.

I decided the first payment I needed to make was to show her how to build a chicken coup. That hen and biddies couldn't live in a cardboard box forever. Not to mention the stink keeping them in a house brought on.

Once I got my own morning work done up, I headed up through the woods to her place. It was late, after six o'clock. She was outside barefoot making tracks in the early morning dew.

"You'll liable to get dew poison," I told her. "Hadn't ought to go barefoot."

She jumped about a foot and whirled around to look at me.

"Do you always move so quietly?" she accused as though it was a compliment.

"Quietly is good," I told her.

She rolled her eyes as though she questioned that. "What's dew poison?"

"Cracks on the feet by getting too wet. Could be hookworms too."

"Hookworms?" she said with a frown. "From dew and cracked feet?"

"Got to enter somewhere. Cracked feet is easy. Nasty things. Linger in the dirt and the body. Worst worms to get rid of."

"I'll buy dewormer medication the next time I go into town," she said as though going into town and buying stuff was the answer to everything.

"Wormwood, walnut hull, and tobacco takes care of it. Does best when mixed with corn liquor. I'll show you how to make elixirs and such when I get time. You need a chicken coup right now. Go get your shoes on so I don't worry about you."

"I was feeling the vibrations of Mother Earth," she said. "I read that going barefoot will help me to feel that I'm a part of nature."

It was my turn to roll my eyes. Hippies. Mother Earth types who didn't know much about nothing, I thought. My Meadow Lark talked about hippies when she was younger.

Envied them, I reckon. Never did get her to believe the real Mother Earth types had lived on this mountain all their lives until the old folks died out and the young folks moved off. She never did understand that being one with nature was knowing how to stay alive.

"You step on one of those rattlesnakes and you're liable to become a part of Mother Nature for certain," I told her.

"Point taken," she said.

Again, I reminded myself how Meadow Lark left this mountain to find herself, while this girl had come to the mountain to find herself. Seemed I was the only person left who was satisfied with who and where I was.

"Tell me more about the Slaughters," she said after she put her boots on and came back outside where I was gathering the supplies I would need.

"What do you want to know besides what I've already told you?"

"You said there were six boys and the father who were known as the seven devils. What did they do to deserve that name?"

"Just about anything they took a notion to do."

"Such as?" she prodded.

"One of the worst things that didn't get discovered for years was what the oldest boy did. He took a shine to a girl down in the valley. She was the uppity sort and let him know right away that he wasn't good enough for her. She called him hill trash to his face. Needless to say, that didn't go over good.

He kidnapped her on her way to school one spring morning and made her walk all the way to the top of this mountain where he bound her arms and legs so she couldn't get away. Kept her in a cave. Visited her every day or so and fed her enough food and water to keep her alive for a long while. Some hunters found her body many years later. She had died trying to give birth. The opening to the cave had been rocked up until nothing could enter."

"If it was rocked up, how did the hunters find her?"

One of the dogs got to sniffing around those rocks, and the hunters seen those rocks looked laid instead of natural, so they took them down and investigated. Found her bones along with the tiny bones of a baby that hadn't gotten all the way out of her. She still had her clothes on along with the rope that was still tied around her arms and leg bones."

"Did he pay for killing her?"

"Couldn't prove he was the one who done it, although everybody knew he was. Truth was nobody wanted to accuse him. Everybody was too afraid of them Slaughters."

"Were you afraid of them?"

"You better believe I was. None of 'em ever bothered me none. For some reason old man Slaughter took a shine to me when I was just a little thing. He told them boys they were to watch after me and not let any kind of harm come to me."

I never told anyone about the young man who did harm to me. I had no doubt old man Slaughter would have had one of the boys kill him if he knew who I suspected done it. It wasn't long after I married George that the remaining Slaughter left the mountain.

"Don't rightly know why old man Slaughter favored me. He once said I looked like a little angel right to my face. He said I looked like my pretty momma."

"Are any of the Slaughters boys still alive?"

"I should hope not. They were older than me. You ought to know more about that than I do. Who did you buy the place from?"

"A real estate broker handled the sale, but she said it was the grandchildren who were selling it. I think there were several of them, but I'm not sure how many."

"If somebody had to buy the place, I'm glad it was you. I was afeared a bunch of investors would buy that big track of land and put in some sort of development. My Meadow Lark was always telling me I should expect it. That it was bound to happen sooner or later. She claimed rich folks living way down in the hot flatlands were wanting mountain houses with a view. The higher up the better."

"She's right," I told her. "Several developers were interested, but they were trying to get the price down to just about nothing."

"You didn't?" I questioned to see if she was one of those cradle rich.

"I saved most all I made with the idea I could buy a place of my own someday. I was willing to pay more than the others."

"I used to dream about owning this entire mountain, but I never had hardly two coppers to rub together." That was one of many reasons my Meadow Lark married who she did. She didn't want to live in poverty all her life the way I had done. I warned her a woman who married for money earned every penny she got."

At the same time, I knew I had not married for money, but I had earned every breath of air I took. I worked like an Irish slave bought at auction. Many a time I tried to work and sleep at the same time. Being a woman wasn't easy. A woman was expected to do every single thing that needed doing and then some. The old saying that men worked for sun to sun, but a woman's work was never done held more truth than anything I'd ever heard said. It still held true for me, and I was all alone. I have to admit it was a pleasure doing things only for myself. The only belittling I had to endure came from myself, and I didn't do much of that anymore.

I couldn't judge my Meadow Lark harshly. There were times when I tried to figure out what it would have been like if I hadn't got attacked that night. I hadn't wanted to marry what fancy folks claimed to be mountain trash. I wanted to marry a smart young man who smelled of clean clothes and after shave instead of sweat and barn manure, but that was only what folks called an Indian pipedream. I knew it could never happen.

I chuckled to myself for wondering what it would have been like to be kissed by a slick shaven man instead of one with a mustache and long beard that smelled like whatever he'd last eaten. But such foolishness as that was years in the past. Old age left only memories of what had once been along with what might have been and never came to pass.

Chapter 19

~~Bennie Jack~~

I had an illusion of how I would be able to do everything for myself by going into hiding on this forgotten mountain. I had been so sure of my ability that I was actually looking forward to everything I would accomplish.

Reality was entirely different.

No matter how hard I worked, very little was accomplished. The worst part was not knowing the best way to do what I wanted done.

Aunt Polly was a God send to me, and yet I almost resented her in an odd sort of way. There were times when I wanted to scream *Momma, I want to do it by myself,* and yet I wasn't able to do it by myself. I had to swallow my pride and accept her help. I tried to convince myself she was what A.J. was to me – my trainer. After all, we were the only two people living on a deserted mountain. It was only right that we help each other.

At least I now had a safe place for the hen and chicks to stay.

"You need to fix a lot next to a barn stall if you're going to get a goat from me," she said as though she needed to tell me such as that.

"Okay," I said. "I'll have a few months to get that done."

"Better to started early than late."

"I will, but I need to work on the house roof first. Some of the tin is loose and it leaks." I thought of all the wet places on the floor from the flash flood my truck got stuck in.

"Can't help you none with that. My old body won't let me climb that high up."

"You're the youngest eighty-one-year-old I've ever come into contact with," I told her.

"No store-bought food," she said. "I believe that food you buy in stores has pizen sprayed on it. Food I always growed never had such as that. Still don't."

"That's why I want to grow my own," I told her. "I want to excel at self-sufficiency."

"Takes a long spell, but you're young enough to learn in time," she added the last two words as a sneaky grin squeezed the wrinkles on her face closer together. "Saw those sacks of fertilize you bought," she said.

"Anything wrong with that?" I asked, slightly insulted by her tone.

"Soon, you'll grow your own fertilize. Chicken and goat manure along with green rot. Ought to dig a hole in the ground and pitch all the weeds and grass you cut in it. Any food you throw out too. Come next year, after it winters over, you'll have good stuff to use. One thing's for certain, you need to remember to never use your own manure on anything. Even animals know not to eat where their own manure is at."

I wondered why she was telling me such things. There was a wooden toilet up next to the woods. It was rather dilapidated but usable.

"Back when I was married to George, there was this family that lived not far from us that used their own manure on their garden. The whole family were sickly with worms and other diseases. They were pale-skinned and right weakly. A lot of the babies didn't survive."

I had no doubt that was true. It wasn't like I hadn't learned about nutrition and diseases, but I allowed Aunt Polly to continue with her advice. She took great pleasure in it.

"I always keep a chamber pot under my bed. Never would let my Meadow Lark go outside when it was dark. You ought to stay inside after dark."

~~~~

It was several days later when I noticed the newspaper I had taken out of the box of chicks the man from the store had put in the bottom. I had read the other newspapers from cover to cover. It was run-of-mill reporting and prejudices to the point of being laughable. There were several instances of victims going to jail for defending themselves from criminals who attacked them. There was destruction of properties, fires, out of control rioting, and even murders going on with what appeared to be little to nothing done about it. I knew most of it had been organized by those who wanted to destroy our country. Many of the rioters were being brought in on busses and paid for doing their crimes. There was no question in my mind, and in others' minds as well, that the destruction of our great country had been planned for years and was now in full swing.

What in this world was going on with the leaders in our country who were letting such stupidity reign over common sense? Was money more important to them than freedom? I recalled what Sargent York once said about killing the enemy. It went something like how sometimes the killing of a few was justified if it could save the lives of many. The more I thought about that, the truer it became. I wondered what God thought of such as that. Was murder not murder regardless of the reason it happened? Was evil not still considered evil regardless of the reason behind it?

I wondered why those I had been working for did not assassinate officials who were committing treason. It might not solve the problem, but it sure would send a powerful message to those who replaced them. I recalled the book "Animal Farm." Those who took their place just might be worse than those who were now in power.

I put the papers down on the porch and walked through the yard. The sun was shining down gentle and warm on my body. Green grass was growing, and tiny bluet flowers were waving delicately where I had mown with that hateful scythe. Dogwood and Redbuds were in full bloom. Daffodils had gone wild and were glowing yellow all over the farm. Forsythia and Lilacs were still heavy with blossoms. Bees were busier than ever as they flew from flower to flower. Bird songs were filling the air. Hummingbirds were zipping about competing with the bees for nectar. This had to be the most beautiful place on earth. It was the life I'd always dreamed about having – except for the lack of a husband and children. Was I wrong for wanting this life and grabbing for it when the chance presented itself?

An unexpected wave of shame suddenly hit me. I had run away from my duty and gone into seclusion. Just because I was declared dead did not give me the right to start thinking of myself instead of the betterment of my country. I should be doing what I did best – ferreting out more incriminating evidence on more of the treasonous higher ups in the government as well as in the private sector. Should I not be willing to sacrifice myself for my country? After all JFK said ask not what your country can do for you, but what you can do for your country. One might conclude he did sacrifice himself for his country. Should I do less?

Chapter 20

One of our best agents, who was known as Badger, sent a message for me to meet with him to update me on what happened at Brigham's office. He was one of our group who had my unquestionable trust. I had been his trainer several years ago.

"First off," he told me. "Word is that all the cash payoff money Brigham had secreted in his office safe disappeared. He has been given a certain amount of time to replace it – or else."

I didn't need to ask what or else meant. "You have him under surveillance?"

"Of course."

"Can he replace the money?"

"He's working on it, but the donors are leery. They fear something is up?"

"Is it?"

"Something is always up," he answered,

I knew that to be true, but we had trouble documenting everything that was going on. "Know more about who took the money?"

"Their surveillance along with our surveillance cameras were taken out for three minutes. It took someone well informed with basically knowing everything that needing doing and what order to do it in to steal the money in that three-minute time period."

"Brigham?" I questioned.

"Perhaps he had something to do with it, but it was documented that he wasn't anywhere near the place at the time."

"Did he have a conspirator?"

"Not that we detected."

"Any speculations on who it was?"

"That's the jackpot question. No one seems to have an answer to that."

"Impossible," I said. "Someone has to know something."

"There's one thing that got some attention," he told me.

"What?" I asked when he hesitated.

"As you know, we have a lot of observation cameras scattered about. One of our cameras picked up something interesting. A few blocks away from Brigham's building it picked up movement of a garbage bag."

I frowned with interest, and he continued.

"It was only for an instant in a dark area filled with shadows, but it appeared that a large garbage bag moved on its own."

"Moved how?"

"As I said, it was only for a second, but the camera caught a glimpse of a full trash bag as it appeared to move from behind a building into a wooded area."

"Interesting," I said.

"We thought so."

"What have you concluded?" I questioned.

"That full garbage bags don't move on their own accord."

"And?"

"We investigated and found scuff marks in the edge of the woods."

"Footprints?"

"Scuffed up place, but no discernible footprints."

"Did you take pictures of the scuff up area?"

"Yes, and then took dirt samples. There was trace elements of actual garbage, but we came up with nothing useable."

"Did you find an empty garbage bag?"

"No empty or full one either. And no garbage pickup."

"And the conclusion?" I asked.

"Could there have been a person small enough to fit in a large trash bag who knew enough about Brigham's building to black everything out, crack his safe, steal the money and then disappear without a trace in three minutes time?"

"Impossible," I told him. "Could Brigham have done it himself to cover up stealing the money?" I asked again.

"Committing suicide would be less painful if he doesn't replace the money."

"If not him, then who was capable of pulling it off?"

"That's what we're trying to find out."

I started to ask him if what Fizz had discovered had anything to do with it, but then I doubted he and the others knew about the documents she had sent me. It was best to keep it that way. Most likely Brigham and I were the only two she sent the information to.

Thinking of Fizz brought her clearer to my mind. Could she have pulled off such as that? I doubted it, although she was ingenious in what she was capable of doing. The clencher to that question was that she was dead along with the two men who were in the helicopter with her. I racked my brain to figure out if she, or the two men, could possible still be alive?

I had personally checked out her apartment and her belongings. Things appeared just as she had left them. Even her bank account and debit cards had not been used. If she were alive, she would need money along with some of her private belongings. We had cameras and listening devices in and around her apartment, but nothing. I was almost positive no one knew about her working for us. She would surely have let Brigham think she discovered the documents of her own accord. But Brigham was smarter than that. A young woman didn't accidently snap pictures of secret documents.

Who Brigham informed about what she had given him, I didn't know, but we were working on finding out.

Because of the tracers I had placed in her shoes, I knew of the missing helicopter along with the occupants before it was reported to the news. My mistake was not taking into account what exposure to salt water would do to the devices. Never once had I taken into consideration she would be dumped into the ocean.

The newspaper spill was that Fizz was taking her annual vacation and hired the private helicopter to take her to Jamaica where she had prepaid for a room in a popular resort. I knew it to be a well-planned set up to explain her disappearance. After all, she was still working as a staffer and would be missed when she didn't show up. There was also the possibility her landlord would report her missing and an investigation would take place.

Evidently, as far as we could tell, she had not given away our mission or information about the Freedom Group. I had no doubt Brigham's hired thugs had planned on interrogating her at some point, but the helicopter had gone down relatively fast over the ocean. Could the accident also have been a setup? My group could not find evidence that the helicopter had not gone down. The coast guard had detected evidence of fuel and chemicals spill in the water, but it was spread over miles of water. The tracers I had in her shoes had stopped working at the approximate location, enabling me to believe the wreckage happened. What I didn't know was why it happened. The news media reported that the search was ongoing, but the small, private helicopter would be more difficult to locate than a larger aircraft.

I feared her death actually happened when she hadn't made any attempt to contact me. She had requested a meeting with me right after she met with Brigham. If she had survived, she would need my assistance and protection, although she had been told if she was caught, she was on her own.

I had put two of the men I had trained on investigating her disappearance. They found nothing. No sign at all of a washed-up body. Neither the pilot nor the other man had been washed up either. It appeared that no agency was searching for the missing wreckage as it was reported to be a private helicopter that had gone down in deep water. There was no indication of where it had gone down other than the miles of chemical slick.

Our group had lost men and a woman in the past. Their deaths had hit me hard. One man's death had been reported as a suicide, although he had been shot in the back of the head instead of in the forehead as reported. Another informant of ours had been shot while walking in a public park. It was determined that a stray bullet had accidently killed him. The shooter was never found. The death of a woman had been reported as an overdose. I knew for a fact she had never used any type of illegal drugs. We had our suspicions of those who were involved, but only Fizz had managed to come up with actual proof.

~~~~

It was two months after Fizz's disappearance when I got the message, or more correctly the warning. DISAPPEAR was the message I received along with the word NOW.

Chapter 21

I was proud of the repairs I did on the roof, although Aunt Polly was involved in that too. She insisted on being right there watching me in case I fell off the roof. She insisted on taking me into the woods to collect pine-rosin to melt on the stove and pour on the nail holes I made in the tin. "Rainwater can seep down the nail holes if you don't seal 'em," she said, which made sense.

I said a prayer of thanks that the rusty tin had only blown loose instead of off the roof. I also had to nail down some of the tin on the barn.

"Did I tell you the barn and outbuildings were just as important as the house to folks who lived on this here mountain," she told me so many times I lost count.

"I can believe it," I answered her.

"Animals were part of survival. Most city folks don't know a thing about such as that. I see that you're keeping that barn door closed in the loft. I reckon that mountain lion has moved on, but I'll make sure I keep my goats and chickens up at night. If I had as much money as you have, I'd get me a dog to watch after things. As for me, I can barely afford to feed myself much less a dog. Did you know poor folks used to always keep a dog? Do you know why?"

"No, why?" I asked as we took a break from working on the roof. It was eleven o'clock and I had warmed up an early lunch since I had built a fire in the kitchen stove to heat up the rosin. I was beginning to think Aunt Polly showed up in the guise of helping me in order for me to feed her. I had no objections. Not only did it save the food she'd canned, but it also provided her with company she hadn't received in years. I could only imagine how lonely she got living on this mountain all by herself. I wondered if I would get lonely when I no longer had Aunt Polly.

"A lot of poor folks didn't have toilets," she said, bringing my mind back to dogs and why poor folks kept them.

"Why not?" I asked.

"Too lazy to dig 'em, or too poor to build 'em. You ever heard of shit-eating dogs?"

I gave her a questioning look.

"Poor folks hardly had enough to feed their kids and themselves, much less dogs. Those dogs were so hungry they ate the human shit. Used them to keep the ground cleaner."

"You're joking," I said with repulsion. I was thankful the Slaughters had a toilet.

"Nope, I hain't. There were also other things they kept a dog for. Those dogs were devil mean. They'd sic 'em on the law and strangers. Law never climbed up this mountain after two of 'em never came back down."

"They were killed?" I questioned.

"I wouldn't call it that. Way back then folks let their hogs run loose on the mountain to have plenty of mass to fatten 'em up. The law was always having accidents on ground they weren't familiar with. Easy to break a leg or fall off a cliff. Wild animals were also plentiful back then. Hogs were known to eat those who were injured. Hogs can digest everything but belt buckles, teeth, and badges."

I cringed at the image she was giving me. I knew about prohibition. Aunt Poly had told me about the Slaughters making moonshine. I also knew how those in power could make victims out of the poor. I commended them for fighting back in the only way available to them – just as I had.

"Does the law ever come on the mountain?"

"No need to. They know I'm the only one living here now, and I'm law abiding. Guess they'll know you live here too when you pay your taxes."

I cringed at that thought. "Did the Slaughter relative show up to pay taxes, or do you know?"

"Don't know, but my guess is that he paid them by mail."

Then that was the way I would continue paying the taxes. No one needed to know I was living on the mountain – or so I hoped.

"Why don't you pay your taxes by mail?" I asked her.

"In case you hain't noticed yet, there hain't no mail service on this mountain. Even if they was, I don't have no checking account. Too risky to mail cash money."

And neither did I have a checking account, nor did I plan to get one.

"It's plain stupid to mail cash. I'm hain't stupid," she said.

Aunt Polly was right about that. "I'd have to get a cashier's check if I paid taxes by mail. At least I had time to think about it."

"Death and taxes. The only two things you'll never get out of. Lawsy, my belly is full. I could take a nap in this warm sunshine, but we had best get back to the roof. Time waits on nobody."

"You're welcome to take a little nap while I'm on the roof," I told her.

"Like I'd do a thing like that," she said with indignation. "The good Lord knows I'll have plenty of time for sleeping once I'm no longer on top of the ground. Want to enjoy the time I got left."

Her words made me think about her daughter and the fact that she hadn't shown up to check on her mother for years. I chose not to point it out as I climbed back on the roof with a fresh tin can of hot pine rosin.

"You be mighty careful up there," Aunt Polly held the ladder and gave me the same warning she had given me a few dozen times.

"I'm always careful," I told her.

"Good. Don't want the sin eater to have to make a needless trip. Hain't seen hide nor hair of him in a coon's age. Wonder where he's at and what he's been doing. Probably been kept busy by all them folks that keep sinning now a days. Ask me, the good Lord's got to blow his trumpet to call all his children home afore long. You do know God promised he'd never destroy people by drowning 'em in a food again. He said the next time he'd destroy them by a fire. Ask me, I'd take drowning over burning. Got an idea it would hurt less."

She went on with her dire predictions as I poured the rosin on the nails. I wished she would talk about something else. I wanted my time on this mountain to be filled with beauty and joy. I wanted to bask in God's love instead of his warnings of hell fire and punishment. I thought God to be a deliverer of love instead of anger and punishment. Was he not a God of forgiveness? I needed to think so.

I was almost finished with the tin of rosin when I heard it. I drew in a breath and climbed down the ladder. "Can you hear it?" I asked Aunt Polly."

"Hear what?" she questioned.

"I heard the sound of a vehicle climbing the mountain."

"You certain it wasn't one of them air-o-planes you heard?"

"I'm certain. It had to gear down and then press on the gas on the steep parts of the road."

"I do declare," she said puzzled before her face brightened. "Do you reckon it could be my Meadow Lark? I hain't heard from her in a long spell. She might show up to see if I'm dead. I'm going to rush back to the house in case it's her. You want to come with me?"

"No," I was quick to tell her. "I need to collect more pine rosin," I told her as an excuse for whoever it was not to see me."

"Might be somebody come to see you?" she said with suspicion.

"No one knows I'm here, and I want to keep it that way."

"Can't say as I blame you. Don't climb back on the roof unless I'm here," she warned and took off through the woods.

I gave her a few minutes head start as I strapped on my Glock. I already had my knife concealed against my leg. I went against my caution about carrying my pistol when I was on the roof. Especially while Aunt Polly was there watching me, but I always took it when we went into the woods. I claimed it was in case we came upon snakes. I wasn't sure she was convinced, but she said, "I started carrying George's little pistol since you shot that rattler. Don't know why since I never did afore, but it seemed like I ought to."

I kept hearing the sound of the vehicle grinding its way up the rough road. I was greatly relieved when I heard what sounded like it was cutting through the woods toward Aunt Polly's place instead of continuing the rough incline to my place. I picked up my pace so I would arrive at the same time as the vehicle.

I hid behind the trunk of a large poplar tree to see Aunt Polly standing in the yard. Her bony hands were adjusting her near ragged clothes and then raking her hair out with her fingers and retwisting it into a neater bun at the nap of her neck. I had to give her credit for a woman her age not breathing much harder than I was after the run through the woods. Oddly enough, I took pride in her physical ability. I hoped living on this mountain would guarantee me the same health and ability when I was her age.

A few minutes later a shiny dark blue range rover pulled into the swept yard and stopped a few feet from Aunt Polly. I could see the big smile on her face when she realized who the driver was. She was at the driver's side door as it opened.

A tall dark-haired woman got out. Aunt Polly grabbed her in her arms laughing and crying at the same time.

"Oh, my Meadow Lark, you've come. You've finally come home," Aunt Polly was saying. "Lawsy me, I feared I'd never see you again. What took you so long?"

"Momma," she said. "I'm glad you're alright. I can't tell you how worried I've been about you."

A daughter who hadn't shown up to see her mother in years couldn't convince me she had been worried about her mother.

"No need to worry about me. I've been healthy and happy just like always. How have you been?"

"Wonderful," she said. "I've been just wonderful. I would have come sooner, but I gave birth to twin boys last summer, and a little girl before that."

"Well praise be," I said, thinking they had to be her change of life babies. "I'd love to see all my grandchildren."

"They're with their nanny. I don't dare bring them to a place such as this."

I could almost see Aunt Polly stiffen her backbone at her daughter's words.

"You'll be able to see your grandchildren once I get you home."

"I am home," Aunt Polly told her firmly. "I'm tickled beyond words at seeing my only child, but don't you dare start in on me about leaving here. I've told you before that I was born in this cabin, and I'll die in it."

"Now, Momma, don't you be like that. I can't live with the thought that you'll die in that falling down shack all alone."

She must not have been too concerned about her mother dying if she hadn't shown up in years. Did she expect to find her mother alive or a pile of bones where she had died in her bed?

"Now listen here, Meadow Lark. You get it out of your head right now about me leaving here."

"How can I do that when you're all alone without one person to look after you?"

"I'm not all alone. I've got a new neighbor. We've been helping each other out for a while now."

"What new neighbor?"

"A young woman who bought the old Slaughter place. She's been fixing it up."

"Are you serious?" her daughter asked. She sounded both surprised and a bit angry.

"I am. She moved in a few months ago."

"Who is this woman?"

"Her name is Bennie Jack. She's from North Dakota. Why do you sound unhappy about that?"

"I got my license as a real estate broker. I had a buyer interested in the old Slaughter place, and now you're telling me someone bought it. Oh well, she won't be here long. I'm sure she bought it to resale. I can guarantee she won't last the winter."

"You could be right," Aunt Polly said as though she was in deep thought. "Let's set down on the porch in the shade. No need standing in the hot sun. I reckon you'll be staying a few days with me."

"No," she said with emphasis. "You and I both will leave here as soon as you gather what you want to take with you."

Aunt Polly steps were spritely as she made her way to the porch and sat down in a ladderback chair. Meadow Lark looked at the other chair as though checking it for cleanliness before she sat in it.

"Let's see now. I have at least a dozen chickens and a couple of roosters. Two nanny goats with babies, and a billy goat who is in stinking rut. Step over to that far field and you can get a whiff of him. I've got my mommie's bed that my daddy made for her along with a dresser and kitchen cabinet. There's the cook stove and the old heating stove and a big pile of firewood. Then there's this cabin and my garden and a good size field of corn and a good size patch of taters. Then there's this mountain with its rocks and trees and clean water and fresh air. If you expect me to leave this place, you'll have to figure out how to take all this along with me."

"Momma, you're talking silly, and you know it. I don't mean to be insensitive, but if you don't come with me of your own free will, I'll be forced to file for guardianship over you. I'll become the executor of your estate and I'll sell this place, so you'll have to leave here and never try to come back."

Aunt Polly laughed, but there was no humor in the sound. "I don't believe my own daughter is threatening to take the only home I've ever known away from me when you know how much I love this place. Besides that, you are willing to claim I am not in my right mind and unable to take care of myself."

"You know I don't want to do that, Momma, but you're too old to stay here by yourself. You're my mother and I've got the responsibility of doing what's best for you."

Aunt Polly shook her head for a full minute. I knew she was in deep thought. "I've told you many a time that I'd rather die than leave this place, and yet you want to take me away from all that I hold dear in my old heart."

"Don't you hold me dear, Momma? Don't you care that I want what's best for you?"

"I've always cared what's best for you, but it don't seem like you care what's best for me."

"I'm not arguing with you on this any longer. I intend to do what's best with or without your permission."

Aunt Polly nodded in what appeared to be defeat. "I understand," she finally said. "Could you see your way to give me a couple of weeks to think on it? It will take me some time to get leaving this place set in my mind."

Meadow Lark looked pleased.

"Finally, after all these years, you're starting to see reason."

"Don't look to me like I have much of a choice, do I?"

"No, you don't."

"Well then, let's have us a nice visit with no more talk of having me declared crazy."

"Okay," Meadow Lark agreed. "So long as you know I'll give you two weeks and no more."

"I know it," Aunt Polly sounded defeated.

"I don't have long to stay," her daughter said. "I'm a busy woman, but it's my duty to take care of my old mother."

I stayed right where I was listening to Meadow Lark brag to her mother about what she was doing and all the good things she had. By the time she was finally ready to leave, I was sure Aunt Polly was as relieved as I was. She walked her daughter to the fancy range rover and gave her a goodbye hug with real tears running down her face.

"I'll be back in two weeks," Meadow Lark told her. "I expect you to be ready to leave with me."

"I'll have everything ready by then," Aunt Polly said in defeat.

"See that you do, or I'll do it for you," were her daughter's last words as she got in the vehicle and left.

Aunt Polly stood in the same spot as she listened to the sound of the engine going through the woods and headed down the rough road.

"You can come out now," she said in my direction. "I know you're there."

I came out from where I was hiding and walked with her to the porch where we sat down in the chairs.

"You heard it all," she said.

"I did."

"What do you think?"

I hesitated to tell her.

"I want the truth," she insisted.

"I think she is selfish. If she was really concerned about you, she wouldn't have stayed away for years."

"I've never seen my grandchildren. Didn't know she was expecting much less has given birth to twin boys."

I didn't know what to say to that. What I thought wasn't fit to say to a mother.

"Suppose you could take off for the rest of the day?" she asked me.

"I can take off for as long as you like."

"How long does it take you to drive off this mountain in your truck?"

"About an hour or less. Why?"

"Then let's get going. I want to get to one of them lawyer's office afore they close."

"Why?" I asked again.

"Don't ask me no questions. I have to think on things while we travel."

With those words she got up and rushed into the cabin. In less than five minutes she came back out wearing what I took to be her best clothes.

Chapter 22

~~Aunt Polly~~

Talk about breaking a mother's heart, Meadow Lark just shattered mine into dust. I loved my daughter more than anybody in the world, but I couldn't allow her to do what she had in mind. What did it for me was seeing her face when I told her the Slaughter place had been bought. As a real estate broker, she was putting into action what she always told me would happen. She was putting together a deal that would be to her benefit. She planned on buying and then selling the Slaughter place along with my place to one of them lowdown developers.

The idea of what my Meadow Lark had in mind had troubled my brain for the last few years. Finally, she had managed to put her plan into action. Before now, she feared I wasn't old enough to be declared incompetent. I had news for my beloved daughter. I wasn't incompetent. My mind and body worked just fine.

Putting the two tracks of land together would double the value of both places. I had an idea my Meadow Lark already had a developer line up. Just as I had feared all these years, she was turning out to be more like the man I suspected to be her daddy than she was me. I'd done my best to turn a blind eye to her conniving ways all these years, but I could no longer do that. My home, the rest of my life, depended on it.

"What are you planning to do?" Bennie Jack finally asked as we bounced down the old logging road.

"Depends," I said.

"On what?"

"On how greedy you are."

"What are getting at?"

"Would you sell the Slaughter place to me for cash money?"

"No," she told me firmly.

"Not if I doubled what you paid for it?"

Her chin lifted a bit in what I took to be defiance.

"I bought my land with the intent of spending the rest of my life on it. There is no way I'll sell it regardless of how much I'm offered."

"Not for triple the amount you paid for it?"

"No!"

She told me with a firmness that I believed.

"You might get married and have children. You'll not want them to be raised on this mountain."

"I'll never get married, and I'll never have children."

"Why do you say a thing like that?"

"I have my own reasons. Private reasons. Now, stop asking about my home. I'll never sell it."

I nodded. Satisfied with her answer.

"Suppose you tell me why you're rushing off this mountain."

"I have my own private reasons," I made a point of repeating what she had told me.

"Okay," she said. "I admit I don't want your daughter to get your land. I bought this place so I can live in seclusion. I don't want neighbors of any kind. Would you be willing to sell your land to me? I'll pay you anything you want and allow you to live in your cabin for the rest of your life."

"I'm like you. I hain't about to sell a single inch of my land. I'm going into town to see one of them crooked lawyers who I've known for some time. I'm going to make sure my Meadow Lark doesn't claim that I'm so crazy she needs to take control over me."

"Good," she told me. "I'll tell him you're more competent than anyone I've ever met if that will help."

"We'll see. Say you'll agree to help me out if need be?"

"Of course, I will."

"Then we'll see what can be done to protect both of us."

I didn't know a thing about lawyering, but I didn't have a choice. There was only one lawyer within a hundred or more miles that I somewhat trusted. He was almost as old as I was, and I'd known him for years. He'd even got one of George's boys out of trouble for beating up a store owner who cheated him. Word was this lawyer was a tough old fellow who stood up for the poor people.

I had Bennie Jack drive through town until she came to a building with the name Kalvin Warsaw, attorney at law on it.

"Stop there," I told her, and she did. "Wait here on me. Don't know how long I'll be."

I got out of the truck and walked right in with determination. A woman around my age was sitting behind a desk. She looked a lot like she could be a Sunday school teacher by the way she dressed and fixed her hair. She looked me over from my shoes to my clothes. I was right glad I'd worn what Bennie Jack had given me.

"May I help you?" she questioned.

"I come to see Kalvin Warsaw."

"Do you have an appointment?"

"No. Didn't know I had need of him until two hours ago."

She frowned and hesitated.

"I wouldn't be here unless it was important," I added. "If he can't see me for a while, I set down in one of these here chairs and wait until he can," I told her respectfully.

"Just a moment," she stood up. "Who shall I tell him wants to see him?"

"Polly MacCallum," I told her.

She went down a short hall, opened a door and walked inside, closing the door behind her. A minute later she came back out leaving the door open.

"Mr. Warsaw will see you now," she said with slight disapproval.

I got up, gathered my resolve, and went in the door she was holding open. A broad-shouldered man with snowy hair and a white beard and mustache was sitting at a desk. He had gotten a lot older since I had last seen him.

"Have a seat, Mrs. MacCallum," he said.

I sat down in the chair on the other side of his desk. "Folks call me Aunt Polly," I told him.

"Aunt Polly," he said. "It's been a while since I've seen you. As you know, your husband and my father were well acquainted."

"You represented my stepson once."

"Yes, so I recall. What can I do for you?"

I came straight to the point. "My daughter recently became a real estate broker. She wants to sell my land to a developer."

"Do you also want that?"

"No, I don't."

"And?' he encouraged.

"She plans on having me declared crazy so she can take over me and what I own."

"Are you crazy?" he asked.

"I reckon that's a matter of opinion, but my mind works mighty fine the same as it always did."

I saw a slight grin come to his lips. "Care if I ask you a few more questions?"

"Go right ahead."

"First of all, tell me about your situation along with your daughter's situation."

I told him exactly what was going on with me and also what was going on with my Meadow Lark.

"Humm," he grunted. "You are still living alone on a mountain with nobody to look after you?"

"I'm mighty capable of taking care of myself just as I've been doing for years, but I'm not alone. I have someone looking after me. I'm looking after her too. It's a mighty fine arrangement for both of us."

"Does she live with you?"

"No. Don't want nobody living with me. I'm finally getting a little peace after taking care of my girl, George, his boys, and my parents. Feels good to be alone, I tell you."

"Who is she?"

"Her name is Bennie Jack. She bought the old Slaughter place and is fixin' the place up right nice like. She plans on living there permanently."

"Does she have a family?"

"She's still young, not married or anything, but she and I have become family. We've been helping each other out."

"What does your daughter think about her?"

"Didn't tell my Meadow Lark much about her, but she'll find out soon enough. She wanted to buy the Slaughter place for little to nothing. She's into buying and selling land."

"Why didn't you tell her about Ms. Jack?"

"To be honest, it's none of her business."

He grinned. "Are you sure about that since she is your closest relative."

"I'm sure about that. I'm here to tell you what I want, so you can tell me how I can do it according to the law." I went ahead and told him what I had in mind.

"Does this Bennie Jack know what you want to do?"

"No, she don't. All she knows is that I ask her to drive me here and wait in her truck for me."

"She didn't put you up to what you've got in mind?"

"Definitely not. If it was her idea, I'd kick her hind end until her nose bled."

He grinned fully this time. "I don't doubt that," he said. "Then why are you willing to do what you've got in mind?"

"Because I like and trust her. I have faith she'll never sell her land or want me to sell mine."

"And your daughter?"

"Don't get me wrong. I love my girl more than anybody in this world, but she only shows up when she wants to take something from me. She hasn't shown up in several years

until today. I hate to admit it, but I have four grandchildren I
hain't never seen. My Meadow Lark hates my mountain so
much she refuses to bring my grandchildren to see me. I
know if I ever leave my mountain to see them, she'll see that
I'll never get to return."

"Don't you want your grandchildren to inherited you
land?"

"No. I don't believe they will care a thing about my land.
Besides, my Meadow Lark will sell it as fast as she can and
put me in an old folks' home."

"How do you know she plans on doing such as that?"

I gave him the name of the old folks' home near where
my Meadow Lark lived and told him to give the place a call.
He typed the name into his fancy machine, picked up the
phone and called.

"This is Kalvin Warsaw, attorney at law. I represent Polly
MacCallum. Do you have an opening waiting for her?"

He nodded as he listened. "Thank you for the
information," he said and hung up.

"You're right," he said. "Your daughter has arranged for
you to take up occupancy there. Did she tell you about it?"

"No. I know my girl good enough to figure out what she
has in mind."

"Did she tell you about the old folks' home, as you call
it?"

"Some years ago, when she was at my place, she told me
about the old folk's home. She claimed it was the best place
next to Heaven. I figured back then what she had in mind for
me. She took time to get her real estate brokers license, got
with child again and had a daughter and twin boys before she
put her plan into action."

"I see," he said. "So, you want to give Bennie Jack, a
woman you've only known for a short time, your land on the
condition she takes care of you until your death?"

"I want to keep a life estate. She won't get a thing until
I'm dead."

"You daughter can contest your competence in doing such as that."

"I know. It's what she already plans on doing to me if I don't agree to her plans. That's why I come to you. I want you to make sure I'm not crazy and am still of sound mind and right sound body."

"How do I accomplish that?" he questioned.

"You ought to know how being you're a lawyer and all."

"Okay. Are you willing to see a doctor and take a competency test along with a physical?"

"I am. Let's do it right now. I don't want to make another long trip down the mountain. I've got too much work to get done to galivant about like a woman of leisure."

His eyebrows lifted and he grinned again. He picked up the phone and dialed. "Say Doc, are you busy right now?"

I didn't hear Doc's answer.

"Then take a break and do me a favor. I want you to do a competency test and a physical right now for an acquaintance of mine. That's right, now, this minute so I can do a little legal work for her. Thanks."

He hung up the phone and looked at me. "So?" I questioned.

"He has an office in this building. He agreed to examine you and do the test. Come on," he said as he stood up. "I'll take you to his office."

"Oh, shit," I said. "I ought to have taken time to wash off in the creek if I'm going to get naked in front of a man."

He didn't comment, but he grinned.

An hour and a half later I signed legal papers after the doctor had declared me sane, competent, and unusually physically fit for a woman my age. He actually said I was in better mental and physical condition than a woman half my age. He didn't mention anything about me not taking a dip in the creek since I didn't have to strip completely naked. I couldn't help noticing he was a clean-shaven man forty years my junior. The thought of what he must think of me entertained my mind.

"How much do I owe you and the doctor?" I asked the lawyer.

He told me the price. "Wait just a minute," I told him, got up and went to the truck.

"Got any money on you?" I asked Bennie Jack.

"How much do you need?" she asked without me saying another word.

I told her.

She reached into her britches pocket and pulled out a small roll of cash. She counted out the correct amount and handed it to me.

"He didn't charge as much as I expected," she said.

"Make sure he gives you a receipt since it is cash," she advised me without asking me questions.

"Promise me something," I said to Bennie Jack. "When my Meadow Larks shows up again, tell her you bought my land and you've giving me monthly payments."

"Okay," she said.

And that was it.

It was done just the way I wanted. In two weeks' time, my Meadow Lark was going to be as mad as a wet setting hen. Can't say I was looking forward to it.

Chapter 23

~~A.J~~

Disappear? Now? I questioned the message I had received. I wasn't about to disappear without finding out what was going on along with why I was supposed to disappear. I hadn't been actively involved in the decisions made by our group. I was a low guy on the totem pole. One of three men who trained recruits how to become a spy along with how to become a spy along with how avoid detection, plus how to survive a multitude of situation. If I had to make a guess, I would say my need to disappear had something to do with Fizz. I feared she had sent the documents to more people than Brigham and me, but I had no way of knowing for sure. I was not subjected to inside information.

One thing I knew for sure, if I was told to disappear, now, I knew it was for the benefit of our group as well as for myself. I had always known there would come a time when members of our group would have to disappear unless we wanted to be added to the list of people who unwillingly committed suicide.

The documents Fizz presented to Brigham could be a setback in exposing traitors. Everyone she had come into contact with would be under scrutiny. What I still didn't know was if she had divulged information to Brigham about our group. Thank goodness she hadn't been informed of the members in our group and their names. However, there were many ways to find out. All she knew was that I was the one telling her who to collect information on. I had drilled into her head that every member of our group was to remain unknown to each other except for assigned contact people. I was her contact person. I never informed her that Brigham was working both ends and the middle. Evidently, she had come to believe he, as a head man at the FBI, would be the one to take appropriate action on the documentation she had discovered. Did that mean she didn't trust me to do my job, or was she the hardheaded *I know better than you type*? The documents she sent me showed she had done searches on her own without my consent.

What was the best course of action I was to take now? I wasn't even sure who I could trust with the information Fizz had sent me. I did know a coverup would be in the works to counter what she had informed Brigham. The information she had discovered would immediately be mitigated. If any of it came to light, it would be considered false information a young, attention-seeking staffer had come up with. The traitors would invent answers for everything. They would also be doing a search on Fizz from childhood to the moment the helicopter went down. Everyone she ever came into contact with would also be investigated – which might also include me.

Was she dead, or was it a planned setup to make those in contact with her accept her death? Was Fizz successful in keeping our group and me as her trainer a secret? If so, why was I ordered to disappear?

I contacted Badger, although I knew I wasn't supposed to unless ordered to do so. I wasn't sure if he would meet me, but he did.

"We're taking one hell of a chance," he told me with irritation.

"Why am I to disappear?" I asked.

"You're going to be found dead tonight?"

"What?" I asked in surprise.

"One of their spies had an unfortunate accident. He'll be found in your car at the bottom of a rock cliff tonight. The car and its contents will burn to ashes. He will be identified as you."

"Why?"

"There is chatter that Fizz and you were in contact with each other on things you shouldn't have been."

"What chatter?"

"Don't know yet. Can't take a chance though. Need anything?" he asked.

"I'm good," I told him.

"Then disappear right now," he said.

We parted as though we were strangers with nothing more than a handshake. He closed his hand over a copy of the flash drive Fizz had given me without any indication he had received it.

He had told me what I needed to know and no more. I had always known to be prepared to disappear if the need ever arose and now it had. A trainer couldn't stay undercover forever.

Chapter 24

~~Aunt Polly~~

Just as I figured it would happen, two weeks to the day my Meadow Lark showed up. I'd heard her vehicle climbing up the mountain. It was eleven o'clock on a warm, sunny day. I had dinner on the stove. I took up a plate of food for myself, and one for Bennie Jack.

"Set yourself down and let's eat a bite." I told her.

"Someone is coming," she said.

"I heard. I figure it's my Meadow Lark. She's right on time." I sat down at the table, but Bennie Jack took off like a shot. I knew she would be in the woods looking and listening. For some reason, she didn't like being seen. I figured she had her reasons. I respected whatever they were and kept my curiosity to myself.

I was watching out my cabin window as my Meadow Lark got out of her vehicle and walked into my cabin like she already owned the place. I could tell she was impatient and maybe troubled by something. Her face showed surprise and then anger when she saw that there were two plates on the table.

"Who were you with?" my Meadow Lark demanded as she glared at the extra plate.

My neighbor. She's the one who bought the Slaughter place."

"Where is this person?" my Meadow Lark demanded as her frown deepened.

"She ought to show up any time now," I told her.

Me and Bennie Jack had been working outside and both of us were still dressed in clothes that were dabbed in good, rich dirt. My Meadow Lark was dressed right fancy with jewelry around her neck, on her wrists and fingers. Appeared she was living the life she'd always wanted. I was mighty happy for her and proud that she went after what she wanted and got it. But I wasn't going to give up my home or the rest of my life's happiness for her ambitions.

"Have you got your things packed?" my Meadow Lark said. "I need to get back home before dark."

"No, I don't cause I'm not going anywhere," I told her. "Have you eat yet? I've fixed enough soup beans and cornbread to share. So, you might as well set yourself down in Bennie Jack's place and eat a bite."

"No thanks," she was quick to turn up her nose. "You promised you would be ready to leave when I was here two weeks ago. Why aren't you?"

"Changed my mind. Decided I'm not going anywhere," I told her.

"I'm your only child. It's my responsibility to take care of you. You're coming home with me just as you said you would."

She acted like I didn't have any say-so in how I spent the rest of my life. "You're right in that you're my onliest beloved daughter, and I'm your onliest mother that still has her own home and land, at least for the time being," I added. "I hain't ever going to leave it neither."

"Don't start talking nonsense, Momma. "And stop being difficult. Like I've already told you, I need to get back home before dark. The nanny needs to leave early."

"Why didn't you bring my grandbabies with you. I'd like to see them."

"Driving on this mountain road is too risky for them. I'm taking a chance on something happening every time I come here. You'll get to see them when we get home."

"No, I won't. Like I done told you, I'm not going anywhere."

My Meadow Lark rolled her eyes in disgust. "Don't start that. I don't want to argue with you. We've been through this before, and I'm not going to put up with your stubbornness."

"Then don't. You can turn yourself around and leave me be. I've done told you over and over that I hain't going nowhere with you."

"Momma . . ." she began, but I cut her off.

"I have no intention of more arguing with you. I have you know I've done sold my land to Bennie Jack. As part of the payment, she's aims to look after me and see to my needs."

"I don't believe a word of it," my Meadow Lark said impatiently.

I picked up my momma's old, worn Bible and placed my right hand on it. "I place my hand on this Bible and tell you I done sold my land to that woman who bought the Slaughter place." Seeing me place my hand on Momma's Bible made her realize I was telling the truth.

"No way," My Meadow Lark almost screeched. "That's not going to happen."

I saw no need to prolong my girl's hissy fit. I'd witnessed too many of her fits when she was growing up to think she would be reasonable.

"I had Bennie Jack take me to the lawyer's office as soon as you left here two weeks ago, and all was done nice and legal."

I took out the lawyer's payment receipt from where I had put it in my Bible and showed my Meadow Lark. She clenched her teeth for a moment before a kind of thoughtful look came to her face.

"How much did she pay you?" she demanded.

"She paid the same amount per acre as she paid for the Slaughter place."

"How much is that?"

I told her the amount. "It's above the appraised price," I made a point of adding.

"Show me the money?" my Meadow Lark demanded of me. "I'll have to put it in the bank for you. It's too risky for you to keep cash in this old cabin," she added as though she didn't trust me with cash money.

"She's agreed to pay me monthly," I told her. "I done used the first month's payment to buy the things I needed." I indicated the few things sitting out that Bennie Jack had given me. "Now, set yourself down and act like a loving daughter who's come to visit her old mother."

"I am a loving daughter, but I can't allow you to pilfer away what belongs to you to . . . to a total stranger."

"What's done is done," I told her. "Now settle yourself down and stop belly aching because you didn't get your way for once."

"For once," she yelled at me. "Momma, I've tried repeatedly to get you to leave this horrible mountain and move in with me. Surely you realize this . . . this woman, or whoever she is, has cheated you. Your land is valuable."

"Really? You never seemed to think so until lately. So might as well accept that I've done exactly what I wanted to do with what was mine to do with."

My Meadow Lark's eyes flashed, her jaws clenched and unclenched. "I'll contest what you've done," she said. "I'll take it to court. You don't have competent mental faculties to sell anything, let alone to the likes of whoever that woman is."

"It's all done nice and legal," I told her. "Not only did I have a lawyer handle the transaction, but I also had a mental competency test at the same time as proof that I still had my mental faculties and knew what I was doing."

"That ridiculous," she shouted. "You've been in dementia for years. It's my responsibility to take care of you. I'm legally executor of your estate."

"My dearest daughter, just because I'm old and I've lived my life on this mountain doesn't mean I'm stupid." I figured now was a good time to tell her what I had my lawyer check out. "I know good and well what you had in mind for me. My lawyer found out you had reserved a room for me in an old folks' home. I wouldn't be living in your house with you and my grandbabies like you claim. You were planning on dumping me off to rot in that place so you could get what little I've acquired through the years. It's best that I went and done what I wanted to do with what was mine."

"I'm only trying to do what's best for you," she said as though she really meant what she was claiming.

I shook my head to let her know she was wrong. I let a little guilt about my daughter slip in. I couldn't help feeling I had failed as her mother by not raising her the way I should have. I had done her wrong by letting her have her way too many times, and not making her realize how blessed we had been to live in a place like this regardless of being dirt poor. Yet, I wasn't ready to give up my beloved life to benefit her finances, which I was beginning to realize was her main concern.

"Are you and your man in some kind of financial squeeze? Is that why you want to get your hands on my land and now my money?"

"Of course not. I'm only trying to make sure you're not being taken advantage of."

"And I keep telling you until I'm blue in the face that living out the rest of my life in my own home is what's best for me. Selling to Bennie Jack has made me able to do that. I've now got enough money coming in monthly to buy what I need in order to live here."

"Momma . . ."

"Don't Momma me, my dear girl. What's done is done and there's nothing you can do about it."

She sure enough didn't like those words.

"We'll see about that," she told me. "I'll sue that woman's pants off for taking advantage of my mother."

I looked her in the eyes. "I suggest you have your lawyer check with my lawyer to make sure all is legal and no cheating anyone has occurred."

"Think you're smart, don't you? Well let me tell you something. No dirty piece of trash such as that stranger is going to take away what should belong to me. I'm your only child. I've got rights."

"That's enough," I told my irate daughter. "I love you with all my heart, but I'll not let you condemn somebody for what I decided to do. What I did was my idea, not hers. Now, either you calm yourself down and act right, or leave 'til you can come back acting like a daughter ought to."

Just as I feared, she let her temper get the best of her. She turned on her heels and marched out of the cabin, got in her Land Rover, gunned the engine, and drove away spinning up the rich black dirt of the yard.

"I hate my Meadow Lark gave you the blame for what I told her," I said to Bennie Jack when she came out of the woods.

"No problem with that," she responded with a shake of her head, "Are you sure she's your daughter? Is there a chance she could have been switched at birth?" she added with an attempt at humor.

I didn't think her comment funny, but I understood. My Meadow Lark had always been on the self-centered side of life, but I had marked it up as being because of George's boys. She had to learn early on to stand up to their picking at her even when they meant no harm.

I couldn't help thinking of the man I feared was her real daddy. She was acting a lot like him. He was determined to get what he wanted regardless of who he hurt or how he got it. I blamed myself again for not being a better mother. My only excuse was that I was always doing what I thought was right back then as well as now. I didn't think it was right for her to institutionalize me because she was wanting something that belonged to me instead of her. I was old and didn't have too much longer to live. All she had to do was be patient and she'd get every single thing I owned. Now, it was too late. I'd done what I'd done.

"You didn't sell the land to me," Bennie Jack broke my thoughts by saying.

"No, I didn't, but my Meadow Lark don't know it."

"If she gets a lawyer, he'll know there isn't a sales contract."

"My lawyer is sworn to secrecy. He'll know how to handle things."

"You trust this lawyer to do what you want?"

"I do," I told her. "I've known him for a long time." She seemed surprised at my words.

"Just because I've spent my life on this mountain don't mean I've not met a few people. I know who I can trust and who I can't."

"I hope so. I just want you to know I'll gladly buy your land if that's what you want. I'll pay you whatever price you ask."

Yep, she was one of those cradle-rich to be saying such as that, but I didn't hold it against her. Money was a good tool to have if you didn't let it go to your head. A child had no choice in her folks being a pauper or wealthy.

"I don't want your money. I hate to admit it, but I'd never see any peace until my Meadow Lark got her hands on every dime of it."

Bennie Jack nodded as though she understood. "I'll back you up regardless," she told me. "I'll be here for you as well."

I nodded, although I thought it kind of interesting that an old woman and a young woman had come to an understanding with each other. Guess it was because we were the only two people living on this side of a high mountain consisting of mostly rock and hard times. I found it mind boggling that a young woman would want to live here unless it was someone who wanted to hide away from someone or something they could no longer face up to.

Chapter 25

~Bennie Jack~

I didn't understand Aunt Polly's logic, but then what she did or didn't do was not for me to judge. She knew best how to deal with her daughter along with her own possessions. What I didn't like was her getting me involved. There was a chance her daughter could expose my existence if she really did act on her threat and sue me. I'd always heard that any person could sue another person for breathing the same air as they did. They might not win the case, but they could cause a lot of trouble for someone. The thing was, if a person didn't defend themselves, they were likely to lose.

Aunt Polly had involved me in whatever trouble she had with her daughter, and I didn't like it one bit. I had moved here to live in seclusion only to discover even here on this desolate mountain there was no such thing as total privacy. I should have minded my own business and never made friends with the old woman. Act in haste, regret in leisure, I reminded myself.

Then again, if her real estate broker of a daughter sold Aunt Polly's land to developers, my privacy was shot. I might never be able to find, or afford, another hiding place as secluded as this one. I had to convince Aunt Polly to sell me her land for real. I had no idea what she had arranged at the Lawyer's office and didn't care until now. The more I thought it over, the more I felt I should disappear from their affairs for a while. Let the two of them figure things out without involving me. I had confidence Aunt Polly could hold her own with her daughter. Surviving alone on this mountain had to make her as tough as this old enduring mountain of rock.

Disappear. It was another word for running away. How many times was I willing to run away? Was hiding on this mountain really the best way for me to handle the remainder of my life? Did I have a choice? These were questions I didn't yet have answers to. I wanted to do more. Spend the rest of my life accomplishing something beneficial.

Hiding away didn't seem like a goal I would be proud of or a goal I might be able to live with. One thing was for sure, I would never become a wife and mother. But then I had never expected to have such a normal life. My goal had been to live and die for the benefit of my country. Such thoughts made me laugh out loud. I had accomplished nothing for my country. As far as I knew, Brigham was still alive, and I might have unintentionally interfered with the Freedom Group's plans.

A feeling of guilt almost overwhelmed me as I walked through my garden. Did I have the right to be here much less be this happy? I had failed my country, but maybe it wasn't too late to rectify my decision to disappear.

Perhaps all I needed time here on this mountain for my head to clear enough for me to make plans as to what I could do that would expose traitors to my country.

In the meantime, I was incredibly proud of what I had accomplished on my new home in the short time I'd been here, although it was only a drop in the bucket of what needed doing. I wasn't sure I had the skills to repair everything that needed repairing, much less accomplish the requirements to become a self-sufficient hermit.

My garden was growing better than I expected. I had to give one or more of the Slaughters credit for not wearing the garden soil out but had obviously put back into the ground what the soil needed to continue producing. The garden spot had been fertilized many years in the past with chicken, cow, and horse manure along with piles and piles of leaves. My

seeds had shot out of the ground the way they should. I
already had lettuce and squash to eat. I had early cabbage
heading, plus a seed bed coming up for late cabbage to bury
in the ground come winter. Aunt Polly had also insisted I
have a late patch of turnips ready to plant so I would have
them this winter. Not to mention the patch of ground where I
had corn growing to winter the goat I was going to get from
her.

Thanks to all my work, along with the help of Aunt Polly,
my roof no longer leaked when it rained. I was surprised at
how much rain fell on this mountain. After each rain, the air
smelled as though everything had been washed clean. It was
entirely different than the tarmac smell after it rained in
Washington D.C. Not to mention what allies smelled like.

I didn't miss the rat race of politicians who thought they
were running our country. I was so satisfied living on this
mountain that I felt guilty for being happy. There were times
when my conscious told me I should be out there gathering
incriminating evidence on those who were destroying our
freedom along with those who were assisting them.

There were other countries that were our enemies.
Interesting how those who hated America the most had the
largest hands out demanding we give them our taxpayers'
money. Why? I wanted to know. Why was such behavior as
this tolerated? How many times did it have to be said that you
can't buy your friends? As for enemies, if you stopped giving
your enemies money, they were even more determined to
destroy you.

Countries who were our enemies had figured out how to
gain control of the weakest of our leaders and focused on
taking advantage of their weaknesses. I was gathering
definite information on who they were along with who was
bribing them. It didn't take me long to conclude it would be
easier to find the ones who hadn't been bribed.

The ones being bribed gathered together and turned on
the few that were actually working for the betterment of our

country. They accused the good guys of doing exactly what they were doing and went about every dishonest means to prove it, including setups and lying. Afterall, they were all too familiar with how bribery worked. The one thing they didn't want was an honest person to be in power.

The good people relied on truth and honor. They didn't accuse without proof. I was one of others gathering undisputable truth. I took pride in what I was able to accomplish. What I didn't take pride in was not being intelligent enough to know who not to trust. I had misjudged Brigham. And that had cost me my life – or so Brigham thought. It actually cost me the life I had always known.

What I now wanted to know was what it cost Brigham, along with knowing what was going on in the world I had escaped from. To do that I would have to leave the mountain.

Chapter 26

In the blink of an eye, I was no longer an active part of the Freedom Group I had worked for and believed in. Someone else would be taking my place in training new recruits. I was now a rejected failure – a disappointment in myself and to my group.

I concluded my ousting was the result of my failure in the proper training of Fizz. For that mistake, she had paid with her life. I failed Fizz.

I didn't go back to my apartment after meeting with Badger. I put into action the plan I had prepared and gone over in my mind many times in case I ever had the need to disappear.

I stomped on my disposable cell phone and then dropped it in the back of a jacked up, mud splattered pickup truck and walked down the street until I came to a well-attended gym. I went into the back door of the gym so I wouldn't have to check-in at the reception desk. I had never entered this gym before, but I had made a point of knowing its layout just in case I ever needed to put my plan into action. I kept my body in tone at my home gym. Not to mention the obstacle courses and rugged terrain I trained recruits in. I took pride in being the most fit and strong person I knew. I ask no one to do what I couldn't and didn't do many times over.

I went straight to the dressing room where other jocks were getting in and out of the shower. I stripped off all my clothes, hung them on pegs near other clothing, and got into the shower making sure I scrubbed my hair and body, although I knew no tracers could be on my body or in my hair without me knowing it. I got out of the shower, grabbed a towel and dried myself off as a sweaty, muscled-up jock stripped off his damp, sweat covered sweatpants and hoody T-shirt, dropped them on the floor and got into the shower without so much as acknowledging me.

I picked up his sweat-stained smelly workout clothes and put them on. When he got out of the shower he would have to dress in my clothes unless he had a change of his own in a locker, which I suspected he did. What jock would enter a gym without a duffle bag to shove into a locker?

I took the fake beard and mustache kit out of my pants pocket and left the room. I made my way back upstairs where I found a room with a mirror that wasn't in use. I entered, closed the door and I carefully glued the fake beard stubble and mustache to my face. I was pleased with what I saw. Neither the beard nor mustache was long enough to draw attention, but scruffy enough to hide my facial features. I looked like a grungy jock who hadn't shaved for several days. Even when I trained recruits, I made sure I shaved every morning. I wanted to look preppy instead of rugged. Undercover cops always tried to duplicate the appearance of the drug-using homeless. Spies were to appear slick and professional similar to James Bond, and in all aspects, I was a spy with a touch of undercover cop thrown in. I chuckled to myself at such illusions. Spies came in all shapes, colors, dress, and sections of life, be it doctors, lawyer, butlers, maids, chauffeurs or well-known politicians.

I walked out the front door and continued walking down the street as if I knew exactly where I was going, which I did. I went inside a store and wandered around like I was searching for something. I had scanned the place on a regular basis as I planned my escape if it ever became necessary. I knew where the service doors were located. I entered one, nodded to stock employees working there as though I belonged and walked out the back door. I quickly entered through the back door of another store and went out the side door of the employees' break room. I crossed the back alley, went in and out of another store and into a small park where I started jogging along with other health enthusiasts. I fit right in considering how I was dressed.

It took me forty-five minutes of jogging and another twenty minutes of walking to take me to the long-term parking lot where I had a beat-up SUV waiting for when this day arrived. I had a key stored in a magnetic box under the rear fender. I bent down to rub my hand over the tire as though I was checking its soundness and discreetly grabbed the box, unlocked the door and got behind the wheel. The car started right up, and I drove to the exit where I paid in cash a hefty parking price for being parked there for an extended period of time. It was an expensive parking place, but necessary for those in need of using it. There were other cars that had been parked there longer than mine. It was one of the few places where people could leave their vehicles while away on extended business trips or vacations. I suspected there were also people such as me who had get-away cars waiting for them.

My main expense was rent. Other than that, I lived like a pauper. What little furniture I had come from second-hand stores, as did most of my clothes. Many years ago, I had purchased what I hoped to become my safe place when this day arrived – and I knew it would eventually arrive. As a trainer of spies, I would come under scrutiny eventually even if Fizz hadn't blown my cover.

I had a tank full of gas along with two full five-gallon gas cans in the trunk of my car. I didn't want to take a chance on stopping somewhere to fill up as there were always cameras in operation. Always be prepared and leave no trace behind was the theory I lived by. That included not having a wife, children, and relatives to take into consideration.

If someone in our group got into trouble, the Freedom Group offered no assistance. Such was one of the reasons our members were selected with great care. Another reason, and equally important, was choosing someone who wouldn't squeal when being tortured. That kind of person was few and far between. Most people would say anything as well as do anything to stop intolerable pain.

I had an idea Fizz chose to take the helicopter down rather than take the torture she knew was coming. I had to give her credit for doing such as that. I still had questions about her death with no answers or way of finding out what happened. As a trainer, it was not my job to seek any kind of information or conduct investigations. I was always to lay low and keep my mouth shut. I did what I was told to do and nothing more. It was difficult for me to accept the fact that I was no longer considered a part of the Freedom Group. The benefit was I no longer had to obey their rules.

My drive consisted of several hundred miles. Never once did I exceed the speed limit regardless of how tempting it was to do so. I had already set up what I hoped was to become my safe identity. Nonetheless, I didn't want to be in an accident. If my DNA was run, it would look suspicious for a man to be declared dead twice in different car accidents.

I drove all night long. Only stopping long enough on a deserted road to pour the extra ten gallons of gas in the tank. It was getting daylight, and the car was running low on gas about fifty miles from my hideaway. I put a fake set of buck teeth in my mouth, looked in the mirror and grinned big. Nothing like fake teeth and facial hair to disguise a man. I considered putting on dark glasses, but that might be going too far when the sun wasn't up. I filled up the tank at a Walmart gas station, found a parking place in the early morning's not so full parking lot, and then went inside. It had been a while since I had visited my hideaway. I had a good supply of canned goods, but I needed to purchase fresh food along with other supplies. It was best I am not seen often purchasing supplies.

I stored the supplies in the trunk of my SUV grinning at the duffle bags I had stashed there. In one duffle bag I had even gone so far as to have extra-large women's clothes and wigs. I doubted I would ever use them as a woman my size would be sure to draw far more attention than a man with facial hair. I would be as obvious as Jethro Bodine dressed up as Jethrene in the Beverly Hillbillies. The thought of watching the reruns of that show lightened my mood for the first time in days. It was a farfetched show, but it did have a touch of realism as far as my long past relatives were concerned.

I had made many short trips to my hideaway in preparation for this day. I sawed down trees and built a small rustic log cabin along with a log barn and several small outbuildings. I made sure I kept my hideaway well supplied for when the time came in case I had been injured and unable to fend for myself. Fortunately, I remained fit and fully functional.

The main reason I chose to purchase this track of land was its location. It was five hundred acres of rocky virgin forest surrounded by thousands of acres of government land, which was the reason it had not already been sold. The previous owner had refused to sell the land to the government. Fortunately, he had managed to maintain the right of ingress and regress that went along with the property. Although the road was only twelve feet in width, it was seven rugged miles long through government owned land. Only hunters and the occasional hikers wanted to invade such rough mountain terrain. The government did not permit hunting, and I had posted no trespassing signs along the boundary of my land. At the entrance of my land, I had hung fake skeleton heads of animals along with other spooky types of warnings. My intent was to make trespassers think some sort of lunatic lived there. One who was unfit to live in society and forced to hide out in seclusion.

I managed to buy the land right before the owner died twenty years ago. I used my real name, Colton Slaughter, to purchase it right after my four-year stint in the army ended. I had spent years trying to purchase the tract of distant family land I had been paying taxes on. If not for me paying taxes, the land would have been sold off at auction for unpaid taxes. Perhaps I should have let it happen and taken a chance on being the one who bought it, but I hadn't.

Unfortunately, and much to my regret, the other Slaughter grandchildren resented my paying taxes on the land and refused to sell to me. And then, on a sudden whim, they sold it to someone else without me knowing it. I discovered my name had been forged on the deed.

As one of the Freedom Group, I had to keep a low profile and would have taken a chance of exposure if I contested the signature. On the deed the woman's name who bought the place was Bennie Jack. What kind of name was that for a woman? I figured no woman would want to live in a rundown, desolate place. Therefore, I still had a chance of purchasing my ancestor's home place from this Bennie Jack.

I also wanted to purchase the land owned by Polly MacCallum, but she flat out refused to sell. I wondered if it was because my last name was Slaughter. I knew a lot of my relatives were a rowdy, unlawful bunch, but she and them were supposed to be neighbors and friends.

I never lived on the mountain homeplace. I was known as the wood's colt offspring of the most notorious of the bunch of Slaughters. Why my sweet mother had given me the last name of my father when I was born had always been a puzzle to me since she wasn't married to him. Her family had been considered rather well-to-do by some standards. I had been provided with a good education along with a loving mother, but it didn't last.

My mother had died young without ever marrying. She once told me she wanted no man other than my father. After her death, the only grandparents I had ever known disowned me, which was something I suspected only my mother kept them from doing from the moment I was conceived. It was hard for me to accept that I had always been an embarrassment to my mother's people through no fault of my own.

When my grandparents passed away, they left their only son everything they owned, which hadn't come as a surprise. I was already in my last year serving in the army and was soon to be discharged. I reenlisted for another stint.

After my second stint, I served as a NYPD police office before becoming a secret service agent assigned to guarding the president of the United States, which I did for both parties as I was registered as an Independent. It was during this service that I learned things that turned my stomach and brought a cold fear I couldn't let go of. If the American people knew about the things that went on, there would be the biggest revolt in existence. Unfortunately, a non-disclosure law passed the year I signed on. Prison would result for anyone who told the truth about politicians and the deep state.

After several years of willingly risking my life to protect politicians I despised, I was approached by the Freedom Group. I had seen enough foul play in our government that I readily agreed to join. Admittedly, I was disappointed in becoming a trainer instead of being assigned a more aggressive role. I was told I was to abide by the rules until the time was right for action. I was still waiting for the right time for action. The book "Animal Farm" kept running through my mind. There was no assurance the next politicians to take control of our country wouldn't be worse than the ones now in charge.

Chapter 27

~~Aunt Polly~~

I figured it was God's plan that the girl arrived on this mountain. She had been nothing short of a blessing to me. Without her my Meadow Lark might have found a way to force me off this mountain before I made my way to the lawyer's office. I had been having bad dreams about my beloved mountain being turned into summer houses for the rich and mighty. I could see the big rocks being dynamited out of the ground with big dozers pushing down the timber. I could even smell the smoke from the burning of the mountain's precious vegetation. Knowing my beloved daughter had turned into one of those real estate people who sought to make a profit from land that ought to be left alone disturbed me greatly. Didn't seem right folks from off could come in to destroy things as though they had the right to do it.

I knew it wouldn't take long until my Meadow Lark showed up again. She wasn't the kind to give up on what she wanted regardless of what was best for anyone else. Sure enough, the thought hardly went through my mind when I heard the sound of her vehicle climbing the mountain road. I could tell it was her by the way she kept pumping on the gas as though she could make the vehicle fly instead of making slow, safe progress the way a person ought.

I sucked in a deep breath and whetted up for the confrontation.

Much to my surprise, she didn't turn in to my place. She kept right on going toward the Slaughter's place. I hurried through the woods in an attempt to arrive before my Meadow Lark did. She was getting out of her vehicle by the time I reached the edge of the woods. I sidled up against the trunk of a large poplar tree to get a better view of what was going to happen.

My Meadow Lark got out of the vehicle, slammed the door loudly and marched up to the porch. I could tell she was mad and ready for a confrontation. Instead of Bennie Jack coming out the door with a double-barreled shotgun pointing at my girl, as I expected, there was total silence. The place appeared deserted. I found that right strange since I knew Bennie Jack had surely heard the vehicle the same as I did.

"Hello!" my Meadow Larked shouted. "Come on out here. I want to talk to you!"

There wasn't a single sound coming from the house or the woods. Not even a movement of the curtains Bennie Jack had found in the attic, washed, ironed, and hung in the windows. Much to my amazement, my Meadow Lark marched onto the porch and beat on the door loud enough to wake all the Slaughter ancestors if they had been buried nearby. When no one answered, she grabbed the doorknob and tried to open the door. It was locked.

"Come out here. I know you're hiding in there," my Meadow Lark shouted to the top of her lungs.

I figured Bennie Jack had to be a long ways off or she would be in a fury about the way my Meadow Lark was acting, and I wouldn't blame her in the least bit.

My Meadow Lark then had the gall to go from window to window trying to look in, but the curtains were pulled together, and sticks were in the upper windows to keep them from being opened. I thought this rather strange as it appeared the place might be empty. I knew Bennie Jack's truck was in the barn hall behind the closed doors. I'd have heard it leaving the mountain if it wasn't.

I jumped at the loud sound of a shotgun being fired. A six-inch limb fell out of a tree not twenty feet from where my

Meadow Lark was standing. She froze in her tracks, not expecting such a thing to happen. It was then Bennie Jack stepped from the edge of the woods at least fifty yards away. I almost didn't recognize her. She was dressed in men's bibbed overalls with a huge felt hat pulled low over her face concealing her features.

"If I was you, I'd be on my way in a hurry," she said in a low and deeper voice than I'd heard her use before. "Trespass on my land again and the shot you'll never hear won't be a warning shot."

"How dare you . . ." My Meadow Lark said in a rage a moment before buckshot kicked up dirt not two feet from her fancy shoes.

"Reckon I'll have to find my burying shovel after I count to five. One . . ." she said. "Two . . ."

By the time Bennie Jack said three, my Meadow Lark was in her vehicle. The engine was roaring by four and she had floored the gas by the count of five. I had to chuckle to myself even though I wasn't sure if Billie Jack would have actually shot my girl.

My Meadow Lark was already out of her vehicle and in my house by the time I got back there. She was searching through everything as though she was looking for something.

"What are you doing?" I demanded of her.

"The contract," she shouted at me. "I want to see it. Where have you been?"

"Well now," I said. "I heard your vehicle go to the Slaughter place. I heard shots. Lucky you're not bleeding or dead. You know better than to trespass where you don't belong."

"I'll have her arrested for shooting at me," she yelled.

"She didn't shoot at you, or you'd be dead," I told her. "That woman don't miss."

"How dare you take up for her," her fury continued.

"I'm not taking up for her. I'm stating a fact."

"I'll have her arrested for attempted murder."

"No, you won't. You were trespassing on her property. You were the one who done wrong," I told her in a useless attempt to calm her down some.

"You're leaving with me right now. She's a danger to you," she shouted at me.

"No, she's not, and you might as well get it through you head that I'm not leaving here alive or dead. I take it you had your attorney talk to my attorney, didn't you?"

She hesitated as her face grew even redder than it already was.

"Meadow Lark," I told her. "I suggest you take yourself off this mountain and not come back until you are calm and reasonable. I'm not going to listen to you until you act like a rational human being."

"I'm not leaving here until I see your contract. She's taking advantage of you and trying to cheat me out of my inheritance."

"No, she's not," I corrected her. "Because you don't have an inheritance from me. Everything I own now belongs to Bennie Jack."

"Then show me the money she paid you."

I suspected money was what she was looking for all along instead of the contract. "What do you need money for?" I questioned.

"I don't need money or anything else from you," she shouted at me. "I'm trying to protect you from that crazy woman," she said, doing her best to change her tune.

"No, you're not. I'm your mother. I know when you're after something that doesn't belong to you. It's best you go back home now and take care of your own children. There's nothing left here for you to get, unless it's my love for my only child. I still love you regardless of how self-centered and greedy you've become, but I'm not too old to give you the tongue lashing you deserve. If you send the sheriff, I'll have to tell him you've been harassing me. I'll don't want to do it, but I'll have no other choice than to ask for one of them restraining orders be put on you."

My Meadow Lark's eyes widened, and her mouth opened and shut a few times before she spoke. "You wouldn't dare. Not to your own daughter."

"I would," I told her. "Seems my own daughter has gone plum crazy."

She glared at me for a few minutes before she whirled around, stormed out the door, got in her vehicle and left.

After she was gone, I sank down on a rickety chair and cried.

Chapter 28

~~A. J~~

I'm settled in my cabin, but I couldn't find my usual contentment. I keep thinking about how life changed. It veers, stretches, as well as retracts and shatters. I cringe at the knowledge that my life could crumble yet again with the slightest alteration. Life is tenuous. Nothing is sure. My life with the Freedom Group had been like fighting a secret war while trying not to be detected. If this kind of war didn't damage your body, it was sure to damage your soul.

These are only part of the sad thoughts I kept having. I still longed to correct the wrongs traditors have done to our country.

I have no doubt my discontent comes from the reason I'm here. I don't like the idea of being declared dead even when it is for benefit. I don't know what went on with the Freedom Group to cause them to make such a decision where I was concerned, unless it was with what Frizz revealed, and that's even more disturbing for me. I do know and keep telling myself the freedom our country has enjoyed is now being threatened by traitors who value their financial enrichment over our nation's freedom.

I was little more than a trainer, although I did receive confidential information that I passed on to higher ranking officials in the Freedom Group. It's a well-known fact that those in government power do nothing about the traitors, which is a good indication they are also compromised. There is no doubt the swamp is filled with deadly alligators who protect each other.

My question now is how I can possibly be a benefit in rectifying the threat – now that I'm officially declared dead.

Stop it! I suddenly heard my inner voice tell me. What makes me think I, one lone man, can accomplish anything? The Freedom Group know what they are doing, and there are many of them. I wasn't the only trainer they had, although I thought I was their best. And then it hit me. Fizz.

How obvious. I should have connected the dots sooner than I had. Fizz had gone to Brigham, and I was her trainer. Either I had failed in my job of controlling her, or the freedom group suspected I might also be a traditor to my country. Surely, they knew better else my dead would have been for real. The Freedom Group was doing their job. Such a realization gave me some relief. Someone better than Fizz and me were doing their job. They knew what was going on.

I wondered who died in my car accident? Someone's body would have been burned into ashes. A fake DNA would have identified those ashes as belonging to me. Nothing was legit anymore. Nothing could be trusted anymore.

You don't need to know everything. I assured myself. You should be grateful that you've been freed to live your own life. I laughed at that thought. Being claimed dead had only a small amount of value. It was a well-known miracle how certain people were able to arise from their graves – usually only for a short time. I would have to remain in hiding for the rest of my life in order to remain alive.

Fortunately, I had this cabin and a portion of this mountain that no one knew I owned. Not even the Freedom Group, I hoped. There definitely were advantages of using aliases. My concern was that I didn't own all of the mountain, which meant others would eventually move here and threaten my anonymity. I had enough money stashed away to buy the old woman out along with the woman who owned the rest of the mountain. Purchasing land would seriously deplete most of my savings, but it would be worth it. This isolated mountain would provide me with what I always wanted and worked toward. Unless it was a family – a wife and children which I would never have. Much like a nun who had given her life to God, I had given myself to my country.

I decided to check on the old woman. I had no idea if she was still alive, but I hoped she was. I knew she had an ambitious daughter who hated the mountain. I did a search on her some time ago to discover she had become a real estate broker. She had done well for herself, but like the old saying, the more a person had the more they wanted. The daughter would want a fortune for the other side of my mountain.

As for the land that belonged to my relatives, I should have no problem buying it as long as I used an alias. Odd how some folks would sell to a stranger rather than a relative. I suppose it came under the theory of jealousy or perhaps even sibling rivalry.

I left my cabin to walk over the other side of the mountain to make sure the old woman was still alive. It had been two years since I had checked on her. Training recruits had taken up most all my time. It was – or had been, my job. I had devoted my life and my time to doing it right. I put my heart and soul into devoting myself to my country. Now, I had been cut loose, cast out, dead in return for all the years of my usefulness. It was shocking to be handed my life on an empty platter before I had accomplished what needed to be done. But what had I expected?

As usual, I didn't want to be seen until I determined the situation on the other side of the mountain. If things were as I hoped, I would have to meet the old woman face to face to buy her land. First, I would need to gain her confidence and comradery. She had a daughter and several stepsons. None of whom seemed to care about the old woman. From what I'd learned about the daughter, she would always be a problem for me. She was both tough and ambitious, obviously from the way she had been raised as well as her own greedy spirit. Her mother, on the other hand, had a very gentle nature about her. Although Polly MacCallum had to be one of the toughest women I'd ever come across both physically and mentally. I knew better than to discredit her on anything. A woman who had managed to survive all these years alone on this mountain was a force to be reckoned with, regardless of her age.

I took time to put on my fake disguise just in case I was seen. One thing was for certain, fake theater makeup and hair was used all the time when a person didn't want to be recognized. Makeup and fake hair had become so refined that it was difficult to tell from the real things. I made a point of using real hair instead of wool along with spirit gum to glue it on, which made it difficult to rip off. The only thing that's hard to change are the eyes. Even when wearing contact lenses that change color, the eyes remain the same. I learned a long time ago to look into the eyes to see the soul.

The few times I came into close contact with the old woman she looked me in the eyes in an effort to see my soul. My soul was something I didn't want anyone to see.

It was for the best that I wanted to purchase the old woman's land. In my opinion this mountain was God's masterpiece. According to my limited knowledge of flora and fauna, there were more herbs and medicinal plants on this mountain than any other place. There were also many endangered plants growing here. It would be a sin against nature if this mountain's treasures were destroyed in order to provide houses with a long-distance view.

I took my time climbing up my side of the mountain and crossed over the top and down to where my distant relatives once lived. I made sure I stayed a long distance from the house, although I could see its roof from the top of a huge outcropping of rock. I wanted to get a closeup look at who lived there, but it would have to wait until I learned more about the owner. I was leery of anyone seeing me. A dead man couldn't be too careful even when he was in disguise. The one time a man dropped his guard was usually the time he would regret it.

I sat on the rock for a while taking in the beauty that surrounded me. I realized again how lucky I was to be alive. I wished they had been able to do similar for Fizz.

Chapter 29

~~Bennie Jack~~

A part of me wanted to leave the mountain in order to find out what was happening in the world I left behind, while another part never wanted to leave this mountain even to get supplies. In the short time I had been here I had found a kind of peace that I never knew existed. I thought of it as Mother Nature soothing what was hurting me. Before coming here, I thought the rat-races of city life were exciting as well as demanding. Being a government staffer made me feel important.

I planned on starting at the bottom and working my way into becoming at the very least a representative of the senate without spending time on my knees. I knew several young women who tried the knee way to promotions. Some of the young women got unfavorable publicity. Others fell to the wayside like unwanted baggage without making a news splash. The rich and powerful men had a way of turning everything to their benefit. Interesting how those in power never paid for the wrongs they did. It was the women who always got the blame.

There was a rare one or two women who accomplished a portion of their ambitions. I knew of one who actually did make it near the top, but it took her many years. Being a favorite sidepiece of a president who was now long dead, had helped her, as did gathering a blacklist of information on those men who might hamper her in reaching her goals. I had an idea she had more information on those who were corrupt than I had ever uncovered.

I wanted her list.

The passing years had taken away her beauty as well as her youth, but not the information she had secreted away. In a way I felt sorry for her because of her continuous attempt to hold onto what she didn't want to lose – including her power as well as her beauty. She had already spent more on cosmetic surgery than most movie stars ever hoped to obtain. Surgery and makeup did wonders for her ego as well as all the liquor she consumed.

I had done everything in my power to discover the whereabouts of her blacklist with no success. I had to give the old dame credit for knowing what she was doing and not being taken down. It was obvious to me, and everyone else, that she had some powerful connections that reached back for years and extended to the present and future. She was a wise old bird who refused to let someone such as me get so much as a blink of her eye.

That smart old bird had taken one young blond male under her wing. She put him where she wanted him to be because he was malleable and potentially useful. He knew to jump to her bidding when she put the squeeze on him. I knew there were more than one man, and perhaps even women, who owed her, but I was still uncovering proof about them when I had foolishly gone to Brigham. From all the information I had gathered, Brigham was serving as one of our agents. I thought he needed to know what I had uncovered the same as A. J. I knew A.J. would veto any contact I might have with Brigham, so I went to him directly. My big mistake. The one I would be paying for the rest of my life.

Lesson learned.

I would never trust anyone again. Plus, I needed my own blacklist, even after I had been declared dead. There was nothing more powerful than knowledge, especially when it was about your enemies.

If I had continued to live, I would have needed to become far better than the old woman. I was astounded and envious at what that woman got away with.

How I would love to get a few more cracks at her information and everyone else's.

I once foolishly expressed my longing to go after her to A.J. He called me off in a hurry. "That woman is pushing eighty," he warned. "She didn't get where she is by being stupid. Mess with her and you'll end up toast in more ways than one."

"Exactly what does that mean?" I demanded of him. He hesitated a moment before he spoke.

"It means you can't uncover anything about her that others don't already know. You're too valuable to fool around with old news such as her."

"I'm not wanting to uncover anything about her. I want a copy of her blacklist."

A.J. laughed. "Most people on her list have died of old age or been otherwise eliminated."

"Then why does she still hold so much power over people?"

"Let's just say there are bigger fish we need to fry than an old woman who will expire on her own before we could take proper action against her. Not only that, but we also don't want to draw attention to our group just yet. We want to have our arsenal fully loaded when we do act."

"But the blacklist . . ." I began.

"We already know most of what her blacklist contains. As I just told you, her information is old news for us."

I wasn't so sure about that. In my opinion he was underestimating the old woman. She didn't get where she was and still remain able to hold onto her power for no reason.

"Your time is too valuable to waste on the likes of her. Do the job you are supposed to do and nothing else," he told me with authority.

I wasn't going to argue considering the fact I was to take orders directly from A.J. He had proven his advice was valid many times over, but in my opinion, he kept blinders as well as a tight harness on me. I could accomplish so much more if only he would allow me to do so.

He went on to explain that the old woman was feathering her own nest, but she was not as much of a threat to our country as others were. He was right in that it would be more productive for me to go for the ones that were of more danger to our national security. The ones who were selling out our country's secrets for their own financial pockets. These were the major traitors to our country. My intuition told me the old woman had a blacklist on every single traitor – old and young. All I had to do was find where it was located.

"It's not as much the people who are supposedly in power as it is the people who are controlling them. Those are the ones we want incriminating information on. Those are the ones you're supposed to discover indisputable information on," A.J. reminded me.

I agreed.

I ran such things through my mind for the zillionth time while I sat on the porch doing nothing. With all the corruption going on, how could I be content hiding here on the mountain? I was a trained spy. I knew how to find out secret information as well as takeovers that were in the first stages of planning. I was capable enough to come up with plans on my own. I hadn't and still didn't need A.J. to tell me what I should and shouldn't go after. In my opinion, A.J. and the Freedom Group were moving too slowly. It was best for the corruption to be stopped before it harmed our country further than it already had.

"What's got you so deep in thought?"

I was so engrossed in my thinking that I startled at the sudden sound of Aunt Polly's voice.

"Thinking of all the things I need to do," I told her.

"Then why are you setting there with your tail end in that porch chair instead of doing what needs to be done?"

"Good question," I told her. "I've just climbed down from checking the roof. I think I've fixed all the leaks. Want to set your tail end down next to me for a while?"

"Don't mind if I do. That is if you'll fetch me a glass of cold water. I got a mighty thirsty roamin' all over creation."

I got up as she sat down. The warm weather. Along with roamin' all over creation, had brought sweat to her forehead and upper lip. I got a glass from the kitchen shelf and caught water straight from the pipe that ran into the troth. Again, I acknowledged whoever came up with having a spring-troth in the room next to the kitchen had been a genius back in the day. It was genius today in a place that didn't have electricity to keep things such as milk and butter cold. When putting food in a Jar and then placing it in the cold water cooled as well as any refrigerator. The only drawback was the lack of a freezer.

"Thank ye," Aunt Polly said when I handed her the glass. She drank the water straight down and then belched as she sat the glass down on the porch beside her chair. "You know them Slaughters were right smart in some ways. It takes a lazy person to come up with ways to get out of work. Don't reckon a one of 'em liked toting a bucket of water."

She was probably right about that.

"Now, take me for instance. I never did mind hard work. It keeps me goin'. I stiffen up if I stay in one spot for long. I can say one thing for certain, no matter how hard I worked it never got me ahead enough to brag about. I was born poor and always expected to stay that way. Notice how you never get the good you want unless you go after it?"

"I've noticed," I admitted. "What about your husband? Did he work hard or smart?"

"My George. Lawsy me, I think he was born plum worn out, but then he was right old when we married. My George did only what he had to do, but I never complained at him. I knew there weren't no use. I never knowed what he'd been like as a young man," she said with a shake of her head. "Ought not to tell a body this, but at my age don't reckon it matters. Don't reckon there's a body you'll be running your mouth to about such things. My George never did satisfy my bodily needs, if you know what I mean by that. Took him less than a minute to grunt like a satisfied hog. Sometimes not even that long." She shook her head again. "I'd just lay there afterwards dreaming about the man I never got to marry. Wondering what it would be like to have a man who did more that lift my petticoat every so often. Sometimes I'd even cry a little, but I reckon sech as that made no never mind. Can't say as I minded when my George got too old to pull it outta his britches."

I watched her face sadden as a faraway look came to her face. I took it to be a mixture of memory and regret.

"My old, worn-out body hain't got no longings no more, but my heart does. I still want for the man I never had."

Aunt Polly surprised me at what she was saying. She'd never talked about such things before. I wondered if her mind was going.

"What was his name?" I asked as she stared out toward the garden going silent for a few minutes. "I mean the man you wanted to marry."

Finally, after a few minutes, she spoke. "Don't know. Never met him during this lifetime."

I must have given her a concerned look without saying a word.

"I reckon I was born picturing the man I wanted to marry up with. I knowed exactly what he looked like – what he smelled like – the feel of him holding me – the way he put a lip-lock on my mouth. Lawsy, I still dream about him during long, lonely nights. Can you believe such as that coming from an old woman like me?" She chuckled a little at herself. "My body is old and wore out, but my mind remembers having a young woman's needs."

I smiled at the way Aunt Polly said that. I never expected to see such longing on an old woman's face. I thought such longings faded away with age.

"To this day my insides ache because I never met him during this lifetime." She turned her head to look at me. "You ever felt that way? I mean has your heart ever cried out for a man that never showed up?"

I thought I understood what she was talking about. I dreamed of having a husband who loved me, but I hadn't imagined what he would look like. Although, I always wanted him to be a proper provider who I could depend on. I had hoped he would be complimentary in the areas I was weak in. I also wanted a man who would honor my ambitions as well as his own.

"I expected him to be a hard-working mountain man, not one of those wussy men who wear their hair in a man-bun and wear funky clothes," Aunt Polly continued. "Got no use for the limp-wristed sort. I wanted me one of those men who knows how to handle his piledriver if you know what I mean."

She surprised me by what she was saying. I found it hard to believe she knew about such things as man-buns and funky clothes considering how isolated her entire life had been.

"My George was a mountain man," she continued. "I figured I got a part of what I wanted, not that I wouldn't have married George if I had to do it all over again. Didn't have much choice in the matter back during my time. Things weren't like they are today. A girl could ruin herself and all her kin without her doin' anything wrong. If you ask me, girls weren't treated right back then. They have it better in today's time."

"Did you and George love each other?" I dared to ask.

"I reckon we did, in our own way. I've heard that true love comes after marriage. I reckon that has some truth to it. One thing I did know for sure, old men liked to bed young girls. I was mighty young back then. You know the saying.

A woman's only as old as she feels, while a man's only as old as the woman he feels."

I chuckled along with her, although I had heard such a remark many times before. She and I both knew there was truth in that truism. I wondered what had made her so talky today, especially on such a subject. Usually, she was focused on gardening, animals, or taking me into the woods to forage and educate me on things that had never crossed my mind. She was determined to teach me things she thought I should know about survival. She told me she wouldn't always be around to fix my blunders.

"I been doing some thinking on it, and it hain't right for a young woman your age not to have a man," she said as though she was overly concerned for me. "What kind of excuse you got to say for yourself?"

I was speechless.

"Well?" she demanded. "Hain't there somebody you've courted? Somebody you might hookup with?"

"Not really," I finally admitted.

"Why not?"

I thought about her question before I answered. I certainly couldn't tell her I would never be able to marry when I was in hiding and afraid to use my own name. No man would be willing to marry a woman without knowing anything at all about her and her past life.

"You're not one of those other kind of women, are you? Your head is nearly shaved slick, and you dress like a boy."

It took me a few moments to realize what she was asking. "No, of course not," I assured her.

"Then why hain't you got a man or boyfriend? You hain't a bit ugly."

Her questions were making me uncomfortable, but I needed to give her some sort of answer that would put her mind to rest. I didn't even want her asking questions about me. "I'm still young and ambitious. I've always dreamed about having a husband and children, but not for ten or fifteen years. I want to make a home for myself and settle down before I get married and bring children into this world."

"Your juices will be dried up in fifteen years," she informed me. "Besides, what man wants to marry an old woman? Only a widower with a house full of hungry young'uns. A man who can't get a young girl who's fool enough to marry up with him."

"Are you suggesting I best rush out and find me someone to marry before my juices dry up?" I asked half in humor and half in irritation.

"You got that right. You're not enough like me to live on this mountain all alone for long. Winter always wipes out everything that's weak."

"You think I'm weak?" I asked with surprise, and perhaps a touch of resentment.

"I think you're mighty determined, but winters are far more brutal than you realize. Being shut in and cold to the bone tears down a body's willpower."

"Are you talking from experience?"

"You better believe it. I've been miserable most all my life, but I'm used to it. You han't suffered much."

"What brought this on? I thought you were happy living here. Thought you were happy that I'm here."

"Oh, I am. I'm mighty happy about both. Don't want you to wake up one morning and declare you've had enough. Don't want you to sell out to some developer who'll cut down the trees and dynamite all the rocks into a pile."

"Are you thinking about your daughter?" I asked.

"Reckon I am. I'm thinking about you too. If you had the right kind of husband, you'd be more likely to stay here."

I wasn't going to question what kind of man she thought was the right kind. I didn't tell her I thought her reasoning was flawed. Few men I had ever known would want to live on this kind of hard-rock mountain with a woman who could never use her own name.

"Don't worry. I plan on living on this mountain for the rest of my life."

She nodded her head as though she was in deep thought.

"I seen that sin eater sneaking about last night after the gloaming set in. I figured he come to see if I was dead yet."

So that was it. She was afraid of dying considering this so-called sin eater was around.

"Where did you see him at?"

"In the woods while I was gathering firewood."

"Did you talk to him?"

"Oh, no. He never says much to me even when he brings me things. Sin eaters don't like for folks to look at 'em, especially at their faces. His hat was pulled down low on his head. His face of hair keeps a body from seeing more than his eyes."

"You sure it was the sin eater you saw?"

"Not exactly," she admitted.

"Then what makes you think it was him?"

"I felt him nearby. I looked up right quick in time to see his shadow as he disappeared behind a laurel hell. If it was a hunter or somebody such as that, he would have showed his self."

I wasn't sure about that. She had no idea how nervous what she said made me. Could it possibly be someone who was searching for me? Had I unwittingly left some kind of trace behind that would be a giveaway that I was still alive? Perhaps I had left traces behind when I went to Brigham's office to retrieve money. I knew I was taking a chance by going there, but it was something I had to do. I needed a lot of money to disappear on. He needed killing.

"Maybe it was the man you've always dreamed about," I said with the intent of joking in order to relieve some of my tension.

"No," she said in earnest. "I've come to accept that the man I dreamed about was my beloved husband in my past life. I think he's been waiting for me to go ahead and pass over so we'll be together again. I'd think he's getting right impatient. You know how things like that go."

In a way that made sense. And yet she was still making me wonder about her mind. Most likely she had started to suffer from some sort of dementia.

"You believe in reincarnation?" she asked me.

"In a way I do, and in another way I'm not so sure," I admitted. It's rather difficult for me to believe there are a lot of souls stashed in one place waiting for a higher power to determine when and if they're supposed to come to live in a human body. And yet something tells me that's exactly what happens."

"I know what you're talkin' about. There're times even I have trouble believing what I believe," she told me.

I wasn't about to ask her to explain, but she did anyway.

"Believing in what you can't see with your own eyes is a hard thing to do, but we do it. Take that sin eater. To tell the truth, I don't believe he's a real sin eater. Not enough people around these parts to die. He'd have starved to death a long time ago if he was for real. The way I figure it, he could be an ordinary man like us. He likes his privacy the same as you and me. Now, I'm not saying he didn't use to be a sin eater."

I cringed at what she might be getting at, but I let her keep on talking without interrupting.

"From what I've seen of him the few times he showed up to help me out, he's a right comely sort of man. Broad in the shoulders and lean in the hips. Appeared strong but not fat. He just might make a good husband to somebody wantin' the same kind of life he wants.

I almost laughed at her obvious insinuation. "Perhaps he's already married," I couldn't resist saying. "Is there a rule that a sin eater can't marry?"

I didn't dare say what I was really thinking. Having a third person on this mountain was causing my instincts to go on alert. The more people who saw me, the more likely I would be identified. I didn't want to go on the run again. I liked the idea of making this rundown place into my forever home.

"Don't know about that," she said. "I hardly think he has a woman. Could be wrong though. I've been wrong a time or two, but not often. I admit I've snuck over the mountain just to see what kind of place he had. Right nice place, but it always looked unlived in. No animals. No garden. Just a log cabin and a few outbuildings. Hate to say it was a better place than my worn-out cabin that was handed down from my folks. Did I ever tell you my George's boys got most everything he owned? I worked my fingers to the bone for 'em and didn't even get a place to live."

I listened to Aunt Polly remembering her past. I could almost see the young girl with hopes of living a good life along with the regrets she had encountered. It scared me to think I would someday become just like her if I lived alone on this mountain, but what other choice did I have? I certainly didn't see living my life with a so-called sin eater in it.

Chapter 30

I stood up on the rock I had been sitting on to get a better view when I saw movement near my relative's old place. Someone was on the roof. It appeared to be a slender, young boy instead of a woman that I'd heard had bought the place. The build and movements weren't that of a grown man. Perhaps she had a son. One thing I didn't want was a family moving in even on this side of the mountain. Such as that was the first step in my beloved mountain being inhibited by outsiders. I took out my binoculars to get a closer look. The boy was climbing down a ladder. I only got a glimpse of a slender back and a head of closely cropped hair before he was out of my sight. I longed to rush closer to the house to get a better look at the occupants, but caution took over.

I thought it best not to take a chance on being seen, although chances were that no one anywhere near this mountain would know I existed. Only fools rushed into a situation they knew nothing about. I would check on the old woman and return for a closer look at who occupied this place after dark set in. That way I could see how many people returned to the house.

I watched Aunt Polly's house for a while. I concluded no one was at home, so I crept closer. I wanted to get a look at the place. It would give me a good idea about how she was doing. When I stayed at my cabin, I would always check on her, especially if it was wintertime. An old woman on this mountain never had easy living, but she did have what few

people had. She was able to live her life without the influence
of others unless her ambitious daughter counted.

Many times, I had provided her with firewood along with
other necessities such as matches to start her fire. Few people
realized the importance of being able to start a fire. She did
have a flint and steel, but it could become almost impossible
to strike a fire in wet weather. Kerosene or lamp oil was
another thing that was difficult for her to obtain. Granted, it
was more of a luxury than a necessity. It certainly was a good
thing to have on a long winter night when the outside world
was dark and ominous. I was well experienced in the need of
that luxury. I had experienced many a night as a child
huddled underneath a pile of quilts during the dark of night
while a raging winter storm roared outside. I promised
myself once I became a grown man, I would always be able
to sleep in a warm and secure bed. Never again did I want to
be afraid of the dark. I had accomplished that to a degree.
Unfortunately, it was after my mother's death.

I remembered promising my mother she would never
lack for anything ever again once I became a man. Much to
my regret, my beloved mother died before I could keep that
promise. There were many questions to the cause of her
death. I thought a broken heart played a huge role. She never
stopped longing for that no account Slaughter who was my
father.

That was water under the bridge and yet it still lingered
in my mind. I acknowledged the fact that part of the reason I
wanted to own the old Slaughter place was because of my
mother. The main reason was I loved this mountain – every
inch of the mountain, was something I couldn't explain.

I realized I hadn't been paying attention to what I should
have after I slipped out of Aunt Polly's cabin and returned to
the woods. I was satisfied with what I saw. Her cabin
contained things she needed to make her life easier. I
wondered if the Bennie Jack woman was responsible for the
improvement.

It was then I realized I had almost come face to face with Aunt Polly. I had seen her moments before she had raised up from where her small, dark form had been hunkered over picking herbs. Thankfully, I was in the shadows and able to slink behind a tangle of a laurel hell before she got a good look at me. I was able to disappear before she moved to where I had stood. I watched from behind one of the huge Poplar trees as she inspected my footprints in the soft mountain soil.

"Show yourself," she demanded. "I hain't dead, but I'll feed you if you're hungry. I han't afeard of no sin eater."

I had to smile at that. I had no idea how she got the idea I was a sin eater, but I wasn't averse to the idea. Being known as such might prove handy someday. I stayed silent as I waited for what she was going to do next. I got the idea that she was somewhat afraid of a sin eater as she hadn't made any attempt to find me. I knew Aunt Polly, and many like her, were steeped in superstitions.

I contemplated the idea of being thought of as a sin eater. There is little I would like more than to eliminate sin even if I was the one to suffer for its elimination. However, I didn't believe any one person could take on the sins of someone else. Back when I was a young boy, I had heard my grandparents talk about sin eaters. Even they didn't believe such a person existed and they were also steeped in superstition and old wives' tales. They believed in visions and signs from God, which I still thought was interesting considering what devout Christians they proclaimed themselves to be. According to my way of thinking, devout Christians would never turn away from a helpless child as my mother's parents had done to me. At least they recognized my existence, which the Slaughters never did.

Rumors of a sin eater might help keep trespassers off the mountain or draw them to it in search of one. An oddball spectacle was always a curiosity. From now on, it might be a good idea not to visit Aunt Polly, but how could I approach her on buying her land if I didn't come face to face with her?

I was pondering on sin eaters along with my childhood as I approached the old Slaughter place. My curiosity as to who lived there was getting the best of me. I didn't like being on the mountain after dark. There was always the chance of coming upon maundering animals during darkness. I had heard the squall of mountain lions several times through the years. I knew that big cats had a wide range they traveled in order to find enough wild game to kill and eat. This mountain consisted of wildlife along with huge rock cliffs on the very top that had caves deep enough to be a perfect place for big cats to bare young. Not to mention black bears along with other wildlife. Most wildlife preferred to stay away from people, but there were always unsuspected encounters.

I sat down on the same rock I was on earlier where I could observe the old Slaughter place. I had no idea why I was drawn to watching that place again as late evening was settling in. I knew it would be better if I went back to my own side of the mountain than to be out after dark. Getting over the rugged, rock formation wasn't an easy job in the light of day.

The image of what appeared to be a young boy wouldn't leave my mind. There was something intriguing about that person and I wanted to know what it was.

I had a good view of the roof, but not the rest of the house. I took a chance on leaving the rock and creeping closer. I had visited that old house while it was vacant, so I knew the layout well. That knowledge, plus using my training skills, should enable me to keep hidden. I wouldn't be as careless as I was with Aunt Polly. Soon, I would change my disguise and pay Aunt Polly a reasonable visit to check with her about selling her land to me. She would also be able to answer my questions about the woman who bought the old Slaughter place. As for now, I had the undeniable urge to get a look at who lived in the house where my rogue father was raised.

I hated the man, and yet I had always been intrigued about him as well as my relatives from his side of the family. Most of all, I longed to know why the man had captivated my mother until the day she died.

Had he still been alive, I would have met him face to face. Unfortunately, or perhaps fortunately, he had died a short time before my mother's death. It had been my feeling of desertion that kept me from confronting either set of my grandparents about their rejection of me. Now that I was a grown man who had come to terms with myself along with my unhappy childhood, I was ready to go back in time in an attempt to recreate knowledge of my father. There was only one person left who might give me insight, and that was Aunt Polly. I would have to present myself to her in my true identity as Colton Slaughter.

I crept closer to the house in time to get a glimpse of the shabbily dressed boy making his way from the barn to the house and closing the door behind him. I heard the sound of one or perhaps two goats bleating in the enclosed barn along with the sound of chickens going to roost in the chicken house. The boy had wisely closed them in the barn for the night the same as Aunt Polly always did. Living on this mountain taught people they needed to take precautions for the care of their animals if they wanted them to survive. Feeling the draw of having animals made me realize I too should get livestock and fowl now that I would being staying permanently on the mountain instead of just visiting my cabin on rare and wonderous occasions.

The necessity of living the rest of my life in hiding had no appeal for me. Yet, I understood the necessity. Fortunately, the Freedom Group created different identities for those who worked for them. With luck I might be able to become my true self again.

I watched the house for another hour, but the boy didn't come outside again. I thought smoke would come out of the chimney from where the mother would be cooking supper,

but there was no sign of smoke or a heat wave rising. I closed
my eyes for a moment as I recalled my own mother building
a fire in a cook stove. I could still smell the wonderful aroma
of cornbread cooking and the sound of mother's voice calling
me in to eat. These were good memories I treasured, but I
would never be able to recreate them. Time moves on and so
do people.

I turned my back to the old house and made my way
toward my own side of the mountain.

Chapter 31

Aunt Polly telling me about seeing someone on the mountain shook me up. I felt a stab of panic before I got myself under control. Hopefully, what she had experienced was an old woman's imagination. The fact she claimed it was a sin eater should have been enough to reassure me that her age had affected her imagination. Her confession about her lover from her past lifetime had solidified she was slipping into dementia. If she told anyone else such things as she had confessed to me, her daughter would have proof enough to put her in an old folk's home, as Aunt Polly called it. Undoubtedly, I would need to watch out for her more than I had anticipated.

At the same time, her talking about the sin eater troubled my mind to no end. If she had actually seen someone, my security could be threatened. I had always heard it was impossible to hide from the government. Was I considered important enough for the government to be concerned about me? I knew I had been declared dead along with the two men in the helicopter. Going down in the ocean left little hope of survival. I was the exception thanks to my training, being in top physical condition along with a lot of luck. I wondered if any part of the helicopter had been discovered. Living on this mountain meant I knew nothing of what was going on in the outside world. Hopefully, it also meant the outside world knew nothing about me.

I sat down at the worn and scared kitchen table and ate leftovers for my evening meal. Like all the other evenings, I did not light a lamp. I had gotten used to the gloaming of late evening settling in. Yet, I was feeling more restless than usual as I peered through the crack in the curtains. I felt as though I was being watched and feared the mountain lion had returned. That was why I had closed up the goats and chickens earlier than usual.

"Paranoid," I whispered out loud in need of hearing another human voice. I grinned at my need to talk out loud to myself. It was something I had never done before. I had been trained silence was the greatest self-protector.

"Reason," I told myself that was what I needed. A reason that would convince Aunt Polly's daughter that I was actually Bennie Jack. I had an uncomfortable feeling that woman was having me investigated.

I had already told Aunt Polly that I was from Killdeer, North Dakota, so I couldn't change that, but I could add to it if need be. I had pulled up all the information I could find on Bennie Jack before I took her name, which was little to nothing. It was only my mother's story that gave me the name. I knew Aunt Polly's daughter would be searching for my background. She would undoubtedly hire an investigator. My consolation was that there were millions of people living in the United States and not all of them could be traced though a background search. Regardless, I had to invent a background for myself that no one could prove or disprove.

A few days later, I heard the sound of Meadow Lark's four-wheel drive rumbling up the rough mountain road. I made a mad rush through the woods to Aunt Polly's place in an effort to arrive before Meadow Lark did. I had reached the edge of the clearing as Meadow Lark got out of her Land Rover. She was alone and not dressed to the nines as usual. She was wearing a pressed pair of pants and a t-shirt.

Aunt Polly was s standing a few feet from the vehicle as Meadow Lark got out. Aunt Polly reached out her arms and took her daughter to her breasts in a hug. The little bent over woman's head barely reach her daughter's armpits.

"I'm mighty glad to see my only daughter," Aunt Polly said. "I hope you have come to visit me in peace and love."

"I have," Meadow Lark said in a sweet, consoling tone of voice. "I don't want to fight with you, Mother. My only concern is for your safety. You're no longer a young woman."

"I've noticed that for myself," Aunt Polly told her with a touch of humor. "So, have you've come to rescue me again, or are you here because you simply love your mother?"

"Finally, you've come to the same conclusion I have by admitting you need rescuing."

Aunt Polly shook her head and her joy at seeing her daughter withered slightly. "Let's go inside and sit down in the cool shade of the house. No need for us to stand outside when the sun is boiling down on our heads."

I watched them go inside and then crept low through the underbrush and weeds until I reached her cabin. I had an idea Aunt Polly knew I would be hiding below a window listening to their conversation.

"What is the real reason you've made this trip?" Aunt Polly asked her daughter after a few minutes of catching up on mother and daughter talk.

"I really do want to make sure you're happy and healthy, Mother. That's one of the reasons why I came to warn you about that woman. That so called Bennie Jack."

"And?" Aunt Polly asked when Meadow Lark hesitated.

"And I can't find anything about her. I even had an expert do a search on her to no avail. He found a Penny Jack who is now living somewhere farther down south, but she didn't turn out to be the same woman who is living here."

"Have you ever searched for me?" Aunt Polly asked.

"I've never needed a search for you. I know all about you."

"Right, and it don't mean a thing when people can't be found on that fancy machine folks are so fond of. Folks have a right to their own privacy, you know."

"Not when they are living on the mountain with my mother they don't. There is something ominous about that woman. If you remember, she tried to kill me."

Aunt Polly chuckled slightly. "Don't be silly. She didn't try to kill you, or you'd be dead. She only did what any mountain woman would do when you were trespassing on her land and trying to break in their house. I can tell you without hesitation that I trust that woman completely. You know good and well that I'm good at judging people, so you can ease your mind. How are my grandbabies? You know – those grandbabies you refuse to bring here for me to see. If I didn't know better, I'd think you are ashamed for your children to know I'm their grandmother."

"Oh, Mother. Don't start that again. I've told you a thousand times I don't want to risk my children's lives traveling on this non-existent road."

"Humph," Aunt Polly grunted. "That's poppycock and we both know it."

"I don't know why I keep trying to tell you anything. It's obvious I'll never be able to talk sense into that hard head of yours."

"I feel the same way about you," she said in her soft old woman voice. "Reckon we'll both have to live with it, won't we? Now, let's settle down and have a nice visit since you've risked your life traveling up this non-existent road. Lord knows how much I've longed seeing my much-loved daughter and grandbabies."

"I also like knowing my mother is safe instead of injured and needing care she won't be able to get."

Aunt Polly ignored her comment. "Tell me about my grandbabies and the newest ones. Did you leave them with that nanny woman? Do you trust her to take proper care of 'em when you're not there? Did you research her on that machine of yours?"

"Yes, Mother. I did a thorough background search on her and got references before I hired her. I love my family and you are a major part of my family. It simply drives me crazy that you're not close enough for me to look after you."

"When I'm not capable of taking care of myself, I'll let you know."

"Oh, Mother," she said in a bewildered tone of voice. "Tell me what you know about this Bennie Jack."

"I know she is a fine young woman. She's a mighty hard worker who wants to live a peaceful life away from the rat race you seem to thrive in."

I heard Meadow Lark let out a disgusted breath.

"Do you always have to put me down? I have as much right to live my life as that so-called Bennie Jack you're unreasonably fond of. I've done good and made something out of my life. Why can' t you respect me for it?"

"I do respect you. We simply don't agree on things."

"That's a fact," Meadow lark huffed. "What would you do, Mother, if our situations were reversed? What if I was living here alone and you were living happily off this mountain?"

Without hesitation Aunt Polly answered. "I'd do the same thing I've done with you wanting to move away. I would respect your wishes and let you do it."

"What if something was wrong with me, and I was unable to take care of myself?"

"There is nothing wrong with either of us. So, drop it my darling girl. Sit down and let's have a nice mother daughter visit. It's not like we see each other every day."

"But . . ."

Aunt Polly quickly interrupted her. "Not another word about me leaving my home or about that little woman who wants to live a peaceful life on this mountain. She has as much right to live her life as you and I do. I see her just about every day, and I can tell you she's a fine person. All she wants is to be left alone the same as I do," Aunt Polly said as though she was getting tired of repeating what she was telling her daughter.

"Is she paying you the way she obligated herself?"

"Are you in need of money?" Aunt Polly asked in return.

"I'm only looking out for you. I don't want you to get taken."

"How many times have you known me to get taken by anybody?"

"Don't try to evade my question by asking one of your own, Mother."

"She is paying me exactly as we agreed."

"What are you doing with the money? You realize it isn't safe to keep it here in this cabin."

Aunt Polly let out a grunt. "You sure are interested in money considering you don't need any. Just so you know, every dime I have goes into a savings account for my grandbabies – those grandbabies I've never got to see. I want it to go toward their education. The good Lord knows I always wanted more book learning. When I die, my lawyer will see what I leave behind will be divided among them."

"Your lawyer? You don't trust me to look after what belongs to you?"

"Hush up about what I'll leave behind, Meadow Lark. I'm starting to think it's you I need to be concerned about instead of Bennie Jack."

"You know better than that," Meadow Lark said in obvious irritation. Almost instantly, she started talking about her children, and that she had brought pictures of them.

For the rest of the visit, they sounded like a mother and daughter sharing everyday talk. I couldn't help wishing I still had parents who loved me as much as Aunt Polly loved her daughter. As I hunkered there, an old pain gripped my chest for the lack of love from parents, a husband, and children I would never have. I have given up my future in trade for trying to aid in the betterment of my country. Worse than that, like our soldiers, I would never so much as get a thank you for it.

I stayed hidden under the window during the time Meadow Lark was there. I had to make sure Meadow Lark hadn't found out anything about me, or about a missing girl by the name of Bennie Jack. Once Aunt Polly walked her daughter to her vehicle, I left my hiding place before Aunt Polly could confront me. I needed to do a lot of soul searching, and then a lot of planning on what I wanted to accomplish with the remainder of my life.

I slunk back into the woods and ran back to my place. I did my best to assure myself that I should be grateful that I was still alive and safe. That should be enough for me, but it wasn't. I didn't want to spend the rest of my life only to return to dust without accomplishing something of importance.

Just as I expected, I had hardly made my way back home before Aunt Polly arrived. It amazed me how fast she could move through the woods. She was faster than I was, and I had spent years in training.

"I knew you was listening," she told me. "I need to teach you how to eavesdrop without mashing down all creation."

"I didn't mean to invade on your privacy," I began to apologize, but she interrupted me.

"I understand why you did it. There's no question in my mind that you're hidin' from something or somebody."

"What makes you think that?"

"It's written all over you, but it's of no concern to me. We all have our reasons for what we do or don't do."

I cringed inwardly at her words.

"Right now, there are a few things I need to find out about. First off, I need you to drive me into town."

"Why?" I certainly didn't want to leave the mountain, but it was the only way I would find out what was going on with our nation's threat to freedom. I realized I was becoming more obsessed with it now that I was rendered useless.

"I need to see Kalvin Warsaw again."

"Who?"

"The lawyer I seen afore."

~~~~

When I first met Aunt Polly, I thought she was a demented witch who was as dumb as a rock, but I learned different. Her mind was as sharp as her tongue could be, except for seeing a sin eater and a longing for a lover who she believed was her husband in a past life. But then, what if what she said was true? Was there some man roaming about the mountain?

"Tell me about the man who lives on the backside of this mountain," I said to her as we bounced down the mountain.

"Don't know much about him," she told me. "He has a fine place that appeared well cared for, but there was nobody there. Nothing to show he had been there in a while."

"How do you know a man lived there if you didn't see him?" I questioned.

"Nothing to show a woman had ever been there abouts. Only man things and such. I got the idea he hain't there often. Things looked right grown up."

"Could he be the man you think is a sin eater?"

"I've thought on that myself. Don't know why it come to mind, but something told me he might be kin to them Slaughters. He couldn't be one of them boys I grew up knowing. They were older than me, but he could be a grandson or maybe even a great grandson."

From what I had learned when I was buying the Slaughter place, there was only one of the slaughter relatives who might want a place on this mountain. It was the one who had been paying taxes on the place for years. The one who didn't get any kind of reimbursement for all his payments.

Her face wrinkled up like she was thinking. "Don't reckon I mentioned to you that my Meadow Lark wanted to buy the place when she got her real estate license. She claims that them rich flat land folks want to build houses with views.

You know good and well there's places on this mountain where you can see all over creation."

She was right about that. Looking down into the deep ravine from the side of the road was proof of the view. It was nothing short of breathtaking. There were places that caused chill bumps to crawl over my flesh.

"There was talk about the youngest Slaughter boy getting a girl in the family way. For some reason, the couple weren't allowed to get married. There was never too much I knowed about the situation. Back then, an unwed mother was a sin and disgrace. They were treated as bad, if not worse, than sin eaters."

Aunt Polly let out a sigh that drew my attention.

"Happened all too often. The woman was the one who paid the price. The man didn't. Folks claimed God made men that away, so they didn't get no blame for what they done to girls."

There was something about the way she said it that sounded personal, but I didn't want to snoop into something she didn't want to tell me about.

"A girl wasn't safe back them. Law was on the man's side. If a man was ever punished, it came from her brothers or her daddy. Knowed a few times when men disappeared, but not too often. Things have changed since I was a girl. Young men don't come to this mountain hunting helpless girls anymore. 'Course you're the only young woman on this mountain now adays."

Finally, the rough road ended, and we were able to ride without being bruised. I hated the road, and yet I was beyond thankful for the difficulty of driving on it.

"Wait here on me," she ordered once we reached the lawyer's office. I grinned at her bossiness. I could understand why her daughter might rebel against her. It also helped with my belief that her daughter would not want her to move back onto the mountain unless she had a powerful reason.

Chapter 32

~~Aunt Polly~~

If I knew my Meadow Lark as well as I thought I did, there was a reason why she was putting pressure on me in order to get control over my land. There was also a reason why she was trying to find out things about Bennie Jack. My girl was smart enough to know it wasn't normal for a young, attractive woman to bury herself on a rugged, almost inhabited mountain without a mighty good reason. My guess was that my Meadow Lark was still hoping to get her hands on both tracks of land dirt cheap.

I was thankful Bennie Jack wasn't demanding an explanation for taking me to see the lawyer. She was good about minding her own business. She was a good companion for an old woman like me. The first thing I did when I saw her was look at her hands. They were hands of a woman that were no longer soft and well cared for, although they might have been at one time. Now, her hands were calloused and almost as roughed up as mine.

Kalvin Warsaw didn't seem pleased to see me, but I knew he always would.

"What can I do for you today, Aunt Polly?" he asked as pleasantly as he could manage.

"I want you to run a financial check on my Meadow Lark."

"Am I allowed to ask why?"

"I need to know if she has money problems."

"What makes you think she might have?" he asked.

"She's visiting me much too often for there not to be a reason."

"Maybe it's because she loves her mother."

I looked him right in the eyes. "You of all people should know better than that."

He let out a long breath of air. "Okay. I'll run a financial check on her. I suppose you want an answer in the next two minutes," he said with a hint of insult.

"There's no such thing as later when you're my age," was my answer for him.

He nodded and let out another breath of air, picked up the phone and started dialing. I had to admit he seemed to know what he was doing along with who to call for information. Less than ten minutes later I heard another one of those fancy machines crank up. Thirty seconds and it spit out several sheets of paper. He retrieved them and handed them to me.

"This is your daughter's private financial records."

I took the papers in my hands. It would take me a long time to go over all those numbers and gobbly-gook. "Tell me what it says." I handed the papers back. He was silent as he studied them. Finally, he spoke.

"It says your daughter made a bad investment and is having trouble recovering from it. The bank is putting her in a squeeze."

"How much money does she need to get her out of that squeeze?"

He told me what I wanted to know. It was an unheard-of amount to me. "How much is my land worth?"

"I'll check and give you a rough estimate," he said as he typed more information into his machine.

I waited patiently for him to come up with something. When he finally did, I nearly fell out of my chair. I'd never seen that much money in my entire life, much less have that much. I was stunned to say the least.

"I see why my Meadow Lark wants it."

"Right, but you already have a legal document giving it to someone else after your death."

It hit me then. The reason my girl was trying to prove the woman, Bennie Jack didn't exist, or at the least, keep her from making payments on the land so it could revert back to me and then her.

"Hold on a minute. I'll be right back," I told him. He nodded but didn't look happy about it.

I went to the truck where Bennie Jack waited. I stuck my head in the passenger window. "Are you rich?" I asked.

"I've got money if that's what you're asking."

I told her the amount I needed. "Have you got that much money?"

"I do," she said without looking shocked.

"I'll give you an IOU for that much with my land to back it up in case I can't pay it back," I told her.

"Is that the amount you daughter needs?" she asked.

I nodded. She was silent for a minute while deep in thought. She then amazed me when she unfastened those too big, bulky britches she always wore to expose a type of cloth purse laying against her belly. I know good and well my mouth was hanging open as she counted out the amount of money my Meadow Lark needed in hundred-dollar bills. She counted it a second time, and then handed me the huge bundle of money.

I felt a bit weak-kneed as I stuck the bulk in my own britches pocket. "I'll bring you the IOU written by the lawyer when I come back."

"Okay," she said seemingly unconcerned about the money. It appeared she had almost the same amount of money left in the purse-like sack. I couldn't help wondering what kind of woman this was who would hand over money the way she did. She had no guarantee I would live up to my word. She obviously didn't know she would get my land when I died regardless if she got repaid the money or not.

"What the hell?" Kalvin Warsaw said when I slapped the cash on his desk. "Where did you get that much money?"

"Never you mind where it came from. I have it is all you need to know. Now, I want you to take me to that bank down the street and trade this cash money for one of them money orders in that amount made out to my Meadow Lark from me. Make sure you add a message saying that's all there is and all there will ever be."

He put the cash money in the inside pockets of his suit jacket and walked with me from the office and down the street to the bank. He did exactly as I asked. Got an envelope and a stamp from the bank and put the cashier's check in it along with a handwritten message signed by him.

"Anything else?" he asked with a touch of bewilderment.

"One more thing while we're here. Write me out a legal IOU to Bennie Jack for the same amount of money. Add that she's to get my land when I die if I don't pay her the money back."

Kalvin Warsaw's eyes brightened, and he gave a slight shake to his head. "You're some kind of smart old bird," he said. "One of the women here can notarize your IOU. I admit I'm glad your girl will get her inheritance."

"Don't reckon she'll get all the inheritance her birthright deserves," I told him. He downed his head and didn't comment further. He and I both knowed it was his uncle who'd done me wrong that night.

I put the envelope in the postal box and returned to the truck. I handed Bennie Jack the notarized IOU that had been witnessed by the lawyer and another woman at the bank.

"Here you go. It's legal and binding," I told her.

"I trust you," she said. "Might as well stock up on supplies since we're already off the mountain."

Chapter 33

~~A. J.~~

I'd been through the grueling, disciplined life of being in the armed service. I'd been told when I could go to bed, when I could wake up, when I could eat, and what I could do. I had gone into private security in order to protect the lives of people I didn't respect. I had also joined the Freedom Group for a similar reason.

Now, it was time I lived for myself.

I had gone over my outbuildings to make sure they were still secure enough to house animals. I didn't want goats, but I would like to have my own chickens along with a milk cow. I wasn't the best of cooks, but I was able to survive as long as I had a garden along with eggs and milk. It wasn't like I could drive off the mountain on a regular basis without folks asking questions about me. It wouldn't take long until someone commented – say you look like them Slaughters. You're kin to them hain't you?

What would be so bad about that? I was kin to them – for better or worse. I was a Slaughter.

Chickens would be no problem, but fitting a milk cow in my old SUV might prove a problem. The answer to that was to build myself a small trailer that was sturdy enough to hold a cow. Fortunately, I knew where a junk yard was located not far from the mountain. I was hopeful I could find wheels, tires, and a frame I could weld together to suffice. If not, I would have to start out with a calf.

I was finding that setting myself up to be totally self-sufficient wasn't as easy as I hoped it would be. I always felt secure in traveling wherever I wanted and buying whatever I needed. If I bought a trailer at a hardware store there would be legal paperwork, I would need to get a tag to put on it. If I made a trailer and traveled without a tag, I could get stopped by a patrolman, which was something I never wanted. If I bought a cow from a farmer and had it delivered, someone would know where I lived.

Okay.

What would an intelligent man do?

Simple. I would have to buy a young heifer small enough to fit in my SUV. I built a rack between the back of the SUV and the front seat. No doubt there would be a lot of cleaning up to do after I hauled a calf, but so be it. I'd cleaned up manure before – of many different kinds.

I headed off the mountain to do exactly that. There were a lot of farms off the mountain in the flat lands, but first, I needed to purchase a supply of feed for the animals I intended to get until I was able to grow my own. It would be too inconvenient to stop at a feed store once the back of my SUV was full of chickens and a heifer calf.

I had put on one of my country man disguises, which consisted of a light beard stubble, bibbed overalls, sweaty, wide brimmed hat and headed into town. When I drove down the street going slow so as not to draw attention, I was surprised to see Aunt Polly stick an envelope into a postal box. I wasn't sure it was her at first, but surely there wasn't another person alive who looked like Aunt Polly.

I found a place to turn around to drive back to make sure my eyes hadn't fooled me. Minutes later, I saw her getting into a beat-up truck and drove by the truck to make sure it really was Aunt Polly as well as who drove her all the way off the mountain into town. I knew her daughter would rather take a whipping than be caught driving such a junkheap of a truck.

My breath caught at what I saw as I drove past the vehicle. It was Aunt Polly alright, but surely my eyes were deceiving me. The person sitting behind the wheel was a young male image of a grungy Fizz. The hair was a buzz cut and the face darker colored than the lovely young woman I had trained, but still yet the resemblance was shocking. I had done extensive research on her before I hired her. There were no siblings, no relatives whatsoever that could be found closer than fifth cousins scattered about. Of course, it was possible that her father could have beget an illegitimate son from someone other than Fizz's mother.

I pulled into another street and made a U-turn. I wanted to get a better look at the driver of the truck and intended to park beside it. I heard the truck start up with the purr of a well-tuned engine. The truck was obviously in better condition than the outside body indicated. It headed down the street, and I followed behind. The truck pulled into the same feed and seed store that I was headed to. I parked close, but not close enough to be obvious. The SUV's windows were tinted making it more difficult to see inside. It was one of the reasons I bought the old SUV to begin with. Tinted windows made it more difficult for curious eyes to see inside.

Aunt Polly hopped out like a rheumatic chicken, while the young boy hesitated. I saw him turning his head as he surveyed the surrounding area. His eyes spotted my SUV right off, but the tinted windows keep prying eyes from getting a good look at me.

"Come on," Aunt Polly called out. "We hain't got all day to fool around. Don't like being away from home too long at a time."

The boy got out of the truck, closed and locked the door, which was a give-away that he was from someplace other than here. I was yet to know of a local who locked their vehicle, especially when it was a beat-up old farm truck.

I took an even closer look when I saw the boy walk a few feet. It wasn't the stride of a boy. It was the stride of a woman I had watched walk many times over. I told myself I could be fooled, but I knew I wasn't. There was no question in my mind that I was looking at Fizz. This was the same woman I had spent an exorbitant amount of time training. I knew her. Knew every movement of every muscle in her body.

Had the Freedom Group pulled the same type of disappearing act for her as they had pulled for me? That was surely the answer considering she and I both were still alive. My question now was how had we managed to be living on the same mountain range. I knew for a fact that the Freedom Group never told anyone where or how to disappear. They definitely didn't want to know. Once a member was declared dead, they were exactly that.

What was now confusing me was that I had personally seen Fizz get on the helicopter and fly away. Had she been parachuted into the mountains somewhere before the helicopter had headed over the ocean? If so, what about the pilot and the other man? Could they also be alive? And the helicopter. Did it actually go down in the ocean?

Those questions led me to wonder again about the break-in at Brigham's building. The building's electric supply had been shut off for three minutes along with all the security devices. I had personally trained Fizz on how to accomplish such a feat. She was a natural.

And then there was the fact that a large amount of unmarked money had disappeared from Brigham's vault. I had remained in the Freedom Group long enough to gather that information. One thing was for sure, Fizz needed more money than what little mad money she kept on her to buy the old Slaughter place. I also found out that her bank account had not been accessed.

Then it hit me. I was assuming that my Fizz was Bennie Jack. She could actually be someone else other than Fizz, but I didn't think so. How could I find out for sure? Was I disguised good enough to keep Fizz from recognizing me? Did I dare get out of the truck and go inside? If she really was Fizz, would her knowing who I was be a bad situation? She was one of the most intelligent and capable spies I'd ever trained. Too intelligent if truth be told. She had found out more than I expected and gone in for a kill using Brigham without giving me fair warning.

Of course. she would recognize me as easily as I had recognized her. She had watched my every movement. Mimicked my way of doing things, thought about things. She had even mimicked my way of getting out of difficult situations she had been put in during training. I had even taught her to change her posture along with her way of walking and holding her body as the situation warranted. She could go from being a sultry seductress to a carefree schoolgirl in the blink of an eye. It was obvious she was feeling too secure exiting the truck to put my training of her into effect. Proof I had failed in my training as well as in her remembering what I had drilled into her brain.

I sat in the SUV until I saw them come out of the store about ten minutes later. I had taken off my hat and lowered myself in the seat far enough until only my eyes and the top of my head were above the dashboard. I could hear Aunt Polly rambling on through the window I had lowered a small crack.

"You didn't have to buy me all that feed. I done told you I grow what my animals eat. Besides, I rather not get my animals used to eating that fancy bagged stuff. Don't believe it's altogether good for 'em either. They need to eat rich juicy vegetation instead of lord knows what's in the bought stuff that's been burnt to a crisp," Aunt Polly was saying.

My attention was focused on Fizz. I took in the way her shoulders shrugged along with the way her body was moving as she pushed a heavy cart filled with feed. I watched as she stopped and hefted the fifty pounds sacks of feed into the back of the truck as though it weighed nothing, but then she had always been strong for her size. Her body was close to being as rock hard as any man I had trained. She was always trying to do a little better in everything. I had to admire her determination. That was why her going to Brigham had puzzled me. Why would she do a stupid thing such as that?

Aunt Polly got into the truck as Fizz pushed the cart back to the store. Her steps were now long and wide like a boy would take. Even her body swayed back and forth the way a cocky youth might do. She had obviously taken note of the SUV still parked near her truck. I also thought she had noticed the slightly open window without ever looking directly at the vehicle. Her training had finally kicked in, but it was too late for her to fool anyone as familiar with her as I was.

I didn't get out of the SUV after she drove off. Instead, I sunk down further in the seat. Sure enough, a few minutes later I heard the sound of the smooth-running engine in her truck. She had doubled back to see if I had driven away. If I had, she would know I was watching her. Since I hadn't, hopefully she would think I was a customer who had come to get feed the same as her.

She drove her truck close to my SUV. I knew she was trying to look inside, but I'd made sure my entire body was below eye level. I listened to her circle the parking lot before she drove away. I waited a while longer before I got out and went into the store.

I got my purchases on a cart and made my way to checkout. "Say, do you by chance know who those two were who just left?" I asked the grizzled old man who ran the cash register.

"Know of the old woman. Seen her around a time or two. Folks call her Aunt Polly. Lives a goods ways from here."

"Who was with her?"

"Don't know nothing about the kid who was with her. Never see 'em afore. I tell you one thing for sure and certain, it's a shame now adays that you can't hardly tell a boy from a girl. Didn't have peach fuzz on the chin or any kind of protrusion on the chest that I could see. Might have been one of them mixed up kind. Good Lord only knows what's to come of this world. Hain't like it used to be, I tell you."

Soon I would make another trip over the mountain to make sure Bennie Jack really was Fizz and not her doppelganger – which I didn't believe.

Chapter 34

~~Bennie Jack~~

I was trained to be aware of my surroundings and instinctively did it all the time. While Aunt Polly was in the lawyer's office, my surroundings were of great interest. My trainer always claimed one of the most important assets was to be aware of the environment around you. It was imperative to know what was happening. You never knew when you would need to use your surroundings to your benefit.

An old SUV drove by and suddenly slowed down after it passed my truck. According to the unkept looks of the vehicle, it should have a rough running engine, blowing blue smoke along with a loud muffler, but it didn't. The engine was running smoothly. The exhaust was almost silent. The difference in the appearance and the running of the engine wasn't enough to draw attention unless you were trained to detect such things. When what appeared to be a junker had an engine running to perfection, question why the contradiction?

Watch out for things that trigger your instincts, my trainer had drilled into me. There are usually reasons why things don't fit together. Reasons that pay to ask questions.

The driver of the SUV was dressed like a farmer with a rugged, unshaved look and a tanned face. Although I only got a glancing view of him through the windshield, something didn't look right about the man's appearance. At the same time, there was also something about him that looked familiar. I became extra suspicious when he turned the SUV around and drove by a second time. The man parked not too far from where I was parked but didn't get out. All my self-preservation instincts kicked in. Something was suspicious about his interest in me. Granted this was a small town, but no one in this small town should be observing me. A lot of men might be interested in gawking at pretty women, but not a grungy boy with buzz cut hair and baggy clothes.

"Here you go. It's legal and binding," Aunt Polly said as she opened the passenger door and climbed into the seat and handed me her IOU.

I had been watching the SUV so close that I had only been vaguely aware of Aunt Polly coming out of the attorney's office. I took the IOU, although I didn't think a woman who had no means of support would ever be able to pay me back, but that was okay. I had given her some of the money I'd taken from Brigham's office. I'd rather it go to her than where it would have gone if I hadn't taken it. I knew the bills were unmarked and wouldn't be traced back to her or me.

"You've both rich and crazy," she didn't hesitate telling me.

"Think so? I've always paid for what I want, and I want your land to belong to me after you gain your heavenly wings," I admitted.

"You didn't loan me nearly what my land was worth. When Kalvin Warsaw told me its value, every hair on my head raised up. Used to be that such a gathering of rocks and laurel hells weren't worth paying taxes on. Seems things changed without me knowing it. That's what happens when a body holes up on the mountain."

I didn't remind her that her daughter was a real estate agent who knew down to the penny what her land was worth. That was why she was trying to discredit me.

"Do you know the farmer in that SUV?" I asked her after I started the truck and drove as close as possible to pass by it.

"No. Never seen the man or the vehicle. Must be a stranger. 'Course I don't get around hardly anymore. Don't know everybody living here now adays the way I once did."

After several minutes of silence, she said: "You know what? Something about the glance I got of him reminded me of a Slaughter. Hain't seen one of them boys around here in years. Got a notion to go back and walk right up and ask him but reckon I won't since we're in a hurry."

She had no idea how her words relieved me. There should be no way a Slaughter would be interested in me. How could he know I was the one who bought his relative's property by simply driving past my truck? Then it occurred to me that he would recognize Aunt Polly. I just might be paranoid for no reason.

When I first got out of the truck at the feed store, I wasn't too concerned at seeing the SUV pull in and park rather near me. I expected a farmer would need feed and other supplies the same as Aunt Polly and I did. It was when he didn't get out of the vehicle and come inside the store that triggered my attention all over again. That's why I kept an eye on the SUV as we gathered our supplies.

I noted he had parked the vehicle in a spot where I couldn't get a good look through the windshield because of the shadows. I suspected it was intentional. The other windows were tinted enough until all I could see was a dark outline of the occupant. My training told me that him being there wasn't likely a coincidence. "Take nothing for granted," my trainer had warned.

Interesting. Too interesting.

When we returned to my truck, I didn't see the outline of the man in the SUV, although I didn't think he had gotten out, although I had been watching. I didn't say a word to Aunt Polly about my suspicions as we loaded the feed, and I returned the cart back to the store. I did make sure I moved like a cocky boy would, but I feared I'd already been careless.

Aunt Polly rattled on as we drove back up the mountain even though the potholes I hit jarred her words.

"You're too quiet," she said. "You worried I won't pay your back that money or that I will?"

"I'm not worried about either," I assured her.

What I was worried about was the man in the SUV. I had even driven back through the store's parking lot, telling Aunt Polly I was making sure I hadn't dropped my list of what I needed in the parking lot. As soon as I passed the truck, I conveniently found the list on the floor where I had intentionally dropped it. We left to go to another store to stock up on groceries. I was shaken to the core as I kept a look-out for the truck following me, but never saw it again.

There was no doubt I had been spotted for a reason – one that chilled me to the bone.

The short hairs on my entire body were standing up, a sure warning that something was off. My worst fear was that Brigham's hatchet men had found me. If not him, then the Freedom Group found out I was alive. I should have known I would be found regardless of where I tried to hide. Should have known my death had been planned, otherwise the helicopter wouldn't have been waiting on top of the building for me.

What was I going to do now?

I should have realized there would be no way I could remain dead much less hide out anywhere while living the rest of my life in seclusion regardless of how much I had planned and hoped. The government had ways of locating everyone. The traitors and their supporters were always vicious about those who tried to expose them.

What I had discovered in the information I had given Brigham, along with my trainer, was proof about the men who were funding the unrest and riots along with dishonest officials who held high positions in the government. As the old saying goes, follow the money and you'll see who is instigating the crimes. I followed the money, and I had answers. What I didn't know the answer to was why the Freedom Group or anyone else was not taking action to wipe these traitors out? My trainer had once told me that the Freedom Group wanted to do things according to the law. Ask me, fire needed to be fought with fire. Good didn't always win over evil. It seldom did. Every decent person needed to step up to do what needed doing, if only it was one person at a time.

Why these evil men were allowed to remain alive, I didn't know. Appeared to me if men such as Osama Bin Laden could be taken out, so could these traitors. They were the ones destroying our country. They were the enemies and war should be declared on them the same as it could be declared on countries.

Why the Freedom Group wasn't doing its job was a mystery. Why hadn't our trainers instructed each one of us to take out at least one of these traitors? In my opinion, nothing short of that would stop the destruction of the freedom American citizens had enjoyed. Why had I not at least taken out Bingham after I survived the dip in the ocean? Even if I had lost my own life with or without accomplishing my missive, my life was worth little compared to the loss of freedom.

As for paying for my sins in the hereafter, I already had the lives of two men on my conscious. One, and hopefully more, would make little difference. I knew of one horrible man at the top of my list, G.T. Sanger. He had funded more criminal organizations than most people could ever imagine. He had sworn for years that he would take down America before he died. He now had one foot dangling over the edge of hell and the other foot was slipping. He bragged that his son would take over after his demise. The way things were now, G.T. Sanger might stay alive long enough to succeed. He did have the help of many foreign countries along with a horde of money-hungry scum willing to sell out their country in return for money and power.

I realized I also had also taken money that didn't legally belong to me. I justified it for two reasons. Part of it compensated for my lifetime savings Brigham would end up getting from my bank account along with what worldly goods I possessed. The second part was Brigham would get what he deserved by it going missing. I didn't know if either of the two had happened.

I dropped Aunt Polly off at her place along with what supplies I could convince her to take. By the time I got to my place, I was going out of my mind about what was happening, while I was living in contentment on the mountain. I had no right to live happily while ranting on about others not taking down at least one traitor each. What made me the exception to my own rule of thought?

If I was a true American citizen who cared about my country, I would put my training, along with the knowledge I had obtained through sleuthing secret documents, into action. I would willingly give up my life to take out a traitor, and I knew who those traitors were.

The best way to kill a snake was by cutting its head off.

Money supply was the snake's head.

I spent hours walking over the land that I now considered mine. I thought about giving it up. About never being able to walk on the grass, look at the garden I had planted, see my animals eating their feed with relish. I thought about not waking up each morning to feel the cool, misty air on my face, not seeing a morning sunrise, or the setting of the sun. I didn't want to give up what I now had, and certainly didn't want to take someone's life. I wanted to do exactly what most people wanted to do. I wanted to live a happy life without worry or stress.

I wanted the life I now had.

I walked through the woods until I came to a large rock outcropping. I climbed to the top where I could see the roof of the old Slaughter house, my home. The ache inside me was more painful than anything I had ever endured.

"What should I do?" I whispered out loud as though the good Lord might actually give me an answer.

He didn't.

What I did or didn't do was up to me and me alone.

Was my life, my happiness worth more than my country?

Was I more important than our soldiers who risk, and gave up, their lives to take out our enemies? I was a spy. I had already risked my life for my country. Did I stop doing it now that I was thought to be dead? Could I live with myself knowing I was now being self-centered?

I knew how to take out G. T. Sanger. I had spent years learning how to assassinate the enemy in ways that would not be questionable. I had been trained to use disguises in order to appear as someone other than myself. My trainer had gone over the art of disguise, along with the art of appearing innocent while being as guilty as the original sin.

My trainer! The man in the truck. The man who looked familiar and yet . . . It hit me then. The Freedom Group had sent him to make my death a reality. I had gone against their rules when I gave information to Brigham thinking he was the one who would finally take proper action. My trainer had spent an unbelievable amount of time training me. I was considered an extension of him. When I failed, he failed.

The warmth of the sun was fading when I finally climbed down from the rock outcropping and made my way to the house.

Tears were streaming down my cheeks as I went inside, got paper and pin, and wrote out my will in hopes it would be honored. I would leave my will and half of the money with Aunt Polly. I would take the rest of the money with me in case it was needed to accomplish my mission.

I knew I couldn't hesitate. I enjoyed the life I was now living too much to linger. If I waited, thought too long, there was a chance I would become Bennie Jack and forget I was ever Fizz.

The gloaming of evening was settling over the mountains by the time I finished preparations to implement my plan. I walked through the garden I had so lovingly dug, planted, and nurtured. I didn't want to leave it, but Aunt Polly would benefit from it. I then said goodbye to the kid goats I had watched grow and thrive. And the chickens. At least their eggs would help provide needed protein for an old woman.

I went back inside with a sinking feeling along with tears I refused to shed. I put the money along with a note in a box and placed it in the center of the kitchen table. I wasn't concerned about anyone else finding it. There wasn't anyone on this mountain other than the two of us. I wondered if she would miss me. Wonder why I left and didn't return.

I had no doubt my plan would end up with the loss of my life, regardless if I succeeded or failed.

I waited until three o'clock in the morning before I got into my truck and left my new life behind. I chose the time in hopes Aunt Polly would be sound asleep enough not wake up at the sound of the truck traveling down the mountain road. The wind was with me. It was blowing down the mountain instead of up the mountain carrying sound with it.

I had prepared myself the best I could knowing I would never drive that sorry excuse for a road again. Such a realization hurt.

Chapter 35

I couldn't decide what my reaction should be at seeing Fizz. Her transformation had been enough to make me question it being her until I got a better look at her. There was no doubt in my mind after I saw her movements. Afterall, all the time I has spent training her, watching her ever move, analyzing her every thought I knew her. She had been an exceptional trainee, capable, competent, along with one of my favorites.

Admittedly, I grew more attached to her than I had any of my other trainees. There were even times when I had to put my own self-control into full force not to touch her firm, muscled body in the wrong sort of way. After all, I was a man, and she was an extremely attractive woman – the kind of woman who appealed to men - even me. I understood how she would make an exceptional spy, and not only because of that intelligent brain of hers. She had what it took, looks, appeal, innocence, and the ability to think on her feet. The one problem I hadn't been able to train out of her was her challenging inquisitiveness in the best way to handle a situation. She didn't like being told what she could and could not do.

As I had acknowledged before, there was something about her that also made men want to trust her. I decided it was a combination of innocence and sex appeal she didn't appear to realize she possessed. I was glad she wasn't dead but puzzled beyond comprehension how she could still be alive. I had personally witnessed her get on the helicopter. I knew she was flying because of the trace I had put in her insoles. The trace was working perfectly until contact was lost during the assumed time of the wreck in the ocean. Debris of the downed helicopter had been found too far out in the ocean for anyone to be able to swim to shore. Articles of identification from all three occupants had eventually been discovered floating in the water.

Even if a person was well trained in survival, it would be difficult to survive the perils of the ocean long enough to make it to land. Not only the distance was a factor, but it was also an area known for shark activity. It would take a miracle granted by God for her to survive, and yet I was looking at her. It was all I could do not to jump out of my SUV and rush over to her, wrap my arms around her, kiss her, and then shake the shit out of her.

It was only the fact that my own identity would be exposed that stopped me. I would need to conduct my investigation of her in secret. Much to my regret, I wouldn't be able to go to the Freedom Group for information. Any contact with them was terminated once my death certificate was issued – the same as Fizz's was.

What I would do next was entirely up to me. I knew I should let things stand the way they were instead of making contact with Fizz, but I knew I wouldn't do that. We were living on the same mountain, both declared dead, both trying to live an isolated life with a different identity.

Too much coincidence to ignore.

I wanted to know what was going on and why.

I had no need to follow Fizz further. I knew where both she and Aunt Polly lived. I would finish conducting my business before I returned to my side of the mountain.

By the time I got to the mountain the dimness of the gloaming was settling in. The sky had lost all its light, shadows were blue-black, and it was too dark to see how to maneuver safely in the woods. I went about my nighttime preparations. I had decided to postpone getting livestock until I found out more about Fizz.

There was no need to hurry with my surveillance. Fizz, or should I refer to her as Bennie Jack, would be there in the morning. It would not be possible to put my mind at ease until I found out what was going on. Hopefully, she would lead me to the answers I sought without having to expose my identity to her.

During the night I dreamed of Fizz and the fact she had betrayed my training along with the strict rules of the Freedom Group. She was only to follow orders I had given to her, instead she went rogue. Could it be possible that someone ordered her else to give away secret information to Brigham? Could the Freedom Group successfully arrange her disappearance? Was there a reason we were now living on the same mountain?

I had tried to keep my true identity a secret as well as the location of my cabin. Of course, the Freedom Group had many spies and ways of finding out things. I was certain the Freedom Group knew every secret I thought I had, and yet was I important enough for them to keep track of me? As for Fizz, they and I both thought there was nothing about her that wasn't known. She had been an open book with no secrets to uncover – until now. These were only a few of the questions I sought answers to. Answers that I was determined to obtain.

I spent a restless night unable to sleep from thinking about Fizz. By the time morning arrived I was determined to find out what was going on with the two of us as well as the Freedom Group. The best place to start was with Fizz even if it meant divulging my identity. Afterall, we had ended up on this mountain together. What was the chance of it being a coincidence? Had she been instructed to by my grandparents' place for a reason?

I got up early and carefully put on my beardy, ragged, mountain man disguise in order to make my way over the mountain. Again, I had mixed emotions about what I should conclude. Part of me was so angry and disappointed in Fizz that I could actually give her a whipping like she'd never imagined. The other part of me was so relieved that she was alive I wanted to grab her and hold her body so tightly that she would never do something stupid again.

Early morning on the mountain was incredible to behold. The temperature was in the low fifties. Chilly, but not too cold for comfort during a long and enduring climb over rocks and storm-downed trees. A gentle breeze was lifting up from the lowlands bringing the spicy scent of mountain vegetation to me. The leaves of the oaks, maples, and poplar trees were moving slightly in the breeze. Birds flitted about as they busily fed their young. Their soft twitters filling the air around me. Sassy squirrels chattered at me from the treetops for invading their privacy.

I loved this mountain and everything that inhabited it. Had ever since I was a child. Even though my father's people refused to recognize my existence, this mountain hadn't rejected me. I always felt it had opened its gigantic arms and wrapped me in their fold. These mountains and hollers and rivers are the blood running in my veins. I came from them and would return to them as surely as I was now walking the high ridges. I had been determined in my youth as well as now to somehow own every inch of this mountain. To protect her from all who would destroy her. My dream hadn't come true, but I hadn't given up.

As for the Freedom Group, I tried to assure myself the group had reasons for doing whatever they did, but I was no longer as convinced as I once was.

I came to the rock where I watched over the place where my rogue father was born. The place that a woman called Bennie Jack bought out from under me. My kin had rather sell to a stranger for less than I would have paid. They doing such shouldn't, and didn't, surprise me. I understood jealousy. I also understood how members of a pack could turn on one of their outcasts, be it animals or people.

For some reason I couldn't put my finger on, the place I was now looking at seemed sad, deserted even. The woman who called herself Bennie Jack had to be there. I saw her with Aunt Polly late yesterday evening. Could she possibly be at Aunt Polly's place?

I climbed off the rock and headed toward Aunt Polly's. I found her outside feeding her chickens and goats. Aunt Polly's soft voice was talking to them as though they understood every word she was saying. I had an idea they did. Her animals were her family. Her reason for getting up every morning and going to bed each night without falling into loneliness and depression. I hid and watched for a considerable amount of time, although it wasn't necessary. I already knew without question there was no Fizz there.

I turned around and headed back to the Slaughter home place. This time I didn't go to the rock. I stayed behind tree trunks and concealing undergrowth until I had a view of the house and surrounding area. Unlike at Aunt Polly's, there was no smell of coffee perking or food being cooked. Not even a whiff of smoke rising from the chimneys.

I eased my way through the undergrowth until I reached the back of the barn. There were tire tracks showing she kept her truck parked in the hall of the barn. I peeked through a crack in the warped, weathered boards to see the truck wasn't there.

I moved from the back of the barn and took a closer look at the tire tracks. She hadn't parked the truck in the barn when she returned home yesterday. Instead, she had parked it in front of the kitchen door. The place she parked had no dew on the grass, while the tire tracks leading away from the house had grass that was damp and still bent down. Indicating she had driven the truck away sometime during the early morning.

Hair raised up on the back of my neck as realization hit. She had recognized me yesterday the same as I had recognized her. She had left out, ran away again, hid from me. I needed to know more. What she had taken would determine if she planned on returning or not. No longer did I try to stay hidden as I walked straight to the kitchen door and opened the unlocked door and went inside. The plate on the table with a box sitting on it was obvious and out of place. I looked inside the box.

"Shit!" I mumbled out loud. There had to be thousands of dollars along with a sheet of paper. I unfolded the paper and read what she had written. I recognized Fizz's handwriting. "Shit!" I said again. Fizz didn't plan on returning or needing the money she had left behind. Which meant what?

It hit me hard.

I knew what she planned on doing as sure as she was speaking to me. I found paper and a pen and wrote my own note asking Aunt Polly to look after the animals for a few days and signed it, Bennie Jack. I placed the note on the table and took off at a run back to my place taking the box, her money and her note with me. No way could I allow anyone, even Aunt Polly, to see the note along with all the money that was in the box.

Chapter 36

~~Bennie Jack~~

The cool darkness of early morning surrounded me with a peacefulness that felt similar to being wrapped in a blanket. It was the kind of comfort I had been seeking when I moved to the mountain. This wonderful feeling made leaving it ever more difficult knowing I would most likely never return.

It had taken several hours and a great deal of determination to psych myself for what needed to be done. Mind control was the key. Mind over matter was what my trainer installed into my brain over and over again. I was to focus on the job that needed doing and nothing else. As determined as I was, I still couldn't eliminate the hurt of giving up the life I now had. Misgiving at what I planned on doing tried to take over, but I ignored them. How many misgivings did our soldiers have before they gave up their lives? I was no better than any one of them.

This mountain had been like finally receiving rest after running beyond exhaustion. I survived an unforgiving ocean, but I feared I wouldn't survive what I was determined to accomplish this time. There was a chance the security was so tight I wouldn't be able to escape after I fulfilled my plan. The only compensation was assuring myself my life was worth nothing compared to saving the freedom of many.

"There is no greater accomplishment than dying for the betterment of your country," my trainer would tell me often.

And yet there was dread – and anger. I wanted to turn the truck around and live out my own life. Let others do the job that needed doing. They were in the know, capable of doing a job better than I could ever do. I was a dumb woman, a nobody, but others were doing nothing, while I was willing to do everything – anything, including giving up my life, I told myself over and over again.

There was the Freedom Group who had others more competent than I would ever be. Surely, they had someone who could do the job I was determined to do. And yet, none of them had. All they did was train spies to gather information resulting in no action being taken. Realizing such was one of the reasons I went to Brigham. According to the information I had uncovered, Brigham was the go-to guy for the Freedom Group. I intended to skip the middlemen and go straight to him thinking he was the one who would take action. I hadn't expected his action would be to kill me.

I ranted on. Asking myself what was wrong with this so-called Freedom Group? What good was gathering secret intelligence to store away in files without doing a single thing about it?

"Patience is a virtue," my trainer told me over and over. "Every single thing needs to be taken into consideration before it's time to make a move."

And yet it was never the right time, nor would the right time come. In my opinion, it was up to a few renegades, such as me, to take action. I ran several scenarios through my mind as I drove for hours on end without stopping to sleep or even rest. I did have to stop to fill up with gas twice, although the old truck got good gas milage.

Finally, I did stop to do exactly what many had done before me. I bought a wig, a fancy dress, and gobs of makeup. I then drove to Westchester County airport's short-term parking where I could leave my truck for a few days without it becoming suspect. I had no fear of anyone wanting to steal the likes of my truck unless it was a trash collector, but I locked it up just the same.

I carried my large purse from the parking lot to the airport where I fixed myself up with the short, blond pixie cut wig. I wanted to look as lovely as possible before I left the bathroom. I hoped I would appear comparable to the rich, elite, young women who lived in the area.

I checked myself out in the mirror. I looked more like a young Bennie Jack than the tempting seductress known as Fizz, which might be a better image to work with. I made my way to one of the many taxi cabs servicing the airport and chose the oldest cab driver. Older drivers didn't bother to remember, or more accurately didn't care to remember who rode in their cabs.

"Where to, Ma'am?"

"The nearest library, please."

He glanced at me, shrugged, and pulled away from curb. I took his shrug to mean not many people asked to be dropped off at a library. Ten minutes later he parked in front of the library and quoted the amount I owed. I paid the fee and left a reasonable tip. Cab drivers tended to remember those who skimp and those who overpaid. I didn't care if he remembered me or not. It wouldn't matter if anyone happened to ask about me.

I silently made my way to a computer and did a search on obituaries. After a few minutes of searching, I was in luck. I found today's viewing of an elderly woman, Marianna Grosnold, who lived near the ritzy, high-class estate of the target I was going after. I researched everything I could possibly find out about her, distant relatives, her husbands, her parents, her children, grandchildren. I found what I was looking for. The one bastard great grandchild whose birth had come close to disgracing the esteemed family name of Grosnold.

I almost smiled with satisfaction to discover the great granddaughter, Nada Grosnold, was close enough to my age for me to identify as the long-lost great granddaughter who just might show up for a funeral along with the reading of a will. She was the illegitimate daughter of the couple's youngest grandson – another family black sheep. Seemed the

Slaughters weren't the only family with what Aunt Polly referred to as a wood's colts. I'm sure it was more common than most families knew about or were willing to admit.

I wasn't trying for a different alias. I didn't plan on being here long enough to need one. What I was trying for was a reason to be in the elite area in case someone questioned my presence before I accomplished my mission. It wasn't a place where a stranger could blend in without sticking out like a crow in the middle of white doves. "Always be prepared for the unexpected," my trainer drilled into my head.

I left the library and walked a few blocks to a high-class department store where I purchased a navy-blue summer dress with shoes and a large purse to match. I wanted to appear prosperous, but not exceedingly so. I needed a large purse to stash the few things I had been wearing in case I had the need for a quick change of appearance. It was surprising how a change of hair and clothes could make all the difference in how a person appeared.

I got a taxi and arrived at the funeral home in time to get in line for the viewing. Several people were staring at me, while trying to appear otherwise. I scanned the guest list to make sure Nala Grosnold's name hadn't already appeared on the list. It wasn't there. So, I wrote down her name in a backward slant that matched several of the other Grosnolds' signatures on the list.

I heard a muted gasp from an elderly lady behind me after she observed my signature. "Well, I never," she said under her breath.

My first thought was to ignore and to pretend I hadn't heard her, but I couldn't resist having a touch of entertainment from this better-than-thou elite snob. I turned to face her. "I beg your pardon. Did you say something to me?" I said as I looked directly into her cataract faded blue eyes. The translucent skin on her face was drawn tight over skeleton-like bones from the many facelifts she had undergone. Her makeup had been carefully over applied. I judged her age to be around eighty or above.

"You've got the nerve," she whispered. "Showing up at a time like this. Have you no respect for those who mourn?"

"Care to explain that comment?" I said in my normal voice.

"Silence! Have enough decency to leave and not to make a scene by further disgracing Marianna by your presence at her viewing. She was a respectful woman," She quickly turned her back to me and marched away with her overwhelming indignation.

I didn't join in the line to give my condolences to the grieving family. Instead, I took a seat in the very back row of chairs provided for the mourners. I simply wanted to watch the people and have them watch me long enough to establish a false alibi for being in the area in case I should need it.

I gave my presence twenty minutes before I got up and left. I had almost made it out the front door when a hand caught hold of my arm. "Nala Grosnold?" an elderly gentleman slightly bent with snowy white hair said. I turned to look at him and then at his hand still holding my arm. He quickly took his hand away.

"And?" I said a bit testily.

"I'm Marianna's attorney. I see you got my request for your attendance at your great grandmother's viewing as well as the reading of her will."

I must have looked shocked, or at least bemused. "I can't imagine why I should be including at the reading of her will," I added.

"You are one of her beneficiaries."

"You've got to be joking," I said.

"I don't joke at a time like this," he told me in all sincerity. "I noticed how your relatives snubbed you, and I don't want you to rush away and go back home because of them. I have an idea that's exactly what you've got in mind."

He surprised me even further when he handed me an
envelope. "Your great grandmother instructed me to give you
this the moment you arrived."

"What?" I questioned as he forcefully shoved the
envelope in my hand and closed my fingers over it.

"She said you'd quibble. She feared you'd not have funds
to remain here for several days. There needs to be a
reasonable time for her loved ones to mourn her passing
before her will is read. Therefore, I have reserved you a prepaid room at the Abby Inn and Spa. I have also rented a car
for you. Marianna said you would have to take a plane to
arrive here on time, you live over two thousand miles away.
I noticed you arrived in a taxicab," he added as though that
finalized my need for a car.

I was speechless as he pressed a car key and hotel card in
my other hand. I started to object but thought better of it. I
had no intention of staying at the Abby Inn and Spa, but I
could use the transportation along with the convenient alias.

Taxi cabs left a traceable trail.

"Thank you," I said.

"It's the black Acura parked out front."

I nod and walk out the door. I'm caught between bursting
out laughing and freaking out. What just happened wasn't
possible. My life couldn't go from Fizz to Bennie Jack to
Nada Grosnold. Was this an Oman? Were the forces that be
telling me I was doing the right thing and therefore helping
me? Luck. I didn't believe such a thing existed. I did believe
in acting upon the opportunities presented. I also believed in
taking advantage of what presented itself. That was exactly
what I planned on happening if circumstances proved to be
miraculously in my favor.

"Plans seldom go accordingly. Always prepare for the
worst and hope for the best," my trainer drilled into my way
of thinking.

If ending up at this viewing at this time didn't beat all the
unexpected turn of events, I didn't know what did. I had to

pinch myself to make sure I wasn't dreaming. I best put my hind end into action before the real Nada Grosnold showed up. I crossed the parking lot, unlocked the Acura, got into the driver's seat, started the engine and turned on the air conditioner. I laughed as I drove away.

I stopped at the library again and did a search on my target.

This time I did pat myself on the back at the timing of what I pulled up. It was the perfect opportunity for me to blend in. My target's daughter was having a huge garden party for her June birthday, which I thought was odd as well as self-indulgent as she wasn't a young girl who longed for fancy birthday parties. She was what I considered an older woman, appearing overweight along with average in all aspects. Maybe this was her last chance to impress herself as well as others.

Regardless, this was an opportunity to easily infiltrate a highly guarded family. I had no doubt G. T. Sanger had far more security than the POTUS did. Whom, if I succeeded with this target and miraculously survived, would eventually come under my radar. In reality, the POTUS was of little importance other than being a puppet who would collapse once the puppeteers no longer had control of his strings. I could almost have compassion for a puppet with such little value. However, if this puppet no longer existed, the puppeteers would be slightly inconvenienced while finding a new one that was in such an obvious position of power.

The media reported that this birthday party was going to be the biggest event ever held. I spent hours researching everything about the party I could find. Finally, before I closed the computer, I made sure I erased my research.

I knew exactly what I planned on doing. What I didn't know was how opportunity would present itself. "Make your own opportunity," my trainer always told me. "Make sure you also take advantage of what is already there."

His instructions had always proven themselves to be valuable to me. In a way I had almost developed a strong affection toward him. There was no question that my trainer was attractive. He was solid muscles without an ounce of fat on his body. His body was rock-hard from all the physical training he put himself and his students through. I admired that in him. I assured myself it was nothing more than my Stockholm syndrome toward him. I didn't believe in love, but I did believe in sexual attraction. I did my best to ignore that I was drawn to his tall, dark, and handsome appeal. I reminded myself that I didn't, and never would, appeal to him as a woman. I was an instrument – one of many.

My trainer's physical appearance was frivolous and of no importance right now. What was important was how I would infiltrate the daughter's birthday party. I knew how I was going to use poison on my target. I almost smiled. Poisoning was a woman's best weapon. It wasn't messy like using a knife or noisy like using a gun, which both were instantly noticeable when used. Poison could take a few hours to a few days before death and diagnosis, which would give the perpetrator time to escape.

There was no question I wanted to escape after I accomplished my mission. I knew the odds were not in my favor. The security was so intense I would most certainly be caught. I had prepared myself for what would surely happen to me once I was apprehended.

Server. That is what I needed to become – one of the catered servers that was required to be at the party. I was ninety-nine percent sure G.T. Sanger's daughter would choose the most expensive catering service in the area. I didn't have time to get hired by them, nor did I want that. Hiring would leave a trace. My goal was to appear as one of the servers. In order to do so, I need to procure one of the serving staff's uniforms. No problem. Entry and stealing were among my specialties. It was what my trainer taught me to do with proficiency. If I could ferret out top secret information, I should have no problem easily acquiring a server's uniform.

I couldn't afford to wait until the day of the party to procure what I needed. I bought a prepaid, untraceable cell phone and called the caterers and pretended I wanted to hire them for a large wedding. The lady I asked questions of was very informative with information such as how much they charged and how many events they catered each day. The more the better. Two a day, seven days a week were their average. Their price was staggering. I told her I would get back with them and disconnected.

I parked outside the catering building and observed how they operated. They had several catering vans equipped to haul preprepared foods. There were also vans used to haul their help to specific locations. I wanted to know how many female servers they had but was unable to do so from observation alone.

Amazing enough, what I hadn't expected happened. Good luck struck again. A man was carrying dirty uniforms from the building and placing them in the back of a van. I watched as he made three trips carrying the uniforms out and putting them in the back of the van. He closed the back door and drove away.

I followed him to the back door of a dry cleaner and parked directly behind him. When he went inside carrying the first load in his arms, I made my move. I got out of the Acura, walked to the back of the van and took a uniform as though I had a right to do so. I got in the Acura and drove away without anyone paying the least bit of attention to what I had done.

Now for the poison I intended to use. Botulism A toxin. The deadliest poison in the world, or at least close to it, and it only took a small amount to be fatal if not treated. It prevented muscles from functioning. Stopped the heart from beating along with keeping a person from breathing. In other words, the bodily functions shut down. People who get Botox injection don't realize the chance they are taking. A tiny bit too much can have devastating effects. As for where I was going to get it. Simple. Plastic surgeons usually kept a good supply as well as certified nurses. Right, I'm good at breaking and entry. Hope my luck holds on this one also.

The cleaning crew was the key to the plastic surgeon's office. I waited outside the office after closing time. As I had expected, a woman near my age, race and size got out of a van wearing a covid mask. She opened the back door of the van and took out an arm full of cleaning supplies. She carried her supplies to the back door of the office, unlocked the door and put her supplies inside. She left the door open with her keys still in the lock as she went back to the van to get out her vacuum cleaner.

How careless some people were.

She had no idea I took her keys as I entered through the open door as though I belonged there. Earlier, I had stopped at a Goodwill store and purchased a set of scrubs along with clear plastic gloves. The right clothes, a short, auburn wig, and carefully applied makeup disguised my appearance sufficiently. To make my appearance even less recognizable I wore a covid mask. How convenient when most everyone wore those masks, and some people still did. Masks were and had always been an unbelievable aide to wrongdoers who wanted to remain anonymous. The covid scare was a blessing for criminals.

The inside of the building was dimly lit since most all the lights were turned off. The air conditioner was still on keeping the place chilly in order to slow down the transmittal and growth of germs. I picked up a file off a desk, opened it up as though I was checking for some information. I carried the file with me until I spotted the room where the medication was stored. I turned my back to the camera to block my attempt to find the right key to unlock the door. The third key opened the door. The glass cabinet door showed me exactly what I wanted. I looked at the file again in hopes it might confuse anyone observing the film if they discovered the Botox was missing. I lifted the file folder to block the camera view as I swiped the Botox. I made a point of shaking my head as though I didn't see what I was after, closed the cabinet door, and left the room locking the door behind me. I returned the file folder to the desk and went out the door the same way I had entered.

I walked past the cleaning supplies sitting inside the door. The cleaning lady was searching in her pockets along with the sidewalk, shrubbery and surrounding area for her lost keys. She was so interested in finding her lost keys that she paid little attention to me if she saw me at all. I discreetly dropped the keys outside the door.

I had carefully checked out the area in advance to know where cameras were located and where they weren't. I chose a secluded area to slip off the scrubs, wig, and mask. I wore shorts and a tank top under the scrubs making me to look heavier than I actually was. I carefully placed the scrubs, wig, and gloves around my waist under the tank top creating a slight muffin top middle. I worked my way back to the Acura I had parked a distance from the doctor's office, got in and drove away.

Luck was still holding. Was that another sign telling me what I was planning to do was the right thing? Never had I planned on intentionally killing a person. I had to work on my mindset to accept that I would committee such a sin, even when it needed doing. I wondered why God allowed such evil men to exist much less committee their diabolical deeds against humanity. He gives people free will was my answer.

I had free will, but was my mission impossible to accomplish?

Chapter 37

If I could get my hands on Fizz right now, I didn't know what I would do to her. I was furious at her as well as myself for what she was about to do. Not only was I angry, she had cost me my job, along with buying my relatives' land out from under me when I had wanted and waited to buy it for years. She had also wormed her way into Aunt Polly's graces, which was another blow to my plans.

And yet . . .

And yet I felt responsible for her and what she did while under my guidance. The Freedom Group let it be known they considered the trainer responsible for their trainees' behavior. They were correct in doing so. If the trainee did not perform according to expectations, they did not gain their clearance. Fizz passed every test far superior to anyone I had trained before. I expected great accomplishments from her, while she had been the ruination of us both.

The more I thought about Fizz, the more red flags started flying for me. I knew without doubt that Fizz was up to something dangerous that I would not approve of. What she left for Aunt Poly was proof she didn't expect to return or remain alive. For my own sanity, I needed to find out what she was planning.

My first thought was she was running away again, but that didn't make sense. She wouldn't have left money behind she would need to disappear again. My second thought was that she planned to assassinate the POTUS, but he had enough security to make that impossible, which Fizz realized.

I put my mind in gear as to how and what she would be thinking. I had told her often the best way to stop a poisonous snake was to cut its head off. I also instructed her to follow a money trail. Without question, money was the root of all evil regardless if a person had it, didn't have it, or wanted it. I had needlessly told her a man's lust for women was equally as strong as his lust for money. She was good at using that lust to her advantage as a spy, but I didn't think lust for a woman had anything to do with her plan this time.

That left money.

Who was it that had enough money to set entire dens of poisonous snakes loose to destroy our country? Other countries were definitely top of the list, but Fizz wouldn't be able to take on another country even though she might give it a try. Most likely she would go for a man she thought was a traitor. If she succeeded, she would go for another and then another until she no longer succeeded.

There was a chance she might accomplish her goal with one or two targets before she was found out and stopped permanently. So, why should I want to stop her from doing what I had also considered doing many times over?

The answer to that hit me hard right in the gut. I had feelings for that fisty, spitfire that had nothing to do with my job. "You frigging idiot," I said as I added a slew of bad words after admitting such a thing. I wanted to have a good life where I was able to live in peace. But I didn't want to live it alone. I wanted a wife, a partner, a soul mate, a mother for my children. Unfortunately, I realized that I wanted Fizz to become that woman.

Impossible!

But it was what I wanted.

I was admitting it to myself now that I knew she wasn't lost to me forever. But she would be if I didn't find her and stop her in time.

Chapter 38

~~Bennie Jack~~

The impossible.

There was no such thing. Even God said that all things were possible if one had enough faith. I added determination to that faith along with the willingness and capability to carry out what no one else had ever accomplished.

My mission was to get rid of a vile, evil snake who spent his entire life controlling what should be left alone. There was no doubt he had always been an evil force who needed to be eliminated. Could it be a good and powerful God allowed such people to exist for a reason. Could it be he was expecting good people to get rid of evil people? Was that my purpose in life?

And if I failed?

There was no one who would grieve my absence. No parents. No children. No husband. Not even a lover. Face it. I was already dead to everyone other than myself.

~~~~

So far, all was good. Not one of Mariann's Grosnold relatives or her attorney had made any attempt to contact me since her funeral. I needed to finish my goal and disappear before the reading of her will – or before the real Nada Grosnold showed up. So far, my luck was holding, but there was no guarantee it would continue.

"There is no such thing as luck," my trainer had told me repeatedly. "You do your research, your planning, and then you act accordingly. You will either succeed or fail depending on what occurs that you didn't foresee. Not to mention the abilities of the people involved. Never, and I repeat never underestimate their ability."

He was right about that, but I still thought good or bad luck had its own part to play.

I did my research again.

"Go over your plans until they are engraved into your brain. Everything you do should become as instinctive as possible without the need for thought. You won't have time to stop and think." That was also what my trainer grilled into my head. "Always remain smooth, controlled, and confident. Never show nervousness or fear regardless of what happens. Always portray innocence or even naivety."

Easier said than done.

My trainer had managed to track me down. Goes to show I wasn't as wily or as competent as I thought myself to be. Why did my failure in disappearing come as a surprise? I shouldn't have expected otherwise, and yet I did.

He had trained me. Knew my responses only too well. It was like he was able to read my mind.

It was a given the Freedom Group had sent him after me, and he had succeeded after all I had gone through to disappear. I had even molded my way of thinking, my way of doing things from being a city-raised spy to a mountain recluse. I had discovered that a different kind of life was giving me a reason for remaining alive. Maybe even being happy.

There was no way of knowing what kind of punishment would await me from my trainer or the Freedom Group, but I knew it wouldn't be pleasant. The Freedom Group had no choice other than to control their members. It was the only way they could remain undetected and functional. I understood that when I joined and now. I had taken a chance going to Brigham and lost. Doing what I now planned meant I would lose again regardless if I succeeded or failed. I understood the precariousness of my actions, and I was willing to pay the price.

I spent one night in a cheap motel as I meticulously step by step put my plans in order and went over them again and again. If there was anything I had failed to plan for, it was too late to rectify it. It was time, and I was primed for action.

Ready, set, action.

I had on the uniform I knew the servers would be wearing to the birthday party. I had chosen a chick, high school girl kind of wig, put on a pair of fake glasses that I had altered, applied, and reapplied makeup until I looked as young and innocent as my age would allow.

I knew exactly where and when the servers would be loading into the van to be driven to the party in order to ready everything for the most ostentatious party ever thrown. All the food and decorations would be delivered in separate vans that we would unload and put in their designated places.

I had wanted to bring along my trusty companions, which were my pistol and knife, but I knew that would be impossible. If we were not stirp searched, we would surely go through metal detectors with guards watching every move we made. There would be utensils in the vans that could always be used as weapons. Even a China plate could be broken and used to slice into a jugular. A spoon handle could gouge out an eye. A fork to the Adam's apple did wonders in stopping an attacker. There was always instant pain with a swift, direct hit to a man's groin. All were ways to stop an opponent momentarily, but nothing could compare to a bullet through the heart.

I parked in the help's parking lot and walked straight to the van where the servers were gathering and joined the women and two young men who were getting in the van. I feared I might stick out like a sore thumb, but no one paid any attention to me. I was another person in a group of workers. I made a point of going to the back of a full van to sit with the two men servers who came along to lift and tote the heaviest items.

"You're new, aren't you?" one of the men asked as he looked me over.

"Somewhat," I answered. "I've worked one other event."

"Which one," the nosy man asked.

Fortunately, I had read about an event the day before, one neither they nor I had attended.

"Surprised that a newbie would be sent to this job," he said as he looked me over from head to toe.

"I'm not," the other young man was quick to add. "Look at her. She'll be eye candy for the old man if he should show up to his daughter's big event."

"But not so for the birthday queen," the first young man said with a chuckle.

"Don't know about that." They both sniggered like schoolboys at that remark. Adding a little insight to the birthday queen. But she wasn't the one I was concerned with, but she might provide an alternative way I could get to him.

"I'm surprised this party has been allowed," I said in hopes of getting any kind of comment about the father.

"Why is that?"

"I've heard a lot about her dad. He's . . ." I left the sentence unfinished to see what either of the men would say.

"It's unlikely he will be there," the first young man said.

My heart skipped a few beats, although I had considered such a possibility and prepared for several scenarios.

"Why wouldn't a man show up at his daughter's birthday party?" I asked.

"Let's just say he's not a public man. He guards himself as though he was all the gold in Fort Knox."

I had heard similar. "Really?" I played naïve. "I heard he loves attention."

The second guy chuckled but didn't comment.

"Love isn't a word connected with him. Hate would be more correct," said the first man.

"Why's that?" Again, I played naïve.

"There's one thing you need to learn early on," the second man said. "And that is you can never trust an angry rich man."

"Angry? What does he have to be angry about?"

"Some people don't need a reason. They were born angry as well as rich as King Midas."

"Yep," said the first man. "The more you've got, the more you want. Makes you mad when you don't get your own way. Interesting enough, this old skinflint has managed to get almost everything he wanted and yet he's still angry."

An older woman sitting in front of us turned around to give us a cold eye. "And men accuse women of gossiping. You know the rules. We're supposed to do our jobs without gossiping about our clients," she told all three of us as though she was in charge of morals.

Both young men laughed. "Since when?" the first man said.

"Since the minute we got in this van."

"Now, Betty, you know we've all gossiped about the participants of this party since we were hired to cater it," said the girl sitting beside Betty. "They are the elite of the elite and there is curiosity about how they got that way."

"Right," said Betty. "But that was before we put on our uniforms and became professional servers for the Sanger. Now, hush up. We're almost there. Remember we're to keep our mouths shut and do our job while remaining invisible."

That's exactly what I wanted. To do my job while remaining invisible.

The van stopped at a check point and every person in the van was asked to get out. A man searched the men, and a woman searched the women. Both searchers wore thin plastic gloves on hands that moved in a professional way over our bodies. I wouldn't have been surprised if they had asked us to bend over for a cavity search, but it didn't happen. Admittedly, I had momentarily considered inserting a tiny vile of the Botox-A poison into a private area. Considering the deadly toxicity, I chose not to take a chance on such as that. I had to come up with a better way of transporting the poison. One in which would never be expected or found.

There were also drug sniffing dogs that checked us out along with the van. The van driver was ordered to park the van in a nearby lot where he had another device to go over the van, and we were put in a different transportation provided for us. I wondered what security would do when the vans of decoration and food showed up. Would the device and dogs be enough? I had no doubt everything would be gone through if not put in different vehicles. Once we arrived in the huge garden of the main house, we went through another security check that was far superior to security at airports. I felt as though my body was being insulted and wondered if the other servers felt that way also.

All this attempt at security reaffirmed this man was terrified of everyone and everything. He realized how many people wanted him dead enough to go through any means to succeed. I had not expected such extreme security. It made my intent more difficult. It also made me more determined to succeed in my mission.

There was an enormous courtyard that opened up to a staggering view of the grand house's expansive exterior. The party was to be set up in a huge U shape surrounding a pool with sparkling blue water next to another house I took to be a bath house for the pool.

I was stunned at seeing the gardens surrounding the main house. They were spectacular. I had no doubt those gardens contained every kind of tree, shrub, and flowers imaginable. Each section of gardens was far superior to any arboretum I had ever visited. There was an oasis of trees, shrubbery, ponds, fountains, statues, and flowering plants. Not only that, but there were also uniformed guards as thick as maggots on rotting meat scattered in the vegetation, paths, rock walls, pool, and buildings. I wondered if there were always this many security guards or if they were hired for this party. I could not imagine what price tag went along with the birthday queen's party.

Follow the money.

"Staggering," the first male server whispered to me under his breath.

I did not respond as I looked about in awe. "Remain innocent and appear impressed," I could almost hear my trainer whispered those words in my ear.

Minutes later, the vans with the decorations and tents arrived. The men were put to work setting things up for the next four hours while we readied the table decorations and prepared for the food that was staying warm or cold in the specialized vans that were allowed to enter. During this time there were no signs of the family members – only an unknown number of security guards surveying every move we made without lifting a hand to help with anything. They reminded me of all the outrageously uniformed guards surrounding the palace of the queen of England. Silent and watchful. These guards were not outrageously dressed for show. They wore regular dark suits with bulges in their jackets where their pistols were located. Obviously, there were weapons allowed on the premises when they belonged to the guards. I missed mine like I missed a trusted friend.

I had followed the money. Now I had to cut off the head of a snake. My mission might be more difficult than I had expected. During my research I had discovered my target was not only the owner of a huge fortune, but he was also the king of mind games. He could convince people of anything. He could turn your own brain against you before you realized what had happened. There was no question about him being intuitive, cagey and a survivalist who used people in whatever way he chose. He was also good at relieving people as well as countries of their wealth. I also found out he was the kind of man who would kill his own grandmother to benefit himself. He was born into the life of privilege and plenty, but it had never been enough for him. He had a crazed need for more – more money, more control, more power.

He owned many huge plantation-type of mansions, apartments, and town houses. It was claimed he never let anyone know where he would be at any given time. He had an abundance of security surrounding him and his estates twenty-four-seven. There were servants to cater to his every whim, although he never paid them well and treated them like dirt under his feet. He was the kind of man who cheats on his wife, mistress, and girlfriends. In my opinion a cheating man was no man, and this was a cheating man with no scruples, no goodness inside of him whatsoever. The kind of man who had everything and deserved nothing.

I had learned early on that assets were both liquid and nonliquid. Assets could be transferred in ways that would make it nearly impossible to trace. My target most likely had more assets, liquid and otherwise, than anyone could possibly imagine. He also knew how to flaunt his wealth to belittle and defeat any opponent who had enough grit to go against him. He was used to getting what he wanted regardless of what it cost a person or a country. There were always the weak and the strong. Those who were strong and in control became the winners, while those not in control became the losers. My target's talent was making sure everyone other than him became the loser.

I had wagered my bet on him being at his daughter's big blast of a birthday party, but I was no longer so sure. The press had covered the birthday party to the hilt. It was one of the largest to-dos ever held. Did he dare subject himself to such a crowd? Did he dare encounter the flack he would get by not showing up at his daughter's grand birthday party?

"Everyone who is anyone is expected to be here. Including the POTUS and first lady," the first male server bent his head and whispered near my ear as we passed each other in our rush to set things up. "Thus, all the extra security."

Reason told me that part was only speculation. The POTUS and first lady would be warned away from publicly being anywhere near this man and his daughter's party. Although, according to the documentation I had discovered, G.T. Sanger was the POTUS's largest supporter and contributor. A contributor who expected his money to get done whatever he wanted done– and it had.

The POTUS had many puppeteers pulling his strings and G.T. Sanger was a main puppeteer, but only one of many who had strings in their hands. To stop a puppet from dancing the puppeteers needed to be eliminated. When that happened, the puppet would become a worthless pile of rags and broken strings.

As the sun was setting and the temperature became perfect – no doubt as the Sanger had ordered, the guests started arriving dressed to the hilt and sparkling with expensive jewelry on fingers and arms, around necks, and dangling in ears.

"Enough glitz to blind a normal person," the first male server whispered to me as we passed. I was beginning to like this young man. He had a way of seeing things in a way I liked.

I was given a tray containing champaign to distribute among the thirsty guests. I had to resupply the tray dozens of times without being allowed to get close to the house where I would need to go if Sanger didn't show up.

I couldn't count the times hands touched my body in an inappropriate way as I mingled through the crowd. There were many times it took all my control not to sling the tray into the face of several men.

"You're a pretty little thing," a man said as he stopped me to take a flute. "Much too pretty to have such a low-paying job. I can remedy that," he said as I hurried away from him. That was only one of the many insinuating comments that were directed at me.

"Get used to it," another of the tray carrying women said to me as we both got new supplies. "It happens to us all the time. Both the men and women think because we're the workers they have the right to insult or proposition us. They see us as less than them. Kind of like we're their slaves since we're not part of the rich elite."

The longer I endured the insults, the more tempting it was to add Botox to several drinks instead of only Sander's.

It didn't take long for the wine and champaign to take effect on many of the guests, allowing their snobbery to slip a notch or two. Women were beginning to openly flirt with men that were married to other women. Men were talking about their business dealings while eyeing the women with what I thought was a degree of obvious disrespect. No doubt they were speculating on which of the women would be the best, or worst, in bed. Me and the other servers included.

Drunk, is what I thought. Many of these people would be slobbering drunk before the party was over. According to the men I served drinks and hors d'oeuvres to, I decided a woman would have to be drunk out of her mind to tolerate any one of these men. As for the women, they had a worse attitude toward the servers than the men. Cat claws were being whetted on us.

The queen bee was strutting about as though she owned the party, which she did. She made sure she had more sparkle decorating her body than any other woman there. Each and every man made sure they paid special attention to her. Giving her extravagant compliments and admiring smiles as the liquor flowed and the party wore on.

I waited, hoped, prayed even that G.T. Sanger would show up. When he didn't, I started to put one of my alternate plans into action. I knew he had his own brand of rare and expensive imported whisky that he alone indulged in. All I had to do was enter the house, find his private supply and drop the Botox A in. A good plan since I would be long gone before he indulged.

I had done my best to plan a way to get into the house and find his private supplies, but it no longer seemed as simple or as possible as I had hoped. There were security guards at every opening of the mansion, including at the many windows. I was checking out every tree, shrubbery, ever flower on the place that might give me cover as I moved toward the house. I even wondered if I pretended to faint from heat and overwork if I would be taken to the house. Most likely I would be tossed into one of the catering vans to recover or not.

Maybe if his son showed up, I could flirt with him enough for him to take me into the house for whatever reason he imagined. A nice kick to the groin along with the choke hold my trainer had taught me could leave him unconscious long enough for me to dump the Botox A into his father's decanter. I also had to take the security guards into account. They would be watching my every move.

His son didn't show up.

I was thinking of all the alternative plans as the party was hitting its climax with a huge birthday cake, surrounded by expensive gifts, was being lit with six-inch candles. My luck held as the crowd parted, and the big man himself showed up to lead the happy birthday song to his daughter.

I was surprised at how old his stooped body and wrinkled face looked. Bags hung from his eyes and his mouth had sunken in. Even his voice had a tremble to it as he sang. His daughter put her arms around him and gave him an endearing hug as though he was her overly beloved father. He hugged her right back and kissed her on the cheek, but I was close enough to see the expression on his face and the coldness of his eyes. I suspected he detested the party and his daughter and she him.

I was momentarily taken back by their cold, calculating expression. If it was true that the eyes were the reflection of the soul, this man was evil to his core and his daughter was no exception. The father standing beside his daughter was nothing other than the devil incarnate. I instantly wanted to be the one who sent him straight to his own kind of hell. I was willing and anxious to pay whatever price it would take for me to put him there.

Much to my surprise, his eyes met mine an instant before I looked away. A shiver ran over me as I felt his gaze go from my face downward and then back to my face again. I pretended not to notice, but all my training came into focus. I knew exactly what was on this despicable man's mind. I also knew his age would prevent him for succeeding in his male-driven desires toward a young, innocent girl. But his age did not mean he wouldn't be able to get his depraved kind of pleasure in other ways. All in ways a young, innocent girl would never recover from.

Much to my surprise, one of the security guards spoke within inches of my ear. "Mr. Sanger would like for you to be the one to serve him and his daughter their special champaign flutes to toast this monumental occasion."

I turned to him with a look of surprise. "Me?" I questioned with such disbelief the security guard grinned.

"Yes, you," he said in a low voice. "It's a tradition for him to pick one girl to serve him champaign."

I saw the first male server standing behind the security guard. He gave me a discrete lift of his brows as if to say watch it.

"He also requested you to be the one who tastes both flutes of champaign before I take them to him."

"Me? Why?" I asked as innocently as possible, although I knew exactly why. In case they somehow contained something he would not want to ingest, like poison.

"He thinks you are very kissable and wishes for his lips to touch where yours have been," the guard said with the slightest smirk on his face as he looked at my lips.

"Uhh," I stuttered. "Are you serious?"

"I am. Do it right now, while he watches you."

I looked toward him – at the hard, cold eyes observing me. I looked confused as I looked back at the security guard, and nodded hesitantly as though I didn't know exactly how to react, much less take a sip from the flutes. The security guard lifted a flute toward my lips, and I sipped as the rim bumped against my glasses. I gave him an embarrassed look as I took my glasses off to sip the second flute. He lifted the second flute, and I steadied the flute with my hand that held my glasses.

"This one is his," he whispered. "Give it a special lingering kiss."

I did as he said, lingering with my lips on the rim of the flute while Mr. Sanger watched. I squeezed the temple tip of the glasses above the flute a moment before the security guard moved the flute from my mouth.

"Delicious?" he whispered.

I nodded.

"You've been chosen," he whispered close to my ear.

I wasn't sure what he meant by that, but I made sure my face turned beet red as I looked down hoping to appear too embarrassed to look at G.T. Sanger or anyone else. I picked up a napkin and touched my lips in an innocent and provocative way as I made sure I wiped the temple tip of my glasses. As I was about to put the glasses back on, the first young man server bumped into me.

"Act startled and drop your glasses," he whispered and then spoke loudly. "So sorry. I didn't mean to bump you."

I hadn't expected that, but I did jump and drop my glasses, which he stepped on.

"I'm so sorry," he said again as he grabbed a towel from his belt, bent down and picked up the broken glasses wiping the dirt and debris from them. "Can you see clearly without them? Do you have another pair in the van?"

"No," I said in total surprise at what he had done. Could he possibly have known what I had done with the glasses? I gave him a devastated look as I took the broken glasses from him, careful to make sure I kept them in the towel, not wanting to touch the broken earpiece that contained the last drops of the poison.

He pointed to a shaded spot under thick foliage of a tree where several people, as well as a security guard, were standing as they observed the security guard taking the champaign flutes to those being honored.

"So very sorry," he said again. "Stand in the shade while you try to fix them as best you can," his voice was loud enough for several people to hear him.

I gave him a real surprised look, but I moved to the shade of the tree with the towel and broken glasses in my hand. This was something I had not planned on happening. Neither was being asked to sip the champaign, but it was nothing short of an opportunity come true for me. I squinted my eyes as though I was trying to see clearer as I watched G.T. Sanger click his flute to his daughter's flute. He looked toward me as his lips touched where mine had been.

"May we both celebrate many more wonderful birthdays," he said, still looking at me.

A roar of applause and cheers filled the garden as he drank a large portion of the champaign as did his daughter.

"Silence. Quick. Move now," a guard whispered as a hand gripped my wrist. My first reaction was a hammer first to his Adams apple, but reason stopped me from delivering it as he eased me behind the trunk of the tree I was standing under, and then into the thick shrubbery surrounding it. "You're safe," he whispered above the roar of the applauding crowd.

There was no doubt in my mind that both he and the male server had observed the drip of liquid into the champaign, although I didn't know how that could have happened. Clear drops of liquid would have been difficult to detect as it entered the flute. I needed to make my escape instantly. I didn't resist being moved along. Actually, I clutched the jacket of the man moving me. I felt the bulge of the pistol beneath his jacket and readied myself to grab it, but first I needed to get away from the crowd before I made my move. I had no doubt I could incapacitate this man when I chose to do so.

"We have to escape *now*," he whispered, putting emphasis on the word now as he maneuvered through the flora and fauna of the garden and around statues until we came to a tall fence that surrounded the private compound. He pushed on a board, and the bottom of it moved upward.

"Hurry," he whispered again. "Before they see us."

Getting away from there was a good idea regardless of the reason he was assisting me. He pushed me through the opening still holding onto my wrist. The board instantly fell back into place. He pulled me next to a concrete column surrounded by azaleas in bloom.

"I've got her," he said into the lapel of his jacket.

Now was the time for me to take action. Just as I moved, he clasped both my arms with lightning speed and tackled me to the ground with my face in the dirt and arms behind my back with him sitting on my legs. I chose not to resist, at least until I discovered more about the situation.

"Don't move or make a sound. I'm a friend. We've both got to disappear right now, or we never will. You were spotted as a non-employee of the catering company."

That I believed. A few moments later a navy-blue SUV drove up and came to a stop within a foot of the concrete column. The back door opened, and the man dragged me to my feet and then shoved me inside and closed the door while he held onto my wrist. I would give myself two minutes, long enough to get some distance from the compound, before I made my move. I was not nearly as afraid of this man and his driver as I was getting caught by G. T. Sanger's goons.

"Glad you're still alive, Fizz," said the driver.

I stiffened as I recognized the voice. "How did you find me?" I asked.

"Where else would a dead woman be?" he came back with. "I always told you that an idiot always leaves a trail."

"I did not leave a trail," I told him. "Neither am I an idiot."

"You did, and you are for what you just did."

"One down," I said with a touch of pride. "It's more than you did for your country," I shot back at him.

"There would have also been you down if it wasn't for us. You wouldn't have gotten away this time, Fizz."

"Yes, I would. I had a good trainer."

"I can't argue that last part."

"Where are you taking me?"

"Away from here as fast as I can."

"And then?"

"And then we both disappear for good this time."

"Drop me off. I have a few things I need to retrieve."

"Such as pistol, knife, along with a dilapidated truck you left at the airport."

"You always claimed to be the smartest trainer who ever existed."

"Still am. That's why we're both alive."

"Ego," I said.

"Truth," he returned. "Watch out for her. She's not to be trusted," he told the man sitting beside me with a touch of humor. "I have your pistol and knife safely tucked away in your truck."

Less than two miles later, he pulled into a Walmart parking lot and stopped beside my own truck. Not only had he figured out where I left the truck, he had found my extra set of hidden keys and driven it to the Walmart parking lot.

"Hold onto her," he told the man beside me. "Let me get in the truck before you put her in the passenger door."

"What? Don't trust me?" I snapped at him.

"I trust you, Fizz? I trust you to make a run for it. I trust that you're at your wit's end as what will happen to you now.

When someone goes against her training, her oath, she pays the price."

What he said was not encouraging. I knew I had to make a run for it, but my escape would have to be delayed until the time was right. This man, my trainer, was no fool. He had made a point of knowing me inside out. Knew what I thought and how I would react to any situation. Yes, he knew Fizz, but he didn't know the woman who was now Bennie Jack. I knew very little about what he had in mind, but I did know he wouldn't hurt me physically. Neither did I know where he would take me or where I would end up as long as he remained in control.

"Want me to cuff her or zap her with my stun gun?" the man beside me spoke for the first time since he's tossed me in the SUV.

"Does he need to do that?" my former trainer asked.

"No," I told him.

"Are you willing to sit here without trying to escape as we leave this place behind?"

"That I'll agree to."

"I'll hold you to it," he said.

"What about him?" I asked as soon as I was in the truck with my former trainer driving. The other man had driven off in the blue SUV.

"He was my plant at the party."

"And the talkative server?"

"Both of the male servers were my plants."

"The glasses? He stepped on them. Did he know?"

"Probably. Since you were searched and not wearing jewelry, those glasses were the only way you could bring in the poison."

"Will he be singled out and punished for what he did?"

"I doubt it. He's a professional."

"A part of the Freedom Group?"

"No. He is no longer part of the Freedom Group, but he and the others are among those I trained."

"Then who is he?"

"I call him a friend who is willing to help a friend. What would you have done if Sanger had not singled you out of the crowd?"

"I had alternative plans."

"I'm sure you did but would they have failed?"

"I was prepared to do what was necessary not to fail."

"Including losing your own life?" he questioned with raised brows. "The guards were told that you did not work for the catering company.

"So I was told," I said. "And yes, I would risk losing my own life. If our soldiers are willing to die to protect our country, then I can do no less."

He shook his head as though my words bewildered him. "I hate to break the news to you, but I think you should know your grandiose effort was futile."

I gave him a puzzled look. I had seen Sanger drink the poison. His hours were now numbered and in a very painful way unless a doctor figured out what I have given him in time to administer an antidote."

"Fizz, you made yourself into murder for no reason whatsoever."

I started to argue, but he held up a hand for silence and continued talking.

"G. T. Sanger has a limited number of days to live. It was discovered several years ago that he had cancer. He tried to keep it a secret as he surged ahead to put his diabolical plans into action. As you already know, he was one of many who wanted to destroy the American way of life to prove he had the power and wherewithal to do so."

I glared at him. Wanted to call him a liar, but I was stunned into silence.

"Sanger learned as a child how to use fear to control others. As I have told you before, the greatest controlling factor is fear. For years, he knew how to put people in powerful positions who feared him enough to do his bidding.

People who have loved ones who are alive will do most anything to keep them alive. They'll go to any means to protect someone they love."

He was silent for a few minutes.

"Love and money," he said. "Since time began, some people will go to the ends of the earth to obtain and maintain both."

"Not everyone," I boldly told him.

"Everyone," he said.

"Not me," I declared with conviction.

"If that's true, then you have never truly loved," he told me with a touch of sadness in his voice.

"Why did you come after me?" I demanded. "Why didn't you allow me to succeed or fail on my own."

"Simple. I didn't want you to be traced back to the Freedom Group. Brigham and his goons are still out there, Fizz. It's best if they remain believing you were drowned in that ocean along with the other two men. By the way, how did you survive?"

"I had a competent trainer," I was quick to answer.

He nodded. "That you did." After a few moments of thought he added, "You still do."

"You're putting me back into the Freedom Group?" I asked with astonishment.

"No. Neither you nor I will ever be connected with the Freedom Group again. They believed you died in the helicopter crash and that's the way it must stay for your own benefit. Surely you realize you were a traitor to the rules the Freedom Group has in place as well as a traitor by going to Brigham."

"I'm no traitor," I told him angrily. "I found information that Brigham was a double agent who was on our side. I thought he was the man who would take action instead of hording information while doing nothing like the Freedom Group was doing."

"If that is what you believed, then I failed in your training. I trusted your judgement, but you proved me wrong."

My hackles raised at his comment.

"I've told you many times that money is the root of evil. The traitors are funneling more money to Brigham than he got from the Freedom Group."

And I had taken a sizable portion of that money.

"They declared me dead for not being able to train the stupidity out of you," he added. "They were right. You were my Achilles heel. You took me down."

"What?" I questioned feeling both anger and puzzlement.

"What you did with Brigham was a reflection on my competence. They arranged for my death, the same as they did for you."

"They arranged my death? They planned for me to die in the helicopter crash?"

"No. They don't kill their members. According to my sources of information, I recently discovered the driver of the helicopter was a member of the Freedom Group. He was to carry out the arrangement for both his and your disappearance. Is that what happened?"

"He died," I told him. The other man slit his throat," I didn't tell him I was at fault for both men's death. I now had three men's lives to torture my soul.

"I hate to hear that. I was hoping he also escaped. He was a good man even though I wasn't his trainer."

Not nearly as much as I hated it, I thought, but didn't say it out loud. "And your death?"

"My demise was in a car crash. A.J., the best trainer who ever existed if I do say so myself, died a horrible death. From his ashes arose a different man. A man who wants to live the rest of his life in peace and contentment."

"As do I," I assured him. "But somebody has to do something since the Freedom Group is sitting on their hind end doing nothing." Again, I spouted out my anger at their lack of action. In my opinion, every traitor to our country should be wiped out, regardless.

"Doing nothing, humph," he repeated. "You're wrong about that."

"Then why aren't they getting rid of the traitors?"

"Have you ever noticed when you kill a snake another takes its place. For instance, G. T. Sanger will be drawing his last painful breath soon, but he has set up for his son to take over. The son is more vicious than his father if that is possible. In my opinion it would be far better to leave the father alive and in control than to clear the pathway for his son to take over to do whatever he pleases. Imagine what kind of man his son is considering who his father is."

I took his words into consideration, but I didn't agree. The son might very well be more vicious, but he didn't have the experience or the knowledge his father had. Plus knowing his father had been poisoned regardless of all the security just might add to the fear of what might happen to him.

"One traitor less is one traitor less," I told him.

He only looked at me and shook his head in obvious bewilderment.

Chapter 39

Again, I wanted to grab hold of Fizz and shake some sense into her. Why couldn't she understand that patience was a virtue. Patience and proper planning were what accomplished lasting results. She didn't even appreciate what I had done for her. Not only had I risk my own life, but the lives of three good men to get her out of the Sanger's compound.

I had done everything in my power to figure out what Fizz was planning. I had called in help from people who had disappeared the same as I had. They had actually risked their new identity as well as their lives to help the spy I had mistakenly determined had the most capability and determination. I had failed in making her realize she was to follow Freedom Group rules instead of going out on her own reconnaissance. I was as guilty as her. I couldn't let her die for my inability in training her.

"What now?" she asked as though I was the one in the wrong instead of her. What now was exactly right. I had at least expected her to thank me for making sure she escaped the torture she would have gone through once security realized what she had done.

"What did you put in his champaign?" I asked.

"Botulism A," she said. "The party would have been over, and everyone left before he started feeling sick. His doctors would have determined it came from something he ate, but it would have been too late for him."

"Not if he was treated in time," I told her. "His doctors will no doubt think there was botulism in his food. Resulting in the catering company being sued for something that wasn't their fault. A dignified catering company will likely be forced out of business, and it will be your fault. Did you not take that into consideration?"

"I did. Everything they served will be tested with no botulism found."

"Leftovers would be disposed of."

"Not necessarily. Besides, he will be the only one who got sick. If any of the food had botulism in it, everyone who ate it would have the same symptoms."

She did have a point. "What if he gets treatment in time and doesn't die?"

"He's old. His body will be rendered useless as well as that already demented brain of his. Plus, even the doctors will most likely think the cancer you told me about will be the cause of his demise."

Again, she had a point.

"And you, Fizz? How will you live with yourself knowing you killed a man?"

"The same way our soldiers do after they've taken out an enemy."

She was too quick with her answer. If I knew anything about her, I knew she wasn't as heartless and unfeeling as she tried to portray herself. I was sure she would have nightmares about what she had done for the rest of her life.

"What now?" I asked her the same question she asked me. "Do you want to go back to the life you were living before you decided to kill a dying man, or do you want my help in disappearing again?"

"I don't need your help in disappearing," she told me with the arrogance I knew so well.

"You didn't do such a good job of it on your own if I was able to find you and then figure out what you were planning where Sanger was concerned."

"Exactly what do you know about me?"

I looked her in the eyes and said the words "Bennie Jack."

She almost grinned before a serious expression took over.

"You're good," she admitted. "Does anyone else know about me?"

"No. I'm the only one who cared enough to look for you. As your trainer, I thought you might have learned enough from me to survive. I wanted to know for sure if my training had kept you alive."

"And now that you found me what are you going to do next?"

"That is up to you." I said and waited for her answer.

"Exactly what choices do I have?" she demanded as though I was the one who did her wrong.

"Like I just offered, I can help you disappear again, or you can go back to being Bennie Jack until you get bored with that kind of life."

"And if I chose to be Bennie Jack, then what?"

"Then you will be free to live the rest of your life on the mountain or leave it anytime you choose."

"You won't interfere with me again?"

"Not if you give me your word of honor that you will become Bennie Jack and never cross the line to become Fizz, the super spy, ever again. That along with your word you'll never try to kill another person regardless of how much they deserve it. Do you think you can do that?"

"And if I can't?"

"Believe me when I say neither of us wants to go there."

"Are you threatening me?" she said as her temper flared.

"No, I'm not threatening you. If I wanted you harmed, I wouldn't have gone to all the trouble of getting you away from the birthday party. I very likely saved your life. Is that too hard for you to realize?" My answer seemed to calm her down somewhat.

"If I become Bennie Jack, what will you do?"

"My time as your trainer, your protector, will come to an end. I'll disappear and become a different man from the one you associated with. Hopefully, I can become the man I always wanted to be – a man with a wife. a family and a home filled with peacefulness and everlasting love."

A frown creased her brows as she gave me a long and studious look. "I believe you," she finally said. "I give you my word of honor that I will never be Fizz again."

I believed her. "I'll drive your truck to the feed store where you'll be able to travel that potholed excuse of road on your own."

"And you?" she asked again as though she just might care a slight bit about what happened to me. "Are you married? Do you have children?"

I chose not to answer her questions as I said: "Forget about me. I'll be living a good life," I hoped I was telling her the truth.

Chapter 40

~~Bennie Jack~~

Once we committed to an agreement, we never spoke of what had been or was to be again. We sat in our own silence as we traveled. The man who was once my trainer only stopped to fill up the truck with gas as he drove toward my mountain. Never once did he stop to rest, and neither did I rest, although I could have closed my eyes while he drove. My mind was going over everything that had happened since the moment he had found me. My big question was had he really saved my life, or would I have been able to escape on my own? I didn't even know if my target had drunk enough of the poison to take him out or if I had actually been spotted as a plant.

My bet was on my own ability, but because of A.J. I would never know for sure.

I did question why he had gone to such great lengths to make sure I was safe. He claimed it was to make sure Brigham and the Freedom Group still believed that I was dead. Something told me it had to be more than that. After taking time to rationalizing his action, I decided he wanted to save face with those who once knew and trusted him – especially the Freedom Group.

Another question that kept me from closing my eyes and resting was if I would be able to make myself become Bennie Jack instead of Fizz. Although I was satisfied now, would I be satisfied enough to live the rest of my life on the mountain? Alone. In seclusion. I had Aunt Polly now, but considering her age, I wouldn't always have her. Once she passed on, I would be alone.

And that reminded me of the box I had left on the table with my note and money in it. I was sure she had found the box along with its contents. What excuse would I give her when I returned? Did I ask for the money back? Would she return it willingly? Did it matter?

Finally, it hit me. "How did you know what I planned on doing?" I asked. He had told me earlier that he knew the way I thought and what I would do, but that wasn't enough of an explanation to satisfy me.

"I wanted to find out more about you and how you were surviving. The only way I could find out was to pay you a visit. I arrived at your house and discovered you were no longer there. I found the box you left on the table. I have the box, your note and your money. I left a different note asking the old woman to look after your animals until you returned."

"You trespassed on my property?" Yet, I was both relieved that I didn't have to explain the note or the money to Aunt Polly. I was also angered that he had trespassed into my private space.

"And if I hadn't returned?" I couldn't keep the sharpness from my voice.

"I would have arranged for the old woman to find your box."

"Do you plan on trespassing on my privacy again?"

"I believe our parting should be our final contact with each other as long as you don't go off your rocker again."

"Off my rocker?" I couldn't keep my anger at his words hidden.

"Exactly. Surely, I trained you good enough to realize you aren't qualified to take matters into your own hands. The Freedom Group knows what needs to be done and when it needs to be done far better than you."

"Knowing and doing are two different things," I told him. "At least I was willing to cut the head off one snake."

"Cutting the head off one snake makes little difference. They have plans to eliminate all the snakes."

"Then what don't they do it before it's too late."

"Timing. By taking action too soon, many of them would be able to escape."

"Taking no action allows them to thrive," I told him.

He shook his head as though reasoning with me was a lost cause.

We traveled the rest of the way in silence.

The morning was new and fresh with shades of gray, orange, and delicate pink rising over the mountain when he stopped my truck in front of the feed store. I saw the beat-up SUV parked in the far corner of the parking lot.

"Have a good life," he said as he opened the door and got out.

"You too," I told him as he closed the door. I slid across the seat, put my truck in gear and drove away. I couldn't resist looking in the rearview mirror. The SUV was disappearing in the direction we had come in. I wondered where he was going and who he would become.

As I drove the rough road, a sadness came over me. It was similar to the feeling of loss I had after my parents died.

Someone I had depended on would never be there for me again.

Nothing had ever looked so good as the old Slaughter place when it came into view. I stopped in the yard. The chickens, the goats were waiting for me right where I had left them. The last few days had felt more like I'd spent a lifetime away from home. All I wanted to do was walk through my garden and make sure my animals were okay. After that, I wanted to go to bed and sleep while my ragged and hyper nerves settled down.

"Where in this world have you been?" came an accusing voice as I stood near the goat lot. "I've been worried sick about you."

I turned to see a worried and yet relieved looking Aunt Polly. Of course, she had heard the sound of my truck climbing up the mountain.

"There were a few things I had to take care of off the mountain," I told her.

"Why didn't you let me know?" she demanded. "All you wrote on that paper was for me to look after things until you returned."

"I'd left a few things undone that required my immediate attention," I told her.

"Must have been right difficult to see to them if it kept you away from home this long."

"It was something important to me."

"Well, did you get 'em done?"

"Yes, I did what needed doing, and now I'm back. I didn't mean to cause you extra work."

"I'm thankful you're back. Taking off sudden-like and leaving only that note didn't sound like something you'd do. Must have been all-mighty important for you to leave out the way you did," she said as she squinted her eyes as though it might give her a better understanding of what I wasn't telling her.

"The more I thought of it, the more important I realized it was," I told her. "I knew I would never be able to rest until I took care of something only I could do."

She nodded. "You look like you've been put through a ringer and then wadded up wet," she added.

"That's how I feel," I admitted.

"Have you eat?" she surprised me by asking.

I shook my head. Eating hadn't occurred to me in a while. I'd had a different kind of hunger.

"You just lay yourself down and take a little nap. I'll get a fire started in the cook stove and cook you up a mess of grits and fry you some eggs. I'll wake you up when it's done, and we can both eat us a bite."

I did as she said.

Chapter 41

~~A. J.~~

I waited until Fizz, or rather Bennie Jack, was a good distance away before I turned around and took the road that led to my side of the mountain. I didn't want her to know who I really was or where I lived. I was determined to never cross over the mountain again unless it was to contact Aunt Polly about buying her place. I still wanted to own the entire mountain, but I wasn't sure how I could make it happen. I didn't think the Fizz I knew would stay put for long. Her seeking type of brain had always come up with some type of new challenge. It was one of the reasons she made a good spy. The excitement of proving she was better than everybody else was the fuel that kept her going. I had an idea it wouldn't take long to get her wanderlust back. She wasn't the type to settle down on a lonely mountain. She was too young and restless, had too much life left in her.

On second thought, maybe I should cross over the mountain often and on a regular basis. Not only did I need to make sure the crazy young woman kept to her agreement, but I also needed to know when she became restless enough to sell her land.

I walked over my little homestead. Looked at all I had accomplished along with what I planned on accomplishing. I had cleared twenty acres of land and used logs and sawed lumber to build a barn, a springhouse, a woodshed, and my very own log home. Just to look at everything gave me a sense of accomplishment. My home, this mountain, represented the place I had dreamed about having since I was a child. It was what I worked for – my reason for becoming a trainer for the Freedom Group, not that I didn't think working for the Group was worthwhile as well as needed. I did, but I was also planning for my future. Unlike Fizz, I didn't think being able to take out one traitor was worth giving up my life.

It wasn't going to be easy for me to stop being A.J., the best trainer of spies that ever existed, but I had to realize that A.J. was as dead and burned into ashes. Like Fizz, I had been only living a make-believe life as a valuable warrior for my country. We weren't even major cogs in a wheel. We had both been easily replaced. That knowledge was rough on a man's ego.

She and I both had a chance to become real people again. The type of people who lived a normal life as private citizens, if normal was possible.

I smiled as I went inside the log cabin that belonged to me, made my way to my bedroom, and laid myself down on my comfortable bed. For the first time since I was a small child, I fell asleep in the middle of a beautiful, sunny morning.

I slept soundly for several hours before I woke up with a startle. I had seen Fizz's mangled and dead body after Sander's hatchet goons got through with her. I was in a cold sweat even after I realized I had been having a nightmare – or rather a broad daylight tortured dream. I was still shaken even after I realized that the crazy, young woman was alive and hopefully safe. I had made sure of it. I had even put the lives of men in a dangerous situation to assure she remained safe.

At least the two male servers really did have a job working for the catering company. Like me, they got new identities as well as a new life. Soon, I needed to make sure all was well with them. I would be responsible if they lost their jobs or suffered any kind of repercussions for helping me with Fizz.

Another thing that was rattling my brain was why had I gone to such an effort to save her? It wasn't like she was the only female agent I had trained. I didn't know what several of them had become or where they had been placed. As for Fizz, I might as well admit I didn't save her entirely to keep Brigham and the Freedom Group from discovering she was still alive. I had always faced truths head on. I might as well admit, at least to myself, that I had feelings for the young woman. The kind of feelings a man had toward a woman he desired. My feelings went beyond sexual, although she did arouse such responses in me regardless of how hard I tried to convince myself otherwise. I wanted to protect her. Keep her safe from any kind of harm.

"Shit," I mumbled as I got out of bed. I had to put Fizz out of my thoughts. That part of life belonged to a dead man. It was time I filled my homestead with hard work and the animals I would take care of. I already had the animal feed stored in the barn. Seeing Fizz had kept me from going after the animals. Getting them was a way to help take my mind off this so-called Bennie Jack.

I hooked up the trailer I had wielded and nailed together, hooked it to the SUV and drove all the way back to the feed store. Who else would know more about where the best farmers were located than feed store personnel.

"Back so soon?" the man at the cash register said as I came in the store.

"Can't stay away," I said, hoping to spread a little humor, but the cashier didn't respond, so I said: "Figured you might know which farmer has the best heifer for sale."

"Know most every farmer in the area," he nodded as he came close to bragging.

"Who do you recommend?"

"Homer Crowder. He's got several little Jersey calves for sale right now."

"What about the old woman and kid I saw leaving here the other day?" I asked, wanting to find out what he might know about Fizz.

"Which old woman? Theres a couple of old women who buys feed here."

"The one who came in right before I did."

"Oh, you're talking about Aunt Polly. I know her, but don't see much of her."

"And the one who was with her?"

"Newcomer. At first, I didn't know if the kid was a boy or a girl. I thought on it some and decided she was a young girl. She's gonna be a looker when she grows up, if you ask me. Makes a man wish he was young again," he said with a lift of his brows.

"Aunt Polly said she bought the old Slaughter place. Know where she come from?" I asked.

"Reckon it's none of my business else she would have told me. Just like where you're from is none of my business," he said a bit sharp. "Seems to me you're a newcomer in these parts."

I grinned at his 'I mind my own business' attitude, which he obviously didn't do. "I'm not exactly a newcomer. I'm Colton Slaughter. My Grandparents owned the old Slaughter Place."

"A Slaughter, humm. According to my recollection, your grandma was a good woman. Can't say much about your grandpa and uncles. I was just a boy back then. Rowdy bunch, if I 'member them right. Hope you didn't take back after 'em."

"I consider myself lucky to take back after my mother and her people. She was a gentle woman."

"Who was she?"

I told him her name.

"Yeah, I remember some talk about her and the youngest of those Slaughter boys. You wouldn't be the Slaughter woods colt, are you?" he said with his direct, matter of fact kind of talk. "I was a boy back when all the talk was going on. Heard your mother's folks wanted to lynch the Slaughter who wronged their daughter."

"Right, but my mother wouldn't hear of such a thing. He was my mother's own true love. Turned out I'm the best one of the bunch."

He chuckled at my comment. "You might be right about that. Say, you come for more feed or more gossip?"

"Both, I reckon," I mimicked his way of talking, but it would take more than talk for a newcomer to fit in even though I was the son of a Slaughter. I had lost my accent during the years I had had been gone. "Can you tell me where Homer Crowder lives?"

He gave me general directions and then added, "Can't miss it."

Newcomers could and would miss it, but I wasn't a newcomer. I'd hung around this mountain ever since I was a boy wanting to own land where my roots were sunk into the good earth. The fact that I paid taxes on my grandparents' place for years and then had my relatives sell the place out from under me was not settling well. I had to figure out a way to get both Aunt Polly and Fizz to sell their land to me. What I needed was a surefire plan of action. I would work on that plan while I stocked my place with the animals I wanted.

I knew where the Crowder place was located, but I had never met Homer. His two Anatolian Shepherd/ Great Pyrenees dogs raised a threatening attack as I drove into his yard. They were definitely better than any burglar alarm. Plus, they had long, threatening teeth. I stayed in the car and waited. A couple of minutes later, the barn door opened and who I took to be Homer Crowder came out.

"Down," he said to the dogs, and both of them hunkered down at his feet as though they were ready to protect him.

"What can I help you with?" he said in a friendly enough manner, yet a bit standoffish.

"Is it safe for me to get out?" I asked.

"Depends," he said, as he looked my homemade trailer over.

"On what?" I asked.

"On what you come for."

I wasn't sure if he was serious or joking. "I came to buy a calf," I told him from out of the window. I knew better than to get out if I wasn't invited to do so.

"It safe to get out then. What kind of calf you looking for?

"I'd like to get a heifer. A Jersey heifer if you've got one for sale."

"Got several," he said. "They're in the pasture behind the barn if you want to take a look at 'em."

"I would," I told him.

He led the way around the barn while both dogs walked at his side. "Nice dogs," I commented.

"Best ever was. Don't know what I'd do without 'em. Keeps all sorts of vermin and pests away. Four legged ones and two legged ones."

"I believe it. Where did you get 'em?" again, I mimicked the speech pattern I knew so well.

"Traveled a good ways into Virginia to buy 'em. Got puppies in the barn if you're interested in buying yourself the best farm dog ever to draw a breath of air."

"I would like one," I found myself saying, although I'd never given any thought to having a dog.

"They're ready to go. As you can see, I've got four fine Jersey heifers that'll make the best milk cows that ever was."

The largest of the Jerseys got my attention. She had a gray colored body with almost a black face and legs. She was older than I had planned on, but there was something about her huge deer-like eyes that said she would be a gentle cow.

"What are the prices?" I asked.

"Afraid I've had to price 'em dirt cheap considering what fine stock they are." He continued to quote a price with the one I liked being the most expensive.

"She's eighteen months old last week. I went ahead and bred her to my fine Jersey bull six weeks ago. I dare say she's the best deal for you, unless you have your own bull."

I didn't have my own bull. The price he quoted didn't seem too much, but I didn't know what Jerseys, or any other livestock were selling for.

"If I was you, I'd buy me two heifers unless you have other cattle. One heifer would get mighty lonely all by herself. That way you can alternate when they calve. Have one cow giving milk while you turn the other cow dry afore she calves."

He had a point. Two cows would be better. I picked out the smallest heifer – a little tan one without as much black on her. She also had those huge deer-like eyes.

"Good choice," he said. "You got two of my finest. Want a bull calf too?"

"No," I told him.

"You'll need a bull to breed 'em too. Get a calf now and he'll be ready by the time they come in."

"Maybe later," I told him, trying not to grin at his salesmanship.

"Don't reckon that little trailer would hold three head of cattle no how. You can come back later if you change your mind. Now, for the puppies. I recommend you get two of them. They seem to do better when you've got two together," he told me as he took me inside the barn to where several white puppies played together in one of the barn stalls. I liked their looks right away.

"What's their price? Don't know if I can afford 'em after getting two heifers instead of one," I told him in an effort not to be gouged.

He asked what I considered to be a reasonable price.

"Appears like I'll be taking two heifers and two female dogs."

"Right," he said. "Back your little trailer up to the barn door and we'll get 'em loaded up."

Chapter 42

~~Aunt Polly~~

Didn't know what to think when I'd heard Bennie Jack leave the mountain long before daybreak. She coasting instead of having her truck engine running, which meant she was sneaking away for some reason she didn't want me to know about. When a body reaches my age, sounds that hain't normal have a way of waking a body up. It woke me up and I couldn't fall back to sleep to save me. The fact she done it troubled my mind until I couldn't get a bit of peace.

I couldn't settle down until I found out what was going on with her. As soon as it was light enough for me to go ahead and do up my own work, I made my way to her place and knocked on her kitchen door, although I knew she wasn't home. Knocking on her door was a matter of respect regardless. Just as I figured, she didn't answer. Curiosity got the best of me. I opened the kitchen door and walked inside although it went against my upbringing. I saw that piece of paper on the table where breakfast ought to be. I had just about got used to eating meals at that table. So, it felt alright for me to check the paper out.

What I read didn't make sense at all. Even the writing didn't look like what I'd seen of her penmanship, but then I hadn't seen enough of it to be certain.

Now she was back and wasn't telling me a thing that made good sense. Reckon I ought to honor her silence without questioning her reason, but I didn't want to. A body needed to know what was going on in order to know how to react. Poor little thing really did look whipped. It would be best for me to let her rest up and pick information out of her a little at a time like I had to do when I was getting the goody out of cracked walnuts.

I would only be right for me to fix us both some breakfast and fill our empty bellies before I headed back home. I hadn't realized how lonesome this ole mountain was until I discovered I was alone again. Even the sound of the birds reminded me that I was the only person who was hearing them. Never thought I would be glad there was somebody living in the old Slaughter place again, but that's the way things sneak up on you when you hain't expecting it to happen.

Odd how lonesome wasn't as noticeable before she showed up. Reckon I got used to having somebody to talk to. Someone to depend on in case there was an emergency. I had even noticed she didn't always carry her pistol when she stepped outside for a few minutes, but she had it strapped under her shirt if she was going outside for any length of time. It was right obvious something or other had put a fear in the girl that wouldn't be letting go of her anytime soon.

I recalled our trip into town. Seemed to me she became oddly silent after the man in the SUV showed up while I was in the lawyer's office. He did remind me of a Slaughter, and she had bought the old Slaughter place. Could they have some sort of connection with each other?

I didn't know if she would ever tell me what had troubled her or not, but there was a chance I might figure it out. I'd always heard a problem shared was a problem halved. I was willing to carry half her load if she wanted me to, but I had an idea her past would always remain inside of her.

The smell of good coffee perking did its magic by waking her up. She came into the kitchen with blurry eyes and an attempt at a fake smile. And yet, there was some sort of relief in her.

"Eat your belly full," I told her as I put scrambled eggs, gravy and biscuits on the table, along with two cups of strong coffee.

"You're a life saver," she said as a strange expression passed over her face.

"A body needs to fuel up after they break their night's fast if they want to get any work done during the day. Have you noticed if you don't eat breakfast, you'll most likely need to take a nap around three o'clock?"

"Yes," she said. "I've noticed."

"Didn't get much sleep last night, did you?" I mention right uninterested like.

"Not enough."

"Must have drove all night by the looks of you."

She nodded without comment, which told me she had been a good distance from this mountain, but she hadn't been gone long enough to go back to North Dakota where she claimed she came from. Her claiming to be from that state didn't hold water for me, but I didn't question her about it. When a person came up with a story that wasn't true, they usually had a reason for it.

I knew all about the need to keep things to yourself. I'd lived a lie ever since the seed of my Meadow Lark had been forced inside of me. A body had a right to hold their secrets silently in their hearts like I had done all these years. Sometimes I wondered what my Meadowlark would do if she found out how she had come to be. I figured it would tear her up a right smart, hurt that overabundant ego of hers. I didn't want to do that to my beloved daughter. I didn't want to do it to myself either. I'd spent my life trying to repent from what happened to me. I didn't know what I'd done to make him attack me, but I felt guilty just the same. I wasn't a beauty or the flirtatious type. I'd done my best, even back then, to be a Godly kind of person. Still did. I'd heard say that bad things happened to good people, and I reckon bad men was what happened to good women.

Had to admit, it was a great relief when George's privates became as limp as a dishrag. All that humping and grunting was disgusting to me. My own momma felt the same way. She warned me that it was a wife's duty to let a man have his way even when the wife didn't want to. She told me I'd have lay still and endure while it was going on. She said it would be over in a minute or two. She was right.

I didn't feel right in telling my Meadow Lark such things my momma told me. I figured my hard-headed girl would find out her own way about such things.

Chapter 43

~~A.J.~~

I had lots of expectations about how I would live my life after I retired from the Freedom Group. It helped my ego to think of myself as being retired instead of gotten rid of. I was torn between being angry about no longer being a part of the Freedom Group and being thankful that the rest of my life could now be my own to live I chose.

As for Fizz, I was still furious enough at her that I didn't know which way to turn. I never wanted to see set eyes on her again and at the same time I wanted to confront her with my growing anger. To think she had put me and three good men in danger was about more than I could take calmly. Why she had taken it upon herself to wipe out traitors was beyond me. She had to know her life could end in a matter of seconds, and yet she was willing to die for the betterment of our country. In a way I had to admire her for that even though it was a stupid thing to do. She considered herself a soldier, which was my fault. I had drilled into my trainees' brains that they were soldiers the same as those who enlisted in the armed services. The only difference was their secrecy.

Even though I didn't want to admit it, I felt responsible for what Fizz did and didn't do. I might as well admit I had brainwashed Fizz to the point where she believed she should do her share to wipe out our enemies. I had never before considered she would need to be deprogrammed until I backed off enough to take a hard look at what Fizz had done.

But I didn't want any kind of deprograming responsibility. I wanted, needed, to stay as far away from

Fizz as possible. Hope she could and would be able to turn herself into Bennie Jack without my interference.

My best action of self-preservation would be to merge myself in the life I now had. I assured myself for the umpteenth time that I should stay on my side of the mountain and never again spy on this so-called Bennie Jack or Aunt Polly again. At the same time, my obsession with owning my relatives' land, along with Aunt Polly's land, was my life-long aspiration. My streak of stubbornness wouldn't allow me to give up that dream. Ever since I was old enough to understand my out-of-wedlock situation, I promised myself I would one day be the owner of what had been denied me.

Another of my ambitions was to own a self-sufficient farm be it my grandparents' place or the side of the mountain I now owned. When I got home from my purchase of calves and puppies, I discovered having animals wasn't as rewarding as I thought it would be. Both puppies had done their business on the floor of the back seat. I carried both puppies to a barn stall and spent time cleaning up their mess in the SUV.

Then I backed the trailer to the barn hall and unloaded the calves. Again, I discovered a short, homemade trailer wasn't the easiest thing to back up, but I managed. I had left a slight space between the trailer and the entrance to the barn hall. None of my training had taught me the smallest heifer could escape through a foot of space. But she did.

I got the other heifer in a stall, moved the SUV and trailer out of the way, and spent two solid hours trying to chase the calf into the barn hall. I never realized how fast a calf could run or how easily one could outmaneuver me. All my previous training had not taught me how to wrangle one small heifer into a place she did not want to go.

I decided I just might have to let that crazy calf run on the mountain for the rest of her life – or mine. She had certainly taught me a few things about endurance and evasion, while she bested me at it. Finally, I gave up, went into my cabin for a cold drink of water and a towel to wipe away sweat and grime. Training recruits and training myself to be a self-sufficient farmer were both equally difficult.

After I had recovered slightly, determination had me scouring the woods and bramble for the runaway calf. The way my luck was going, that heifer would be all the way back to Homer Crowder's place by now. The sun had set, and darkness was settling in by the time I gave up searching and went to the barn to give the pups and heifer their evening feed and water. There in hall lay the little heifer calf in front of the other heifer's stall. It appeared she had been lying right there while I searched all over creation for her. I felt like giving her a kick right in the hind end. Instead, I quickly pulled the barn door closed, leaving only shadows in the barn, opened the stall door and ran her in with the other heifer.

She acted as though it was where I should have put her in the first place.

I thought about naming her Fizz.

Chapter 44

It was a relief to be back on the mountain, and at the same time I was suffering from deep down disappointment. I had done what I thought was my duty, but I didn't know if it had been successful or if my effort had been wasted. I blamed A.J. for that. He had no right to interfere with what I did. I was no longer owned by the Freedom Group, and according to him, neither was he.

If I wanted to know if I had killed the 'snake', I would have to leave the mountain to find out. Being isolated had its drawbacks. What was the most shocking to me was even on this mountain I had not been hidden well enough. If my previous trainer could find me, so could others. My big question was what I was going to do about it?

Leaving here to find a more secluded place was obviously the answer. The question was where would I go? Was there any place on earth I couldn't be found? A.J. had indicated we both were now free to live our own lives, but I would be a fool to believe such as that. I feared belonging to the Freedom Group was similar to belonging to the mafia. Only death would set a person free. A.J. and I were both declared dead, but we weren't free and feared we never would be as long as we lived. Not only that but A.J. knew where I lived, and he had even trespassed on my property and entered my house, left a fake note for Aunt Polly, and hid my money.

"What you looking so down in the mouth about?" Aunt Polly asked as I did my best to eat the breakfast she had cooked.

"Lack of sleep," I told her in hopes she would accept it.

"Does it to a body," she told me as she shoveled biscuit and gravy into her mouth. I knew she wasn't seeking more information about where I had gone. "Ruins my whole day when I don't get a good night's sleep. Will you have to leave here again?"

"No. I don't think so. I've made this my home and it's where I want to stay," I told her and hoped it would be explanation enough.

"You had another home before you got here. A body always carries their past with them regardless if they want to or not."

She was right about that. Never had I thought joining the Freedom Group would end up with me where I was today.

"Reckon there will always be somebody left behind who is wondering what happened to you," she probed.

"I doubt it. Like I told you before, I was an only child without any close relatives."

"Don't seem likely a pretty little thing such as you didn't have boyfriends and a whole pile of friends," she continued.

"I didn't," I told her more firmly than intended. "I valued my privacy then the same as I do now."

Aunt Polly didn't seem offended by my comment. If anything, it only made her more curious. "Don't want to talk about your past, do you? Reckon you know that talking about things sometimes helps get rid of them."

Irritation flew all over me. "If you must know, I left here to cut the head of an evil snake."

She nodded as though my words hadn't surprised her in the least. "Did you have any success at it?" she asked as though it was a logical question.

"Wasn't able to hang around long enough to find out."

"I always wanted to cut the head off an evil snake who did me wrong. Never did have a chance to do it. Helped by telling myself God didn't want me to harm myself by doing such as that. I figured it would hurt the snake more if I went on to live a happy life. Reckon you can live a happy life right here in God's country the same as I have."

"That's why I moved here," I told her. "To live my life and nobody else's."

She gave me one of her looks. "Just about everybody has secrets they've buried deep inside them. Secrets they have a right to take to the grave with them."

"Then why are you digging for my secrets?"

"Right good question, that one," she admitted. "Seems I'm a snoopy old woman who's sticking her nose where it don't belong."

"I suspect you're right."

She chuckled at that. "Reckon I'll shut my mouth about such things. If the need arises, you and I both have a good set of ears. In the meantime, I cooked breakfast. You get to wash up."

"Agreed," I told her. "I do have one question. Did anyone show up while I was gone."

"Not that I seen or heard," she said with a speculative look at me.

Okay. She answered one question, but I had many more questions. How and when did A.J. come to the mountain and enter my house? If he didn't drive up the mountain, it meant he had walked here. That meant he had to drive somewhere nearby. It would take hours to walk up this mountain even for someone in as excellent condition as A.J. was in.

"That sin eater you've mentioned. Do you have any idea where he lives?"

"Don't know the answer to that."

"Can you describe him?"

"Already told you what he looked like. Average size man maybe a bit on the tall side. He appeared to be fit and well portioned. Flat belly. No beer gut. He always had a mop of hair on his head, a thick beard and bushy mustache and eyebrows. He usually wore a hat pulled low on his head, but he had intelligent eyes. Something about him was kind of familiar. Like I'd seen folks he resembled, but I couldn't get a good enough look at his face to figure out who they were. Why do you ask?"

"The thought of a sin eater makes me kind of leery," I told her. "Can't understand why he would be hanging around here."

"I wouldn't call it hanging around here. He kinda shows up every so often. Mostly when I'm in need of something right bad like."

"What made you think he's a sin eater?" I asked her the same question I'd asked before.

She cocked her head to the side as though she was trying to make a decision on something difficult. "Some folks claimed there was a sin eater living on this mountain. Seemed like that's who he was the first time I saw him sneaking about. Dark. Silent. Appeared right shabby and didn't want me to get a good look at his face," she answered the say way she had answered before. Had I really expected a different answer?

And then it occurred to me. She had mentioned someone living on the backside of the mountain. "Could this sin eater be the same person who you said lives on the backside of the mountain?"

Again, she thought about it a minute before she answered. "The few times I've set eyes on that man, he didn't resemble the sin eater. The man living on the other side of the mountain had light brown hair and short redish beard and mustache. He always had on a flannel shirt and bibbed overalls. The sin eater had long, almost black hair with a thick black beard and mustache. He had slumped shoulders underneath layers of ragged clothes that didn't appear or smell too clean."

So, there were actually two men who roamed, and perhaps lived, on this mountain. There was no question that I had to find out more about them. "Do you know who the man on the backside of the mountain is?"

"Don't have any idea."

"Didn't you ever cross over the mountain to get a look at him and his place?"

"Never did cross over to get a look at him."

"Why not?" I asked.

"For the same reason I never went snooping about this old Slaughter place. Weren't none of my business. Never believed in trespassing where I don't belong. Not only that but going over the mountain is a mighty hard trek. It's rougher than a corn cob with rock cliffs steeper than a horse's face, and it's easy to get yourself turned around and lost. A lot of death traps when you don't know what you're doing or which way you're going. Even my own daddy refused to go over the mountain. Too dangerous he always claimed. If timber rattlers and preditors don't get you, the mountain will. I reckon I come to believe him."

I didn't remind her the red bearded man evidently crossed over several times. I had no fear of rough terrain or getting lost. A.J. had trained me to survive in a hostile environment. Interesting how I appreciated him and hated him at the same time. "I understand, but walking and looking about on public land that's not posted isn't considered trespassing," I told her, although I didn't know if it was exactly true.

"Matter of opinion," she told me with a shake of her head. "How would you like somebody spying on you and yourn?"

She made her point, but still yet, it paid to know what was going on around you. Knowing who lived on the other side of the mountain was something I needed to check out.

"My mammy was a God-fearing woman who taught me right from wrong. She always said it weren't right for a body to stick their nose where it don't belong. That way folks are able to get along with each other. Reckon her advice still holds."

I didn't disagree with what her mammy had taught her. I didn't disagree with her. What I disagreed with was accepting the lack of knowledge.

Aunt Polly left me to wash the dishes, while she headed back home. I knew one thing, and I suspect she knew it also, I wouldn't rest until I crossed over the mountain to get a look at the other place and who lived there.

~~~~

I woke up before dawn lit the sky and fed my goats and chickens. From what Aunt Polly had told me, I knew it would be a hard day's trek that would take me near dark to get back home. I took my Glock, knife, pepper spray and compass.

After an hour of walking on ground that had obviously been cleared or simi-cleared a generation or two ago, I began a steep climb upward.

After two hours of rapid climbing upward, I came to realize what Aunt Polly was talking about. Crossing the mountain looked easy from a distance, but once I got into thick forested land with clusters of undergrowth along with massive rock outcroppings, I realized how difficult the mountain was to navigate, and yet the red bearded man had evidently crossed over several times.

It occurred to me that he probably had a map of the mountain when I didn't. I should have asked Aunt Polly if she had a map, but most likely she didn't have one, or she would have mentioned it. I had gotten a rough sketch of the property I had purchased from the Slaughters, but it didn't show anything of the mountain terrain I was trying to cross over.

Thinking of the Slaughters and the rock cliffs I was climbing over reminded me of the girl who had been held captive until she died from childbirth while her hands and legs were still tied with ropes. I hoped the Slaughter responsible for such a crime suffered the rest of his life by what he'd done.

Much to my surprise I discovered my leg muscles were starting to burn as I struggled to climb over a monumental rockface cliff that appeared to be half a mile wide and taller than a city Highrise. I came close to regretting my decision to climb it instead of taking the extra time of trying to find a way around it. The hundreds of huge boulders surrounding the cliff appeared to be as difficult to maneuver, not to mention falling down a crevasse or twisting an ankle, as climbing the cliff would be.

It took only moments for me to discover one of my mistakes was not wearing a pair of leather gloves. My hands were scraped and bleeding before I got halfway up the cliff. My baggy pants only protected my legs slightly as I tried to find footholds to place my feet. At least I had worn good hiking boots. I found that many of the rocks broke away when I placed my weight on them causing me to hang on with my hands while I scrambled for a secure foothold. I could already feel the bruises and scrapes on my legs and body that protruding rocks had caused. The long-sleeved shirt I wore gave me some protection, but it didn't stop bits of trash, dirt, and bugs from covering my shirt and finding their way down my neck. Even my arms and fingers were trembling with exhaustion by the time I finally reached the top of the cliff.

Heaving my exhausted body over the final rim of the cliff took all my energy as well as determination. With a prayer of thanks, I sank down on the hard surface of the moss and bramble covered rock as I heaved in deeps breathes of oxygen. I said another prayer of thanks that I hadn't fallen during the difficult climb. The rockface cliff was much more difficult to climb than it appeared. I was both thankful for the training I had received, while being surprised at how the last few months without intense training had lowered my stamina.

I thought all the hard work I had done on my new place would continue my endurance, but I was wrong. I had quickly started to become soft. I wondered if A.J. had also become soft after he had been declared dead. Most likely he was the type to keep up the training until the moment he really did drop dead.

It even took me longer than I thought necessary for me to catch my second wind enough to continue making my way over downed logs and through twisted growths of laurel hells. The further up the mountain I got, the more it resembled a war zone of upturned tree roots and crisscrossed logs. Several times my feet sank into rotted logs as I stepped on them. I had to be extra careful to make sure I didn't twist an ankle or even worse, break a leg. I should have left a note telling Aunt Polly where I was going, but what good would that have done? She would never be able to find me by climbing over what I'd already climbed over.

The next huge rock cliff I came to had me maneuvering over the boulders to skirt around the cliff, although it ate up too much daylight time. I didn't look forward to being caught out during a long, dark night in a hostile environment.

I had been trained to survive all situations I might encounter, I assured myself. But I certainly wouldn't be looking forward to it.

Finally, when I came to a spot with less boulders, I took out my compass to discover I was way off the direction I had figured to get me over the top the fastest. I thought about climbing a tall hemlock tree in an effort to get a better look at how the land lay ahead of me, but all the trees were now short and leaning in the same direction. Wind, I thought, along with the pull of gravity had the trees leaning downhill. I might get a better view of the downhill terrain, but I would not be able to tell much about the uphill climb.

So, I kept on climbing by clutching onto whatever grew, including the abundance of rocks. It would be my bad luck to grab hold of a rock that had a timber rattler under it. If I ever made my way off the mountain again, I would be certain to purchase a snakebite kit. Maybe even a dozen of them.

I was trying to muster up more determination when I rounded a huge oak tree to find that I had stumbled upon a path of sorts. It ran up and down the mountain. I wondered if it was an animal trail or perhaps even a path Indian tribes had traveled long ago. Whatever the cause of the narrow path, I was thankful for it. It was slightly off the way my compass pointed but taking it would be faster and much easier on me. Going over the very top of the mountain might not be the best idea after all. Not only that, but the mountain also contained more acreage than I thought, plus I didn't know exactly where the man's house would be located.

I felt like getting down on my knees and kissing the ground when I finally reached the ridge on top of the mountain. I thought going down the mountain would be easier than climbing up the mountain. It was, in a way, since I had come across the rugged path. The drawback was the soil was of a shell rock consistency. The loose soil caused my feet to keep flying out from under me. I would slide long ways on my rear end. Oddly enough I seemed to always slide, roll, or tumble away from the path and down steep banks and ravines. I alternately slid into green berry briars, deep holes where trees had uprooted, or into poison ivy. There was no doubt I was and would be paying for my curiosity.

Each time I fell and got back on my feet, I made sure I hadn't lost my Glock, knife, or pepper spray. Being without them would leave me too helpless. I didn't like that feeling. In a way it was worse than being at the birthday party where I hadn't been allowed to have them on me.

The faint coolness of the wind that blew up the mountain became a blessing to me. My clothes were already wet with sweat after the difficult climb. After falling down and wallowing all over the black woods' dirt, they were also completely soiled.

I hadn't gone far when the blessed winds brought the sounds of calves bawling and chickens cackling. I followed the sounds until I found my way near the edge of the large clearing. I had no doubt the trees that were once growing in the cleared area were now the cabin and outbuildings. Interesting how those log buildings looked both old and new. I assumed the old looking cabin had been built several years ago, while the newer outbuildings were built recently. There were large enclosures for two calves with several chickens milling about.

I sank down in a large clump of concealing undergrowth to watch the place until the owner came out. I wanted to get a good look at the man.

I hid there for hours without seeing any indication of human life. From one clump of undergrowth to another, I slowly made my way closer to the house. Still, I saw no indication anyone was home. After several hours of watching, I kept in a hunkered position as I snuck to a window. Hearing no sound from inside, I eased my head up until I could see in the window. I saw no one. I continued creeping around the house looking in the windows until I determined no one was inside the cabin.

Chapter 45

I woke up in the middle of the night with a restlessness that wouldn't allow me to fall back to sleep. A feeling came over me that I had to make a rushed trip to visit Aunt Polly if I wanted to buy her land before her daughter got her way. I didn't want to make the same mistake I'd made with my grandparents' place. After tossing and turning for a restless hour, I finally got up and fed my livestock and fowl with my trusty flashlight. After I had finished, I used the flashlight to put on the fake scruff of beard and mustache I wore as my farmer disguise.

Aunt Polly has seen me like this several times when I made a trip over the mountain to check on her. Every time she had seemed thankful to see me along with whatever assistance I was able to give her. Little things such as matches, and lamp oil were worth more than money when they were badly needed. Another thing was firewood during a bitter winter. I tried to make sure she had enough wood along with a down sleeping bag to keep her from freezing to death. Each time I showed up I could tell how much she appreciated what I brought her, although she also resented the fact that it was badly needed. Maybe, just maybe she approved of me enough to let me buy her land, or at least give me a first refusal on it.

As for Fizz, or rather Bennie Jack, and the old Slaughter home place, I suspected there would come a time when she would run again. Knowing I had found her would become a great incentive for her to make another attempt at

disappearing. I didn't blame her in the least. She had no way
of knowing I would always protect her identity regardless of
how badly I wanted that tract of land.

What would I do if she up and disappeared while the land
remained in her name? How would I be able to ensure the
land became mine? I would think about that more after I
talked with Aunt Polly.

Once my disguise was finished, I turned off the flashlight
and went into the brisk darkness of early morning. I carried
the flashlight although I didn't really need it. I had traveled
the pathway over the mountain to Aunt Polly's and the
Slaughter place so many times I could find my way during
the darkness of night. I often thought I must have a small
degree of Indian blood running in my veins that aided in
making me love the solitude of this mountain.

Every day while I was in the armed services, I braced
myself to survive long enough to accomplish my dream.
Working with the Freedom Group had allowed me enough
money to buy my dream. How ironic when I discovered Fizz
had bought the place out from under me. It took all my
control to despise my cousins instead of Fizz. She had no way
of knowing I intended to buy the land I had spent years
paying taxes on.

Get over it, I told myself harshly enough to get my own
attention. You don't need to go over your disgruntled plans
repeatedly. Do something about what you want or shut the
hell up. That was exactly what I was doing – something about
it.

I arrived at Aunt Polly's at the break of dawn. The
wonderful, crisp, aroma of morning, along with the song of
birds, had lightened my mood and brought a smile of near
contentment to me. As usual, I found Aunt Polly feeding the
few animals she cared for. I couldn't help but notice how
feeble her brittle looking little body appeared as she moved
about. Her shoulders slumped, her head hung, and her steps
were slow and deliberate as she shuffled over the land. How,

I wondered, did she manage to survive all alone on this mountain after everyone had left out. If I remained alone, would I become anything like her? Would I come to understand her way of life more than I already did?

"You're out and about mighty early," she said without me realizing she had seen me.

"I like getting out and about early of a morning. You got eyes in the back of your head?

"Nope, but I got mighty good hearing. No animal pit-pats on the ground the way a big man's feet does. Not only that, but the wind is blowing toward me. I smelled the soap you use before you ever got close."

"I'll have to remember that," I told her. I had always told my trainees to never use anything that had an odor to it. I was no longer going by my own advice. Seemed I was getting more careless as time passed.

"What you wantin' this early of a mornin'? Must be mighty important considering how early you had to get up."

"It is," I told her with sincerity but hesitated to come right out with it.

"Then come inside while I pour us both a cup of coffee. I think it's perked to perfection by now. Don't have to water it down none now that Bennie Jack keeps me a good supply."

"Small pleasures become treasures," I said, surprised at her offering to take me inside her house, which was something she had never done before.

I was also surprised at how small along with how scrubbed her little cabin looked. She had her little bed in the living room close to the heating stove. She noticed my looking at his.

"Old bones need heated up even during the summer," she told me as she took two cups off the shelf and sat them down on the small, worn-smooth wood of the little table. "Sit yourself down."

I carefully pulled out the only other chair and sat down. She used a rag to lift the coffee pot from the top of the heating stove and poured the boiling brew in both cups.

"What's your name?" she finally asked me as though it had just occurred to her that I had one.

"Cole," I told her. Colton Slaughter. I believe you knew my grandparents right well."

"Ahh," she grunted as she sipped at the boiling hot coffee. "I knew you looked familiar, but I couldn't put my finger on it. I'd of figured it out the first time I seen you, if it wasn't for all that straggly hair on your face."

I chuckled a little. "It's my attempt at a rugged man look," I told her.

"You've done right well then. Now, let's stop dilly-dallying so you can tell me why you're here."

"Okay," I would come straight to the point. "I would like to buy your land. I'm willing to pay you up front, while you continue living here with a life estate."

She took another sip of coffee. "I can't do the likes of that."

"Why not?" I wasn't really surprised at her answer.

"Cause my land is already committed to somebody else."

I shouldn't have been surprised, but I was. How could she allow her daughter to have the land when she knew she'd sell it faster than the blink of an eyelash? I'd have to pay her triple what it was worth, but I'd do it if I had to.

"Perhaps your daughter will sell it to me. I'll still allow you to stay here as long as you like."

"She can't do the likes of that," she didn't hesitate to tell me again.

"Why can't she?"

"She'd do it in a minute if you offered her big money, but she hain't the one my land is committed to."

"She's not?" Came out of my mouth in surprise before I could stop it.

"Nope."

"Who is it committed to?"

"Can't tell you that."

"Why not?" I asked real soft like.

"It's a secret," she said as she took a good swallow of the slightly cooler coffee. "Why hain't you drinking your coffee? Cost too much not to drink it."

"It's a little hot for me. Why would it be a secret?" I wanted to know.

"If I up and told you, it wouldn't be a secret."

I opened my mouth and the words "Bennie Jack" came out. I saw the tiniest flicker of humor touch her face and knew I was right. "Why would a single woman want with all the land on this side of the mountain?" I said it a little harsher than I intended.

"Same reason you'd want to own the entire mountain, I reckon."

"She'll end up selling it," I did my best not to grit my teeth after I said those words.

"Hain't saying she's the one or not. Like I done said, it's a secret."

I lifted the cup and took a swallow of the too hot coffee.

"You could marry her," she surprised me by saying.

Her words caused me to strangle on the coffee. It was all could do not to spew it out of my mouth.

"Why not? You hain't wearing no wedding band."

"I don't want to marry her. I want to own the mountain to keep it from ever being developed," I feared my voice held the desperation I was feeling.

"Marrying her would right much get you what you're after. More I think on it, the more I like the idea."

She might like it, but I certainly didn't. "I have no intention of doing such a thing," I said with conviction.

"Then you don't want to own the mountain very much. Don't deserve it either if you're not willing to do what's needed to get it."

I almost said I didn't even know the girl, but I did know her. Maybe too well for my own comfort. If she'd been anybody other than Fizz, I would consider doing exactly what Aunt Polly suggested. After all, Fizz was a beauty. Even I had felt a few pangs of sexual attraction toward her, which was only normal for a man who still had the want too.

"What makes you think the likes of her would be willing to marry me?"

"Same reason you'd want to marry her. She wants to own the entire mountain to keep it from being developed. Put you both together and you'll both have what you want."

"And if we get divorced?'

"Won't. You both would lose too much if you let that happen."

I didn't say out loud what ran through my mind. I wouldn't put it past Frizz to do to me what she'd done to G.T. Sanger.

I drank my coffee, shook my head, and stood up. "If something happens with your secret, I give you my word of honor I'll give you far more than your land is worth, plus allow you to live here without having a worry in the world."

"Afraid you're too late where I'm concerned, but you'll think long and hard on Bennie Jack. Love of land is more powerful than what folks call being in heat. Land will always be there. Heat cycles come and go."

"That's a fact," I told her as I went out the door, surprised at her analogy.

"You left signs where you been watching her," she said with a knowing chuckle. "Don't know about her, but I'd say you might be in heat."

I ignored that as I hurried to disappear into the shelter of the forest. I headed straight to the Slaughter homeplace. I needed to get a better idea of what Fizz intended to do. If she was ready to run, she would need a lot of money in order to do a good job of disappearing. There was a chance she would be willing to sell the land after all. The big question was would she be willing to sell it to me?

The more I thought about it, the more reasonable the idea seemed plausible. I had spent a lot of time training her. I knew how her mind and body worked better than anyone else did. I could use my knowledge and skill to convince her she needed to head to a different country if she wanted to remain alive. It wouldn't take much to convince her that her whereabouts had been discovered and I was willing to help keep her alive. The same as I had done with G.T. Sanger.

I secretly observed the Slaughter place for several hours before I concluded she wasn't there, but her old truck could be seen through a crack in the barn doors.

Where could she be? What could she be doing for this length of time?

And then it hit me.

Aunt Polly had said Fizz wanted to own the entire mountain to keep it from being developed. Could she possibly know I owned the other side of the mountain? I doubted it. Thankfully, Aunt Polly only knew me as Colton Slaughter, while Fizz only knew me as A.J., her trainer. I had to keep it that way.

I left my observing rock and headed back toward my side of the mountain where I could do some positive thinking about what my next course of action. I hadn't gone far before I found her tracks in the soft woods' dirt. I started tracking her while listening carefully to make sure our paths didn't cross.

I hadn't tracked her long until I realized, according to her direction, she just might be heading over the mountain to confront me. Could she possibly know who I actually am? I didn't think so. I had even gone to the extreme by concealing the SUV she had seen me driving in a pine thicket. I'd made a point to buy a slightly newer model farm truck with a rack.

I tracked her to the largest, most daunting rock cliff on the mountain. I expected to see her tracks skirting around the rock cliff, but her footprints went straight to it. The places where she had placed her feet and clung to the rocks with her hands were easily spotted. I knew I had trained her well, but I never expected her to take such a dangerous chance on rock climbing when it wasn't necessary. Going around the cliff and huge boulders might have taken her thirty minutes or an hour longer, but she would not have taken a chance on falling and fatally injuring herself. Climbing that cliff was something even I shied away from.

I took my time as I went around it and made my way to the top. She had left her body print in the moss while kicking away some of the bramble. I wondered how her hands were after clinging to the rough rock face to keep from falling. They had to be painful.

It was obvious she wasn't trying to hide the tracks she left behind in any way. The climb had to have been a strain on her physically if not mentally. The fact she wasn't trying to cover her tracks was a good indication she had no idea that I was crossing the mountain to spy on her and Aunt Polly. Which meant she didn't know I was A. J.

My plan of buying her out just might work if I played it right.

I found the place where she had discovered the path many deer had made during years of meandering their way through the rocks from one side of the mountain to the other. She was really going to be mad at herself if she followed the easy path all the way back to the Slaughter place. I made sure I stayed far enough away from the path so I would not be spotted if we crossed paths before I saw her.

That didn't happen. I heard her grunting and groaning as she made her way over the top of the mountain. Evidently, she had discovered no one was home and decided to return to the Slaughter place. From where I hid, I could see her plain enough to get an idea of what she had gone through. She had certainly chosen the wrong way to cross the mountain until she hit the deer path. I suspected she had continued to follow the path down the mountain, which was a mistake. Deer hooves were smaller and more dexterous than human feet. I could only imagine all the miss-steps and tumbles she would take. I had once taken the same path and quickly learned my lesson.

I was rather disappointed to think someone I had trained was returning back home without succeeding in her mission. I reminded myself this was now Bennie Jack instead of Fizz. It had been many months since I'd had a training session with her. During that time, she was capable of deprogramming herself. Still yet, intensive training never completely disappeared.

When I got back to the house, I discovered her training was still with her. She had lifted a window and entered my house going through everything I owned while trying to make it look like nothing had been touched. Most people would not have noticed, but as her trainer, I noticed. I chuckled without being amused. I'd made sure there was nothing connecting me to being A.J. I made sure every item of identity I had left lying about indicated I was Colton Slaughter.

Chapter 46

Colton Slaughter. I found his name on a farm magazine next to an easy chair. I also found his name on receipts in a drawer where he had bought animal feed. Made sense that a Slaughter would be living on the back side of the mountain. Like Aunt Polly's and my place, there was no electricity, but I had come across a large generator at the backside of the cabin. I wondered if he was the same person Aunt Polly thought was a sin eater, but that didn't make sense considering the two men had a different appearance and different colored hair. A moment later I had to grin at that thought. I knew only too well how easy it was to use stage makeup and artificial hair to change one's appearance. The art of disguise was taught to members of the Freedom Group.

Once I had carefully searched his house, I checked his outside buildings. Finding his truck parked in the barn hall made me more cautious. There was a chance he was somewhere on the mountain and would return soon. I had found out who he was, and it was time I headed back to my place before I was caught trespassing.

I followed the almost invisible path which made my return much easier and faster than using a compass to keep to a straight line over the mountain. Still, the twisting, rock spued path amounted to a workout almost as intense as A.J. used to put me through. I had to watch my every step to make sure I didn't sprain an ankle or get bitten by a poisonous snake. I arrived back home covered in dirt, blood-streaked and exhausted. At least I'd found out a Slaughter lived on the back side of the mountain.

"Fed your animals for you. You're a bit behind time."

I was startled at the sound of Aunt Polly's voice.

"Weren't as easy as you thought, was it?"

"Shit!" I mumbled at seeing the grin on her face.

She chuckled. "Did you find his place?"

"I did," I told her as I went into the house to get some water.

"What got hold of you?" she asked as she followed me inside.

"Nothing."

"Then what did you get hold of?"

"Rock cliffs, dirt, and briars." I said, remembering the poison ivy I rolled in. I'd be taking a soapy, hard scrubbing, all over washing as soon as I could get some privacy.

"Colton Slaughter come to see me earlier," she told me.

I just about spued out a mouth full of water. "He was here?"

"Yeh, while you were at his place. "He wasn't as dirty as you are."

She had to add that just to aggravate me. "What did he want?" I said a bit sarcastically.

"To buy my place and yours."

"I'm not selling," I told her firmly.

"Me neither," she said. "Told him such."

"And?" I questioned.

"I suggested he marry you."

I dropped the glass on the floor. It broke.

She grinned. "Best idea I've had in years. Marry him and you'll own the entire mountain once I die off."

"So will he," I shot back.

"Right. When you have two people who love the same thing, it'll be taken care of twice as good."

All the things that ran through my mind weren't suitable for saying out loud. "I have no intention of marrying anybody," I almost shouted.

"No need to get all hot and bothered. You ought to think on it a while. Guess you already know intentions amount to farts in the wind. It's the doing that counts," she told me with her own kind of logic.

"You can't be serious." I added in disbelief.

"I am. If I was young again, I'd marry him."

"You'd marry a Slaughter in return for getting his land?" I accused.

"Folks marry for all kinds of reasons. If nothing else, you ought to meet up with him and work up some kind of agreement. According to his looks, he could make marriage right pleasant."

My mouth had to be hanging open. My mind was buzzing with disbelief along with anger. How could she possibly suggest such a thing? I came here to escape. To live my life the way I wanted – in seclusion.

"Now, don't you go getting on your high horse. I only want what's best for you. Having a man around, even if you don't love him, makes life easier on a woman. I know that for a fact. Being a young, pretty woman alone on this mountain makes for an easy target for all sorts of things."

"That's why I'm well-armed."

She drew in a long, drawn-out breath. "Sun's long set. I best get my old bones back home. Showed up to tell you about the Slaughter man. Found you gone and started to worry. You might ought to build a fire in the stove and take a good, hot washing up. Looks like you've been rootin' with the pigs."

That was good advice.

I watched as she hobbled off through the yard and disappeared into the woods. It hit me how old she actually was. The remainder of her life was limited to years at best. And then I would be living on this mountain alone. Wasn't that what I wanted? But I wouldn't exactly be alone. There would be a man I didn't know who wanted my land. I had no idea what lengths he would go to in order to get it.

Hadn't Aunt Polly told me how lawless that bunch of Slaughters was? If she cared anything at all about me, why would she suggest I tie myself down to one of them? I would have to think about that. Even sleep on it for a while.

Chapter 47

~~A.J.~~

Having been Fizz's trainer was difficult enough, being married to her would be pure hell for any man. Aunt Polly's suggestion of marriage to her had me shaking my head in disbelief. I could only imagine what it would be like having such a spitfire as a wife. A man would never know what she might get herself into next. Be it poisoning someone she thought should be taken out or breaking into my cabin the way I had trained her to do.

Such an attitude had made her one of the best spies I had encountered, but it also made her a risky one. I had seen the same kind of attitude in applicants the Freedom Group considered bringing in. Most of whom I had turned down. Why hadn't I turned Fizz down? If I was honest with myself, not only did I think she could and would do the job intended, but I also admired her spunk and determination. Plus . . . and I hesitated as I realized such, I had deeper feelings for her. What name to put on those deeper feelings, I wasn't sure. Affection. That might be the best word I could come up with. Bewilderment also ranked high on the list.

One thing I did know for certain, us living on both sides of the same mountain wasn't a good thing. It wouldn't take long until she found out A.J. and Colton Slaughter were the same person. I might as well confront her with it. That might be incentive enough for her to let me buy her out and convince her to move on.

I thought of options concerning Fizz for several days before I decided to take action. What did I have to lose?

Sooner or later, she was going to discover the truth about me. Hopefully, before that happened, I might be able to convince her to move on, while selling me her land. I wasn't sure what kind of deal, if any, she had arranged with Aunt Polly, but I wanted to find out.

I walked down the mountain from my cabin and got the SUV out of the pine thicket. I practiced all the angles I wanted to present to Fizz as I drove up the poor excuse of a road. I hadn't driven far when common sense hit me. Both Fizz and Aunt Polly would hear the sound of the SUV. If I drove to the Slaughter place, Aunt Polly was sure to show up, or at least hide in the woods and eavesdrop on the reason I was there.

I managed to pull off the road in a slightly wide place, made a lot of backing up, pulling forward as I maneuvers to get turned around, and drove back down the mountain. Hoping they would think whoever was driving saw the condition of the road and changed their mind about driving up the mountain.

I wasn't pleased by the long walk I would have to take to reach the Slaughter place, but I convinced myself it was nothing more than continuing my fitness training. One thing I didn't want was for my body to go flabby.

I ran, jogged, and rested for a few moments, and then I did it all over again. The air on the mounts was brisk and contained less oxygen than down in the valleys, but I was used to breathing thin air. I always informed my trainees they could experience altitude sickness if they climbed mountains. Altitude sickness was almost a sure thing above 8000 feet. This mountain was over 6000 feet. Not high enough to assure altitude sickness, but high enough to make breathing more difficult when not used to it.

My first stop was at Aunt Polly's place. I used thick undergrowth as a hiding place while I made sure she was home. Using my skills to remain silent and undetected, I continued to the Slaughter place.

Chapter 48

~~ Bennie Jack~~

I was clearing away a section of brush and undergrowth near the barn to add grazing space for the goats. Once upon a time the area had been a fenced in lot. I assumed the Slaughters used the area to graze their milk cow or run hogs. The area's soil was the most fertile spot I'd come across. It grew giant ragweed twelve feet high or more. The goats loved to eat them. I had been staking them out and decided it was time to repair the old hog wire fence.

Suddenly, chills ran up my backbone and the hair stood up on the back of my neck. I grabbed my Glock out of the holster and looked for poisonous snakes. Saw none. Didn't smell a cucumber or burnt bean scent. Instinct had me take cover behind the nearest tree trunk big enough to serve as a shield.

"Don't shoot, Fizz, or rather Bennie Jack. It's me, A.J. here."

The sound of his voice startled me enough for me to shoot him, or at least splatter the ground beneath his feet. Surely, he realized how jumpy I was after I had poisoned that no account snake of a man.

But I didn't shoot him.

I didn't want to waste my ammunition regardless of how aggravated I was that he had shown up.

"Is it safe to show myself?" he asked, although we had parted on civil enough terms.

I detected a faint touch of humor along with seriousness in the tone he used. "What are you doing here?" I demanded.

"I brought news you'll be interested in."

"Really?" I did want to know what had gone on in the world I'd left behind. More so, I wanted to know if I'd eliminated the snake. "Show yourself," I called out the term we had been trained to use.

He came into the yard looking sweaty and pleased with himself. I felt the old familiar twinge of showing respect to my trainer, but he was no longer my trainer. We stood on level ground with each other. We were both Freedom group cast outs. Both assumed dead.

I left the lot and joined him in the open yard. "Okay," I said as I looked him over. I saw that he also had a holster and Glock concealed underneath a sweat-dampened shirt. Old habits die hard for a reason. No question he was still fit and muscled to perfection. His hair was longer than the nearly shaved head he usually preferred. "Lont hair can be used to take a man down," he always claimed. If anything, he sported a darker tan than I'd ever seen on him. He'd obviously been outside more now while training his recruits. Again, I understood how women would swoon over him, while other men became envious. He was the epitome of tall, dark, and handsome with enough of the outdoorsy type to appear rugged.

"Climbed the mountain," I said as a statement and not a question.

"Started to drive up that horrible road but decided against it considering how sound can travel. Didn't want Aunt Polly to be part of our conversation. She doesn't know anything about your past, does she?"

"No," I told him.

"Good. It's best to keep it that way."

On that I agreed. "What was so important that you climbed the mountain to confront me with?" I came straight to the point.

"Let's go inside in case the old woman shows up. Our voice won't carry as well."

I considered refusing, telling him he could say why he came and then get back off my mountain. Having him near made me nervous as heck. He had some sort of reason to find me in the first place. I needed to know what and why. I held out my hand to indicate the kitchen door and let him proceed in front of me. "Never turn your back on the enemy," he always drilled into me. I did allow him to hold the door open for me.

He'd always been considerate like that.

I was still facing him. My Glock was still in my hand but not pointing toward him. "Okay, I said without sitting down or inviting him to take a seat.

He drew in a breath and didn't hesitate to say, "You're in danger of being discovered if you stay on this mountain. Both Sanger and Brigham have put out a hit on you."

Which I figured could be true. Both would like to get their assassin hands on me if I were still alive. "Are you indicating I wasn't successful in my Sanger mission?"

"Not entirely."

"What do you mean by not entirely?"

"His cancer treatment didn't mix with what he ate and drank during the birthday party. He vomited up the food along with the poison you gave him."

"Shit," I said. After all the work and planning I went through, I failed at what was extremely important to me. "Then why does he have a hit on me?"

"Enough entered his system to be detected. Not to mention his vomit was analyzed. As you can imagine, it wasn't the first time he had been poisoned. According to my information source, it probably hastened his inability to fight his cancer. He's in a weakened state and not expected to last much longer."

I thought of his son and the need to eliminate that snake also.

"No," he said firmly, as though he knew my thought. "Leave that up to the Freedom Group. They know what they are doing, even if you don't want to admit it."

"They're known for sitting on their thumbs without doing a single thing about what's happening to our country."

"You're wrong. You don't know everything that's going on, Fizz."

I only looked at him without acknowledging he still considered me part of the Freedom Group, or he wouldn't have referred to me as Fizz.

"I should have said Bennie Jack, right?"

"Right. What's your name now?" I asked.

"It doesn't matter."

"I assume it was never A.J."

"Right."

"But you know my real name."

"Of course. You used your real name when you worked as a governmental aide."

"She, along with Fizz, died in the ocean," I informed him. "So how is it I have two hits on me when I'm supposed to be dead."

"Surely you realize there were more security cameras on the Sanger estate than in the White House. Your face was seen."

I had thought of that. That's why I made sure I wore a good disguise that would have fooled my mother. Not only that but I had waxed my fingertips, plus wore a pair of gloves as did all the servers. Yet, I had not fooled A.J., but then I wouldn't have. He had seen me in a lot of different disguises, along with a variety of circumstances. Not all of them becoming.

"Such comes with the job," I said a bit sarcastic.

"Neither you nor I are any longer on the job."

"Then tell me the truth of why you're here."

"I already told you."

"And what do you suggest I do about it?" I asked as my suspicion rose.

"Whatever you decide to do. I only wanted to give you a head's up on what's going on."

I gave him a skeptical grunt. Not only had he been my trainer long enough to read most of my thoughts, I also had learned to second guess him. I knew there was more than a warning on his mind. "Why don't you stop procrastinating and tell me the entire truth," I demanded.

"The truth is I thought you might need more money to disappear than you have. The amount you left for the old woman wouldn't be enough for you to leave the country and disappear for any length of time."

"And you're going to give me enough?"

"Not give," he told me firmly. "I thought I would offer to buy this useless piece of rock in return for the money."

I laughed right out loud. "If I can be found on this mountain, you can also be found."

"I'm not wanted for any crimes," he pointed out. "My only failure was not training you to abide by the rules, while you're up for spying, theft, and attempted murder."

"How much would you give me for my place?" I asked.

He quoted me a price that was within low-end reason.

"Your land along with Aunt Polly's would be worth more if both parcels could be sold together," he made a point of saying.

He then gave me an estimated price for both tracts of land.

"What would you do with the land? Divide it up and sell tracts of land to have a compound for other Freedom Group members who've been declared dead?"

A surprised look came to his face. "No," he told me firmly. "More than one person living in an area would be easier to locate. Track down one, find them all."

My answer was a flat no. I wanted to yell at him to get off my mountain and never come near me again, but I knew better. Plus, he should know I wasn't as stupid as he was assuming. What I needed to know and didn't, was how he found me in the first place along with why he wanted my and Aunt Polly's land. To find out, I would have to string him along for a while.

"I'll have to think about it," I told him. "I need to talk to Aunt Polly before I make a decision."

"The old woman indicated you also own her land, is that true?"

"Aunt Polly will never sell her land. She was born here and wants to die here."

"I would have no problem with her staying in her cabin, or even moving into this old house after you leave if she prefers. That cabin of hers is barely hanging together. A winter storm with heavy snow could collapse it on top of her."

I didn't respond to what he said about her cabin because it was true. "I thought you wanted to live here."

"No, I don't want to live here. I'm offering because you need money to disappear, but I won't give you money without something of equal value in return."

"Why are you willing to be so accommodating?"

"I failed to trained you sufficiently. Such failure on my part leaves me responsible for putting you in the situation you're now in."

His expression softened a little as he looked me in the eyes. I got the feeling he might have some kind of feelings for me other than his regret for training me as a spy.

"Do you feel responsible for all the recruits you've trained?"

"In a way," he said. "But they weren't my pick. You were."

I had to admit we did seem to have a repour with each other from our first encounter. Almost to the point of inappropriate feelings that were not allowed between Freedom Group members, although we never admitted it much less acted on it. At the same time, my gut instinct told me there was more to his so-called generosity than he was telling me.

Much to my and his surprise, Aunt Polly walked in the kitchen door as if she had the right to do so.

"If you've come to propose marriage, you ought to be down on your knees," she told him.

I saw the flicker of an *oh shit* moment in his eyes before he could hide it.

"I came to make an offer to purchase both her and your land," he said in a calm tone of voice that sounded reasonable. "Now that you're here, we can sit down and discuss how that would benefit all three of us."

"Good idea," she said as she pulled out a kitchen chair and sat down. She nodded toward me and the other chair. "Why don't you bring in a chair from the porch, Colton," she made a point of saying Colton as she looked him in the eyes for a moment before she turned to me. "Colton Slaughter. His grandparents owned this place," she informed me.

I felt like ice cold water had been thrown in my face. "Colton Slaughter?" I said the name in almost a whisper.

Aunt Polly nodded. "That's who he is," Aunt Polly said. "I had an idea it was him I heard tromping through the woods a short time ago, but I wasn't sure. So, I came to make sure you were okay."

He said nothing as he turned and went out the door. A moment later he returned with a chair, placed it at the table and calmly sat down. I stared at him in disbelief while trying to subdue the rush of anger I felt at realizing that A. J. was the man whose cabin I had been in – the man who lived on the other side of the mountain.

"So," Aunt Polly said. "I take it you two know each other from aways back."

I looked at him and said nothing. Neither did he.

"I got here about the same time you did," she explained to him. "I'm right good at eavesdropping. Heard everything the two of you said. I take it you decided to try and buy us out instead of marrying her the way I suggested."

"Marriage would be too complicated. Buying the land would be more reasonable," he told her as though she was the one who was being ridiculous.

"Only if it was for sale. Now, suppose you tell me why Bennie Jack is a spy, thief, and attempted murderer?"

"Such as that is confidential," he told her. "We're not allowed to divulge such information."

I decided it was time to tell Aunt Polly a little truth. "He was my trainer. I gathered secret information. I made a foolish mistake and got discovered. Unknown to the criminals, I escaped their attempt to kill me. I got revenge by taking my own money they would retrieve from my checking account, plus other ill-gotten money waiting to be laundered from evil people. After all that, I decided to disappeared. And then a short time ago, I tried to poison one of the men who was a funding contributor to the destruction of our country," I told her, pretty much summing up what had happened.

"Thought it had to be something. Wasn't sure what." She turned to him. "Well, are you going to ask her to marry you?"

"You can't be serious," I said before he could.

"Oh, I'm serious all right. Makes perfect sense to me."

"What makes sense is her selling me this place while she moves somewhere out of the country where she'll be safe."

"I may be old, but I'm not daff. Don't believe for a minute they've found her. She's safe right where she's at. You found her because you live on the other side of the mountain, and you've been spying on me for years. Now that's the truth, hain't it?"

"Not entirely."

"Then you tell me what is."

"You're right that I want to own the entire mountain. Not only because my grandparents lived here, but because I want to preserve this mountain with all its beauty. That's what's important to me."

"But not important enough to marry Bennie Jack."

"Wait a minute here," I interrupted. "Did it ever occur to either of you that I don't want to marry him or anybody else." I repeated what I had been saying, and Aunt Polly refused to hear.

"Such as that shouldn't matter in the least. Folks get married all the time when they don't want to. You both out to be willing to do what's best for everyone involved," Aunt Polly was quick to tell us. "What's important is that you both have your own place to live in. Just because you get married don't mean you have to live with each other. All that piece of marriage paper means is the two of you can control who owns this mountain. Two people stand stronger than one. Plus, if one of you dies, the other one can stay in control."

She had a point, but what about our wants, our future. I still had a dream of children and a loving husband to share my life with sometime in the future, and A.J. had indicated he wanted the same thing.

"If I ever get married, I want a real husband," I told them.

"I want a real wife. One I can trust," A. J. added with an intended insult toward me.

Aunt Polly shook her head in a sad sort of way. "That would mean bringing in strangers. Sounds to me like folks would find out who you both really are. Don't reckon either of you can afford that to happen. You'll both end up losing what you're trying to preserve. Perhaps even lose your lives from what I've heard. Oh, well, I reckon you'll both have to think on it a while before you get enough sense to know I'm right."

I sat there stunned as I tried to take in A. J. and Colton Slaughter as being the same person. "I don't believe it," I said mostly to myself other than to Aunt Polly. "My trainer is living on this mountain. At least now I know how you found me," I said to him. What I didn't know was if he'd somehow arranged for me to buy this piece of property with the intention of getting it from me.

"You really were a spy?" Aunt Polly asked as though she didn't believe what I'd said earlier.

"I'm not sure what I was," I told her.

"Like I'd pass something such as that on. Folks would committee me for being plum crazy if I claimed such as that. At least you're not a murderer. God might not forgive you if you killed somebody."

I didn't argue with her or ask her if she though the soldiers who were forced to kill during war would never be forgiven by God. I always considered myself as also being a soldier who was fighting the enemy for our country.

"Don't know why you didn't own up to such as that to me in the first place," she said. "It wouldn't matter to me what you were. What matters is who you are now. And more important is who you will be in the future."

I let what she said wash right over me. What had me stumped was why she wanted me to marry Colton Slaughter. Saving the mountain didn't seem like reason enough.

"You really want me to marry him?" I demanded.

"I do."

"Why?"

"He's a good man. The kind that will take care of you."

"I can take care of myself."

"It helps to have a man for backup. A lone woman can be a target. Daddy once said a man will get the shit beat out of him if he messes with someone's girlfriend, but he'll get killed if messes with a man's wife."

"That might be true, but what about loving the man you marry?"

"Love don't matter much. It's overrated. What matters is how he's going to treat you for the rest of your days. I've knowed of women who married for love only to be beat on until the day they died."

"How do you know he wouldn't beat on me?" I came back at her as I glared at him.

"By the way he's treated me all these years?"

"By the way he's treated you all these years?" I questioned what she'd said. "What are you talking about?"

"He's the sin eater and the one who'd showed up when I was in need. No matter if he put on disguises, I got a good look at his eyes this time. I seen what I should of seen sooner. Folks can't disguise their eyes."

"He's your sin eater?" I questioned.

"I reckon he's one and the same, aren't you?"

He didn't admit or deny it.

Chapter 49

We were getting nowhere with marriage talk. Although, Aunt Polly's way of thinking did have some merit to it. There was one big drawback where Fizz was concerned. She would never be able to use her own name. Not only that, but she would not be able to legally change her name without making her identity public, which was something she didn't want. If she did get married, there would be a question of its legality. If I were to marry a woman who did not exist, would I still be considered the joint owner of her property?

Another consideration was the fact that I wanted a real wife with legitimate children. Most of all, I wanted a home where two people loved each other. Trouble was that I had never met a woman I had fallen in love with. In the few years I had been in contact with Fizz, she hadn't found anyone either. The only time she ever spent with a man was with one of her targets. The ones I had assigned her. Again, I acknowledged how good she was at her job. That was until she decided to go over my head with information. I simply couldn't trust her any longer.

"What name would she use on her marriage license?" I spoke my thoughts out loud.

"Bennie Jack. That's my name. That's who I am," she told me with a lift of her chin.

"Not legally," I reminded her.

"Yes, legally. I have a birth certificate, driver's license, social security number since birth and the whole works."

"You faked them," I said, knowing her claim wasn't legitimately possible. I had checked her out thoroughly. I knew all about her since childhood until the moment she got on that helicopter, or so I thought.

She gave me a slight grin. "You don't know everything about me," she said triumphantly.

"I believe I do," I informed her.

"Keep believing whatever you like," she shot back at me. "If you know so much about me, you already know I wouldn't marry you if you were the last man on earth and the alarm on my time clock was screaming," she added childishly.

"I'm not asking you to marry me," I returned.

"Will you both stop bickering," Aunt Polly said. "If you won't listen to what's best for both of you, then so be it. Colton Slaughter can stay on his side of the mountain, while Bennie Jack can stay on this side of the mountain. At the same time, my land will remain mine to do with as I please."

"You're right," I told them both. "It appears we'll have to be satisfied with what we have regardless of how much we want to protect the entire mountain from outsiders." I turned my back to them and headed out the door and back to my side of the mountain.

I did my best to curb my irritation and do some logical thinking. What Fizz said about being Bennie Jack kept nagging my mind and I couldn't put my finger on why. Call it intuition or even the results of always being suspicious enough to look for an underlying meaning to everything. As soon as I crossed the mountain to reach home, I found the non-traceable, burner phone I kept nearby at all times and called Badger.

"Who's calling?" Badger answered after several rings.

"What took you so long to answer?" I asked, knowing he had to retrieve his own burner phone from its hiding place. The sound of my voice told him who was calling.

"What's the problem?"

"No problem. I need you to find out something for me."

"Same as always," he said a bit irritated. "What is it this time?"

I didn't want him to know Fizz was now using the name Bennie Jack. Therefore, I couldn't very well ask him to gather information on a Bennie Jack. I couldn't take a chance on Fizz being discovered using the alias of Bennie Jack. I gave him Fizz's real name. "I need you to find out everything about her from her conception until her death."

"Could I ask why being you've already done such as that?"

"No."

"Figures. What is your deadline?"

"Tomorrow."

"Figures," he said again. "Anything else."

"Later on, perhaps." I hung up knowing I would have whatever information he could dig up soon.

I already had all the information on her I thought possible, but not to the extent what Badger would have access to as I was no longer privy to all the spy equipment and devices. He definitely deserved his moniker. He was one of the best men I had trained. Plus, I trusted him to have my back - regardless.

Chapter 50

It didn't take long for Badger to get back in touch with me. Did me good to realize I had trained him sufficiently. One failure was enough to erode my confidence in my own judgement. With Badger I'd had success. I could trust him to have my back when the need arose.

I answered my burner phone to hear his voice.

"Anna Burnstine was born to Helen and Calvin Burnstine. Her mother was forty-nine years old at the time, and her father was fifty-six years old. It was a home birth in the remote hills of Kentucky. I assume by a midwife or more likely by her husband. It took several years later before her birth was reported by a census taker. She was four years old at the time. Shortly after her birth, the Burnstines moved to Virginia where the father got a job that paid fairly well. They made an effort to have their daughter well educated. It appears she had an ordinary city girl childhood with not so much as a traffic ticket. Her parents are dead. I could find no living relatives beyond distant cousins. As you already know, she became a congressional staffer before she was recruited, and you trained her. From that point on, you know all about her."

I was disappointed in what he told me. I already knew most of that information. "Nothing unusual stands out?" I questioned.

"No, not really. According to her elementary school records, she was unusually intelligent when she entered school. She could already read and write. It was noted that her mother had spent a lot of time teaching her. Her height and weight were also slightly above average for children her age. She became a straight A student who was interested in law and politics. As I said, you already know such as that since you researched her."

"I do," I told him. "You found nothing that stood out? Nothing that caught your attention?"

"Nothing. Other than the fact she was reported to have drowned in the helicopter crash, which you already know. Neither her nor the two men's bodies have been discovered, which surprises no one. She is definitely considered deceased. Of course, you are up to date on all that information as well."

I almost asked him to do a search on a girl named Bennie Jack, but I hesitated to do so. If I wanted to find out about that girl, I'd have to do it on my own.

"Thanks," I said.

"No problem." He disconnected and so did I.

That wasn't the information I wanted, but it was what I expected. I was hoping he would find something that I had missed. He hadn't.

I would have to make a trip to Kentucky to do some research on Bennie Jack which would require me to leave the mountain. I discovered my plans had a hindrance in the form of two heifers and puppies. Even an attempt at being a hobby farmer required time and presence. It meant I would need to feed the animals and then leave as early in the morning as possible. I would make sure I left them enough food and water for a day and overnight.

After I fed the animals, I put on what I considered my best ordinary-man disguise and left long before daylight. By the time the sun was up, I was nearing Kentucky in what was obviously a rural area. The hills were tall, wooded, and close together much like a giant hand had squeezed the earth hard enough to squirt the terrain up between giant fingers. I got a really good idea of what a deep holler was because I was driving in one.

Between the towering hills, there was only room for a narrow, paved road and the clear water of a twisting creek. I thought this just might be a stream of water clean enough to drink.

I got the tranquil kind of feeling I associated with a hundred years in the past as I observed the flora and fauna of the area. It was beautiful in a primitive way. Few houses could be seen as I rolled down my window. The soft wind brought bird songs along with the sound of the rushing creek to my ears. In a way the area had an unrequited feeling about it as though time had and would continue to stand still in this place, while spirits of the past lingered.

I found myself wondering how the few people living in the scattered houses made their living. I didn't see any businesses or manufacturing plants where people could be employed. It was miles of similar scenery before I came to a very small town.

I arrived at the courthouse in the county a few hours after they opened where Bennie Jack and Anna Burnstine were born. I didn't want to be the first one there. If I was lucky, there might be a lot of people conducting what they thought was urgent business. If so, I might not get a lot of recognition by being a stranger.

It didn't work. There were fewer people in the courthouse than in a coroner's dissecting room. A lone woman sat behind a worn oak desk situated behind a room-dividing counter. She looked up when I came in the door.

"What are you needing?" she asked without getting up.

"I want to check birth records," I told her politely.

"Whose?" she wanted to know as she slowly got up and came over to the dividing counter as if me being there was an inconvenience to her.

"Jack is the last name. I'm not certain about first names," I told her. I hadn't expected her to question me.

"Why's a stranger wanting to look at our birth records?" she asked as though she had the right to do so in what I took to be a conversational tone of voice as she looked me over from my face down and then back up.

I had to come up fast with something she might accept. "I'm into genealogy and I want to find out more about my relatives."

"You a Jack?" she asked. "You must be the cream of the crop. Odd how some of them were good looking, while others were hog ugly," she added as she leaned against the counter as though she and I both had all the time in the world to stand there doing nothing other than gossiping.

"My mother was before she married. Some of her ancestors lived here," I told her in my friendliest and slightly gossiping tone. "She never told me much about them while she was alive."

"Can't say as I blame her. Those Jacks were a rowdy bunch. No offence intended. What did you say your name was?" she asked as though I had told her, which I hadn't.

I did some quick thinking. "George, George Burnstein," I told her in hopes she would also comment on the name Burnstein.

"Oh, yeah. I remember the Burnsteins, although I was still in grade school when they left out. Are you kin to them too?"

"That's another thing I wanted to check on. I think my dad was a long-lost distant cousin or something like that. Seems there aren't many Bernsteins around that I can find."

"Far as I remember, the Burnsteins were decent folks. Minded their own business and never bothered a soul. Didn't have any kin living around these parts. Don't remember exactly where they came from before they moved here."

"The weren't native to this area?"

"No, they weren't, but they lived here for a few years or so."

"Where did they go?"

"Don't rightly recall that. Like I said, I was little back then."

"What about the Jacks? Are they still living in the area?"

"Birdie is still living in their old home place. Old man Hencle died about ten years ago. All their kids scattered to lord knows where. What I remember best, is that youngest girl of theirs disappeared off the face of the earth when she was still little. Nobody ever figured out what really happened to her. There were a lot of different opinions on the matter, but that was years ago."

"Do you suppose Birtie would be willing to talk to me?"

"She'd be willing to talk alright, but I'm not sure she'd make much sense. She was always kind of odd in the head if you know what I mean. Oh, me," she suddenly added. "I don't mean no disrespect to one of your relatives."

"Oh, no, I didn't take any offence. I'm not the sharpest tack in the barrel myself."

"Know what you mean. We all have to do our best with what the good Lord granted us."

"You've got that right. Where does Birdie live?"

"Oh law, it's not far from here the way a crow flies, but you'll have to ramble around all creation to get there by road. Being a stranger, I best draw you a little map unless you have one of them little machines that tells you where to go."

"I've got a GPS," I told her.

"I'll draw you a map anyhow. I've heard those things tend to take you all over creation. Don't have one myself. Not many folks around here do. They already know where they're going."

She got a sheet of paper from under the counter, took a pen, and proceeded to draw fairly reasonable directions. Finally, when someone else came in, she opened a gate in the counter and pointed me to the room where records were kept.

"Hey, Hilda. How are you doing after your surgery?" I heard the clerk say as I headed into the records room. I hesitated inside the open door long enough to hear the Hilda woman say, "Who was that?"

The clerk answered by saying, "Some stranger claiming to be kin with the Jacks and the Burnsteins. He's doing research on them."

"Poor man," Hilde said in a loud whisper. "He hain't going to leave here happy."

From there, their conversation ignored who I was interested in and went to their own interests.

I was pleasantly surprised to find the records were organized although most of them were handwritten instead of being computerized. I was able to find both Anna Bernstein and Bennie Jack's birth certificates. Bennie Jack was two years older than Anna Bernstein. They were not the only ones whose birth was reported a length of time after they had been born. It appeared to be the custom of babies being home birthed instead of at a hospital. Doctors were required to report home births, but self-proclaimed midwives didn't. A lot of people thought it was nobody's business how many children they had.

Once I researched everything I could find about both Jacks and the Burnsteins and took pictures of the documentation, I left the records room and went into the office where the clerk was.

"Find what you were looking for?" she asked from where she sat at her desk.

"I'm not sure exactly what I'm looking for, but I thought here would be a good place to start."

"I never wanted to find out much about my relatives. Most folks end up mighty disappointed. Not saying you'll do the same or nothing like that," she made a point of adding. And yet her attitude indicated that I would.

"Is there anything else you can tell me about the Jacks and the Burnsteins?"

"Not much to tell. Times were hard back then without all these rules and regulations the government is forcing on us these days. Back then folks did the best they could and minded their own business. Don't know what good has ever come from snooping around in other peoples' business," she made a point of saying.

I got an idea she was indicating I should mind my own business instead of butting into the past.

"Thank you for all the information," I told her in my most appreciative demeanor and left to pay a visit to Birtie Jack.

Using her map and the GPS I found myself on a one lane dirt road with huge old growth tree on both sides with their limbs touching overhead. Occasionally a low hanging limb would brush against the top of my car scraping at the paint. The road to my grandparents' place was a highway compared to this road. Its enclosed and unused appearance had the feel of cold air creeping into my chest. Admittedly, I was feeling slightly apprehensive, and I wasn't the kind who never got spooked. I had no doubt bad things had happened in this neck of the woods.

It seemed as though the enemy was watching me, waiting for the moment when I was less attentive, more vulnerable. At the same time the place had its own kind of beauty. A beauty that took the mind back to a different time when the spirits of these people who once dwelled there still lingered in the shadows. Good people. Bad people.

Bad people were almost always able to overpower the good people. Why? Because they had no soul. No value to anyone other than themselves, while the good people cared about others. Good people wanted to do what was right regardless if it wasn't beneficial to themselves. Ah, well. Enough of my philosophizing. I had come here for a reason, and I needed to keep my mindset in the right place.

I was beginning to think I was on the wrong never-ending dirt path. I stopped and picked up the clerk's map from the passenger seat. After studying it for a while, I decided I was still on the right path, although it no longer qualified as a road. I started the car and continued on hoping if and when I reached Birdie Jack's place there would be enough room for a vehicle to turn around. I even cringed at the thought of backing out of this place.

Finally, after the dirt path turned into a weed strewn grass path, I saw a slight clearing ahead. A little further and I spotted a shack clinging to the topside of a bank. The shack was of weathered sawmill boards with batten nailed over the cracks between the boards to keep the wind and snow out. A rusty orange tin roof sagged atop the shack and over a narrow porch leaning precariously downhill. Regardless of the downhill incline, an old woman sat on the porch in a ladderback chair.

This had to be Birdie Jack, although she appeared to be closer to a hundred years old than in her seventies.

I stopped the car in the only wide space and got out. The huddled form of the woman appeared not to be any more interested in me than if I was a squirrel.

"Mrs. Birdie Jack?" I questioned.

"It's who I be," she finally answered in a deep, smokey voice far stronger than the frail body I was looking at. "What's your purpose?"

"I wanted to talk with you if that's all right."

"Talk's cheap," she said. "Got any good eats in that fancy automobile of yourn?"

"I do," I said as I recalled the energy bars and trail mix I had brought with me to keep from stopping for greasy, unhealthy junk food. I turned back to the car and got an energy bar and a pack of trail mix and held it up.

"Bring 'em on up here," she said in that same husky voice. "Been hankering for more'n beans and turnip greens lately."

I climbed the bank and felt the give of the lopsided wooden steps leading to the porch. Thankfully, they held my weight. Her bony hand reached out for the *good eats* before I stepped onto the porch. I let out a breath of relief as the worn porch planks held my weight.

Birdie grabbed the bar and trail mix with fingers that reminded me of hawk-like claws. Her hands and fingers were long and slender with yellowed fingernails. My first thought was she had never eaten enough beans and turnip greens to put an ounce of fat on her bones. There was another ladderback chair leaning against the wall. Without being invited, I sat down in the chair.

"That be Hencle's chair," she said over a mouth full of energy bar. "Won't like you takin' it."

"I thought your husband was dead," I said without thinking my words might hurt.

"Body be dead. Spirit hain't. He still haunts me."

I sat anyway as I watched her gum down the bar and stuff the trail mix in her pocket.

"What you a wantin'?" she finally asked.

"I want to ask about your daughter, Bennie Jack."

"I named her afore she was born. Thought she'd be another boy. Don't have her no more. She was my onlyest girl. I'd already spit out a house full of boys. Wanted her so she could help me out some, but it didn't come about. Why you askin' about sech as that?

I decided it was best I continued the lie I'd told the clerk. "My mother was a Jack. She never talked about her ancestors. Had me curious is all."

"I relate to that," she said without any emotion. "Never was a Jack any account. Mine included. Married a Jack afore I growed body hair and good sense. Who's your pa?"

"Bill Burnstein. I'm Bill Jr."

She shook her head as she took a tin of snuff out of a different pocket than the one she'd put the trail mix in, pulled out her lower lip and dumped powdery snuff in, put the lid back on the tin, and replaced it in her pocket.

"You got two smacks in the face, didn't you?"

"Were the Burnsteins no good also?" I ask with a slight touch of humor.

"Both of them Burnsteins shore was lazy. Neither of 'um worked a lick. Wouldn't help me out if I'd a been in a ditch a'dyin'. Moved into the old McIntyre's fancy place over the hill yonder. Fixed it up a right smart afore they left out. Always actin' like they was God's gift to all creation. Looked down their noses on me and mine, they did."

"How long did they live here?" I asked without elaborating on what she'd just said.

She squinched her eyes making her abundant winkles deepen as she went back in memory. "Not long. Let's see now. Seems like I recall the man leaving out about the time my baby girl went missin'. Had her in my old age, I did. After givin' birth to seven Jack devil boys, I figured my juice had dried up years a'fore, but it hadn't. Never had another 'un after her even though Hencle kept pesterin' on top uh me."

"Did Mrs. Burnstein and her baby girl go with him?"

"I reckon that snobby woman followed him shortly after he took off. Don't know nothin' about a baby. Never seen her big or nothing like that when she lived over the mountain there. Don't know nothin' about them after they pulled outta here."

"I thought she had a daughter."

"Not that I knowed of," she said. "Coulda had a bunch of 'em once she left here. She was right on in years when she lived here. I'd of thought she was past her breedin' years."

Interesting. I had done a thorough search on the Burnsteins before my approval of their daughter. According to the information I had obtained, Anna was two years old when they moved.

"How old was your daughter when she disappeared?" I questioned.

"Comin' onto four years," she said. "You got any more of 'em candy bars?"

"I got another one if you want it."

"I want it uh sight," she said.

"I'll get if for you, but first can you tell me what you think happened to your little girl?"

"Never knowed for sure, but I'm thinkin' somebody took her when she was out in the woods playin'. She liked to traipse off after Hencle's huntin' dogs. Me and all my young'uns searched these hills for days without findin' hide nor hair of her. They did find scuffed up footprints in a soft spot of dirt. Looked big enough to belong to a man wearing shoes instead of brogans like Hencle and the other men around here wore. My young'uns all went barefooted most of the time. My boys tried to follow 'em footprints but couldn't."

"I know you and your family were devastated."

"Was, but I reckon God knows what's best. You gonna get me that other candy bar instead of sittin' on your hindend gabbin'?"

"I'll do that right away. By chance did your girl have any birthmarks that might helped identify her if she'd been found?"

"The looks of her would have been enough. She was a pretty little thing. Come to think on it, one of them huntin' dogs bit her once on her right jaw near her ear when she was about two-years-old atter she pulled its ears. Left a little scar but that was all."

I got up out of Hencle's chair and carefully went down the rickety steps. I got her another energy bar along with the last pack of trail mix and climbed back onto the porch long enough to hand them to her. "Thank you for talking to me," I told her.

She nodded. "When you come back bring more good eats," she said. "I get right tired of nothin' but them beans and turnip greens."

I managed to do a five-point turn around and head back down the path. At least this sorry excuse of a road didn't have as many potholes as the road to my grandparents' place. It wasn't as high up on a mountain top either, but it sure was isolated.

I analyzed the information I had gathered on the long drive back to my cabin. According to the girls' birth certificates Anna Burnstein was two years younger than Bennie Jack. According to the school records I'd obtained, she was taller and more advanced than the other children when she started school at six years of age. If Bennie Jack was four years old when she disappeared, then Anna Burnstein would have been two years old. Surely the Jacks would have known if the Burnsteins had a two-year-old.

Interesting. A four-year-old girl went missing the same time as a family with a two-year-old girl arrived in another area. Especially when the two-year-old started using the other girl's name when she was grown and gone into hiding.

I considered turning around to go back and do more research but thought it best not to do so. I didn't want to call more attention to myself than I already had. Neither did I want anyone else to start thinking about the two girls or what happened to one or both of them. Hopefully, the clerk and Birdie Jack would soon forget about me, or at least, put the crazy man looking for his heritage from their minds. One thing was certain, if I ever went back, I'd take Birtie Jack a huge box full of good eats.

The more I analyzed the situation, the more positive I became that the Burnsteins moved away with the little girl. All I needed was to see that little scar on her cheek as concrete evidence. I had no doubt the Burnsteins were the best thing that could have happened to the girl. I shuddered to think what she would have gone through if she had remained with Bertie Jack and her bunch of devil boys. Just about the only thing good that I could think of about Fizz being Bennie Jack for real was that she could get married and it would be legal, just as my marriage would be legal as Colton Slaughter.

I arrive home right before dawn. I checked on the animals and fed them before I hit the bed for a couple hours of sleep. I woke up determined to get a closer look at the right side of Fizz's face. I needed to think of an excuse to pay her a visit. I got my best bag of 8-O'clock coffee and a large box of kitchen matches and headed out over the mountain to Aunt Polly's. After I had visited with her for a while, I would come up with an excuse to stop by to get a look at Fizz's face.

I considered taking a different path over the mountain because the one I had always taken was getting a bit worn. It was obvious it was being traveled. I wondered if Fizz was taking it to spy on me more than that one time. I didn't see any evidence of her footprints, but I did see several deer tracks and what could have been a large cat. Most likely a bobcat was prowling about. It was the time of the year when a deer could still be giving birth to late fawns. Their rut season was usually between September and November, but there were always those who were young or slow to take. Years ago, there were neither deer nor other game left alive on the mountain. They became food for both mountain dwellers and people down in the valley when times were hard. In the last few years, the wildlife had returned. I hoped I would be able to keep it that way.

I told myself I was in luck when I heard voices I recognized. Aunt Polly along with Fizz were in the woods gathering stinging nettle.

"I'm itching like crazy," Fizz said. "I can't stand this any longer."

"I told you to wear long sleeves, didn't I."

"I didn't know stinging weeds would sting this bad."

"If you think it's bad now, you ought to get in them when you're wearing a dress like I am."

"We've got enough," Fizz said. "Let's get out of these things."

"Stop your belly aching. The stinging will stop in about ten or fifteen minutes."

"Why don't I believe I'll ever stop itching. I'm in big time misery.?"

"Goodness me. You're a timid one. Step over there in that clearing while I fill the sack."

"I'm not timid," she said. "Although I'm itching to death right along with you, but you're too stubborn to admit it."

"Want to borrow my shirt?" I asked Fizz as I eased up to them. They were so busy arguing that not ever Aunt Polly heard me approach.

"So, you finally decided to show yourself," Aunt Polly said. "You've been hiding behind that clump of undergrowth for a full ten minutes watching us.

Okay. So, maybe she had heard me.

"What are you doing on our side of the mountain?" Fizz demanded.

"I got supplies and thought Aunt Polly might could use a few things."

"Trying to bribe her, aren't you?"

"I would if I thought it would work."

"Turn around and go back where you came from. You're not welcome on our land," Fizz said angrily.

"Now, Bennie, you just calm yourself down a bit. You two got no reason to be at each other's throats. Seems to me you were mighty good friends at one time not so long ago."

"We still are," I said.

"Not since I learned you're trying to steal my land along with other things."

"I'm not trying to steal your land or other things," I told her.

"There's three of us on this mountain," Aunt Polly said. "Every one of us would like to own this whole mountain, but neither one of us do. In my opinion we ought to stick together as neighbors and friends. The three of us joined together would have control that one of us won't have."

"Makes sense to me," I said.

"I don't trust him. I know how sneaky he is. All he wants to do is take advantage of me."

"Since when have I ever taken advantage of you? Name me one time," I said.

"When haven't you?" Was the best she could come up with.

Fizz puffed up like a toad frog. She couldn't think of a time. Actually, I'd always had her back on everything, and she knew it. I even had her back when she went to deliver her documents to Brigham. I had even planted bugs in her shoes so I could track her. What I hadn't counted on was her getting in a helicopter.

"Your face is dirty," I told her as I took my handkerchief out of my back pocket and wiped at her right cheek moving her hair aside. Sure enough, before she could jerk away, I saw there was a tiny white scar. It was so small that I'd never paid any attention to it before. "When did you get that scar?" I questioned. "I never noticed it before," I asked as I let my finger touch it.

"It's none of your business, but my mother told me I fell and hit the edge of a coffee table when I was little."

"I always knew you were awkward."

She hit at my face with a handful of stinging weeds. I blocked with my hand and arm. She was right. Those weeds stung. I took a step back. "Want me to help you fill your sack with those weeds or not?" I asked both her and Aunt Polly.

"I reckon we both do, if the two of you will stop fighting long enough to be of use," Aunt Polly told us.

I paid closer attention to this Bennie Jack than I had paid to Anna Burnstein when I was analyzing her as one of my trainees. I was trying to see anything about her that would remind me of Birtie Jack. She was so different it made me wonder if I could be mistaken about her identity. The clerk had indicated Birtie Jack was less than intelligent. After talking with her for a while, I concluded the same thing. And yet Fizz was intelligent. Maybe too much so. Highly intelligent people often lacked common sense. I hadn't observed that to be the case with Fizz. She had common sense along with an abundance of conniving. There was something about her that made me trust her as well as want her, and that made her one hell of a spy. Even I wasn't immune to her appeal. More than once I'd wondered what she would be like in bed. Pure fire, I thought.

Hard to handle.

Hard to satisfy.

But some kind of fantastic pleasure in the trying as well as the doing.

"I'll carry that heavy sack home for you," I told Aunt Polly.

"No. you won't," Fizz shot back.

"Yes, he can," Aunt Polly said in her kind voice. "It pays to have a strong man about even when he lives a long piece away. Like I done said, we need to become friends with each other. Sticking together is the right thing for us to do."

I took hold of the sack Fizz had clutched in her hands. She held on tight and jumped backward a couple of steps. Her foot caught on a log causing her to lose her balance and flip backward. Her head hit a rock with surprising force. That's what you get for being so stubborn, I started to say when I realized she wasn't moving.

"She's done knocked herself out cold," Aunt Polly said as she bent down and started slapping at Fizz's jaws. Regardless, she didn't move.

"Wait a minute," I said as I pulled Aunt Polly away and bent down to check Fizz. I felt the back of her head where it hit the rock. No blood. That might or might not be a good thing as I felt a knot growing. Outward bleeding was most always preferrable to inward bleeding.

"Lordy, is she dead?"

"No. She'll be all right after a while," I hoped. I'd seen several people with concussions after they receiving a hit to the back of their heads.

"She needs to wake up," Aunt Polly said. "It hain't doing her no-good laying on that wet ground like she's doin'."

I checked her pulse and then her eyes. Her pulse had slowed down and her eyes were rolled back. Her body was trembling. I feared she was going into shock.

"I'll carry her to the house. She needs to stay warm."

"I'll tote that sack."

"Can you carry this coffee and matches too. I'll come back after the sacks of nettles."

"I can tote 'em both. I'm stronger than you think I am."

I picked up Fizz and cuddled her head and body to my chest. She didn't weigh as much as I remembered the few times I had picked her up during training. Either she had been working too hard or not eating enough protein and carbs. I had the oddest feeling that I needed to take care of this girl the same as the Burnsteins had surely felt.

I got an image of Calvin Burnstein coming across a hungry, dirty, crying child lost in the woods all by herself. I imagined his pity as he picked her up and felt her bony body as he cuddled her in his arms. He evidently knew the Jacks and their seven devil sons. Even their mother referred to them as seven devils. I can understand how he would carry the pitiful baby girl home to his wife. Evidently, they wanted to do what was best for the child, and that wasn't returning her to the Jacks. They surely decided it would be best if Calvin Burnstein left the area with the child.

The research I had done on them to qualify Fizz had shown that Calvin and Helen both returned several times to Kentucky in order sell their house along with other matters, but never together. I now knew why.

Chapter 51

I opened my eyes to discover I was in bed. At first, I wasn't sure what bed or even where I was. I did know that I had one heck of a throbbing headache. It surely had come from duress and dehydration after all the hours I'd spent in the ocean after the helicopter went down.

Of course, it did.

There was no way I could ever forget the salt water and broiling sun beating down on me.

"You're finally awake," said a familiar voice. At first, I wasn't sure if it came from my trainer or if I was hallucinating. Floating in the ocean for days on end would do that to a person. I closed my eyes and then opened them again. This time I saw his face hovering above mine.

"Got a headache, don't you?" he said.

"You finally found me," I mumbled. "I thought I was going to drown."

"In the ocean?" he asked. "How did you manage to escape?" ask my trainer. I had no qualms about telling him what happened.

"Brigham is a traitor. A double agent. He planned on the big man killing me. The big man cut the pilots' throat. The helicopter sank in the ocean when it ran out of fuel." Self-preservation kept me from telling him what I had done to the big man.

"So that's what happened," he said. "I suspected such as that, but I wasn't sure."

"Do I hear you talking? Has she finally come around?"

I heard a woman's voice coming from the other room. A.J. quickly placed his finger over my lips to hush anything I might say and slightly shook his head. I knew he wanted me to say no more about what I had endured.

"Yes, Aunt Polly. Bennie Jack has finally come around," he said as he looked me in the eyes as if to communicate silently with me.

"Is she alright?" the old woman asked as she came into the bedroom to look down on me.

"She is. Just a headache where she fell and hit her head on a rock."

As I looked at the old woman's face, I started to recall what had happened. "I'm fine. Just a little addled. What happened?"

"You fell and hit your head on a rock," he repeated what he had told Aunt Polly.

"That's why my head hurts." I started to sit up which made a sharp pain shoot through my head. I laid back down. "How about a few aspirins,' I said.

"Not until I determine you don't have any internal bleeding. Got any liquor? It will work as good as aspirins."

"No," I told him, making sure I didn't move my head.

"I have some medicinal shine at my place," Aunt Polly said. "I'll go get it."

"No, I'm okay," I assured them both.

"That might be a good idea," A.J. told Aunt Polly. "If it won't be too difficult for you to go after it."

"Hain't difficult. I do it all the time. I'll be back as fast as my old legs can travel," she said as she gave me and A.J. a look before she went out the door. He went to the bedroom window and looked out for a few minutes.

"I watched her go into the woods, She can't eavesdrop on us," he said as he turned back to me. "How much do you remember about becoming Bennie Jack?"

It hurt my head to think, but I did anyway. I forced myself to recall the helicopter and the ocean. I cringed as I remembered what I went through before and after I was washed up on the rocks. Slowly, memories of everything else came back like scenes on a movie screen.

"I did what I thought was best," I told him, slightly apologetically. "I never intended to cost you your job."

"I understand that. I'll have to admit I've come to enjoy being a free man."

"A free man?" I questioned.

"Right. You and I both have been set free."

He had a point. I hadn't thought about it exactly like that before. I needed to keep telling myself I'd been set free instead of being in hiding.

"You don't hate me?" I asked.

"Perhaps I'm still angry at you for going against what the Freedom Group allowed, as well as my training of you, but I certainly don't hate you."

"You kept me alive," I told him.

"How's that?"

"I kept hearing your voice telling me what I should do in order to stay alive."

"Didn't always listen to good advice, did you."

It wasn't a question, but he was grinning.

"Now, Bennie Jack. No more secrets between us. When did you discover you really were Bennie Jack with an alias of Anna Bernstein?"

"What are you talking about?" I said, trying to play innocent.

"You know what I'm talking about. Stop playing innocent. We both know Helen Bernstein was never able to have children."

"She had me," I told him.

"Yes, she did have you. You were four years old when she had you and faked a birth certificate for you. Have you forgotten I do a complete search on the people I train?"

"You knew all along?"

"Why do you sound so surprised?"

"You should have told me."

"Why should I? You were my Fizz regardless of who gave birth to you. What I want to know is when and why you found out?"

"Does it matter?"

"No. It doesn't matter in the least. Except for the fact that you and I both can use our real names when we get married."

"I'm not marrying you."

"Might as well admit I'm the only man you've ever loved."

"I don't love you," I said with conviction.

"Truth is, we have loved each other since the first time we looked into each other's eyes."

"Oh, how romantic. You're just trying to get my land."

"I do want to own the entire mountain, but not enough to tie myself down to a hardheaded spit fire of a woman unless I was crazy in love with her."

"Bull shit," she said.

"How about telling me how long you've known you really are Bennie Jack."

I wasn't going to answer that question, ever. The main reason was because I hadn't known, not for a fact. I had only suspected. Mother had surely told me about little Bennie Jack's disappearance for a reason. I suppose it was a mixture of guilt and truth that was bothering her. Regardless, Helen and Calvin were my parents and always would be.

After my parent's death, I had gone through their private papers. I'd found Bennie Jack's birth certificate along with Anna Bernstein's. There were several pictures of a pitiful, ragged, dirty, small child with huge eyes and tangled hair. Someone had taped those pictures on the underside of a drawer along with a notarized copy of her birth certificate.

The little girl resembled pictures of me.

Without a reason for doing it, I made a point of using Bennie Jack's birth certificate to get a social security number along with driver's license in her name with a picture of me on it. Why I needed such when I also had the same in the name of Anna Burnstein, I wasn't sure. I only knew it was something I should do.

Chapter 52

Bennie Jack

It took the realization of a long, cold winter in the making before what Aunt Polly had been telling me made sense. Life would be a lot easier on a woman if she had a good man to help her out. A.J., or rather Colton Slaughter, became that man, although I continuously refused to marry him. He was making sure Aunt Polly and I had enough firewood to keep us from freezing to death during sub-zero temperatures.

I watched him as he cut locust trees with a chainsaw, hauled the cut blocks of firewood in a wheelbarrow from the woods into my yard. I stacked the firewood after he had used a double bitted ax to split the blocks of wood. Sweat soaked his shirt. His hair grew wet, but he didn't stop working. He took every task as seriously as he took training his recruits. I came to admire him more each day.

"See what I've been telling you," Aunt Polly said as she did her best to help with stacking wood. "You ought to marry him."

"He hasn't asked me," I told her without adding *again.*

The wrinkles on her face deepened as she grinned. "He would if you gave him a little more encouragement."

"I don't want a man to boss me around."

"From what I've seen, you hold your own where bossing is concerned."

I suppose she was right about that.

"Let's go inside the house and get us a nice cold drink of water," Aunt Polly said. "I'm getting a mite thirsty."

I started to tell her I wasn't thirsty, but I thought she might need to rest. As soon as we got inside, she filled a glass full of cold water and handed it to me.

"Take this to him," she told me. "After he drinks it, kiss him like you've wanted to do ever since you set eyes on him."

"I . . ." I began to object.

"No need to deny it. The two of you look at each other like two hungry dogs smelling cooked meat. You're both all but slobbering at the mouth."

"That's not true."

"It's the truth if truth was ever told. Now go out there to him."

I had to be work-addled because I went without arguing further. He stopped chopping when he saw me with the glass of water.

"Thanks," he said as he reached for the water.

I watched his lips touch the rim of the glass. I imagined what it would feel like to have those lips on mine. I shivered.

"I needed that," he said with a slight smile.

He held the glass toward me. Instead of taking the glass from his hand, I stepped up to him, put my arms around him and pressed my mouth to his like a woman who had finally found what she sought.

The glass dropped onto the ground.

Never had I expected how tight his arms held onto me. How the electric fire shot through me, through him. Finally, we were both going after what we both wanted. It was only the thought of Aunt Polly watching that kept me from ripping the sweat-soaked shirt off his body.

"Hell fire," he surprised me by whispering.

"No. It's heaven," I whispered back.

"Finally," he said.

I agreed.

Chapter 53

It was a fact that I had gone from a living hell to finding heaven. Colton Slaughter had realized his dream of owning his grandparents' place along with the entire mountain. I owned it as well.

Aunt Polly had signed her property over to me free and clear. There was no way she could ever pay off the IOU she gave me. I had gone ahead and paid her daughter more for the property than it was worth. She stopped harassing her mother after she got the extra money.

My husband moved himself and his animals into the old Slaughter place, leaving his cabin empty for the time being. Someday we knew one of our future children would want to move in.

I'd had mixed feelings as we stood before a justice of the peace to say our wedding vows. Aunt Polly stood with us as a witness. I wasn't sure if I was making the biggest mistake of my life or not.

The *or not* proved to be the one that won out.

I won't go into explicit details about our wedding night, but it was far more than I could have imagined. Again, he proved to be my trainer who kept me alive and happy. I might have shown him a few moves he hadn't expected as well. We spent a sleepless night and the best part of another day in bed doing what newlyweds do with each other.

When I finally got out of bed, I went to the window to see that snow was softly falling. There was at least a foot of snow that had already fallen. My outside world was silent and beautiful. Inside I was unbelievable happy except for one small thing. I knew neither Colton nor I would be fighting for our country. We were dead to the Freedom Group, but at the same time, we were also free. I hoped everyone else would be able to continue living in freedom.

"Fizz," A.J. softly said my previous name as if he knew what I was thinking. "We have no choice other than to let the Lion sleep."

He came up behind me and closed me in his arms. I knew we were safe here on our mountain, but there were many others that were only safe as long as the lion slept.